MICKY O'BRADY

CRIS PARR
~~CRISPR~~

CRISPR
Copyright © 2024 Micky O'Brady
Cover Design: www.KimG-Design.com
Interior Format: Dorothy Dreyer

Published by Snowy Wings Publishing
PO Box 1035, Turner, OR 97392

ISBN eBook: 978-1-958051-86-3
ISBN Paperback: 978-1-958051-87-0

CHAPTER ONE

News flash: Standing in the spotlight can cause temporary blindness.

While that could be a deep metaphor for life, it's actually nothing but an accurate description of my current situation: I can't see a thing.

Three spotlights shine onto me. One from the left, one from the right, and one from the front to make sure I can't make out anything of the audience other than absolute blackness.

And geez, does it get hot up on stage.

A drop of sweat runs down my neck and disappears between my shoulder blades, joining its buddies that have traveled down this path over the last ten minutes. Wearing a wig and double-sweaters under my business-style outfit wasn't my brightest idea, maybe.

But, if heatstroke is the price I have to pay to be allowed to present, then so be it.

I straighten up and smile down into the audience I can't see. "To sum it up, alterations in gene function can be caused by more than just changes in sequence. Epigenetics is a fascinating and promising addition in the field of genetic engineering. By identifying and targeting the correct gene, we can affect gene expression in many ways. While more research is obviously needed," *hint-hint-give-me-that-internship,* "this is a fascinating start into a new area of genetic engineering. Thank you very much for your attention." I take a quick bow as the audience applauds. Maybe it's my imagination, but I feel they're clapping louder than with the other finalists. Especially louder than with *him.*

Apparently, that's what *he* thinks too, or else *he* wouldn't be standing backstage, waiting for me, leaned against the wall with his arms crossed in front of his broad chest and a scowl on his face.

I brush past him and ignore him. No way he saw through my disguise—

"Nice job there, *Cassidy.*" The snideness in his voice makes me twitch once before I can suppress it. Dang it, he kno—

With two quick steps, he has caught up with me. "You're not fooling anybody with this, Nya. What the hell?" He grabs my arm and stops me. "You know you're not allowed to participate—"

I turn on my heels and rip my arm out of his grasp. "Shut up, Gabriel! None of your concern."

A muscle in his for once clean-shaven jaw ticks. At nineteen, other guys might look softer or younger without the bit of stubble they can grow, but not Gabriel. He always looked older, courtesy of his tall stature, muscular frame, and what I would call a testosterone-boosted facial bone structure. Meaning, he has high cheekbones, a prominent jaw, and deep-set gray eyes under heavy brows. Mother Nature went all out and gave him thick, wavy, blond hair he wears open, or in a man-bun, like today. I've heard other girls say he's cute. Obvs they don't know the idiot.

Said idiot presses his lips into a thin line. "It is my concern if you're cheating." At least he has the decency to drop his voice, but come on!

I keep mine low and level. Barely, though. Anger-control is not my thing. "I'm not cheating. I'm presenting my research at the Advangen Junior Scientist Symposium. That's all. Not my fault your splicing idea came a dime a dozen." I can put as much snide behind my words as him. Anybody who saw us would be hard-pressed to believe we used to be friends. Used to. As in *until seventh grade*. Heck, I even had a huge crush on Gabriel. Again, past tense. Now, four years later, there's nothing left of that friendship, or that crush, and for a good reason.

I brush off the lingering memory of his touch on my arm and give him my best acidic smile. "May the better person win. And we both know who that is." I spin on my heels and strut away from him, head held high, steaming on the inside. Not my fault the company my dad works for offers the best summer internship for young and upcoming bioengineers. Not my fault it's an annual competition where only the winner gets the spot. *Totally* not my fault they excluded employees and their families from participating—it's just super unfair. Ever since I was young, I've been reading about biochemistry. Chemistry. Physics. *Anything* science related. Guess that happens with a dad high up the food chain in one of the leading bioengineering companies of the world, and a mom who was a doctor. It's in my genes, so to say.

One could think Dad would support my choice and passion, but no. Over the years, he's done nothing but discourage me. Cue pink stuffed unicorns for my birthday when all I wanted was a microscope. Or the summer I spent horseback-riding instead of at science camp. Or that he cancelled my subscriptions of *Genome Biology and Evolution, Genes*, and *Journal of Biological Engineering* and got me *Shape Up* instead.

Yeah.

Daddy-O would rather have me a stay-at-home parent than a

scientist, it appears. So, in a way this is me rising against the oppression. Okay. That sounded bad. I love my dad, but boy, can he be stubborn. And yes, I know they're never going to give me the internship. For one, I'm still in high school. Happens when you barely turned seventeen a week ago. In the history of Advangen's internship program, they've accepted nobody who wasn't in college yet. Yes, I've checked.

For another, as much as it pains me to admit it, Gabriel is right. Officially, I'm forbidden to participate. The wig and disguise won't do squat should I really win.

Obviously neither catch changes the fact that I *want* to win— if not for the internship, then to show Dad I *can* do this and I *want* to do this, even if he'd rather have me, I don't know, going into interior design, or whatever else he can come up with.

Let's call it fighting for my freedom. Has a nice ring to it.

The overhead speakers click and squeak once. *"Contestants, please assemble backstage. Contestants, please assemble backstage."*

Showtime.

Adrenaline spikes as I follow the other ten finalists to the backstage area. Making it this far is already an achievement. Even more for me than for Gabriel, I'd say. While I have to rely on our school chem lab after hours, the golden prince has his own lab set up at home, courtesy of a rich—and proud—dad. Must be nice to feel supported.

We all gather in the area behind the stage entrance. Sophie, one of the assistants in her early twenties, greets us with a smile. "All righty, guys, gals, and non-binary pals. Mr. Delacour will announce the financial support for third place and runner-up first, and then we'll find out who'll be joining us this year." She winks at us—actually, mostly at one of the cuter guys around her age, but oh, well. He's one of the few who could be dangerous to me. Him, the girl in the pink blazer, and, unfortunately, Gabriel. They all delivered strong work, whether I like it in Gabriel's case or not.

I shake out my hands. Okay. Okay. Here it comes. Out on the stage, Mr. Delacour, Advangen's recruitment director, paces back and forth. "…which is why we are honored to present financial funding over five thousand dollars to…" He pauses for effect and glances down on the little card in his hand. "Joseph Marcello! Congratulations, Joseph!"

Amidst our little group a guy pumps his fist. "Yes!"

Huh. Not the cute guy. Not the gal in pink. Not Gabriel.

Didn't even have this one on my list of serious contenders. Dang it.

Everybody claps in front of the stage and behind it, although back here it sounds a bit forced. I'm pretty sure my research was better than his, but still. Makes me nervous he came in third. What if I—

Delacour is on a roll. "And this year's runner-up, the second-best presentation with the potential to bring movement into our scientific world, goes to…" The same pause, the same look down onto his cheat-sheet. "Gabriel Hargrove! Come on out, Gabriel! Congratulations!"

Aww, dang it. Keeping my smile borderline sincere is hard work. Why did it have to be him? Granted, his abstract was good, and so was his poster, but mine was better! It was! Plus, that still leaves cute guy and pink-sweater girl.

"And now the winner of this year's Advangen's Junior Scientist Symposium for bringing new ideas to the field of genetic engineering…" No glance needed this time. Crap. That means it can't be me. My fake name is anything but easy to remem—

"Cassidy Sibagatullin! Congratulations, Cassidy, and welcome to our club!"

Cassidy—

Somebody claps my shoulder. "Nicely done! Seriously great paper! You'll rock that internship!"

Huh? Wait—wait, that *was* me! I won! "Wooo!" Like a crazy person, I pump up both fists in the air. I really won! *Me!* All by myself! With research *I* conducted! I'm *bringing new ideas to the field of genetic engineering*, how amazing is that?

I all but storm past the others onto the stage. This time, the spotlight doesn't bother me at all. Nope. I was born for it. Shaking hands with Delacour is a pleasure. Bowing to the audience the same. Holding that trophy, an artsy interpretation of a double-helix structure, feels better than anything in my life. In fact, I'm on a high, riding it for all it's worth.

That is until Mr. Delacour leads me backstairs to meet with Dr. Sherman, CEO extraordinaire, to discuss the details of my internship.

In retrospect, one could say I might've handled this a little bit naïvely. I mean, did I want to accept the summer internship and wear a wig and three sweaters on top of each other every day? Tell my dad lies where I was going, then jump off the bus across the office while he pulls into the parking lot in his Beemer?

Well, doesn't really matter how I wanted to play this, because the game is over the second Dr. Sherman shakes my hand and the door opens behind him.

"Sorry I'm late," my dad says as he walks into the room. "But appears I'm just in time to welcome our newest—" He freezes in mid-sentence and mid-step.

Uh-oh.

Busted.

CHAPTER TWO

Never have I seen Dad move this fast. "Nya!" he hisses. "What the—" For the second time within thirty minutes, I get grabbed by the arm and spun around, away from Mr. Sherman. "Tell me this is a joke."

Dr. Sherman lets go of my hand as it gets ripped out of his and throws my dad a confused glance, coupled with a slightly annoyed undertone. "Steve? Care to elaborate?"

Crap. My face turns crimson. No other way out but full steam ahead. "No need. Dr. Sherman, hi. It's Nya Bennison under this disguise." I give a shy wiggle with my fingers.

Mr. Sherman's eyes pop open wide. "Nya Bennison." He pronounces my name correctly—*Nee-Uh*—which, to be honest, many people mess up even after I just said my name. Plus, Dr. Sherman and I have never met, despite him having been Dad's boss for twenty-something years. For a moment, I wonder if Dad talks about me at work, but I doubt it. According to him, work is work, and family is family. He doesn't talk about work at home or about home at work.

Well, at least he's consistent.

Dr. Sherman's gaze darts back from my dad, green from anger, and me, red from embarrassment. His brows scrunch down into a V. "I can't say I understand what's going on."

Dad straightens up and stands halfway in front of me. To top it off, he and his boss aren't always on the best of terms, and me pulling the stunt I just did… Yeah. Not helping.

"Nothing, Brian. I apologize. Nya knows very well she's not allowed to take part. Obviously, she will withdraw the submission and the internship will go to the runner-up."

Aww, man. I groan internally. Yes, Gabriel may deserve it, but I'm pathetic enough to not be happy for him.

Dad squeezes my arm hard, and I respond the way he wants me to. "I apologize, Dr. Sherman. I shouldn't have entered under a fake name." But I wanted Dad to see that I can do this. That I *want* to do this—research—and nothing else when I'm done with school. That no one can persuade me otherwise.

To my utter relief, Dr. Sherman chuckles. "In our twenty-year history of hosting this symposium, this might be a first. Or, well, we didn't catch the other guys." He chuckles again. "But, Steve, if I may. I really liked Nya's approach."

"You did?" my dad and I say simultaneously, one of us slightly more enthusiastic than the other.

"Yes, I did. She's right, epigenetics is an important field we've been neglecting. In fact, I liked her idea so much that I'm willing to overlook that Nya is technically excluded from participating."

"You are?" Hope rises inside my chest. Does that mean—

Dad presses his lips into a thin line. "That's very generous, Brian, but it would be unfair to the other contestants. Nya cheated. I don't want her rewarded—"

"But I really want her on our team, Steve. I believe she will learn lots, and maybe even show some of ours how it's done. Right, Nya?" He winks at me.

Oh heck, yeah! "Of course, sir. Thank you, sir." I'm beaming ear to ear and stepping from one foot to the other like a little Energizer Bunny kept from running around.

Dad gives it one more try to ruin my future. "But the rules—"

Sherman waves him off. "We made them, we can change them. This summer, Nya will be our intern—one of our *two* interns, to be precise. The second internship goes to the runner-up. I think that's more than fair." He holds out his hand. "What do you say, Nya? Are you in?"

Am I in?

Am I in?

What kind of question is that?

Yes, there'll be hell to pay later, once Sherman isn't acting as a referee between me and Dad anymore, but I'll take whatever punishment Dad dishes out, as long as I get the internship. No matter if Gabriel is there or not: I won.

I take the hand held out for me. "I'm in, Dr. Sherman. I won't disappoint you."

My dad sucks in a sharp breath of air and makes this sound like I punched him in the gut.

Yeah.

Maybe I won't disappoint Dr. Sherman, but I'm pretty sure I've already disappointed my dad. Or angered. Probably both. The entire way out of the auditorium, through the lobby, and to the front of the line parking spot his Beemer's parked in I can practically see the steam rising from his ears.

He unlocks the car and close to rips out the door when he yanks it open and sits himself into his seat as if gravity were stronger on his side than mine. "What in the name of all that's holy were you thinking?" He pulls the car door closed so hard, the whole car shakes. "The rules are explicit, and I know for a fact you can read.

I also know for a fact that I asked you more than once to please drop this and find some other hobby!" He rams his thumb onto the starter-button.

"Hobby?" I click my seatbelt into the buckle and turn to face him. "You're calling this a *hobby*? Do you know how many hours I've worked on this project? How long I stayed in school? I—"

"You said you stayed in school because you joined the cheerleaders!" He sets the blinker with so much force, it makes an unhealthy cracking noise.

"Because you wouldn't let me stay to do actual work!" I throw up my arms. "*Of course* I didn't join the cheerleaders, Dad! I have absolutely no interest in joining them, not now, not ever! The only thing I *am* interested in is research, and like I have told you a million times before, you should understand that! Research is your life!" How can he fault me doing the same thing he's doing? How's that fair?

"Yes! I know it's my life! And did it ever occur to you that maybe I have good reasons to keep you out of this line of work? That maybe you weren't... made for this?"

Ouch. I suck in a harsh breath through my teeth.

I wasn't made for this? Like, I'm too stupid? A girl—so I can't do research? What would be hurtful from anybody stings twice as much now that it comes from my dad. Tears fill my eyes, but I refuse to let them fall. "What are you saying, Dad? That I can't do research? That I can't do science?" I cross my arms in front of my chest. I won't cry. Won't. Will. Not. Cry. "Look, it's not my fault I am this way. Sorry if I'm disappointing you, but I'm not the type of girl you want me to be. I don't care about cheerleading. I don't care about horseback riding. I want to do scientific research, and I want to be good. I *am* good already." Or else I wouldn't have won today.

Pressure clamps around my head. Ugh. Not tough to guess where the headache is coming from. Thanks, Dad.

But hey, maybe there's hope, because Dad doesn't flatten me with another rebuttal, but deflates. "Nya, I… I'm sorry." He glides one hand over his short brown hair. I wouldn't be surprised if today gave him a few new grey ones in addition to the ones sprinkled in already. "I'm not disappointed in you, not at all, I just… I just would've wished for a different career for you."

"But why if that's what I want do?" My voice breaks at the end. Good job keeping my emotions reigned in.

A small smile plays around his lips, but he doesn't look over at me. "Maybe because I know how hard this job can be. And at our company. Just because I'm high in the food chain doesn't mean it's the best place to work at. Sherman is nice most of the time, but…"

"I know you're not besties." Although I don't get why Dad didn't switch jobs years ago. Anybody would've taken a scientist of his caliber and his number of publications. *Anybody.* And the patients he says depend on him, wouldn't he be able to continue working on their cases if he switched to a different company, one with a less hostile work environment? Sherman must be paying Dad really well to stay, but from my point of view, I'd rather have a less-stressed and slightly less-paid Dad, than vice versa, but that's just me.

"No, we're not besties. Never will be." His voice hardens, and I cringe.

Yikes. Whatever happened between them must've been a biggie. Dad never said what drove a wedge between them, but he usually isn't one to hold a grudge. This one though, he nurses.

"Anyway." Dad comes to a stop at a red light and looks at me. "At least Dr. Sherman will be traveling to work with our sister companies in Europe a few days after your internship starts, so you don't have to worry about him."

Or rather, *he* doesn't have to worry about him.

"So, what about a compromise? I let you do the internship, now that you have been officially accepted"—a muscle in his jaw twitches with those last two words—"but only under two conditions." He gives me an expectant glance and I nod like a bobble-head figure, hope rising. Anything if he lets me go.

"One, you promise me to give something else in your life a chance. You're barely seventeen, Nya. While it's good to have something to focus on, you need to broaden your horizon." He waits for my reaction.

"Okay. I'll try something else. Maybe I'll try out for the cheerleaders for real." Dad would love that. I'll probably get hives, but oh well. The things I'm willing to do…

"All right. Two, you stay on the down low at Advangen. I don't want you to get any special treatment because you're the COO's daughter. You don't come up to the executive floor, in fact, I will make sure your badge will be restricted to the lower levels. You work like everybody else, keep your head low, and stay away from the exec floor. Understood?"

A wide grin spreads across my face. "Done." That's easy. I'd keep my last name quiet anyway. This is *my* personal achievement. Not my last name's.

Dad rolls his eyes. "Well then, welcome to the club."

CHAPTER THREE

The Club, as Dad phrased it so nicely, is not as exciting as I would've thought. At least not on the first day. Quite the opposite. It's kind of annoying—although to be fair, that would mostly be because of Gabriel. I was so happy he's a year older and graduated high school a couple of weeks ago, which means my life was and would have been blissfully Gabriel-free from that point on. Only now he's here. Super.

And he's in such high spirits.

He glowers at me during orientation. During the tour we get. During lunch.

I can totally ignore it and hide behind the ten other new recruits, but it's a bit irritating. Our dads were always so happy we got along well together, despite the almost two years between us. After all, we were the only connection left to their respective wives. Our moms met in—yes, I'm not kidding—cake decorating class and became best friends. Somewhat surprisingly, our dads hit it off, too, even though one is a nerdy scientist and the other a famous sports star. Enter family BBQ-dates and dinners at their respective houses, even way before I was born. When my mom died after giving birth to me and Gabriel's mom left him and his dad a few years later, our shrunken families stayed close—so close, I didn't stand a chance but fall for Gabriel. And how could I not have? He's a good-looking guy, a parallel-universe-version of Thor, including long, thick hair in an off-blond, and the grayest eyes I've ever seen. Usually, he's nice too, charming even. Just not to me. Not since I was in seventh grade, when our friendship—and also family BBQs, for that matter—found a very sudden end after he started spreading rumors about me. Yeah. Didn't need that, especially not on social media, for the world to see.

Dick move.

Anyway. Of course, our guide for the day, a gal in her early twenties by the name of Penelope, is a big fan of Gabriel's. And he's milking it for all it's worth.

Ugh.

Get a room.

Dad needn't worry my last name would give me an unfair advantage, because as it is, Mrs. Penelope has a list of favorites, and I'm not on it. More than once, Gabriel has this look on his face, the equivalent to showing me the middle finger. He knows he's got her. And he knows my dad and his stupid rules, so he could probably bet I'm supposed to stay under the radar.

Whatever.

After lunch, we're getting our ID badges printed down in security. Penelope reads our names off a list, and although I could bet it's alphabetical, Gabriel gets his ID first. "Gabriel Hargrove," reads the security guard. "Access levels one and two. Restricted." The way she rests her hand on Gabriel's arm, I can only imagine what other access she is thinking about. Gag.

Once Gabriel is done, she discovers the power of alphabetical order and goes with Abbott, Rowyn, and then Bates, Hunter. Which means after that—

"Bennison, Nya?" Another glance at her paper and then at me as I walk up and take a seat across the security guard to have my picture taken. Yeah, I know. Dad and I don't look that much alike. He's tall and wiry, I'm more short and… not quite stocky. Sturdy. Yup. That sounds better. Dad has brown hair, mine is reddish, and the fair complexion I must've gotten mostly from Mom brings me a total of fourteen and a half freckles.

Penelope's eyes narrow and her cheeks turn pink. "Bennison? Any relationsh—"

I shrug, like, no biggie. "My dad." Can't say it doesn't feel good to, uh, *casually* mention that. Yeah, Pennie, how 'bout that? You ignored the boss' daughter. Good job, really. And hey, *she* asked about Dad. He didn't say I was supposed to lie.

"Oh, how nice." Penelope tries to save the situation and turns to the security guy. "Uhh, Adam, make it access levels one, two, *and* three for Dr. Bennison's daughter. *Un*restricted." She gives me a quick, only slightly fake smile. "Or else you can't visit your dad upstairs."

She doesn't know he for one doesn't want me to get access to anywhere besides my floor, and for another will never want to see me, but hey, I'll take my access, if only to rub it into Gabriel's face. "Wonderful. Thank you, Penelope." I take my badge and walk back to my seat, whispering at Gabriel in passing, because yes, over the last years, I've become that bitter person who dishes out when she can. "Have fun with the foot peeps, loser."

I swear little puffs of steam rise from Gabriel's ears, declaring me the winner for this morning's round.

Nya—one, Gabriel—zero. And only a whole summer internship to go, but what do I care? Not at all, because the rest of the day runs much smoother and much, much better. I get assigned to my team in Genetic Engineering, far, far away from Gabriel in

Applied Medical. Can't say I mind it. Bad enough we're on the same floor. But after a couple of hours, I've forgotten about him. Completely. Gabriel is gone from my thoughts, banished and erased by the most amazing afternoon I've ever had: doing research with the pros.

Okay, granted, it's not like I was working on the actual project, but I'm *right there*. I get to help with set-ups, prepare slides, restock reagents, and enter the data into the computer. Not glamorous work, but uh, hello? I'm *right there*.

"Hey, Nya?" That's Shawn, the oldest of the scientists I'm assigned to. He looks the part with his sparse hair and thick glasses, no offense. "Would you mind doing a quick run for me? Down to the computer lab? I need a new pack of DVD-Roms to burn the latest data onto them." He points at the computer I used for the data entry until a moment ago. "I don't trust those USB-things."

I jump up and salute, taking a second to stabilize myself when a bout of dizziness hits me. Happens a lot lately, usually when I sit for too long, I think, but it doesn't hamper my uber-motivated spirits. "Sure thing, Shawn. No problem at all. My pleasure. Where is it?"

Shawn chuckles at my enthusiasm. "Easy. North elevators, as far down as they go. Exit, turn left, past the vending machines, then it's where you hear heavy metal music and where the coffee scent's coming from."

Sounds easy enough. "Back in ten." I slide out of my lab coat, hang it on its hook, and sanitize my hands before I sneak out of the lab and down the hallway. Knowing that behind every door some of the States' brightest minds are conducting experiments... I wanna skip down the hallway, but common sense stops me. I might be the youngest ever accepted into the program, but that doesn't mean I need to act like it. Still, it *is* exciting. The only lab worldwide to keep up with Advangen is WissenSCHAFFT in Germany. Funnily enough, its owner and lead scientist is a woman named Johanna Friedrichs, who was Mom's roomy in college. She went into—*tadaaah*, genetic engineering, but for plants, not humans, like Dad. Seriously, science touched my life before I even knew what it was.

Once I reach the North elevators, I check the buttons. "Second, first, Lobby, S-One, S-Two, S-Three..." S probably means sub level, I assume. Shawn said *down as far as they go*, so I hit S-3—and nothing.

I hit it again.

Nothing.

Harder.

Nothing.

Grrr.

Whatever, I'll try S-2 and find stairs or use another elevator. Once I hit the S-2 button, the doors close and I'm on my merry way. After maybe thirty seconds I arrive at S-2, all ready to make it obvious I'm a newbie and ask people for the stairs when I see the vending machines and the sound of heavy metal music hits my ear. Smells like coffee, too.

Huh. Look at that. It turns out I was right after all.

I follow the scent and music to the right, and lo-and-behold, there are the tech guys. I stop at the reception desk. "Hi, I'm from Genetic Engineering. Shawn sent me. He'd like some more DVD-Rs, please?" I only feel slightly old-school asking for DVD-Rs. They were old when I was born.

"No problem. Give me a moment." The guy whose name tag reads *Howard* gets up and looks through the drawers in the ceiling-high cabinet behind him. "There you go." He hands me a full pack. "You new here?" He gives a pointed glance at my sparkling new, shiny name tag.

"Yes, I am. Won the summer internship. I'm Nya." I hold out my hand and he shakes it.

"Nice to meet you. Howard. And congrats, that one's hard to get." He chuckles. "But you must be a smart one. You found us. We've had interns get lost in here. For months." He sticks out his tongue at me and I laugh.

"Naah, finding you wasn't that bad. I mean, they told me where you were, although it would help if the last floor you're on was really the last floor. That S-3 button is confusing."

Howard rolls his eyes. "Yeah, right? There is no S-3. Construction error in the elevator. Anyway. Call me if you guys up there need anything, ok? Shawn knows his server is due for maintenance, so he better secure his data. Any way he chooses." He points at the DVDs again.

I wiggle the box. "Will do. Thank you!" With a small wave of my hand, I leave. Okay, got my DVDs and a message for Shawn. I'm so productive. I press the button to go up, and right away, the little up-arrow above the door comes to life. The doors slide apart.

"... went totally nuts on me, I mean, if that's what—"

The moment I step in, the two guys in there fall silent. "Hi." I nod a short greeting and push the button for the fourth floor.

"Hi," one of them says back, and that's it.

Usually no big deal, nobody really talks in an elevator, but this time the silence… it's heavy. Awkward.

I throw a quick glance at the shiny metal doors in front of me— and then do a double-take. Wait, does he have—?

The elevator slows down and the doors open. Both guys push past me, no, *elbow* their way past me. "S'cuse us," one of them says, while the other one covers his face, but not well or quickly enough: A black eye and busted open lip, both looking fresh, like it just happened. I cringe. Looks painful. What did they do in that elevator before I entered? Practice for an MMA cage fight?

Only when the doors have closed and I'm whisked up to the fourth floor does it click in my mind.

Those two guys, including the guy with the beaten-up face—they came *up* in the elevator to my floor.

Up from S-3.

S-3 that I was told doesn't exist.

"Hey, Dad?" I take another helping of mashed potatoes. My second. No way the cheerleaders are going to take me after that dinner, even if Dad fell onto his knees and begged. Plus, even if I was super-skinny and not more on the sturdy side, they wouldn't let me join. I'm pretty sure Bethany Alcala is no fan of mine since she made fun of Gabriel in third grade and I beat her up for it. Not my proudest moment, but Gabriel was a shy, skinny kid, and I was the exact opposite. That was also before he grew into Thor and became all cute and manly and stuff. More importantly, it was before he turned into an a-hole. These days Bethany could say what she wanted about him, and I'd applaud her. Only that now the tables have turned one-eighty she's totally into Gabriel, like everybody else, and I'm on his shit-list.

Correction: He's on mine. Top position.

But no matter what, Bethany wouldn't let me on her precious team if I had an Olympic medal in cheerleading. Makes me feel moderately safe buying my freedom with the promise to Dad to try out for cheer. I don't think he knows they only do that once a year. Win for me!

I put the spoon back into the bowl. "Dad? Da-had? Father of

mine, hello?" It still takes Dad a good five seconds to realize I'm trying to talk to him.

"Huh?" He looks up from his plate. Whenever there's some kind of meat, potatoes, and veggies, he's in heaven and completely focused on the meal. His holy trifecta of nutrition. Me, I'd stick to mostly veggies if I could. Meat and I don't do so well together.

I cut up a thick carrot. "Gee, Dad. Why so distracted today?" Usually, Dad isn't the cliché of a scatterbrained scientist, although today he fits it perfectly.

He takes a second to process my words, as if his RAM was busy with other thoughts, then shakes his head. "Sorry. I've been working on a serum, and it's not going the way I want it to."

He's talking science to me? Gimme more, Dad! "What kind of serum?"

"I'm trying to rewrite an area of a gene that's already been overridden for a patient who's otherwise going to die, and— Never mind." He waves me off.

I pout but give it one more try. "Is that why you've been working late so much over the last few months?" Why he's been so grouchy, I mean, more than his usual level? I figured it had to do with work. Dad is a perfectionist, and something not working the way he envisions it would easily get him to an elevated grump-level. Especially if it's life-or-death.

He nods, so I carry on.

"Then the serum is for the delivery vehicle?" Usually, a modified virus that won't cause an illness, but is perfect for bringing the tools for genetic editing into the cell, CRISPR to select the area to be modified on the gene, and Cas9 as the scissors to cut. And I have to say, I'm happy Dad is on the case. He's good. He really is. If anybody can insert a new, functioning gene, it's him. He'll figure it out and that patient will be better in no time.

My deduction makes him smile. "It is for the delivery vehicle. I got that ready, but my modifications to the genome aren't doing their job. Anyway." He shoves another forkful of meat into his mouth. The topic of work is done.

Thing is, it's not. "By the way, my team sent me down to IT today, and I was just wondering…"—how two people could come up from a floor that doesn't exist and why they would bleed—"What's up with that weird north elevator?"

Dad's brows scrunch together. "Nothing. Why? Did it get stuck? Somebody got stuck in the south elevator last month, but they checked them all over after that."

I shake my head and swallow fast. "Nah, I mean because of that S-3 button."

Dad's hand freezes in the middle between the plate and his mouth. A drop of gravy falls onto the cloth. And another. And another. *Another.* He blinks twice—and shoves the food into his mouth, chewing like it was the sole of a shoe, not a tender steak. "Oh, *that.*" He washes the food down with a sip of water. "Don't ask me. When we took over the building it was already wired like that. Maybe they got it cheaper." I get a wink and sly grin with that one. "In any case, I stand corrected, now that I think about it. The north elevators were the ones acting up. So, I suggest you stay away from them. I'd prefer to keep the COO's daughter out of daily gossip." He balls up his napkin and throws it onto the table, for a moment lost in thought. A small smile pulls the corners of his mouth up. "Did you know your mom once got stuck in an elevator?"

"Mom?" A warm, fuzzy feeling comes over me. Dad rarely talks about Mom. All I know is pieced together from seventeen years of begging for information scraps and committing them to eternal memory. I can't really hold it against Dad, though. From what I know, my mom was the love of his life. The perfect woman: A scientist, just like him, only devoted to clinical medicine, not research. A tad crazy, according to the skydiving pictures I found in Dad's drawer. Also a cook, writer, inventor and avid hiker. My mom did it all. So, when she died in childbirth after seventeen hours of labor when my large head got stuck in the birth canal and the emergency C-section only saved me and not her… it would have been a blow to everybody, but to my dad it destroyed his life.

Correction: *I* destroyed his life.

Maybe it's subconscious—well, I hope, or else it would make him one heck of an ass—but the way he acts with me, that distanced, careful way, I'm sure it stems from that. I'm sure somewhere deep down, he blames me for something *I* had no control over, and all his issues fall back on that one moment *he* had no control over.

I've always assumed he didn't want to be reminded of my mom, and that's why he pushed me in a totally different direction and away from science. Problem is though, I don't like to get pushed. I tend to push back.

Dad still carries that small smile, and it lights me up. This is a rare treat. This connection between us brought upon us courtesy of my mom's memory.

"You know, that was at university. Years ago. There was a power outage, and she got stuck. And I was waiting for her to come to our date. Nothing. I call the hospital, and nobody knows where she is. At that point, it's been hours, the power's long back on. So of course I worry. That wasn't like your mom. Couldn't get a hold of her. Long story short, after I got together a couple of friends, we found her in the elevator that had literally gotten stuck, despite the power being back on. So, once the firefighters pulled her out of that shaft, I got down on one knee and asked her to marry me."

I squeal once. "You did?"

His smile widens. "I did. The worry and fear I had when I couldn't find her showed me that my life without that woman would be incomplete, so I did it." A shadow crosses his face and he clears his throat. "Well. Anyway. Finish… finish your food. I still have work to do."

And with that, he gets up and walks out on me, the daughter who killed the woman his life is incomplete without.

CHAPTER FOUR

Today is the first day I feel like a real-deal adult.

It's my sixth day at Advangen and the first I'm going to start my own little project. To top it off, Dad is sick—not that it's a good thing—but since he can't drive me-slash-us to work, I get to take the bus. Nothing says adulting more than prepping your lunch and getting ready without a responsible caretaker nagging you to do stuff.

Unfortunately for me, my good mood goes *poof* the second I arrive at the bus stop, and that would be thanks to the tall, lean figure propped against the lamp pole next to it.

Gabriel glances up from his cell for about a split second. That's all he needs for the muscles in his jaws to tighten. "Ah, look. It's the COO's daughter." He clicks his phone off and shoves it into his back pocket.

"Shut up, Gabriel." I stare in the direction the bus is coming from, which, coincidentally and thankfully, is also the other direction from Gabriel. Why the heck doesn't he take his BMW? Daddy sprung for a fancy new electric one. I'm sure if Penelope saw him in it, she'd be all over him, again.

"Sure. Bit sensitive today?" He picks up his bag from the

ground and stands next to me. "Maybe because daddy's girl has to go alone to work today? Without her puppy protection?"

I wrap both my hands around the lunch bag I'm carrying. There's a glass Tupper in there, if I swung it really hard…

Alas, my self-restraint is commendable. Part of me wants to clock him in the head, but I don't. Yes, that's partially because the bus chooses to arrive at this very moment, but also because I'm in control. Gone are the times where I got into school brawls over differences in opinion. I'm a well-functioning almost-adult.

There you go.

I hold my head high as I enter the bus and fall into a window spot on the left. The second my butt touches down, I realize I made a tactical error. I should've taken the aisle seat.

"Nice. Thanks for saving me a spot, Nya." Gabriel slides into the seat next to me.

"Bugger off, Gabriel."

He places one hand over his heart. "Ouch. That hurt. We're going to the same lab, Nya. We're colleagues. Granted, one of us has been invited to co-author a paper—"

"What?" My head whips around. "You're kidding me." They invited him to write a paper with them? Him? He came in *second*! *I* came in first! What the heck is wrong with people?

Gabriel looks down at his fingernails, a smug look on his face. "Oh, wait—no. Your team didn't ask you?" The smug look turns into some kind of superiority complex. "Maybe they figured out the boss' daughter was really only that: the boss' daughter."

Hot anger shoots through my veins and ignites every cell in my body. Gone is my oh-so-commendable self-control. I scoot in my seat to face Gabriel, gripping my bag so hard my knuckles turn white. It's that or ramming my fists into his face, and I have enough common sense left to know that's not a good idea. *Barely* enough common sense left. "Shut up, Gabriel," I hiss at him. "You can be an ass all day long, I don't care, but you insinuate one more time I got this spot because of my relationship with the COO, I'm going to make your life hell." Not an empty threat. He used to be my best friend, now he's my best enemy. No doubt he started it, but I know I'm not innocent in keeping the feud alive. Easier to attack first than to deal with being attacked.

His eyebrows fly up to under his hairline. "You—"

"Correct. You think my name got me here? You think it wasn't all me working hard and spending hours in the lab? You're wrong, and you know it. So shut up and stop bullying me."

"*I'm* bullying *you*—"

"You—"

The woman in the row in front of us, mid-forties, turns halfway around to us. "You go, girl. Show him who's boss." She glances at Gabriel down her nose that shuts him right up.

"Thank you," I say. *Show him who's boss.* Okay, easy-peasy. I brush off something invisible—i.e., Gabriel's presence—from my left shoulder and face forward. My heart hammers like crazy, because I was *this* close to losing it. And here I thought maturity had finally won. Nope. Not even close. And by the looks of it, it won't win anytime soon either, because as I do my very best to ignore Gabriel, a plan takes shape in my mind. I'm nothing if not motivated, and competition has so far always made me better.

Once the bus arrives at Advangen, Gabriel scoots out of our row without a look back, or a look at me. I'm not even making a snide parting comment. Sometimes I surprise myself, especially because I stay calm and collected throughout the entire morning.

Granted, I work even harder, but that's par for the course in making a good—an even better—impression. Eventually, the moment has come. I take in one long, calming breath, then take off my medical gloves and throw them into the biohazard trash. "Hey, Shawn? Say, can I ask you something?"

"Sure thing. What's up, Nya?" Shawn does the same and takes off his safety goggles as soon as his hands are freed of the gloves. Wouldn't want any contamination of the equipment.

"Just wondering if you could give me an eval and tell me what I could improve on." I give him an innocent blink.

He chuckles and shakes his head. "Nya, you're doing beyond well. I mean, I can check in with Lillian and the others, but I don't think either of us has had an intern this professional before. We didn't have to spend hours teaching you the one-oh-one of lab etiquette, you've read all the important articles—heck, even more than Jules, if I'm not mistaken, especially on Epigenetics—so, yeah, I'd say you're doing really well." He beams at me, and I'd be lying if I said it didn't make me proud. Alas, that's not what I'm going for.

"I'm so glad to hear it, really. If there's anything I can improve on, please let me know. I want to be the best I can."

He claps my shoulders. "You're doing fantastic. No complaints at all."

Commence happy face. "Thank you, Shawn. And, well, if that's the case…" Pause for dramatic effect, widen eyes, suck in lower lip… "Do you think I could co-author the paper you're working on?"

His face falls. "Uhh—"

"I mean, at the very end. Obviously. I don't mean to take anybody's spot. But I can do my fair share of work, you know that. I have already. So, if I crank it up, could I…" The sentence trails off, because Shawn's face says it all. "That's a no, I take it?"

He cringes. "Nya, it's complicated."

"Complicated." I can't see why. I do the work, I get mentioned. I do more work, I get mentioned further up front.

"Yes. Complicated." He sighs and works a hand through his hair. "Listen, I'd love to have you co-author. Or use you more. With your skills…" Another sigh. "But… my hands are tied—"

Click.

The pieces fall into place. "My dad." I cross my arms in front of my chest. "It's my dad, am I right?"

Shawn looks at me apologetically. "He kind of made it clear where the limits are. I'm sorry," he adds. "Maybe if you talked to him—"

"Oh, I will talk to him." Don't know if it's going to change anything, but I'm flipping mad. Flipping, steaming, stinking mad. How dare he ruin this for me! How dare he! I got in here on skills, not his name! On skills I worked hard for! How dare he spoil this for me!

I feel a vein pulsating in my temple and rub my forehead. Headache. Of course. Thanks, Dad, as always.

With all the self-control I have, I force my features under control. "I'll let you know what he says. Would it be okay if I took my lunch break now?" Because I need to put some distance between us and blow off some steam.

"Sure. Sure. Take a bit longer, and… Listen, I'm sorry. Really."

I believe him. Nobody here has given me any indication otherwise. It's all my dad. I force my face into the resemblance of a smile. "Thanks, Shawn. See you soon."

And then I'm out before I blow up and lose all maturity and bonus points I have.

I stomp into the elevator to go down to the first-floor cafeteria.

So. Mad.

Dad's lucky he's out sick, or else he could bet I'd be storming into his office right now. How dare he? Why the heck can't he stop meddling? This is my life. My decision. My work. Gah!

"Hold the elevator!"

Before I've even pushed a button, I shoot my hand out to keep the doors from closing. Unfortunately, my anger-clouded brain hasn't quite realized I should've done the opposite.

"Thank you. That was—oh." Gabriel's eyes widen when he sees little me.

"Unintentional." I complete his sentence and glower at him, my headache pulsing with my spike in blood pressure.

"Figured so." He shrugs it off and leans against the wall of the elevator as the doors are closing. "But so nice of you, nonetheless. I only have a few minutes for lunch. Those retroviruses are impatient, and we're *this* close to a breakthrough." He looks down at his cuticles and blows on them.

Wrong thing to say. I can barely stand Gabriel the way it is these days, and even less so when he teases me like this morning, but doing it now, after what Shawn just told me? Not cool at all.

And it turns me into a sore loser. A petty person.

I pull off my best condescending smile. "Aw, so happy for you. But sorry, this elevator is going up first." I whip out my key card and swipe it across the reader, then punch the button for the 8th floor. "Some of us have important things to do—oops, wait, you're not allowed access up there." I fake surprise and cover my mouth with my hand. "So sorry, didn't want to rub that in your face, but ouch, that must sting. I'll talk to the guys from human engineering up there over lunch. I know you're a big fan. Maybe they'll give me some tips."

Gabriel's face turns red. "Shut up, Nya."

Gotcha. That hit his soft spot. "Really, a pity you're not

allowed up there, Gabriel. So much to see. So much to learn." The doors open. "Bye, now. Have a wonderful lunch." I give him a royal wave and sashay out of the elevator and walk around the corner like I owned this place—only to deflate the moment I'm out of sight and the elevator whisks Gabriel away from me.

Crap.

"Dang it." I kick the wall. Stupid, stupid, stupid. Now I'm stuck on the executive floor, no food anywhere, no ibuprofen for my poor abused head anywhere either, *and* I can't very well go down to the cafeteria after the show I just pulled off. To top it off, Dad isn't here, so I can't visit and yell at him either, so I don't have a clue what to do here with my frustration. Ugh, ugh, *ugh*. I got no-freakin'-where to go.

Pinching the bridge of my nose, I evaluate my limited options. I could go down to the second floor and see if my friend from years ago still works here, Mr. Yannic. Poor guy had to babysit me on the few and far-between occasions when Dad took me with him to work, because God forbid I'd bother anybody on the executive floor. Better keep Nya out of sight. While that part annoyed me, I liked Mr. Yannic. Always had candy, always had squirrel food, because he was the only one with a tree reaching his window and squirrels coming by for the occasional snack.

But yeah, or rather, no: I won't go and catch up with Mr. Yannic either. Grr.

After one more kick against the wall, I decide to call it defeat. Well, to a degree. Call me pathetic, call me small-minded, but I can't get over the fact that I was demoted to a useless intern second class, while Gabriel gets to co-author a paper. Maybe call me resentful and bitter, too.

I sigh so loud it would've been embarrassing had anybody been around to witness it.

Sheesh. Pull yourself together, Nya. Whining never helped anybody. The measure of a person isn't always how successful they are, but how they handle defeat. Correction, because as I said, this is not defeat, merely a *temporary setback.*

Thing is, to handle any setback, I need some external support: chocolate. And while Dad told me the executive lounge up here holds tons of healthy food, nothing chocolate-y can be found anywhere. Apparently, they've never heard about healing powers of dark cocoa. Amateurs.

Still, I'm not going to the cafeteria and risk looking stupid in front of Gabriel. I have other options: vending machines. Good thing I know my way around here and where to find vending machines.

An office door, the one closest to me, opens and a man steps out sideways, still talking to somebody on the inside of the room. "—and then send me a memo when the cell lines— Oh!" He startles when he turns around and sees me, but so do I, because I know that slightly older, gray-haired gentleman.

Heat swamps my cheeks. "Dr. Sherman. Hi!" It comes out more as a squeak than a greeting. Could it be any more embarrassing than me standing up here like I had nothing better to do when the CEO of Advangen runs into me, literally? And didn't Dad say something along those lines that he was gone most of the summer, to Europe? Clearly, he isn't yet. Sigh.

Dr. Sherman narrows his eyes and tilts his head to the side, as if he was trying to figure me out. He lets his gaze roam across my face so thoroughly, I wouldn't be surprised if he counted all my fourteen and a half freckles. Eventually he looks at my ID clipped to my revers, and understanding flashes across his face. "Nya Bennison," he says, drawing out the words. "And boy, do you look different from last time I saw you."

My blush intensifies by the nth degree, because yeah, we haven't really met under normal circumstances yet. "Well, uh, this is the real me." Without a wig and fifteen thousand sweaters.

His gaze travels over my face in a slow and perusing way, as if he hadn't just counted every freckle and looked at every single strand of my red hair that has escaped my hairdo. "Yeah." He stretches the word out. "This is the real you, I can tell. You're... your father's daughter, for sure."

That sounded weird, especially since we don't look that much alike. I clear my throat. "I was on my way back down. Sorry, Mr. Sherman." I lift a hand and wave, about to turn.

"How do you like your internship?"

I stop mid-motion. "I love it. I'm learning a lot."

He chuckles. "That was the plan. Has anybody already let you analyze your own genome? That's always thrilling."

I shake my head. "No, not so far. We're busy with Shawn Bushman's project."

"Ah, okay. That makes sense. But then, you are a budding geneticist. It's kind of a rite of passage to extract your own DNA and visualize it. It's the highlight for most interns." He smacks his lips as he tilts his head. "I'll tell you what. Why don't you do that in my lab, right down this hallway? I can't have my COO's daughter miss out on all the fun. Come on." He slaps my shoulder and nods his chin toward the hallway behind him.

Holy cow, the CEO of Advangen wants to freakin' work with me! That's like being knighted while receiving the Nobel prize at the same time! Excitement rushes through me—until I remember I hold myself to a certain standard, and that I don't want nepotism as a driving force behind whatever I do at Advangen.

So, I do the morally right thing and shake my head, even though it feels like working against a force stronger than my neck muscles. "Thank you, Dr. Sherman, but I'm really involved in Shawn's project. It wouldn't feel right to abandon it mid-work. But..." I bite my lower lip and peer up at him, hopeful. "But maybe in a week? We should be done with most time-sensitive work at that point, plus, I could give him some heads-up." *Please say yes, please say yes...*

Dr. Sherman laughs out once. "You are your father's daughter, indeed. Always thinking about work. All right then, I see your point. Today in a week? And don't cancel on me. Yes, yes, I know Bushman's always busy, and he could always use your undivided attention and help, but like I said, you gotta play a little bit. You can't only be working." He winks. "What do you think?"

What do I think, besides that holy cow, the CEO of Advangen is really willing to work with me? A huge grin splits my face. "I would love to do that. Thank you, Dr. Sherman! Today in one week."

"4:00 P.M.?"

"That's perfect." Any time would be, but this way he's right. I can finish helping Shawn and then do my thing.

"Love it. Just do me a favor. Don't tell your dad. Knowing him, he'd get his knickers in a bunch if I took you out of your regular duties."

I huff. "You know him well, sir." That's Dad in a nutshell. "I won't mention it to him."

"Then we have a plan. Even better, a secret plan." Sherman gives me a thumbs up. "I haven't had the chance to impress an intern for a while, so I'm looking forward to it."

"Looking very much forward to it myself. But, anyway, please don't let me keep you." I wave again. "Thank you again, Dr. Sherman. Have a great rest of your day." With that, I walk back around the corner toward the elevator, hearing Dr. Sherman take off in the opposite direction after a few more seconds.

Once I'm sure nobody sees me, I pump a fist. Squee! I get to work with Dr. Sherman! I've got to come up with a list of questions, and not just about genetic engineering, but his career. No use asking Dad about his, but Dr. Sherman… He seems to actually want to teach me. That conversation could've been super awkward with me being caught on the executive floor but turned into a lucky coincidence.

Hah! Take that, Gabriel!

I push the down button to call the elevator, and its doors open right away, letting me enter.

"Hold it!"

Before I can suppress the reflex, I have yet again shot out my hand to block the doors from closing, like I did for Gabriel. What is it with me and—

My gaze falls on the two men trying to catch the elevator, pushing a cart loaded with everything a scientist's heart desires.

Whoa.

That cart? It literally holds heaven on earth.

"Thank you." Guy number one breathes heavily. "This thing otherwise takes forev—" His eyes fall on me, brows pulling down into a disapproving scowl—until he gives me the once-over and notices my badge. That's when the scowl morphs into confusion and his eyes jump up to my face again.

I sigh. I know. Young woman, on the executive floor, must be a mistake. I wave at him. "I'm allowed to be up here." I point at the stripe at the bottom of my ID. "I won the Summer Internship this year."

Pause.

"Ah," guy number one says eventually.

Ah.

No *nice to meet you.*

No *cool, congrats.*

Nope.

Nothing.

And it's a tad awkward.

I clear my throat. Awkward-shmawkward, who cares. Curiosity wins over awkwardness any time of the day. I nod at the cart. "Is this… are you… I mean, is this for the CRISPR-directed integrates study? The one that's been on the news?" Because it looks like it might be. A-mazing. So, so cool. That study can help us figure out how to use CRISPR for larger edits, not just short sequences, and looking at their table… Well, maybe not. Huh. It's also loaded with tourniquets, vials, needles and IVs, slides for microscopes and what not. On the other hand, they're coming from this floor, the executive floor, where all the really important things happen and Sherman has his own lab.

The two exchange a glance. "Yeah. Yeah. Part of it," Guy number one says. I peek at his ID: Dirk Boldt. Never heard of him, not that it means anything. The only thing that means a lot is that this is an opportunity, served on a silver platter. *Cart.* Silver cart. But still.

I point at the materials. Gene sequencer as well. Whoa. "So exciting, seriously! I'm on lunch break—would you mind if I gave you a hand? Watched what you're doing?"

The guy shoots a quick glance at his colleague, and neither he nor I miss the slight shake of his head. "Actually, sorry, it's not something we—"

As much as I hate it at times, now is the moment to use my very own Open Sesame. I smile at Dirk's colleague. "Sorry, so rude. I'm Nya Bennison, Mr. Bennison's daughter."

One Mississippi.

Two Mississippi.

Three—

The elevator pings and opens its doors to the S-2 floor.

Yeah.

Well.

That'd be my cue to scatter, because the one sentence I'm waiting for doesn't seem to come from them: definitely no invitation to join them.

But hey, at least I made a fool of myself after all. Not in front of Gabriel or Dr. Sherman, there's that, but in front of Dad's colleagues.

I give it one more attempt to save this from a complete disaster. "Well, if you change your mind and need a young, motivated scientist, call me." I step out of the elevator, but hold my arm out to stop the doors from closing into those two guys.

"Sure. Thank you," Guy number one says.

And stays put.

His colleague looks straight past me, unblinking. Waiting. "You can let go," he says.

Huh?

Oh.

I pull my arm back and the doors close.

In the very last moment before they shut, I see guy number one touch his ID to the pad and select the very first button next to it.

S3.

Heat flows through my chest. They're going to the very floor my dad insists doesn't exist.

And they're taking all the material with them.

CHAPTER FIVE

No matter the rest of the afternoon running smoothly, I can't forget about those guys going down to S3.

The quote-unquote non-existent S3.

Yeah. Non-existent my butt.

The longer I think about it, the clearer it gets: It's all Dad. He doesn't want me to find a footing in research, so he makes sure his employees know to keep me on a short leash. He also makes sure I don't venture off the beaten path and find even more I'd be interested in, namely, cutting-edge research I've been dreaming about. *Dreaming!*

Alas, this dream is slowly turning into a nightmare.

The entire way from the bus stop to our house, I stomp like a mad elephant in a stampede. I wonder what he told them. Did he ridicule me, like I didn't know what I was doing? Threaten them? A mix of both?

More importantly, does it even matter? I slam the door closed. "I'm home!" Home and mad.

Coughing comes from my dad's bedroom down the hallway. I drop my work bag next to my dad's and slip out of my shoes before I tip-toe over the cold tile floor toward germ-central. California is nice in fall, only our AC cools it down to freezing.

I knock twice on the door frame before I enter. Dad's propped up on two or three pillows in his bed, reading glasses on his nose, the latest copy of *Scientific Unlimited* in his hands. Could be any other day if it wasn't for him wearing sweatpants and a T-shirt instead of slacks and a dress shirt, with or without tie, depending on the day. With a tie on a workday, without on a weekend.

His face lights up when I come in, and for a moment, I'm not mad anymore.

For a *brief* moment. Like the length of a heartbeat.

I lean against the wall and cross my arms, and that gesture alone brings the smile on my dad's face to falter. "What is it, Nya?"

My lips press into a thin line. Keep it calm. Don't yell. Don't accuse. It won't lead anywhere. We're going for professionalism and maturity, or else this is a dead end.

I cock my head to the left. "Dad, what are you going to do when I move out?"

"Huh?" He blinks twice.

"No, really. When college comes around and I move out."

He lets the issue of *Scientific Unlimited* sink down onto his legs. "Regarding…?"

"Me. When I'm at college, how are you going to control me? Or my life?"

"Control—"

"My life. When I'm gone. Different city. Far away. Nobody you know in the faculty, nobody to influence and to tell what to do with me."

Dad cringes. The pieces have fallen into place. "Nya—"

I hold up a hand. "I'm mad, Dad. You know how hard I worked—actually, you don't, because you make telling you those things freakin' hard. But you can at least imagine how hard I worked to come up with the data that won me the internship. I got in on my own, and then you have the audacity to meddle behind my back? You're sabotaging me before I can even get a leg off the ground." I walk over to the little table he has under the window and grab the bottle with the Ibuprofen.

"I wouldn't call it sabota—"

Deep breath. "You wouldn't? I would. What about drilling your employees to hold me back is not sabotage?" I unscrew the bottle and count three pills into my palm.

Dad takes off his glasses. "Do you want to transfer?"

"Huh?" Transfer what?

"I can talk to Mike or Joe at CenterCure. I'm sure they'd be happy—"

Oh, come on! I set the medication bottle down with a bang. "But I wouldn't, Dad! It's Advangen who has all the cutting-edge research! Not CenterCure! Maybe WissenSCHAFFT in Germany, but one, their focus differs from Advangen, and two, I doubt you'd like to send me there, right?"

His lips press tight. "Not going to happen."

That was a safe bet. Anything that reminds Dad of Mom is a no-go, and her former best friend at WissenSCHAFFT would fit the bill. "See? So just let me do my thing! Dr. Sherman even said today—"

Dad grows completely still, as if he was frozen in time. "You met Dr. Sherman?"

"Yes, I ran into him on the exec floor—" I snap my mouth shut. Dad didn't want me up there, and yet I still got access. Telling him I still got up there is the fastest way to get all my access revoked.

But to my complete and utter surprise, Dad doesn't latch onto that. He chooses a different target. "He saw you?"

I roll my eyes. "Yes, Dad. He did. And he seems happy that I have this internship." That might be stretching it a bit, but he wasn't unhappy to see me, so there we go. I mean, he offered to work with me—which I won't tell Dad about, unless I want him to meddle with that, too. No idea, he might just tell his boss I have the cooties or something. Wouldn't put it beneath him.

I pop the three Ibuprofen capsules into my mouth and take a sip from Dad's water bottle on the table.

An alarmed look creeps into his face. "I drank from that!"

I swallow and wipe my mouth with the back of my hand. "So what? We've shared bottles and glasses and even ice cream cones before."

He gives me a deadpanned look. "I'm sick, genius."

"And I never get sick." I shrug. "Your germs don't touch me."

Dad snaps his mouth shut and closes his eyes, taking one slow breath, like praying for patience. He exhales just as slowly. "And yet you're taking Ibuprofen."

"Minor headache."

The alarmed look on his face grows. "Again? Since when? How bad is it? Any other symptoms with it, like—"

"No, Dad, don't freak out, I'm fine. It's just a headache, because I'm stressed. Oh, and do you want to know why I'm stressed by any chance? Because I saw your lie go up in smoke, Dad."

He chokes on his next inhale. "What?" It comes out with a wheeze.

I take a step away from the wall into the room, arms crossed in front of my chest, chin up high. "I saw a team take equipment for the CRISPR-directed integrates study into the elevator—down to S3. Which, wait—which doesn't exist. I was told. By my father, who's apparently doing all he can to keep me out of the loop."

Dad pales. "There is no S3."

"Right." Of course there isn't. "Maybe my clearance isn't high enough, but then don't lie to me but say—"

Dad's hand slams down on the mattress next to him. "Damn it, Nya, there is no S3! And for once in your life, can you please just listen to me and back off! Trust me as your father that I know what I'm doing, at least most of the time, and running around talking about stuff you don't understand—" He stops himself mid-sentence, but the damage is done.

My jaw drops open. "Stuff I don't understand? Stuff I don't understand?" I stomp down hard, then freeze, only my harsh breathing disturbing the strained silence between us. "You know what, Dad? Never mind. This is useless. We both know I'm going to do what I do best, and you're going to do your best to keep me from it." I pause to look at the man I wanted to see me for who I am all my life. "Guess it's on then."

I turn on my heels and walk out, the last bit of dignity I still have left keeping me upright until I hit my room and fall face-forward onto my bed.

Then, I cry.

The next morning I'm up early. Tough to get a good night's sleep after a fight with your dad. It's still dark outside when I'm ready to go. Of course, I could stay home longer, but then Dad would wake up. Since he's not going to work today either, I might be lucky and he might sleep longer, but usually he's like clockwork. So no, I won't stay. The first bus leaves in five minutes. What if I started the setup already and maybe even worked ahead? Wouldn't that show Shawn how good I am? Maybe he could talk to my dad and put in a word for me, because this nonsense, it has to stop.

I grab my bag from the table next to Dad's—and pause.

What if—

Naaah. I'm not that kind of—

But…

With a silent groan, I snatch Dad's Advangen ID-card from the pocket of his bag and slip it into mine.

Apparently, I *am* that kind of girl.

The entire way to work, Dad's ID burns through the bag, through my jacket, through my shirt, right into my skin.

Proves I at least still have a conscience. Not a clean one, but a conscience.

I wrap my fingers around the innocent little plastic card. I'm only going to use it for one teensy-tiny peek. A quick in and out. Verification and evidence of my theory. Exactly. That's all this is. Verifying a thesis, only the thesis statement is *my father is lying to me,* and its objective is *to find out if and why Nya Bennison's dad is a lying s.o.b.*

Makes me feel better already.

When I arrive at work, it's barely five thirty a.m. The lights are on, and the janitor's laying out skid-proof mats in front of the automatic sliding glass doors. It's supposed to rain today and I guess the company doesn't want to get sued by employees who slipped and broke their necks.

I nod a quick greeting and enter the elevator. Taking a quick glance around, I swipe my ID and press S3.

Nothing happens. *Because there is no S3.* Right.

So, with a little twist of my body, I pull Dad's ID out of my bag and swipe it in front of the reader. Even if the janitor had peeked, he wouldn't have seen anything. I hit the S3 button with my index finger—

And the doors close.

S3 doesn't exist my butt!

A small smile works on the corners of my mouth, but man, the way down to S3 feels way longer than it should. Maybe that's because my heart's beating a tad faster than normal, courtesy of my possibly illegal way of access.

Eventually, the elevator jolts to a halt, and in that split second before the doors open, I curse myself for not having more of a plan in place: What do I do if there's a checkpoint? People? When I go back up? What do I tell Dad? That I stole his card? What do I tell Shawn? *Look, dude, downstairs looks more interesting, I know I shouldn't be there, but can you transfer—*

The doors hiss apart and my eyes pop open wide.

Whoa.

Oo-kaay…

I'm not in Kansas anymore, it appears. The elevator opens into a small room filled with metal lockers, shelves, and hooks on the wall—all empty. And that's not what has my heart beating faster: That honor would go to the air tunnel installed across from me.

Excitement makes my next breath wheezy. *Gotcha.* This air tunnel is proof they're working on something awesome down here. The only reason to have this thing is to move between two areas and have it filter out any kind of contamination. Usually, there are suits to go with that, like white, all-body-dress-up-things, but I don't see any. I assume they'd usually be in the empty shelves, which must mean level of contamination is not important at this point in their studies.

I take a couple of small steps forward until I'm at the metal door. A light blinks on and off on the reader next to it. Okay then. Dad's ID comes in handy today. Here's to hoping Dad doesn't get a daily log of his swipes via email or whatever.

One swipe and the lock gives an audible click. I blow out a puff of air. In for a penny, in for a pound. Let's add trespassing to the charges of stealing my dad's ID.

The door to the air tunnel is much heavier than I thought when I pull it open. Okay, yes, it would have to keep whatever might be toxic in this lab out if needed, so I get it. Once it closes behind me, a short wave of claustrophobia washes over me, because this is *small.*

And quiet.

No hiss of air, no fan running.

Complete silence thanks to the hermetically locked doors and isolation. My heartbeat sounds like a steam train, my breathing is even worse. Raspy.

Anyway.

After about ten seconds, another audible click announces the outgoing door to be open.

Here we go.

My heart speeds it up, be that because of the illegal entry, or because of the prospect of seeing cutting-edge set ups. I open the door and step out—

—into a regular hallway.

A disappointingly regular hallway.

I look left. I look right.

No super-secret lab equipment.

But also no cameras that I can see—nothing but a regular hallway.

Well, not quite. I mean, the walls are white, and it looks like the same blueprint from upstairs—hallway to the left and right, doors in the same location they'd be on my floor—but movie posters cover the walls here. *Star Trek. Star Wars. Back to the Future. Avengers. Dune.*

Uhh…?

I take a tentative step to the left and let the door fall shut behind me.

Not what I expected.

Instead of the usual medical, sterile air, I pick up on something fresher, like fresh-cut grass or so. What the…?

I tip-toe down the hallway. The doors have labels, like upstairs, where the rooms have numbers depending on level and location: L1-12, L1-13, L1-14, or L2-12, L2-13, L2-14. Here? Not so much.

Door one: Storage.

Door two: Kitchen.

Door three: Library.

So what—S3 is nothing but a less-fancy version of the executive floor? That's it? With an airlock? Seriously, WTF?

Door four: Bathroom.

Door five: Cris' Room.

Wait, what? I do a double-take. Cris' room? Who is Cris? I mean, besides, obviously somebody high up the food chain, or else he wouldn't have his own secret floor—and maybe whatever happens here, he is the man behind the research? If that's the case, how can I meet—

The door behind me opens and I jolt. Crap I—

Some whistling, soft steps—

I whirl around, ready with an explanation, an apology, anything that will keep me out of trouble—and I freeze.

So does the person three feet across from me.

A… boy.

My age.

A boy, about my age or a tad older, naked besides a towel around his waist, secured with one hand while the other rubs a smaller towel over his short, wet hair.

Not. What. I. Expected.

The boy stares at me, frozen, like I stare at him.

I know I should say something, apologize, explain, but my brain short-circuited the moment my eyes fell on him.

Why is there a barefooted, half-naked boy standing in the hallway on the secret level of my dad's company?

The boy blinks. "Uh… hi?" His voice is deep, but rises in the end as if he weren't sure this was the right thing to say.

I open my mouth, only to close it right after. Then, I shake my head, but it doesn't do a thing to clear my mind. That half-naked boy is still there. Wide shoulders, a couple of scars and scabs on his breastbone, framed by nice pecs. Nice biceps, too. Impressive abs, like eight-pack. A fine trail of hair from his belly button to—

Yeah. Uh, stop it right here.

The boy tilts his head. "Do you… speak English?"

Shit. My cheeks burst into flames. "Yes. Yes, I do. I'm sorry."

His eyebrows shoot up to under his hairline. "Sorry for what?"

I raise one eyebrow in response and pointedly look at his towel. "You're coming out of the shower."

"Yes." He says it more like a question, like *yes, so what?*

"And you didn't expect me."

The boy laughs and drops the hand that worked the towel through his hair. "No. Can't say I did." He gives me a once-over.

And again. Narrows his eyes. "You're a girl."

Aw, come on! "What's that supposed to mean?" I've had enough misogynistic crap to deal with in my life, I don't—

"Sorry!" He all but jumps back, both hands raised, like in

defense. "Sorry! I just… it's just—" His towel slides, and it's all he can do to grab it before it shows me way more than I've already seen. "Whoops." The look he gives me, a mix of apologetic and… I don't know, *young*. Somehow, it makes up for the blunder he just landed. Barely so.

I sigh. "Nobody expects a girl. I know. Guys, yes. Girls, not so much."

"I didn't really expect anybody, like I said. Nobody's really allowed down here."

About that… "But you are?" A boy. My age. Repeat: *A boy. My age!*

He shrugs. "Yeah. Somebody has to run all this." The hand that holds the smaller towel waves through the air toward the hallway I came from.

My hands ball into fists. No freakin' way. *This guy* runs the lab down here? This *boy*? WTF, indeed! I mean, what are his credentials? He can't be much older than me, maybe Gabriel's age, but how can he be so much better than Gabriel or me? Because we're *good*! We exceed what others tackle for their PhDs—and if there was a genius my age in my dad's company, wouldn't I know about that?

I answer the question the second I ask it: No, of course not. Dad wouldn't do anything to encourage me, and if this is top secret down here, then he wouldn't be allowed to share that information anyway.

Still.

I'm mad.

The boy doesn't seem to pick up on it. He smiles wider, dimples and all, and throws the smaller towel over his shoulder to hold out a hand. "I'm Cris, by the way." He takes a small step forward to reach me, a cute little ankle bracelet jingling on his right foot.

I take his hand. "Nya." Kinda proud of not squishing his bones to mush.

"Nice to meet you, Nya." His hand lingers too long in mine, so I pull it out.

I nod my chin at the shower. "So, you're just off a night shift, or what?" Dad used to do that. Work the nights in the lab, take a shower at work, go to university and teach. That was when he was working on his thesis, before I was born. He still talks about it like it was the best time of his life.

Cris shakes his head. "Nah, just woke up half an hour—"

"Wait, you sleep here?" Aw, come on! He's not just running this lab, it's basically his? *His* responsibility, *his* baby?

"Yes." He nods, like, *of course.*

And it makes me mad. This is getting worse and worse. Here I am, working my butt off for some kind of success, something— anything, really—and this guy has it all. Heck, they allow him to stay right in the freakin' lab, while I can't even co-author a minor paper! Envy-green doesn't look good on me, but man…!

I blow out a long breath of air. Easy, tiger. Blowing up won't help. It's going to get me the opposite—

Oh.

Idea: what if I got him on my side? And let *him* work on Dad? If he's their genius, the guy who runs *this*, isn't his word bound to have some kind of impact, no matter his age?

Cris might be my ticket to the in-club.

I turn my frown upside down. "That's awesome. You've got everything right here." I motion around. "Can you give me a tour?" Because I want to see it all, especially the lab.

His brows narrow as his face takes on an amused look. "My pleasure, but I believe it would be customary to get dressed first? Or would you prefer—"

This time it's my turn to jump back, both palms up. "No! No! I mean, whatever, but of course, yes. I mean, no." Crap. Totally butchered that one.

Cris chuckles. "Get dressed first, you say?"

My cheeks burn. *Burn.* "Yes."

He chuckles once more. "Okay—"

A loud siren blasts through the ceiling-mounted speakers. Cris flinches. "Crap. I'm late." He shoots me a glance. "Want to help?"

OMG, do I ever? Excitement shoots through me. "Of course. I assume it's...?" I let the sentence trail off, and Cris doesn't disappoint.

He rolls his eyes. "Saving the world one button at a time, you know how that goes. If we both log in, it could shave one or two hours off the work."

Oh, crap, logging in! I flinch. Whatever it is we're logging, if they—no matter Dad is sick—see me log in from here, under Cris' work, I'm out. Cris has no reason to stand up for me, none at all. I haven't shown him my worth yet.

I come up with an apologetic smile. "Actually, can't make today, but... can you do me a favor?"

He shoots a nervous glance at the door that says *Office*, then back at me. "What?"

"Would it be okay if I came back tomorrow, and you showed me around?"

"Wait, you want to go back up?"

"Well, yeah."

"Why?"

D'uh. "Because I have work to do."

He shakes his head. "I don't get it. You... are upstairs, but you also have access here?"

Strike! He assumes already I'm assigned here. I hold up Dad's

ID with my thumb on the picture. "Yeah, of course."

That earns me a slow, measured smile. "Okay. Then I'll see you tomorrow. Same time?"

"Same time."

"I'll try to be out of the shower by then."

"I'd appreciate that." Although… he has a nice body. Added bonus for today.

The same alarm tone rings again. Cris twitches once. "I really gotta go."

"S-sure." Sometimes cultures can't wait, I know that much. I turn to leave. Oh, actually, one more thing. "Hey, Cris? Could you please not mention me? I… I haven't gotten my official orientation for down here yet, and I don't want them to know—"

He holds up a hand. "Say no more. I know how it is with protocol. You've been cleared and you have access down here. That's all I need to know." He gives me a mischievous look. "See you tomorrow, Nya."

"See you tomorrow, Cris." I turn away from him and walk down the corridor. Guess once I come clear I will have some apologizing to do, but then… I'm hopeful he's going to understand. I bet it's the same for him, the struggle because of his age. His advantage is he's a guy, so at least he doesn't have to deal with all the misogynistic crap, but still.

One swipe of the ID unlocks the heavy swing door and I pull it open. Just before it closes, Cris calls out my name.

"Nya?" He's still standing where I left him, one hand on his towel, the other raised in greeting, or rather, goodbye. "Be careful up there, okay?"

The door falls shut and locks me into complete, all-encompassing silence, where nothing rings louder than his last words: *Be careful up there.*

CHAPTER SIX

I'm distracted for the rest of the day. Preoccupied, basically. It's not like me, but I can't help it. My emotions circle from anger to self-pity to go-getter-attitude and back, but in the end, I come up with a plan: get on Cris' good side. Get him to put in a word for me, preferably directly with Dr. Sherman, get noticed, get promoted, and rock the science world.

Easy-peasy.

Setting the plan into motion: "Hey, Shawn?" I keep my gloved hands on the adjustment dials of the microscope I'm working with.

"Huh?" He doesn't look up from his, but scribbles something with his right. Wonder how he can read it after, but experience has shown he can.

"I'll be in a bit later tomorrow, around noon or so, if you don't mind. Working on a project my dad gave me." Kind of. Or not. Not really.

"Sure. I'll wait with the new setup until you're in." He goes back to scanning through his slide, and that's that.

Like I said: Easy-peasy.

But why is it then that I can't get Cris' words out of my ear? *Be careful up there.*

Careful with what? To not tell people? Keep it a secret? That should be easy, because I ain't ruining my chances by blabbering about what I did—what I'm about to do.

Once I get home, I only check quickly on Dad. For one, I'm still mad at him, for another, I'm sure he'd take one good look at me and know that I took his ID. Or did something. I'm not the world's best liar, sue me.

"Sorry, Nya. You've got to take the bus tomorrow again." Dad coughs hard, the last one ending in a wheeze. "I won't make it back to work yet."

Can't say I mind at this point. I definitely need his ID one more time. "No problem, Dad. Did you COVID-test again?"

He gives a small nod at the small, rectangular plastic tester on his nightstand. "Negative. My antibodies are still holding strong. This is just a regular, boring virus."

I'll take regular over COVID any time of the day, not that I ever had COVID, or frequent colds, that is. It's from all the veggies I'm eating. Healthy as a horse. "Anything I can get you?"

"Unless you can make me recover quicker so I can get back to work on my serum and help my patient, no thank you." He waves a tired hand, my sign to retreat. I lock myself into my room, power up my laptop and start my Pubmed search about everything related to Advangen's research, because if I want to impress Cris tomorrow, I better be prepared.

Be careful up there.

This morning I make it to work even earlier. Part of it is because I want to make sure nobody sees me—after all, this is still trespassing and breaking the rules—the other part is that I want to get started as soon as possible. To say I'm eager is an understatement.

Once I pass the airlock, I announce myself. Seems like a fair warning, considering yesterday's way of meeting. "Cris? It's Nya. Good morning!"

"I'm over here." His voice comes from the end of the hallway close to where I ran into him a mere twenty-four hours ago. This time, I pay even more attention to the doors. Where is that lab? Unless it's behind one of the rooms I pass, I wouldn't know where they're hiding it. Oh. Maybe they are. I'll find out soon enough.

I find Cris sitting in the room labeled Living Room—watching TV. A movie, actually. *Avatar.*

He mutes the sound. "Morning. You made it back." A smile spreads over his face, and for a moment, it makes me feel special and cool.

Until I remember I tricked him into this.

"Yeah, I'm back." I drop my bag close to the door and fall onto the couch next to him. "Didn't take you for a TV-in-the-morning-person." To get where he is, he must've been on top of things 24/7, and from experience I know that affects both social life and free time. Massively.

He sighs, then gestures at the shelf next to the TV, loaded with DVDs. "Not much else to do here."

Everybody needs a break, I get it. "What about the gym on three?" Or the masseuse on the same floor. Or the small park outside. All courtesy of Dr. Sherman's attempt to imitate the real big companies, like Google and Apple. All that's missing is a bike track for the office hallways.

Cris throws me a questioning glance. "Upstairs?"

I point my finger up.

Cris laughs out once. "Good one." He searches for something

on the coffee table in front of the couch. All right, I get it. He's important. Grr.

He finds the remote and switches off the TV. For a brief moment, as he's focused on the remote, head held low and curly hair falling into his face, I allow myself to look at him: deep-set eyes under a prominent ridge. A straight nose slightly widened at the root. Together with his high cheekbones, it gives him a strong, masculine flair, kind of like those models when they're aiming for the mysterious look, and somehow the familiarity of it tugs on my core. His hair is lighter than I thought yesterday, but then, it was wet. Instead of black, it's more a brown with some red in there, depending on the way the light hits it. And, if I'm not mistaken, I see some freckles. Hah! A fellow freckle-person!

Cris throws the remote back onto the table. "So, where'd you transfer from?"

Uh, transfer? I drop my gaze and fumble with the zipper of my hoodie. How do I play this? "You know, I've been all over the place. Why?"

He scoots back and pulls one leg up so that he's facing me. His right arm rests up high on the couch's back, making his biceps pop. Can't fool me. He knows where the gym is.

"Because you're the first transfer ever. I thought we were spaced too far."

Spaced— "You mean the other locations?" Advangen has several daughter companies throughout the world, all Dr. Sherman's. Dad has been to many of them over the years, much less when I was younger and needed a sitter, much more over the last years as teenage-me annoyed him more and more.

Cris nods and wipes that resistant lock of hair out of his face. "Yeah. So far, I've only seen people leave for one of the other locations, but never transfer here."

I give him a skeptical glance. "Really? Why would they? This is by far the best one of them all." Headquarters.

His fingers drum a rhythm onto the couch's fabric. "I figured the radiation was at its worst here."

The— "Radiation?" What kind of radiation? Everything's genetic research, not physics. No need for anything more than, let's say, an X-Ray machine.

He nods. "Makes me sad I never got to see the surface. I mean, you traveled it on your way here. What does it look like up there? Still mostly barren?"

Still mostly—

What the what?

"You're kidding me, right?" There is no radiation.

His brows pull together. "No. Did it sound like I did?"

"Radiation."

He nods.

"On… the surface."

He nods again, face straight and serious.

I sit up straighter. "Is that your idea of a joke? I mean, payback because I surprised you yesterday? Wanna see how far you can play the little girl?"

His brows pull down into a V. "No?" He scoots back a bit, creating distance between us. "I was genuinely interested. I get it if you don't want to talk about it, doubt it was fun making your way here." A shadow of empathy creeps over his face as he keeps his eyes locked with mine, waiting for a response.

My mouth opens and closes.

Again.

"Uh, Cris?"

He nods. "Huh?"

"Are you being serious? I mean, have you sniffed too much

formaldehyde or something? Or been hit on the head?"

He flinches. "Well, that—"

"Because you know there's no radiation, right? Like, for reals?" What a phony.

His eyes widen for a moment, then narrow. "What are you saying?"

"That. There. Is. No. Radiation." I take it slow. Maybe he's delayed or something. Maybe I was wrong, and he isn't a genius they keep here. Maybe he's Dr. Sherman's nephew and not quite right in the head, and they allow him to stay. Or whatever.

He scoots back even farther and pulls the leg on the couch in, widening the distance between us. His face takes on a look of pity. "Uh, sorry. But, I mean, you know that… I don't want to be patronizing, but you know you can't see radiation, right? It's still there. Has been—"

I jump off the couch, hands balled into fists at my side, fury powering me forward. "Seriously? One can't see radiation? Seriously? Care to mansplain anything else to me? What the heck is wrong with you?" Because *something* is. Un-be-freakin'-lievable. That one-liner about me being a girl yesterday, and now this. Hello McFly? Anybody home?

I'm so caught up in my rage it takes me a second to process Cris' reaction to my outburst: hands up, as if he wanted to make sure I don't clock him in the head, said head ducked under his protectively raised forearms, face losing its color, a look akin to fear flickering over it.

And it makes me stop dead in my tracks.

My chest is heaving up and down in heavy breaths. I'm not good at holding back, I know that. But I didn't know I delivered such a good show I would scare somebody twice my size. Taking one slow breath, I focus on relaxing my fists. Misogynistic or not, something's off with him.

"Cris?"

The look he gives me is careful from behind his protection.

"Cris, why do you say there's radiation?" This is me being the bigger person and reaching out. There's this knot of *something* in my stomach, and it weighs heavier by the minute. What am I not getting here?

He lets his hands sink down one inch at a time, but only when I take a seat again does he relax. Sort of. He clears his throat and glides one hand through his hair. "Because it's there. Has been for decades."

"From the sun." That must be what he means. UV radiation and stuff. But—

"No. From the war."

"The—"

He looks at me like I was stupid. "The *Atomic* War?"

I want to jump up again and call him on his game, but something in his expression keeps me from it. A shudder runs down my back. "Can… can you tell me more?" Careful. If he's crazy, he might be volatile. Or his mind might. I might've stumbled into something I have even less of a business being in than I thought.

Cris sighs. "The Atomic War of two thousand. Destroyed almost everything on the surface. Whatever survived is severely irradiated, think Chernobyl times one thousand. Human survivors stay underground. Food's grown underground. Leaving your shelter without a radiation suit will kill you within two minutes. With it, it takes an hour." He counts it off like in a school quiz.

Holy cow. He's serious. I scoot forward, knees together, hands on them, the picture girl of careful attentiveness. My palms are sweaty, and I wonder why, but maybe my body picked up on what my mind hasn't fully progressed yet. That this isn't normal. That this is big.

I have a floor that's officially non-existent.

On that floor is a boy.

A boy who insists the surface is rendered uninhabitable by nuclear wars.

Either he's crazy and locked away, or... or he's just locked away.

A cold layer of sweat breaks out and brings me to a shiver. "Cris?"

"Yeah?"

"When did you last go up?"

He huffs. "Up? Nya, I was born down here, and I will die down here. I've never left this place."

My jaw drops.

He didn't say that.

He can't mean it.

I mean, it's crazy talk. It must be—oh. "Then what about TV?" I nod at the screen.

"My movies and stuff?"

"Yeah. How do you explain the shows on there? They're mostly on... the surface, right?"

He shrugs. "Sure they are. Most are from before two-K, the others are AI-generated."

"AI—"

"It's our only pastime, right?" I get a small smile, although I feel like he's holding back. Maybe he thinks I'm as crazy as he is—and maybe he really and truly is crazy. That would be the most logical explanation: Advangen has the best options to keep him here, like under surveillance. Maybe this used to be a lab, and maybe there's still some storage here, which is why I saw them bring down supplies, and I jumped to the wrong conclusion. If he was Dr. Sherman's nephew or whatever, it would make sense. Sherman has the money to have private arrangements for him. Better than the looney bin.

Let's test that theory. "What's your last name, Cris?"

His brows crunch together. "Parr. Why?"

Parr. Not Sherman. But could be the other side of the family. "Just wondering." And the question is, where to go from here. I probably should go back upstairs and forget I ever intruded here. I bet Dr. Sherman wouldn't be thrilled if I spilled the family secret.

I slowly get up to standing. Don't want to spook him again. "Okay, I better get going."

His face falls. "Really? I mean, already? You could… don't you want to stay a bit longer?" I could bet his cheeks take on a reddish color, but then he's pale already. That would do it.

He sucks in his lower lip. "It's dangerous up there. There's nowhere you'd have to be that urgently. I mean… couldn't you stay?" Something in his voice unravels that knot in my stomach and turns it into mush. Crazy or not, Cris is lonely. It's that easy.

I close my eyes for a quick second. Dang it. Dang it, dang it, dang it. Shouldn't be doing it. Shouldn't. Should not. *Not.* Still, when I open my eyes, I give him a smile. "Would you like me to come back tonight?"

The corners of his lips kick up. And dang it again, if it didn't make him look cute. "Yes. I'd like that."

I ignore the tingling feeling in my stomach. "Okay then. I'll see you later."

CHAPTER SEVEN

f I thought I was nervous the last time after I met Cris, it's nothing against this time.

What am I doing? I'm messing with stuff I shouldn't be messing with. I have no business down there. Gah!

Interestingly, I didn't feel any of that when I thought there was a secret lab, or when I thought Cris was running it. Nope. Only now that I've discovered a mental case hidden away do I get these second thoughts.

But those second thoughts get replaced and overwritten by third thoughts: he's alone. Whatever they told him, or whatever his mind made up, he clearly doesn't have enough company. Who knows when he last left, and if he even remembers—well, apparently he doesn't, or he chooses not to—and who knows how often he has services and therapy down there. I would think Dr. Sherman could afford somebody to be with him twenty-four-seven, but maybe that's not recommended. Maybe being supervised and babied all day long would delay progress.

As the day moves on, I find my mind more and more occupied with Cris, and less and less with my work. And it shows.

"What's up, Nya? You seem distracted today." Shawn hands

me another slide for the microscope.

I sigh. "Sorry. Lots on my mind."

"I get it. Because of the project your dad gave you?"

The project? Oh. Okay. Right. Proves how bad a liar I am if I can't keep track of my false stories. "Kind of." I scroll through the magnifications to find the right view of the slide.

Shawn chuckles. "Say no more. Your father can be a very intense man."

"Yeah, he—" *Idea:* "He can. And since it's only the two of us… It's obviously different from bigger families. I sometimes wonder how other people do it. Deal with stress. Like…" Pause for emphasis. "Dr. Sherman. I mean, he must be super busy. He has a big family to rely on, right?"

Shawn shakes his head. "Not at all. I agree with you. I don't know how he's doing it. Mr. Sherman is literally the loneliest person on the planet I know. Maybe that's why he is so successful. He only focuses on work."

I look up from the microscope. "What do you mean, loneliest?"

"He has no one. No partner. Parents gone. I think they died when he was a young man. No family. No—"

"No family at all? Not even, I dunno, a distant cousin, some nephews…" *Hint-hint.*

"None. He's a golf club member, that's all there is regarding a social life." He sighs. "So, in the grand scheme of things, your dad can be lucky to have you."

"Huh?"

He winks at me. "To have you in his corner. It makes a difference."

"S-sure." I focus back on the slide. No family. Shawn has been with the company for decades, wouldn't he know? But then, would Dr. Sherman announce a mentally unstable relative living in the basement?

I flinch. That sounded bad.

And it feels even worse.

Shawn focuses back on his work, leaving me to mine and my thoughts, or rather, to my thoughts. It's not as if I got anything decent done this afternoon.

Alas, that might be a good thing today. Around six thirty, Shawn taps my shoulder from behind. "You're the last one here, Nya. Go home."

I sigh and lean back, rub my forehead and look over my shoulder. "I should stay longer. Today's not my day. I didn't get half of the stuff done I needed to."

"But you're also an unpaid intern. Go home." He squeezes my shoulder, and I appreciate the sentiment, but today I have different plans.

I smile up at him. "Only a bit longer."

The older man sighs. "All right. But remember to cut yourself some slack, okay? I'll see you tomorrow."

"See you tomorrow, Shawn." I wave, then focus back on my slides, or rather, pretend to focus. As soon as the door closes behind him, I lean back and take off my gloves, blowing out a big puff of air.

Okay. Six thirty. From what Dad tells me, most employees leave on time. Some stay longer, but according to Dad, who stays the longest most of the time, especially over the last months, to work on his patient-life-saving-serum, by seven this is a graveyard.

I shudder.

Don't want to be spooky or pessimistic, but I don't like that phrasing at the moment.

So, I spend a good thirty minutes by pacing back and forth until I deem it safe enough to take the north elevators down to S3.

Luckily for me nobody else rides with me, so I don't have to perform my elaborate *oops-I-forgot-something-and-have-to-go-back-up-routine* I planned for.

Small favors, really.

When I finally get out of the airlock, Cris is already waiting for me. Leaned against the wall, one leg up and foot propped against it, arms folded across his chest—he looks normal. Not like a mental case.

"Nya." His face lights up when he sees me.

I take it back. He doesn't look normal. He looks hot. Not my type, but undeniably hot. Those deep-set eyes, muscular body, they make him look like a million bucks. Too bad his sanity is questionable.

"Hey, Cris." I close the door behind me. "How was your day?"

He pushes off the wall. "Meh. Uneventful, so far. It's getting better right now." He glances at me from under his long lashes. "How was it… up there?" A longing creeps into his voice, enough to convince me my idea is only half crazy.

Half as crazy as Cris.

"Actually, I wanted to show you something." I walk past him to the living room and wave at him to follow.

"Show me something?" Like a puppy, Cris follows me.

"Yup." I take my cell out of my back pocket, fall into the couch, and tap the spot next to me. "Sit down."

With a little plop, he falls into the couch next to me, so close, I somewhat lean into him when his weight shifts onto the sofa.

"You know, I figured I give you a brief glimpse into the world up there." I unlock my cell and Cris whistles through his teeth.

"You've got a cell. I'm impressed."

"You are?"

"Hard to get, resources and all."

Yeah. *That.*

Anyway, back to business. I swipe a strand of hair behind my ear. "So, I'd like you to keep in mind that things can change, right? And that we all forget stuff. All the time. I'm, like, the worst with that." I give him what I hope is an encouraging smile. "To jumpstart your memory, or at least give you some food for thought, I want to show you a little video I took over lunch break today."

My thumb hovers over the play-button. Here's to hoping it doesn't trigger some kind of mental melt down but helps him recover whatever he's lost.

I hit *play*, and mini-me in the video smiles into the camera. "Hey, Cris it's me, Nya," I say and wave. "I'm on lunch break, and I wanted to show you what a nice day today is." I cringe. While Cris doesn't pick up on it, I sound like I'm talking to a baby. He's glued to the screen, jaw dropped, eyes wide.

"You… are you *out*?" He shoots me a look to confirm.

I nod. "Yeah. Look." In the video I turn the cell in the slightest, so that he can see me walk through the park. It's a nice day, tons of people are underway. Moms with strollers, people jogging, kids playing in the playground. I kept myself in the picture with the front camera as I walked along the park—

Cris all but rips the cell from my hand. "How did you do that?"

"Do what?"

"AI? How'd you insert yourself into that? I see your thumb covering the camera sometimes—"

"That's because it's real." I emphasize every word, because boy, his delusions are baaaad.

He shakes his head. Fast. Again. Again. "No. No, no, no. *Shit.*"

"Cris, really. I was there. I *am* there every day, when I pass there on the way to work."

"Damn them. It's real." The head shake cranks up its speed.

"Damn them." He jumps up and drops my phone on the couch. With two quick steps, he is over at the shelf in the corner and pulls out a folder. "Here. It's all here."

He comes back and falls into the couch, this time so close, our legs touch. He doesn't seem to pick up on it, but I do. People who just met usually keep more distance between each other, especially boy and girl.

With shaking fingers, he opens the folder. The first two pages he has to try twice before he can turn them. "Look. Memos. Everything." He flips through the pages, and all I pick up on are fragments of headlines:

… Radiation Risk…

… Do not open air lock…

… No survivors after hull breach…

… Food reserves growing thin…

"What the heck?" I whisper. Who does that to somebody? Who comes up with a backstory that convincing to—

Cris slams the folder shut and lets himself fall back onto the couch. His chest heaves up heavy, and his breath comes out in puffs. He pinches his eyes shut and closes his finger so hard around the folder, like a bench vise, his knuckles are turning white.

"You know, I was hoping this day would come, and yet I feared it. It was more like a dream. Sometimes… Sometimes I wondered. They come back, and their skin has a tan. Or dirt drops from their soles. One time, somebody was wet on the shoulders and down the back, as if…"

"As if he had run through rain?"

"Yeah." He gives me a pitiful look. "And then I think it can't be. Who runs through radioactive rain, comes in here, and doesn't set off the alarms? Who does that?"

"Who does that?" I echo in a whisper. Who does *that?*

The muscles in his jaw pop as he chews on his lower lip. For a while he says nothing, and neither do I. Because right now, I don't know what to think.

"Do you think I'm crazy?"

"Huh?" My gaze jumps over to him.

"Do you think I'm crazy? I mean, obviously you've been up there. You've seen the surface. And here I am, holed up, telling you about radiation. Do you think I'm crazy?" He holds my eyes, and I swallow hard.

"Well, it has crossed my mind." The outrage I expected doesn't come. Instead, he nods once.

"It has crossed mine, too." His gaze doesn't waver. "And I've considered the same about you."

"Me?" It's more a squeak than anything else. Why would he think that about me? I'm as sane as they come!

Oh.

Well, said every insane person in the world.

Cris nods. "Yeah, you. Not easy to make sense of you. First, because you're the only new person to come down here in years. The first female, by the way, too. Nobody comes down here besides the same people, because we're the only ones who *survived in this location.*" At least he gives himself air quotes. "Second, you don't know what you're talking about. Dodged my question about transfer, which, by the way, was a fake. Third, you show me an ID. Nobody carries one down here. Fourth—"

I hold up a hand. "I get it, thank you." No need to rub it in. "So, since when did you know I wasn't who I said I was?"

"Honestly? From the first second I saw you. I just didn't know what to make of you."

"Ouch."

"Actually, it was quite the pleasant encounter. Unexpected, but pleasant." His gaze softens. "Doesn't happen every day that your only hope for freedom walks in on you coming out of the shower."

My face warms up, but I ignore it. "Hope for freedom?"

He nods. "Hope for freedom. Do the math for me. What do you think is going on here?" He gestures around the room.

I work on a dry swallow. Good question. It doesn't look good. At all.

Cris raises an expectant eyebrow. "Humor me."

Okay then. Deep breath. "If I assume you're not crazy and locked in here for your own protection—sorry—then it changes everything." And it ain't pretty. I look up at him, waiting, then count off my fingers. "We have a secret floor. Yes, this floor is well hidden. Access only for high-ranking employees of Advangen."

"Advangen?"

"The company this building belongs to. Genetic research."

"Research?"

"Yeah. Anyway. You're hidden. You've been fed lies. You've..." This one is hard. "You've never left this floor. So... I mean, I don't want to accuse anybody, but at this point it looks like... like they're keeping you locked up here."

His fingers drum a rhythm onto his thigh as the apple in his throat moves up and down once. "That's what I'm thinking too. Have been considering it for a while."

Holy cow.

The magnitude of what we pieced together is overwhelming. A prisoner. In my dad's company. A young prisoner. A boy who has done nothing wrong, as far as I can tell.

I lean forward. "Why? Why are you here, Cris?"

He huffs once and rubs both palms over his face, then falls back into the couch. "I think you've given me the answer when you told me who owned this—"

A click coming from the hallway. Voices.

Cris' eyes pop open wide. "Shit! They're early. Nya, hide!"

My heart skips a couple of beats. "Wait, who—"

"No time," he hisses and jumps off the couch. "Get behind the door and stay silent. Watch. I'll distract them and make sure they don't see you. They *cannot* see you. Do you hear me?" He grabs me by the sleeve and yanks me up, dragging me over to the door.

"Cris—"

"Shh!" He places a finger over my lips. "Not a sound. Believe me. Get out of here and promise me… promise me you'll be back." His voice takes on a pleading tone.

For a moment, our eyes connect. *Fear. Hope.* "I will," I breathe against his finger. I will.

Cris' eyelids flutter shut. "Thank you."

The steps come closer. Two people.

Like lightning, Cris pushes off and darts to the other end of the room, close to the desk.

And not a moment too soon.

The door opens and almost hits me in the face. "Whazzup, Cris?"

Cris spins around from the desk, as if he was surprised they were here. "You're early."

The two guys step farther into the room—

Holy cow! The guys from the elevator! Guy number one, Boldt or whatever his name was—and guy number two is the one I met on my first day, the one with the beaten-up face!

Wait—was that… Cris? Did I get that right? Cris gave him the shiner? With as little movement as possible, I retrieve my phone from my pocket, silence it, and press record.

"Well, after last time we couldn't be sure how long it would take us. Thanks for *that*, by the way." That's the second guy. He lifts a hand and points at his face.

Cris crosses his arms in front of his chest as his only response.

Boldt sighs. "So, you're going to make it difficult again?"

"I don't see why we need to do this so often."

The man steps forward. Only now do I see he's holding a little carrier with vials and syringes. "And how often do we need to spell it out for you? Radiation affects everybody, and we need to make sure—"

"But I'm not even leaving the compound."

"Doesn't matter. Contamination happens through food and water, you know that. You want to stay healthy, you let us check—"

"My bone marrow? What about a plain old blood draw?"

"Can't have your stem cells affected, you know that."

Oh my freakin—

I can't believe what I'm hearing. They're truly feeding him those lies. It's not Cris, it's *them*.

And they're not here to play games.

"Listen. Easy way or not, what do you choose?" Boldt holds up something that looks like a small drill.

Cris keeps his arms crossed in front of his body. "Not." For a split second his eyes dart over to me in the corner, maybe to check if I'm seeing it all, but he needn't worry. I'm glued to the scene in front of me.

"All right then." Boldt shrugs and pulls something out of his white coat's pocket. "We gave you a fair choice." Two small darts shoot out of the device in his hand, burrowing itself into Cris' chest before he has a chance to step back. The moment they hit him, Cris stiffens and jerks as he falls down to the ground. A harsh *tictictictic*-sound comes from the device—

"Get him! Now!"

Guy number two runs over to Cris as Boldt lets go of the taser.

Together they roll Cris on his back, stunned, and needless to say, neither of them is gentle.

I know what's coming next. They gave me enough hints to draw the conclusion.

Boldt rips open Cris' shirt. "Fast. He's getting better at handling it."

Guy number two disinfects his chest bone. "Done"

"Good." Boldt readies the bone marrow drill and rams it into Cris' sternum.

I want to stay and watch, because I'm frozen to the spot—frozen by the sheer horror of human beings doing this to each other.

But when they turn around to leave, they'll see me, no doubt about it.

My soul and heart scream to run and help Cris, but my brain overrules them both: he knew what was going to happen. He played tough to get so they'd be distracted and I could get out.

I take all my courage and sneak around the door into the hallway.

Then, I run.

CHAPTER EIGHT

I can't get my brain to work.

My most prized possession, my thinking machine, my idea-generator, it's running on empty. It can't process what it has seen. It can't add one and one and arrive at two, because two… two is unbelievable. Two must be wrong, and yet every time I recalculate, I arrive at the same result: Advangen is keeping Cris locked up and using him—but for what? Why? What's so special about him, and how the frack can they do that? How can they keep another human being locked away? Since birth, maybe even?

I wrap my arms around my shivering body as I all but storm out of Advangen's employee exit. It's a good thing that I'm by far the last one to leave. I don't want to be seen; I don't want to be asked questions.

I only want to go home.

They tasered Cris. They *tasered* him! Two adult men tasered a teenager held in the basement of my dad's company. How crazy does that sound?

Super crazy.

And that exactly is my problem: What am I going to do about that? What *can* I even do about it? Go to the police? *Oh, hi, there's this teenager kept prisoner in Advangen's basement—in their* secret *basement, to be precise, which I accessed with a stolen ID-card—and they're drawing bone marrow on him, like, experimenting probably.*

Right. That's gonna go over well. I skid to a halt somewhere around Main Street. Didn't even realize I didn't take the bus. Too worked up.

Breathing hard, I lean against a wall and press a shaking palm against my forehead. Dizzy. Headache. I'm clearly out of shape, but man…! Straightening myself up one vertebra at a time, I wait for the dizziness to retreat.

I can't believe it.

They tasered him.

And coming to think about it, he knew that was going to happen. *I'll distract them and make sure they don't see you.* How often have they done this to him? What else have they done to him?

Nausea rises and brings bile to my throat. *What else* have they done to him? I saw the scars on his chest bone. *How often* do they do this to him?

I don't think I've ever felt as helpless as I do now. Usually there's always science, a logical explanation, a natural next step for me to take. Now, not so much. The police are out the window, obvs. Somebody working at the lab, maybe Shawn—nope. I doubt he knows about it. Who then does? Mr. Sherman. He's the boss. My dad—

Holy Guacamoley.

Dad's ID got me into Cris' Lair.

Does that mean he knows about Cris? Or does it work, because he's the COO, and has access literally everywhere?

The nausea brings another wave of bile.

Dad can't have known. He wouldn't do that. He wouldn't be part of keeping a teen holed up for life.

No.

Nu-uh.

But no matter what, I can't talk to him. If he doesn't know, I doubt he'd believe me. If he does, well, wouldn't put it past him to cut me off from Advangen, and then I'd have no way of reaching Cris.

So, in the grand scheme of things, there's nobody I can trust. Nobody who can help me figure out what's going on and help Cris. Nobody who'd be crazy enough to listen to me and—

I groan when finally—*finally*—an idea flashes to life, even though it's one of the stupidest of mine in a while.

Aww, come on. Is that really my only option? Really? *Really?*

I close my eyes and suck in a big breath. Yeah, I guess so. No other choice. Better put on my big-girl panties, because no way this is gonna be easy. Or fun, for that matter.

I push off the wall and turn left onto Schoen Street.

For this, you owe me, Cris.

I ring the bell to the separate apartment off the main house—main mansion; I apologize—precisely twelve minutes after I came to my momentous conclusion and decision.

And nobody opens.

So, I ring the bell again.

And again—until I hear cursing from the inside. "What the hell? I'm coming." He rips open the door—and there he is. A strange déjà vu hits me, because Gabriel is… wet.

Wet, with a towel around his waist.

"What—oh. Nya." Can't say Gabriel sounds friendly, and I didn't expect him to.

"Uh, hi, Gabriel." I do my very, very best to keep my eyes straight up and trained on his face. Not looking down. Not checking out his chest. Or his abs. Or… Nope, not happening. What's up with guys taking a shower when I show up? Seriously.

His lips tighten. "I'm just done working out," he says. "What on earth are you doing here?"

The tips of my ears burn. "I'm sorry to bother you, but I was wondering…" Big girl panties, big girl panties… "I was wondering if you could help me with something." There we g—oh. "*Please.*" There we go.

For a moment, Gabriel stares at me. Then blinks. Again. "Excuse me?"

"If you could maybe help me—"

He looks behind him, then faces me again. "You sure you're talking to me?"

I roll my eyes. "Yes, idiot. You."

"Oh, really." His voice turns sarcastic. "Because I wasn't sure you still knew where I lived. And also, not sure I heard you right calling me an idiot about ten seconds after you asked for my help."

Damn it, so much for keeping it together. The burning spreads from my ears to my cheeks. "I'm sorry," I push out through clenched teeth. "Force of habit. But can I please—"

"No."

My eyes pop wide. "What?"

"You heard me. I'm not the type of guy you can treat like shit and then use when you need him—"

Oh, come on! "I didn't treat you like shit! You started the whole thing when—"

"Well. Maybe I did, but you for sure made it hard to apologize or—"

"As if you ever tried!"

He grunts and throws his head back. "And here we go again. Ever noticed you're the one rubbing it in my face whenever you do something better than me? Who couldn't shut up about that freakin' scholarship last year? That she passed college biochem? The—" With every accusation, with every example, he steps forward closer, until he all but towers above me. And Gabriel is tall. I have to crane my neck to look up and not at his partially naked body, and it puts me at a disadvantage.

And Gabriel isn't done. "Or when Principal Sanchez gave you the Citizen Award? Did you then win graciously, or did you rub it in my face? I can't remember, Nya, so why don't you tell me? Huh? Tell me what you did and then ask me again if I'd like to help—"

"Gabriel." I lift both hands up. "Gabriel!" Nothing. "Gabe!"

That shuts him right off.

The apple in his throat moves up and down hard. "What... what did you call me?"

Yeah, that... "Gabe," I whisper.

He sucks in a big heap of air. "You haven't called me that since—"

"Since seventh grade." I don't know the exact date. It was more of a progression. Can't even say what the first straw was that broke the camel's back, or rather, my trust and adoration for Gabriel. I try not to think about any of it, but it was more annoying than harmful in the beginning. Comments to my classmates, about whom I hang with. My clothing. When I called him out, he got defensive in a way I wasn't used to, so I distanced myself for a bit, and that made it worse. Let's just say I got my mental defenses up and ready just in time for when Gabriel poured the bucket of ice water over me when I was in seventh grade, and wearing a white T-shirt. What I was not ready for was him taking a picture of that. And posting it on Insta.

Needless to say, I made school talk for a couple of days. Weeks. Months.

The laughter, the finger pointing, the way Gabe laughed with them… Also needless to say, his actions hurt me beyond belief. Which could be why I always have my claws out when it comes to anything Gabriel-related. But, because I'm mature like that, I won't let it interfere with the reason for coming here: Cris is more important than my hurt feelings or an old vendetta.

Gabriel nods once. Twice. "Yeah. It's been a while." The way he looks at me is… odd. More like Gabe, less like Gabriel. So familiar, yet so foreign.

But nonetheless, I take my chance. "*Gabe*, please. I need your help. Really. I don't know whom else to ask and… You're kind of my only hope. The only one I can bounce off ideas with."

Gabriel stays silent, so long that I'm about to turn and walk away.

But no more than a second before I'd given up, he steps aside and makes room. "Let me get dressed."

Oh. Okay. That actually worked! I'm admittedly a tad flabbergasted, but still manage to get my legs to move and enter his home.

"You know your way to the living room." Gabriel points past the kitchen and struts toward his bedroom, closing the door behind him, leaving me alone in the hallway.

I blow out a puff of air and take a few steps, then stop. It feels weird being here, like a blast from the past. Haven't been in here in such a long time, yet… yet his apartment is still about the same as it was when we and our families were friends. Slowly, I let my gaze drift over the walls and furniture on my way to the living room.

With a professional athlete for a father and an interest in

biochemistry, Gabriel has always been walking a line between two worlds. Sports-memorabilia sit next to organic chemistry books in his shelves, posters decorating the walls could either be of some kind of athlete or a nerdy Schrodinger's Cat meme. That's Gabriel in a nutshell.

Eventually, I have a seat in his living room, which feels oddly adult, too. We used to hang in his bedroom most of the time, but that was when we were younger. Now it wouldn't feel right, and not only because he's getting dressed in there but also because our, uh, *relationship* has kind of outgrown his bedroom.

So yeah, like a real visitor, I sit down on his couch, and I don't have to wait for long. Not even a minute later, Gabriel walks back in, slipping into a shirt. The way he stretches emphasizes his abs—

My cheeks warm up.

Well.

He could've done that in his room. Dang it.

Gabriel falls into the couch at the other end of it, one arm up on the rest, one leg pulled up and tugged under his other knee pit. "So? What was so important that A, you had to ask now, and that B, you had to ask me." Of all people, is the unspoken addition to his sentence.

I sit up straighter. Here goes nothing. "Okay. Promise me to give me the benefit of the doubt, will ya?" Because, like I said, super crazy story.

Gabriel nods. "Oo-kay…"

Good start. Anyway. "In my first couple of days at Advangen, I found that the north elevator had another low-level floor, S3. Didn't think much of it. Dad told me there was no S3. It was an error in the design, so whatever. Then I see somebody bring a push cart down there, full of lab supplies. Vials, syringes, etc." I swallow once. Knowing they were for Cris… It changes things.

Gabriel uses my break. "So, you're thinking there's a secret lab down there."

My eyes pop wide. "Dude! Exactly what I was thinking!" Out of reflex and years of old habit, I hold out a hand—and out of years of old habit, Gabriel slaps it.

The moment our palms connect in an epic high five is the exact moment we both remember we're not doing this stuff anymore. He yanks his hand back so fast I briefly wonder if the contact with my skin burned him or something. Then, he works the same hand through his hair and drops his gaze to the floor, while I… scoot back in the most awkward way and clear my throat.

"So, yeah, anyway. I figured if it's a secret, the only way to get in is to use Dad's ID. And since he's sick—"

"You took it." He still keeps his gaze lowered, but at least we're talking like two mature people. And the way Gabriel is thinking proves I chose wisely in my confidant.

"Yes. I took it and went down there."

"And what did you find?"

I blow out a big puff of air. "Not what I expected."

Gabriel rolls his eyes. "*I* kinda expected that with that start."

Okay, here goes nothing. "First, an airlock. Non-functioning air-part, well-functioning locking-part. Then a small hallway, half the size of the area you're in at Advangen, and, well, room designations that threw me off: Living room. Bathroom. Office."

"So what? There's an apartment down there. Maybe Sherman stays there when he's working late. No big deal."

Another big breath. "It wasn't the apartment that concerned me. It was the boy."

Gabriel's brows scrunch together. "The boy?"

"About our age. Cris. He…" I close my eyes, the image of Cris on the floor, tasered, as fresh as when I saw it.

"Spit it out, Nya."

"He lives down there."

Gabriel stares at me.

And blinks.

And blinks again. "That's what has your knickers in a bunch? Somebody living there?" He huffs once. "Wow, Nya. Are you jealous somebody has 24-7-access to the lab, and it's not you?"

His snide brings more color to my face, mainly because it's annoying how well he knows me. "Shut up, Gabriel. And yes, in the beginning I was mad, until I wasn't anymore."

He sighs, like he was bored. "And why would that be? Pray tell, I can hardly wait."

I keep my gaze drilled into his. "Because I think Advangen is holding him prisoner down there and is experimenting on him."

Gabriel's jaw drops.

Pause.

His eyebrows slowly march up to his hairline.

Pause.

He blinks hard, then gives one small shake of his head. "Wow. *Wow*, Nya. For a moment, you got me. For a moment, I thought you really needed my help, but obviously, I was wrong. Yes, you need help, but I'm thinking a psychiatrist with very strong medications at their disposal might be the better choice." He wipes his palms on his jeans and is about to push himself off the couch when I dart forward and grab him by the sleeve.

"Gabe, sit. I told you to give me the benefit of the doubt."

He falls back into the couch from my unexpected pull, one eyebrow remaining raised. "I thought I gave you that when I let you into my apartment."

"Oh, shut up. I have proof."

"Proof."

"Kind of." I pull out my phone.

"*Kind of* sounds even better." But hey, he stays seated. I count that as a win. As fast as I can, I unlock my phone and thumb open the photos app. "Here. Look." I hit play, and the entire scene unfolds in front of Gabriel. How they enter, how they taser Cris, how they tackle him and try to access his bone marrow or whatever.

When the video ends—with my feet and the floor in the frame as I'm running out of my hiding place—Gabriel slowly looks up at me. "You're not trying to play me." It sounds more surprised than anything.

I shake my head. "No."

"You witnessed that today."

"About an hour ago."

"You've talked to him?"

"Yeah."

"And what's his story?"

"His story is crazy. They fed him lies, Gabriel. Atomic war, earth uninhabitable, can't leave the apartment. He's never been outside. When I showed him a video I took over lunch, he almost freaked out. He has folders, binders, with instructions on what to do in case of a radiation emergency. *They fed him lies.*" Too late do I realize that my hand slid from his sleeve onto his thigh.

Carefully, Gabriel picks up my wrist with two fingers and drops it onto my thigh. "Right. He may believe that, but do you? It's crazy front to back."

Right he is. "At first, I didn't. But… the way he reacts, the way those people treated him… I believe him, Gabe." *Gabe.* Dammit, it's slipping out again.

He blows out air through pursed lips. "I don't know. There must be another explanation. Maybe he's mental—"

"He isn't."

"Really?" He gives me a skeptical once-over. "How'd you know?"

I shrug. "I'd know. And you know what? So will you." I jump off the couch and pull him off with me. "Come on."

Gabriel looks at me, dumbfounded. "Come on—what?"

"Please?" I wiggle my fingers at him.

"No, come on *where*, Nya!"

"Well, duh, genius, what do you think? To Advangen, of course. It's time for you to meet Cris."

CHAPTER NINE

"**I** honestly don't think this is a good idea," Gabriel whispers for the umpteenth time in the last ten minutes.

I pull myself over the fence in the back of the parking lot, right where the old oak I used to climb on reaches across the properties and makes it really easy to overcome this very much unnecessary obstacle. "Maybe you're right, but now it's too late. Watch it!" I jump down and land in a crouch next to him. Hah. The cheerleaders should be proud if they got me.

"It's not too late, we can still—"

"We won't." I walk ahead across the lot toward the back entrance. "No cameras on the outside and only a few in the main lobby and the really important floors." Like the executive floor, where we're not going.

"And why would you think that S 3-floor isn't monitored?" he hiss-whispers to me.

"Because then they would've known I was there. And they didn't." I fish Dad's ID out of my pocket and open the door to Advangen's shipping area. "Come on."

Gabriel groans but follows me. "Seriously, if this gets me fired—"

I stop dead in my track. "Gabriel. There's a guy who's been locked in here for what could very well be his whole life. You getting fired over this won't be what people remember if this case ever goes public." Compared to Cris' problems, ours are ridiculous.

Gabriel's mouth opens and closes. "Touché. Even so, make it fast."

I nod and lead the way through the night-illuminated hallways to the north elevator. "Now watch." I press S3—and nothing happens. Then I take Dad's ID and swipe it in front of the reader. This time the elevator accepts my choice and jerks to life, lowering us level for level, until it halts at S3.

"Welcome to the secret floor." I motion for Gabriel to go ahead and follow him into the little reception area. He takes a good look around, mainly at the airlock. Not much to see with the empty lockers on both sides.

"It's professional grade." He turns and looks around. "But I'm missing hazmat suits, decontamination equipment—everything else."

"I know." I open the airlock and walk in. Only when the door closes behind us do I realize how small this room really is. Like, barely made for two. Barely.

I hear Gabriel swallow behind me. "Why do I not hear anything?" he whispers.

"Because, like I said, I don't think it's on. Or it's fake. It still doesn't unlock until fifteen secs or so are over, maybe so that Cris believes it's real, I don't know. But it's never made any noise for me." Never, as in the last two days.

Finally, the outgoing door unlocks. I swing it open. "Cris? Hey, Cris? It's me, Nya. I brought a friend with me. Cris?"

No answer.

I tip toe forward, not because I'm worried about anybody else being here, but mainly because it's kind of creepy entering a secret floor in the middle of the night.

As I lead the way, Gabriel looks around, taking everything in with the curious, evaluating eyes of a scientist.

"Cris?" How long does it take to recover from being tasered? Minutes? Hours? He should be back to normal—

"Hey."

Jeez! I twitch, a little squeak breaking from my throat. Where'd he—

I turn on my heels, and there he is. Half-hidden behind the door toward the bedroom, a blood stain on the shirt dead-center of his chest, hair chaotic, and dark circles under his eyes.

"Cris!" I dart over to him, grabbing him by the upper arms. He looks like crap. "Are you okay? I mean, are you? Seriously, they tasered you, they—"

He ignores me, eyes boring straight into Gabriel. "Who's he?"

Oh. Right. "That's—"

"Gabriel. I'm a… friend of Nya's." Gabe steps forward and extends a hand to Cris.

"Hi." Cris' tone is more reserved than when he met me, and his eyes dart from Gabe to me and back. "You're *not from here* either, am I right?" They shake hands.

Gabe's eyebrows shoot up. "Nice way of phrasing it. No. Or rather, yes, I'm from… Don't know, what do you want to call it— the real world?" He cringes. "Sorry, that sounded bad. But Nya told me what they told you, and it's—"

"Bullshit." A muscle in Cris' temple twitches. "All they fed me was bullshit."

"Pretty much." Gabe sighs. "So…"

My turn. I take Cris by the hand and lead him to the living room. "Come on, guys. We've gotta talk." And we should do it fast, just to be on the safe side. Even though it feels right, we're still doing something forbidden by being here. I fall onto the couch like a few hours before, pulling Cris down with me. Gabe lowers himself onto the coffee table in front of it.

I let go of Cris' hand and point at his shirt. "Let's start with the obvious: What. Was. That."

His face falls. "That was my weekly routine. Sometimes more often."

My jaw drops. "Excuse me, what? They get bone marrow from you every week? Why?"

"You know as much as I do. It used to be less often, but in the last few months it's gotten way more frequent. All the tests they do, all the meds they give me, they always say it's to check or treat the effects of the radiation, but I haven't believed it in a while. See, their problem is they taught me to read, and they let me. I'm not stupid. Or, well, maybe I am, or I wouldn't still be trapped down here, but too many things they said didn't make sense."

Gabriel leans forward, supporting his weight with his arms on his knees. "What Nya showed me… they've been doing that for how long?"

Cris nods. "For as long as I can think. When I was little, they accessed my shins." He pulls up the leg of his pants and points at the front of his shin, right under the kneecap. An area of at least quarter-size is darker than the rest, irregular, pigmented and odd-looking. "When I got bigger and started not… *complying* as much, they moved to other, easier controllable spots." He points first at his shoulder, then his chest.

"Jesus," Gabe mumbles. "And they don't even numb you?"

"They used to, but a few months ago I refused to be prodded. Didn't want any of these draws anymore. They respected that for a week or two before they insisted they had to resume checking my marrow. And when I still refused…" Cris shrugs. "They just took it."

"Without numbing." Gabe says it as a statement, not a question. A muscle ticks in his jaw. "So much for respecting your wishes."

"Well, I was fighting them pretty hard. And have been ever since." Cris raises his chin in a defiant motion.

Drilling into his bones without numbing him… For months. Nausea swells in my stomach. The more I hear, the worse the story gets. "Wow. Just… wow. I can't even. What's their game? I mean—"

"Stem cells."

My gaze flies to Gabe. "Huh?"

"Stem cells. The only reason they would prefer marrow over blood. It's the better source and gives them a nice, big serving of stem cells." His voice turns bitter.

Okay, makes sense. "But what would they want with his stem cells? Every freakin' week? They could take them once, keep a batch in the incubator, and grow new ones. And it's not like it's a kidney—people donate stem cells. What's so special about yours they do *this* to you?"

Cris rolls his eyes. "I don't know. Nothing, as far as I know. But speaking of special. Do you mind if I see that video again? From your lunch break?" There it is again, the longing, the facial expression that makes him look so much younger than he probably is.

"Of course." I unlock my phone and hand it to him. "Feel free to look at the other pictures on there." With a flick of my finger, I show him the motion to switch between pictures, then look at Gabe.

"So, what do we make of this? Stem cell extraction, kidnapping

—oh. Cris, do you know who your parents are?"

"Nope." His eyes and focus stay glued to the cell.

Gabe pulls one leg in and under his butt. "I don't like it. It screams illegal—I know, it's kind of obvious with a teen hidden in the Advangen's basement—and it screams shady."

"I'd look for a stronger adjective." *Unethical* would come to mind.

"True." He sighs. "Question is, how to proceed from—"

"Ugh. Why is *he* in your photos?" Cris face twists in disgust.

I cock my head to the side. "Who now?" I highly doubt there's anybody—

Cris turns the screen over to me, and my heart stops. A man in his early fifties, chopping onions. Gray hair. For a change, no tie or suit, but jeans and a shirt.

"Steve. He's been my primary caregiver since I can remember."

Gabriel's gasp is drowned out by the blood swooshing in my ears. *He's been my primary caregiver since I can remember.*

I look up from the screen at Cris, forcing down a swallow.

"That… that would be my dad."

Silence.

"Oh," Cris says eventually. "That's awkward."

"That's impossible," Gabe answers. "I know that man and—"

"And that's him. I'm sure. I've seen like six or seven people in my life. Believe me, he is one of them. The one who comes by the most often. He taught me how to read. Math. Even how to tie my shoelaces when I was little."

Oh, holy everything.

I wrap my arms around my upper body to stop myself from shaking.

It was a distinct possibility. I'm not stupid. The ID granted me access here like an open sesame. No alarms went off—that suggests a certain level of involvement. But I'm also human. Trusting people and thinking the best of them is in my blood, and imagining my dad…

I close my eyes. "And you're really sure?"

Cris is nice enough to not sound annoyed. "Yes. I've known him all my life. Since I can remember. He was a fixture in my life when I was little, but lately he comes by less often now after I—"

"After what?" I shoot a look at him under my lashes.

He grimaces. "After I busted his lip open. In my defense, he tried to get marrow from the arm. It *hurts*." He holds up both palms.

A groan escapes me. "Please, don't apologize for punching him. I can't even imagine—wait." I blink twice. Busted lip… "I remember. I remember! That was about two months ago! Dad said he ran into a glass door—"

"Ran into my fist," Cris mutters.

My voice drops to a whisper. "I can't believe that was you. I can't believe that was him." My dad. Keeping Cris prisoner. Who else is involved? Dr. Sherman must know about it—come on, it's his company!

Gabriel clears his throat. "Not to be a party pooper, but no matter your dad's involvement, Nya, we've gotta come up with a plan. I, for one, would like to not be caught down here, because… because a company who has the means to keep one teen might not hesitate to keep three."

My eyes pop wide. "Keep us?" Didn't even occur to me that was an option.

Cris picks up on a different part of Gabriel's statement, though. "A plan?"

"Yes, a plan. Nya didn't come to me to get you more company. She came to find a solution to your problem, so let's brainstorm."

Once upon a time, before our fallout, when Gabriel was in eighth grade and me in seventh, once upon a time, I thought the sun revolved around him. He could do no wrong—at that point, at least—and I had this uncanny sensation that no matter what, I could count on him.

I'm surprised to say that right now, in this very moment, a tiny flicker of that sensation springs back to life and sparks something I haven't felt in a while, especially not for Gabriel.

Which is why I absolutely do not smile. No need to give him a big head. It's ginormous the way it is already. "He's right, Cris. We need to talk about options."

Cris huffs. "*Options* sounds like I had a choice."

Well, true… "I'd say not in the classic sense, but now that you have us, we have options." I look from him to Gabriel. "I would want to know first what's going on. Why are you here? What's so special about your stem cells—no offense—that you're kept here under an enormous amount of pretense to keep you at least somewhat cooperative?" Maybe they pretended he wasn't a prisoner, but let's not kid ourselves: you take the option to leave from somebody, no matter how you sell it, they're your prisoner.

Gabriel folds his hands. "Good questions, but what I would like to know is, have you tried to run? Did you ever leave this place, like maybe they took you somewhere? What's their schedule? What are we up against?"

Definitely chose wisely, bringing Gabe. He thinks big picture.

Cris nods. "Okay. All good questions. Welcome to Cris' life, the introduction. I've never left here. Whenever I try to break open the door, an alarm goes off. To keep contamination out, they say, or rather to keep me in." His voice turns bitter. "They've told me that once I'm twenty, I'm allowed upstairs. That's when my *genome won't be as sensitive to the effects of radiation anymore.* Other teens are kept *deep underground all the time*, they say. We *need young people for the survival of the human race*." He continues to give himself air quotes.

It sounds odd, though. "Why do they tell you it's gonna change at twenty?"

"To give him hope and keep him cooperative, Nya." That's Gabriel. "How old are you, Cris?"

"Eighteen, they tell me. But anyway, you wanted to know their-slash-my schedule. Easy. Predictive. Always been the same. Mornings are for work—you heard that, Nya."

Oh. "The siren when I met you?"

He nods. "Yes. I log into a computer system and check all the safety measures around the compound. Any leaks, any break-downs, then I measure the radiation levels in the ground water and atmosphere. The usual."

"Wait a second. You do that every day?" I lay one hand on his arm but look over at Gabriel. "I assume it's to keep you busy—"

"And to give him purpose and reason to not run." A muscle tenses in Gabriel's jaw when his eyes fall on my hand on Cris' arm, then focus on me again. "No offense, but I can't imagine your dad being so inventive. Who came up with all of that?"

"Ever seen this person?" I scroll through my cell until I find the picture I was looking for, me and Dr. Sherman after I won the internship.

"Not him." Cris shakes his head.

"Oh." All right. "Not Dr. Sherman then, Gabe."

"Don't know if that makes me feel better or not."

Same here.

Cris takes a deep breath. "And no, I don't know anybody else. It's always implied there are others, but I've seen nobody else besides Steve and the guys who draw my marrow."

"So, we're thinking very elaborate game versus something way, way bigger than you." Sounds thrilling, really.

"Like I said, I wouldn't know. I always felt very alone though, if that means something. Anyway, back to routines. I usually do independent study or watch movies all day. Before I had the DVD-player, I usually read. Pretty boring, but *standard*." Again, the air quotes come out. "I had more interaction when I was little, but now it's draws, check-ups, or the occasional visit by *him*," he nods at my phone, "and mostly that's after six or seven."

Translation, when most employees will have gone home. And Dad stays late. Right—like, working on his serum. Sure.

Gabriel and I exchange a glance, and like when we were younger, I can read his thoughts as clearly as if they were written on his face. Good to know we're on the same page. Adrenaline spikes, because this, this is big. I suck in a sharp breath. There's no going back. We're doing this. I stand up and hold my hand out to Cris.

"Let's go."

His brows scrunch into a V. "Go where?"

"Well, what do you think? We'll take you out of here."

"Out of—" His mouth drops open. "You'll… take me?" Hope colors his voice, and it breaks my heart.

"We won't leave you here. It's not right."

Gabriel gets up. "I agree with Nya. My apartment is big. We can hide you there for now and then come up with a plan, but leaving you here… nope."

The apple in Cris' throat moves up and down. "Okay. Okay. Thank you, I—"

"Never mind." I wave him off. "I feel so guilty for what my dad did. I can't even… Anyway." I lead him through the door and into the hallway. "It's the middle of the night, now's our chance. You tried to break open the door, and the alarm went off—we don't have to use force, we've got the magic key." I wiggle Dad's ID. "Everything's quiet. Stick close to us up in the building and watch what we're doing. You'll be fine." I give him what I hope is a reassuring smile. We're kind of flying by the seat of our pants here.

I swipe Dad's ID in front of the reader and the lock for the air lock clicks open. "See? No alarm. We're official, so come on in. This is going to be tight." I hold the door for Gabriel, who scoots in all the way to the back.

Cris stares at the air lock like it was his enemy. The apple in his throat moves up and down. Then, his fists ball and he nods once to himself. "Okay. Okay."

He takes the first step into the air lock—

Alarms blare, sirens howl, a cacophony of noises assaults our ears.

"Shit!" Cris jumps back into the hallway.

"Alert. Alert. Breach detected. Breach detected. Alert. Alert. Breach—"

Holy cow—

I reach for Cris. "Come on! We've got to be fast! We—"

"Nya!" Gabe yanks me around on my arm. "Look!"

Look wha—

Crap.

The elevator.

It's coming down.

Holy freakin' cow.

My breathing turns raspy.

We've just been made.

CHAPTER TEN

No.

Can't get a breath in, can't—

Gabriel can.

He forces his way past me. "We'll be back. Come up with a story. I *promise* we'll be back." He rams the door shut, trapping us inside the airlock.

"No!" I fly forward, both hands against the glass. "Cris! We can't leave him!"

"We won't, but for now, we have to." He yanks me away from the door. "Be ready, Nya! We have to be hidden before the elevator comes down, or it's anybody's guess what's gonna happen to us." His breath comes out choppy. "We need to—"

I know. Hide. "The lockers. For the hazmat suits."

The air lock clicks open at the same time as the elevator makes a pinging sound.

No words needed.

Gabe darts to the lockers on the left, me to the ones on the right. As the elevator doors slide open, both of us slip into a locker, careful to close the doors from the inside without a sound.

Doesn't mean my heart wasn't hammering so loud, it probably

will give me away.

Steps. Voices.

"Man, really? Why can't he act up with day shift?"

Someone chuckles. "Right? But hey, imagine he was out already. Heard he beat up Sayer a few days ago. Don't wanna mess with him if I can avoid it. He's strong."

A beeping noise, a pause, then more beeping noise.

"Huh. His bracelet is still active. How'd he get the door to open?"

"Don't care. Let's make sure he doesn't try again."

"Okay. You—"

The voices drop off as the air lock closes behind them.

Counting down from thirty. *Fifteen. Fourteen. Thirteen—*

The silence inside my little locker is deafening. Dea-fe-ning. Blood swooshes in my ears. The guards were right freakin' there. Alarms. What triggered—ah, the bracelet that's *still active* around his ankle? Saw it on day one. *Nine. Eight. Seven—*

Must get out of here. To the elevator. There are no stairs. Get out, get out-out, come up with a plan—

Two. One.

The air lock should be open to the other side now.

As careful as I can, I open the door and peek out.

The room's empty.

A glance to the left: two men, exiting the airlock toward Cris' rooms. *"Cris. What's up with this craziness?"* The voice is soft, muffled, hard to understand—and moving away from the only area where they could see us in the elevator.

Now or never.

I push the door open, careful not to ram it into the wall, and scurry out of my hiding place, bent low, soft steps—

Gabriel catches up with me in the elevator.

I swipe the card, then press my back against the side. He does the same. The doors inch closed slower than any elevator has ever functioned.

As my wide eyes meet Gabe's even wider ones and the doors are about to close, a pained scream pierces the silence.

Then, nothing.

"What the fuck?" Gabe slams his hand against the steering wheel of his car. "Damn it, that—"

"Keep your eyes on the freakin' road, Gabe!" I yell at him, holding tight to my seat belt. He isn't quite flooring it but isn't quite following the speed limit either. We just want to get away. Put distance between us and what could've been our downfall.

"What the hell was that?" This time it comes without the outburst of aggression and instead with a quick glance over at me. His eyes are still as wide as in the elevator—wide, panicked, and full of fear. "What did they do—"

"I don't know. Maybe I don't want to know. It didn't sound good." Nausea rises, courtesy of my mind's replay. That scream… I swallow hard. "We have to get him out."

Gabriel huffs once. "No kidding, but how? Did you see? The alarm went off when he stepped into the lock—"

"And the men said he still had his bracelet, so yeah, it's an electronic ankle lock." Crap. That cute little bracelet he wears. It's not really that cute, on second thought. "They must be monitoring—" Oh, double-crap.

"What?" Gabriel does a double-take over at me. "Shit, Nya, don't scare me. What?"

So. Not. Good. "Monitoring. I told you I thought it wasn't,

because nobody picked up on me being there, but now that Cris tried to escape—"

Gabriel pales. "You're right. Now they need to check what happened. How he could open the lock. They'll check the database, and of course every ID-log-in is going to be registered for every door. Which means—"

"Which means they'll see my dad log-in although he's home, sick."

Crap, crap, crap.

My next breath comes out wheezy and brings a bout of piercing headache. "Not good." At all. It's not an automatic deduction it was me, but— "Do you think they'll have video?" That would top it off. A video of me—with or without Gabriel—entering the Forbidden Floor.

Gabriel shakes his head. "Don't think so. Not with the level of secrecy. Imagine something—anything—ever happening at Advangen, break and entry, and the police collecting all the surveillance data. They'd be curious to hear about a non-existent floor and the boy kept there. No." One more shake of his head. "This is it. The ID only, and they'll be hard pressed explaining that one if they ever had to."

Deep breaths, in and out. I can handle this. Totally can. Must handle this. "Okay then. Plan. Drop me off at home. I put the ID back in his bag, where it belongs. Will play it by ear tomorrow, but maybe I can get him to see a doctor. That would give us a couple of hours to snatch the ID and—"

"And what? We can't go in while it's broad daylight."

Crap. He's right.

"Okay. Then we back off during the day. When he's asleep, we go back in."

"And how would you like us to counter his ankle lock? You

know, the one that sets off the freakin' alarms?"

I give him my sweetest smile. "We have one day for a thorough google search. We'll figure it out."

We'll figure it out.

We have to.

CHAPTER ELEVEN

When I wake up the next morning, it's not because of my alarm clock.

It's because of the smell of coffee.

And that can only mean one thing: Dad is going to work.

Crap.

I'm up and at the door in no time until I remember to slow it down. Act innocent. Nothing happened.

And boy, is that difficult to pull off.

I walk downstairs. Barely four o'clock. I stifle a pretend yawn. "Morning, Dad. You're up early."

My dad looks up from his iPad, a mug with steaming coffee and a slice of toast on a plate next to him. "Nya. Did I wake you? I'm sorry."

"No, it's fine. Wasn't sleeping well, anyway." Not a lie. I slide behind a chair. "So… you're feeling better?"

Dad swallows a sip of his coffee. "Yes. Kind of. The company called an hour ago and woke me. Figured might as well give it a try with work today."

Don't even know where to start. "They called you at three in the morning? That's new."

He nods. "Some kind of security breach. They read my ID and checked in with me. It's nothing. Somebody must've messed with our systems when they tried to break in." He shrugs, and a motherhood of worry falls off my shoulders. Break in—rather, break out, but okay, at least nobody is suspecting something going on. Cris must've told them a good story.

Cris.

What would I give to go and check on him right now. I can't imagine how he must feel, knowing he's being kept, knowing we were almost out, and then got derailed in the last possible moment.

"Dad, why don't you stay home another day? You were really sick. Maybe go see a doctor." Which will take time. Which will give me and Cris time.

"I'm fine, Nya. Much better. Wanna ride with me, or take the bus?" I get a smile, and while normally I'd jump on it—*he wants to be seen with me, he doesn't mind taking me!*—today I don't.

Nope.

I come up with a plan. Lights, camera, action. One jittery hand swipes across my forehead. "Actually… I'm probably gonna stay home today, Dad. Not feeling so well." I force a shiver, like chills. "That's why I woke up. Maybe I caught what you had." Logical, right?

Dad's smile turns into a mask of worry. "Shouldn't have sipped from my water bottle. Any fever? Headaches? Dizziness? Palpitations? Any—"

I hold up a palm. "Geez, Dad, no, nothing that severe. And no thank you. It's nothing, but I don't want to be sneezing into my face mask all day and risk getting anybody else sick, or worse, risk contaminating the cultures."

He sighs. "I get it. But you'd tell me if you had a headache or if it got worse, right?"

"Yes, mother hen." I roll my eyes, followed by Dad rolling his in response.

"Okay, okay. Stay home, recover. Call me if you need anything, okay?" He pushes the chair back and stands up. "COVID tests are in the bathroom, upper right drawer. If you caught what I had, it won't be that, but better safe than sorry. And then… Anything you need, or is it okay if I leave already? Lots to catch up on."

Oh, no. I'm fine. Actually, the sooner I'm alone, the better. I give him a small, oh-so-brave smile. "Don't worry, Dad. I'll be better in no time."

He grunts and shuffles out into the hallway. Yes, he's just been sick, but can't he speed it up? My self-control is stretched to its max. Waiting for Dad to leave the house, open the garage, get into the car, turn on the engine, and finally—*finally*—back out of our driveway takes what feels like eons.

I switch off the light in the living room and peer out of the window, catching his tail lights turn around the corner. Good. He's gone.

And I'm *on*.

Like a madwoman, I dash up the stairs into his office. Dad always takes work home, always—there must be something that tells me what's going on. Something. Anything!

Alas, where to start? I fall into the more-than-expensive leather office chair behind the old, sturdy wooden desk. Everything is nice and neat. That's my dad. *The state of a man's workplace reflects his state of mind.* Okay then, where would he have anything on Cris— *if* he had anything on him?

Probably not out in the open—on the other hand, he feels safe here, and sometimes it's best to hide stuff wherever people could see it. Makes it seem more harmless.

I crack my knuckles and get to work.

The first stacks of paper are boring with a capital B. Duty rosters, cell cultures, blah blah. Nothing worth mentioning.

The same holds true for the first drawer on the left. And the second. And the third.

Grr.

The drawers on the right… Not much different. I even tap their floors to make sure I'm not missing a secret hidden compartment or whatever, although that's a tad too spy-movie for Dad.

Nothing. Nada. Nichts. Rien.

Dang it. I mean, I didn't expect to find an envelope labeled with *Cris' Secret* in cursive, or whatever, but a little something, at least.

Alas, no such luck.

Frustrated, I shove the third drawer closed. Something rattles in the back of the desk and clutters down. With a sigh, I open the door under the drawers. Better make sure I leave everything in order, or Dad is going to notice.

All the way in the back, a ruler, one of those nice, old, wooden ones, must've come out of its drawer when I shoved it closed a tad too forcefully. It slid halfway down, held in place by the last drawer still firmly closed against the desk's back. With my left hand, I fish for the ruler while opening the third drawer with my right hand to release it. There we go.

I flick the now freed ruler onto my palm twice. Okay. Okay. Do I need to get down on my knees and start tapping floorboards for secret compartments? Or is that too crazy? What do I do next?

What about searching the attic? Would he have stuff there? And why did I think Dad would have anything on Cris lying here on the desk? I stuff the ruler into the top drawer, or rather, I try. It hits the wooden back of the drawer and won't fit.

Anyway. Of course, I could go through all the one million binders in the shelves next to the door. That might only take me about half a lifetime.

Just great.

I yank open the second drawer, throw the ruler in with the envelopes, and slam it shut.

Okay, here's the plan. I'll start with the folders the highest up, assuming Dad wanted whatever compromising material might have tucked far away and not easily accessible. I got at least until 5:00 P.M. if not later to find something that's an obvious-yet-not hiding place—

Wait.

All of a sudden, it feels warm in here. I tug on the collar of my shirt. That stupid ruler—it slid right into the second drawer. It hit wood in the third, as if that drawer was shorter.

But it isn't.

Or at least, it shouldn't be. I drop to my knees, all but ripping that bottom door out of its hinges. Craning my neck, I activate my phone's flashlight and angle it up. Nope, I was right. The third drawer reaches all the way to the desk's wooden backing.

A puff of air escapes through my pursed lips. I might be onto something. Little by little, I inch back up again and take a seat in Dad's chair, as if any fast movement would make this idea—this chance—go up in smoke.

I open the top drawer. Like before, there's nothing of interest in it: Pens. Tape. Stapler. Eraser. Sharpener. No ruler, though, because it won't fit. I swallow dry and pull the drawer out as far as possible.

Tap Tap Tap.

Jeez.

It sounds hollow. The *back end* of the drawer sounds hollow. My heart races and stumbles over its own feet. Maybe I judged him wrong, maybe Dad is spy-movie enough to hide something—and hide something better than I thought.

Within ten seconds, I've taken all the office supplies out of the drawer, but not without taking a picture first to remember where they were. Beginner's mistake to mess up.

I roam my shaking fingers across the back of the drawer. The wood feels rougher, not the same as the sides or front of the desk, so maybe… Maybe I'm really onto something.

I give it a slight push.

Nothing.

Shove to the right.

Nothing.

Shove to the left.

Nothing.

Gah!

Frustrated, I drop my hands, fingers sliding down on the wooden panel—

And *click*, I feel resistance, like from a loaded spring, and then a thin wooden flap falls open and clatters into the now empty drawer.

I'm not breathing.

Really, I'm not.

My dad has a secret compartment in his desk. *My dad.*

I turn on the flashlight on my phone again, although I need about five attempts to push the right button. Once it's lit, I shine it into the depth of the drawer—

The next breath gets stuck in my throat. Won't come out.

Because there is a small manila envelope in there, folded up and squished, but it's there.

It evades my grasp two times. That's how much I'm shaking. My dad is involv— No. It must be something else. Love letters from my mom. That's it. Nausea rises, courtesy of the very real possibility that my father plays an even bigger part in keeping a teenager hostage in the basement of his company than I already know.

I drop the cell onto the desk and unfold the envelope.

Not sealed.

"Okay, here goes nothing." I reach inside, pull out a card with a few folded papers stuffed inside of it.

A card.

A *Congrats, you're having a baby*-card.

Not exactly what I expected. Not exactly something most people would keep hidden.

I take the folded papers out and turn the card sideways to read it:

> *Congrats, Jessica! Please let me know where*
> *you're registered! +49-555-8181409*
> *Love, Johanna*

Jessica. These papers, they're memories of my mom. Can't get my throat to work and swallow. I glide a finger over her name, written some when in the nine months before my birth. *Mom.*

Feels funny when the past is catching up with you out of the blue. And adding one and one, that would be why Dad hid the card. He's too sentimental to throw it out, but still too messed up from the death of his wife to keep it somewhere where he could see it once in a while, especially because I'm pretty sure *Johanna* is Johanna Friedrichs, my mom's oldest friend and the woman who was supposed to become my Godmother if my mom had survived giving birth to me.

Anyway.

Back to business.

I take the papers I dropped onto my lap and straighten them out. Let's see what other blasts from his past my dad can't face out in the open.

Okay, paper number one. Yeah. Not helpful. I turn it over, but the back is empty—and it's not as if a list of what looks like places my mom wanted to work for would help me. All names listed are labs. Many of them crossed out, some of them commented on with her handwriting. Sigh. I get it. Sentimental value.

On to the second paper: A scientific article theorizing about why Neanderthals went extinct. Fascinating, truly. *Not.* At least not now.

The next one is a print-out of two sets of chromosomes, a couple of areas marked on the upper one, one on the Y-chromosome in red. Okay, cool, but also not the game changer I was hoping for.

Then another article, pre-publication, with—whoa—my dad as first author. *Genetic splicing and integration of non-human DNA via CRISPR.* From like almost twenty years ago. That sounds like my dad. But why didn't he end up publishing it? I've never heard of this one, and yes, puh-lease, I've read all his publications, or at least I thought I did.

I scan over the abstract and my jaw drops. *Integrating Neanderthal genes into human genome is the future*, Dad wrote? What the absolute…! Where would he even get—? And why—? How—?

With shaking fingers I move that page away, and the next one lands like a punch to the gut. I suck in a harsh breath.

Oh, for all that's holy—

An ultrasound picture. Black and white, blurry, like a

snowstorm, and yet it's easy to recognize.

It's a baby.

A baby in its mother's womb.

That's the game changer. Right there.

At very first glance, I think it's me, because duh, a baby-congrats-card for me-slash-mom *and* an ultrasound? Pretty easy to come to that conclusion. Only there are two things jumping right at me that don't look like me. For example, that little…uh, *thing* between the baby's legs. Girls don't have that.

So yes, that would be one hint. The other is that somebody—looks like Dad's handwriting—has taken a sharpie to it and scribbled "CRISPR is growing" under the baby's butt.

CRISPR?

CRISPR!

Holy cow. I don't like the connection my mind comes up with.

CRISPR. As in *Clustered Regularly Interspaced Short Palindromic Repeat.* As in *genetically modified.*

But that's not what's sending shivers down my spine.

CRISPR.

CRIS PR.

Cris Parr.

Holy freakin' cow.

My eyelids flutter shut.

Unless this is one ginormous coincidence, it looks like Cris is… is a… is a genetic experiment.

And worse, Cris is *my dad's* genetic experiment.

My dad made Cris part Neanderthal.

CHAPTER TWELVE

"'m not sure I enjoy seeing you this early in the morning." Gabriel holds the door open wider for me. His hair is more tousled than usual, pulled into a messy man-bun high on top of his head. Can't help but notice he's still in his PJ-pants, and that apparently, he sleeps without a shirt.

I notice, and I ignore it, like his little verbal jab.

"Easy, Gabe. Lemme help you: You don't enjoy seeing me early in the morning. Especially not when I'm bringing this." I hold up the pages I copied *and* took pictures of before I hid the originals right where they came from and made everything look as spiffy as before I got my fingers on it. Won't lie. I was close to throwing up for about ninety percent of the time.

"Shit." Gabriel's eyes pop wide. "You found something? Do I even want to know?" He falls onto his couch and adjusts his bun.

I take a seat in the opposite corner. "I would say, no, you don't want to know. It's that bad. Problem is, we *do* know too much already. We can't un-see what they did to Cris, so no matter how much we'd rather let it be, we're in for a penny, in for a pound." Sure, we could ignore everything and never return to Cris. Easiest way for us. Turn a blind eye, stay passive. Everybody does it a million times a year—taking the easy way out, I mean. Sometimes we tell ourselves it was the only option we had, sometimes we come up with reasons, but in the end, we humans choose the easy road.

Unless our conscience overrules that reflex. And mine is screaming at a deafening level.

Gabe holds out a hand. "All right, let me see." He takes the copies from me and scans over the first one. I kept the papers in the same order as the originals were. For effect, so to speak.

If somebody had recorded my reaction, I'm sure it mirrored what Gabriel is going through. Some confusion, then the point where suspicion sets in—and with the last page, the pieces fall into place.

"Shit," he whispers and shakes his head. "I can't believe it. Your dad— I mean, he designed Cris? With non-human genes?"

"That's what it looks like. And he wasn't even especially good at naming him. I should've seen it. Cris Parr. I mean, I've worked with CRISPR for, like, how many years? My dad only mentioned it about five hundred million times." I ram a frustrated fist into the cushion on my right. Seriously. I should've made the connection when I heard his name. But it didn't click for me. Grr.

Gabe scans over the papers again. "Where did you find them?"

"Hidden enough that I'm sure it's not a joke. Secret compartment in my dad's desk."

His gaze shoots up to meet mine. One eyebrow pops up high. "That's kind of spy-movie of your dad."

"My thoughts exactly." Gabe knows how my dad ticks, and vice versa, of course. If I remember correctly, Dad came up with Gabe's eighth birthday present, a biochem-kit for teens. "Gabriel has the potential to become a brilliant researcher," he said. "He should be given every opportunity to work on his skills." Funny, though, the same never applied to his daughter. Oh, well.

Anyway. I let my head drop back into the cushions. "What do

you think of it?" Gabe blows out a harsh puff of air, and I give a sarcastic chuckle. "Yeah, that's what I thought too."

"Well, to be honest, this is a mess. For many, many reasons." He looks at the first and second pages again. "If you wanted me to make sense of it, I'd say your dad—and bear with me here, I know it sounds crazy—your dad integrated certain parts from a Neanderthal genome into human DNA when he designed Cris. The Neanderthal-report, his article on integrating non-human DNA and how that's the future…"

I close my eyes and let go of a groan that's been building up since I found those papers. "His un-published article. He must've known he'd be in trouble if that came out, and yes, all of it sounds crazy, but it's Dad's specialty. He's been playing with CRISPR since forever." He's more the old-fashioned genetic engineer, all about replacing and exchanging genes, while my focus is on epigenetics, turning genes on or off when needed.

I blow a raspberry. "Also, it's not undoable from a technical point of view. After all, we're doing similar genetic engineering in other areas of medicine all the time, but adding Neanderthal genes? That's new. Thanks, Dad."

Gabe takes a big breath. "I mean, there are two sets of chromosomes here, one male, one female. The areas marked, I assume, are the areas where CRISPR integrated the foreign genes." He dabs a finger at the Y-chromosome and some other areas. "Don't know why there are two sets, but maybe the female one was a dud, because this," he holds up the ultrasound picture, "is definitely a boy."

Heat invades my cheeks as I look up at the tiny body part Gabe points to. Well, yes. A boy. That's what I thought as well. Glad we agree on that.

I clear my throat. "Question is two-fold. Why did he do that, and what do we do about it?"

"Not just two-fold, Nya. The *why* we can explain. I mean, they draw marrow from Cris every freakin' week. Something in his stem cells must be special. What's Advangen's biggest research area?"

My brows furrow. "Developing genetic therapies for everything, from cancer to infectious diseases." Like, boosting the immune system and teaching it how to attack certain cells that are cancerous, or restoring function after spinal cord injury. They recently started a trial doing gene-therapy on children born deaf. It's all cutting edge and world-leading. Only the Germans' WissenSCHAFFT is equally well known for genetic engineering. Happens when you come up with the first draught-resistant super grain.

"And there's your answer." Gabe falls back into the cushions. "And the way things are going, I bet it's about immunity to *something*, given the fact that we think certain parts of the Neanderthal genome made them less susceptible to illness. Cris is their unlimited supply of modified cells. We've always had a hard time multiplying those in vitro, and they grow slowly."

Oh, geez. I cover my face with my hands and shake my head. "Makes sense," I mumble through my fingers.

"Why, thank you." Gabe gives me an amused glance. "But in the matter of what to do about it—that's where it becomes complicated."

"No, it doesn't. We have to get him out." We can't just leave him there.

"Agreed, we do. But what then? Maybe we've been going at it a tad too naïvely. Yes, he can hide in my apartment. But for how long? I assume he has no papers at all. And while I doubt they will call the cops when Cris disappears, they will be on the lookout, and if they ever find him, they won't just let him be. They'll want him back."

Damn. "So, we'd have to hide him, which means he'd exchange one prison for another."

Gabriel sighs. "Yes. Unless…"

I sit up straighter. "Unless what?"

"Unless we play this smart. And smart means it's going to be painful for both of us. Not a walk in the park. And for you… it's gonna be the toughest." He gives me an apologetic look.

Well, I'm not going to back out because it's tough. Cris is a prisoner of Advangen—how bad can it get for me in comparison? "Okay, spit it out, Gabe. What's your idea?"

Gabe's eyes meet mine, dead serious. "We get him out. We hide him. And then… we go public."

"Public?" I choke on the word and cough, my next breaths coming in with a wheeze.

"Geez, Nya." Lightning fast, Gabe fishes a Coke Zero from the mini-fridge next to the couch and pops it open for me. "Please don't choke to death. Seems like I have enough problems without you dying on me."

"Uh-huh," I wheeze and take the Coke, but I need about half the can and thirty seconds of deep breathing before I can think clearly again. "Go public. You're serious about that, aren't you?"

Gabe takes a sip of his Coke. Comes in handy to have a mini-fridge right next to the couch. Only children of rich dads. "Yes, I'm serious. Keep in mind, my family has played this game for a while."

"Being in the public eye?"

"No, managing public opinion. Managing the press. And you have to manage them, or else it gets messy."

Well, he's right with that. With a famous basketball-player for a father, Gabe has experienced all kinds of crap. And I know what he's referring to, and despite years of mutual annoyance, my heart goes out to him. "You mean messy as in… the divorce?"

He flinches. Even after over a decade, mentioning his mom still stings. "Yes. You know how ugly it was when she left, Nya. But that was the controlled version. I remember overhearing them fight, the day she walked out and never came back. I know what happened behind the scenes. She promised Dad the most dirty fight unless she'd get what she wanted. And she tried. God, there was so much mud-slinging…" He drops his head and shakes it.

I lean forward and lay a hand on his naked shoulder. "Forget about her, Gabe. Tell me about your plan."

For a second, he freezes when my hand touches his skin. Then he exhales with a little sigh at the end and takes my hand in his, turning it over, but holding on to it.

Uh—

"Nya, here's the deal. This is a battle we can't win alone. If we want to succeed, we need public outrage and support on our side. We're two teens—well, three, counting Cris—we're three teens against a gigantic corporation like Advangen. Our strength isn't in numbers: Three teens missing, and nobody beyond our county line might bat an eye. An international company like Advangen ignoring human rights and the law and keeping a genetically modified boy hidden from birth, to abuse him as a guinea-pig? That's what we need to play, that angle, or else we don't stand a chance. But going public means—"

Oh, I know. "Going public means you're going to lose your internship. I'm going to lose mine, and my dad—"

"Who knows what your dad is going to do?"

"Well, he won't be happy, that's for sure." I roll my eyes. "I expect him to cross me out of his will and never talk to me again." Crap. That sounds… bad.

Silence hovers, and it's heavy.

"Possibly," Gabe concludes. "Question is, are you willing to take that risk?" He squeezes my hand in his, and I have to work on a dry swallow. B-because of his question, of course. Because I'm not used to being the source of his concern. Of his amusement and ridicule, yes, but not of his concern.

One more squeeze for my hand, and admittedly, it feels nice. "Actually, let me rephrase, Nya. The correct question is, are you willing to break with your dad to help Cris?"

And there we go again. That's the big question.

Imagining not having Dad in my corner, despite our differences in opinion for my future, feels wrong. We're a team, always have been, and I figured we always would be. Dad is my only living relative. There's no mom for me to fall back on, nobody else to support me, who'd have my back. But if I break out Cris and we make public what we found… how can we be like we used to?

But even if I decided to not help Cris, could I look Dad in the eye the same as I did a few days ago, knowing he hid a teenager in Advangen's basement and experimented on him?

The answer is easy: No, I couldn't. And neither could I look myself in the eye.

I wish I could choose the easy way out and not do anything. Call it somebody else's problem, not mine, ignore it, and convince myself there's a reason why Advangen is doing what they're doing, and that it's all gonna be all right. But I know it's not. My part in this was laid out the moment I discovered Cris in the secret basement. I can't back out now. I'd never forgive myself for turning a blind eye when I should've looked closer, no matter what or whom I'm going to lose.

Nausea rises as I meet Gabe's eyes. "I'll survive. Priorities. Let's get Cris out of there."

He gives me a solemn nod and a small, somewhat sad smile. "I knew you were going to say that. And I think and hope karma is giving you a bonus point for that decision."

I huff. Doubt that's how it works, but I sure hope he's right.

Gabe stares at a spot somewhere behind me, lost in thought and chewing on his lower lip. "Okay then. Let's brainstorm. We need a plan we can set into action within a day." He opens the fridge again, takes out a pack of Oreos and throws them to me. "Brain food."

I catch the pack and chuckle. "Still keep them in the fridge?"

He levels me with a cool glance. "Obviously, they're best when cold. Now sit, and think."

So, I do, and the rest of the day flies by in no time.

Needless to say, neither of us goes to work: I'm officially sick, and Gabe calls out as well. We're busy though, as in *really* busy. And the weirdest thing? This truce that we seem to have since I told him about Cris. It feels nice. Like the good ol' days. Like we were back to being normal with each other. There's a big fat elephant in the room we don't talk about, but it's for the better.

Twice I catch myself checking Gabe out as he's focused on something on the phone or the computer. The messy man-bun is still there. He didn't bother doing anything with his hair, and I like it. Always liked how Gabe was effortlessly cool, while I wasn't— wasn't even cool when I put in an effort. It's weird, I mean, I haven't really looked-looked at him since he was at the beginning of puberty, and now the old Gabe is there, clearly so, but also this new Gabe. This man-Gabe, with muscles and a wide chin and stubble on his face.

I blink hard and shake my head to clear it. Whatever. He's good-looking, but still an ass.

"Okay, here's the deal." Gabe hangs up the phone. Must have been the umpteenth phone call for him. "My dad's not gonna come back from his trip for another two weeks. He doesn't mind me taking the RV, besides the usual *behave yourself*-crap."

I pump a fist. "Yes! So we can take the RV?"

"We can, and we will. The plan stands. Once you and I go MIA, they will check your house. They will check mine. Won't take much time until they add one and one. Our best chance for now is to take the RV until we set things in motion."

Until we set things in motion—until we've gone public, he means. "And you're sure you can get our story out. Like, really sure." Because I doubt the New York Times, L.A. Times, or even the local small newspaper would hear us out if we called and told them about a teen we freed who'd been held captive in Advangen's basement.

"A hundred percent. Told ya it pays to have a famous dad. There are at least four reporters I can list top of my hat who'd jump at the opportunity. I give the word, they will meet us, they will publish our story."

Deep breath. "Okay. Okay. We've got that part covered. All that's left is the details, right?" Like, packing for days or weeks on the run—fun—and how to get Cris out of there, despite the ankle bracelet.

"Right. I figured you and I both pack, then meet back here. It will take you longer, since you have to go home, so I might go grocery shopping to stock the RV. And then..." He shrugs, shoving his hands into his pants' pockets.

"Then, when everything's set, I steal Dad's ID, we get out Cris and turn ourselves into fugitives on the run."

"Heroic fugitives." Gabe grins and winks. "After all, we're saving Cris from being experimented on."

I return his grin. "Yeah, alright. Heroic fugitives."

But heroic or not, I've got the lingering feeling the fallout of what's coming is going to be more than we're anticipating.

CHAPTER THIRTEEN

My dad lets the door fall into its lock. "Nya, I'm home."

I wrap my fingers tighter around the mug with steaming hot broth in it. "I'm in the kitchen. Hi, Dad."

Heavy steps come down the hallway. Slower than normal. I hear him drop his bag onto the bench close to the stairs, as always. Good.

The door opens with its typical creak half-way through. "Hey, honey."

"Hey, Dad. How was your day?"

His mouth opens and closes once. He pulls out a chair and falls into it. "Rough," he eventually says. "There's... lots of stuff to catch up on when you haven't been in the office for a few days." The smile I get is weak. He looks kinda pasty, too.

"Are you okay? Maybe you should've stayed home another day."

He leans forward onto the table, like he had aged a decade or two over the last half day. "Nah, I'm fine. Just... lots of work, like I said." He reaches for my cup. "What'cha drinking?"

"Broth." I let him take the cup and warm his fingers on it. "Tried eating, but nothing wanted to go down." True dat, albeit for different reasons than I'd like him to believe. "So I figured, a bit of broth to warm me up and help me get over this. Plus, they say chicken broth contains anti-inflammatory properties."

Dad chuckles. "I'm pretty sure they're talking about home-made fresh chicken soup, not store-bought broth."

I pout. "Aww, man!"

He gives the mug back to me. "Worth a try, though, I agree." He leans into his chair and looks at me.

And looks at me.

And looks at me.

Uh…

"What, Dad?" I'm not a big fan of his scrutiny. Not normally, and especially not now.

A quick smile appears on his face, the kind that doesn't reach his eyes. Five minutes in, and I've seen plenty of those already. "Nothing. Nothing. Just worried. You're never sick." His eyes bore into mine, and I do my best to stay nonchalant, because he's right. I'm never sick.

"I know. But I brought it on myself, I know. Guess I didn't know how lucky I was until today. So. Annoying." I sip on the broth.

Pause.

"So… How are you feeling?"

Anxious? Scared? Completely blindsided? I shrug. "Just not good. Under the weather."

Dad narrows his eyes. "Headaches?"

There he goes again with those. I shrug and decide to be honest. "A bit."

That gets his attention. "Fainting? Seizures? I mean, you'd tell me if—"

My eyes pop open wide. "Geez, Dad, chill! No seizures, no, why would I have seizures? But yes, I'd tell you, I'd probably call you in a panic once I woke up from fainting or the seizure's over. Not that you could do anything, but still."

His expression turns serious. "Don't underestimate your old man's determination when it comes to your health. You're sick, I'll fix it. I would do anything for that. For you. *Anything.*"

I know that. Dad is a worrywart, and health always, always came first for him. I've learned to keep it on the down-low whenever something hurts, just because he goes kind of nuclear on me, every single time. Which sucks, because sometimes, sue me, I just want to mention my head hurts, or that I, I don't know, stubbed my toe. Just to get some pity-points, some TLC. But doing so will send Dad into a spiral of worry, so I say nothing unless I have to. Like, now, even though most of it is fake.

Still, I appreciate the sentiment. "Thanks, Dad, I know. But no, no need to activate your savior-complex, I'll be fine." I say it with a wink at the end, because while I need to make fun of his uber-worry, I also understand it's part of his job description as a father.

Dad chuckles and lifts both palms. "Okay, okay. Just making sure." He pauses and smacks his lips. "Still… *odd* you're so under the weather."

A chill snakes down my back. *Play it cool, Nya. Play it cool!* "Not odd, Dad. Annoying."

He gives a slow nod. "Indeed. Very annoying."

"Yeah." Slurp, slurp.

Pause.

I swallow. "But judging by the way you look; work was more annoying."

Dad sighs. "Definitely. Anyway. So, what have you been up to today, then?"

I cock my head. What? We just established I was sick. "Like

staying at home and trying not to puke?" Because there's no way he could know what I've been up to. Nope. Still, my heart speeds up a bit. Damn adrenaline.

"Right." He holds my eyes, but two can play this game.

"Yeah. Thank for giving me that virus, Dad."

"Well, you took it yourself, honey. And I'm sure you'll be better soon. You have the immune system of a horse. Which is why you usually aren't sick with measly viruses."

I ignore the potential insinuation—because how would he know? He cannot know!—and set the mug down. "One, yes, my fault. We've established that, and two, even a horse can get sick once in a while. Speaking of, this beautiful pony needs to go to bed. It's eight already, and I've been feeling crappy all afternoon." Also true.

Pause.

Then, a slow nod. "Okay then. I'll see you tomorrow. Feel better, honey."

I get up and leave my mug on the table. "Thanks, Dad. Hopefully I will."

I could swear I feel his gaze bore into my back all the way out of the kitchen. A shudder runs down my spine. He doesn't know. There's no way. Maybe he's suspicious, but he doesn't know.

I *hope.*

Heart hammering, I retreat to my bedroom. Everything feels surreal, like going through the motions of brushing my teeth, so Dad hears the water flow in my bathroom and doesn't wonder why I'm skipping on my routine. But then, my heart won't calm down at all once I'm in bed, pretending to sleep and waiting for Dad to go to bed as always, at 10:30 P.M. sharp.

Meaning, my brain has two and a half very torturous hours ahead of it to freak out—for many reasons, but mainly because

Dad felt *off*, for a lack of a better term. Yes, maybe he's still sick, work stressed him out, he's in trouble because of the ID, or whatever. Point is, it feels different. *Off*, like I said. Although, if he knew, or if he truly suspected I had something to do with the ID and Cris, he'd say so. Dad doesn't beat around the bush. Not his thing. So all things considered, I'm safe.

I think.

Well, again: I *hope*.

Still, lying here and waiting for him to finally go to bed and then wait another thirty long, long minutes until I'm sure he fell asleep deep enough that he won't wake up is not what I would consider fun.

Usually, Dad's a good sleeper. Lays down, falls asleep within minutes, and then wouldn't wake up if the house came down, but… well, would be very inconvenient if today was the exception.

Once I'm sure I should be safe, I sneak out of bed and get dressed in the dark. Black pants, black shirt, black beanie. Black sneakers as well. I pat my back pocket. My phone stays here, but I got my wallet with all my cash and ID. My other stuff's already at Gabe's. That should be it.

I look around my room, only the light from the moon illuminating some of my furniture's outlines. "Bye, stuff," I whisper. "Hope to be back soon." Although I can't say when that will be, and in which capacity. Can we go to jail for freeing Cris if Advangen called the police on us for damaging their property on our way in or out? Would they dare, even after our story came out? Either way, leaving here today feels like a big step with huge consequences.

Deep breath.

Little by little I turn the doorknob.

Open the door.

Tiptoe out.

Close it softly.

No Dad standing here with a shotgun ready to keep me in my room. See? Good.

At a snail's pace, I sneak down the stairs, staying to the outside of the steps and skipping the ones I know creak like crazy. Not a single sound disturbs the silence, if you don't count the drum beat of my heart, because that's seriously making some very distracting noise.

I slip down the hallway onto the tile floor: quieter than wood.

Dad's bag is still where he left it. I don't need lights for this. My dad's a creature of habit. His ID is always—

Got it. Right side pocket. Easy-peasy.

For one moment, I let my fingers hover over the small plastic card. I take it, there's no going back. My relationship with Dad will never be the same. I'm stealing his ID, going behind his back—well, seems like he went behind mine, too, but still—and probably breaking several laws. Or not, since I feel Gabe and I are the good guys here, but even Robin Hood wasn't technically doing legal stuff. Either way, my actions will drive a wedge between us.

I swallow hard. It's not as if I had a second parent to fall back on, or to be on my side. Dad is all I have, and despite our disagreements, I love the man.

A bitter taste comes up my throat: But what has he done that I don't know about? To Cris?

In one fast movement, I snatch the ID up and curl my fingers around it. Priorities. I've had seventeen years of more or less harmonious growing up. Cris had none. Whatever my fallout is, it's worth it.

So, let's get this party started.

As carefully as possible, I creep back to the front door. Turning the lock is tricky, but I keep the noise down.

Open the door, squeeze through, close it—

And I don't lock it, because the electronic number lock would beep if I did.

Just gotta hope nobody will break and enter at our house while I'm doing the same at Dad's company.

I keep to the bushes lining our walkway. Movement catches my eye, but when I turn, there's nothing there. Geez. Way to go to give me a heart attack. I sneak on, and once I'm off our property, I fall into a light, slow jog.

We're coming, Cris. We're coming.

"This is *whose* car?" Seriously?

Gabe sighs. "Jordan's."

"Why the heck did you take Jordan's car?" Jordan is an idiot. One year above me, so just graduated, like Gabe.

Gabriel stops the black Camaro at a red light. Not much traffic besides us and the occasional other car. We're a small town, after all. "Because if they catch us on video, they'll get Jordan's license plate, not mine. That'll give us some time."

My jaw drops. "But he's gonna get in trouble."

He shrugs. "Do you mind? I don't. I remember Prom."

My cheeks heat. Prom. Yeah. Let's just say my low-cut dress plus too much to drink for Jordan was not a good combo. Add a crush he had on me, and two of my classmates had to get a bit... *forceful* to convince him to keep his hands off me and that it was time to leave. And he wasn't even my date. But wait... "You saw that?" Because Gabe was there with Alexis, volleyballer extraordinaire, and they looked very... *busy*. Ahem.

"Was hard to overlook." He keeps his eyes straight ahead.

"Right." I figured Gabe probably got a good laugh out of it.

He clears his throat. "Anyway. Jordan's car is perfect. Black tinted windows. We're getting Cris out. We'll drive to the empty lot on 5th Street, and that's where Jordan will wait."

A groan leaves my throat. "Really? Why, why, why, Gabe?"

He cocks an eyebrow at me. "Because I'm using him. He thinks he's helping me and a buddy to hook up with you. Hence, he let me use his car. Once we're out, he'll drive ahead to Point View and wait—"

"Because you told him you'd sneak me to the club on 5th, get me drunk, and bring me up there for a make-out session he hopes to join in on." I cross my arms in front of my chest. "That's disgusting. You know that, right?"

"He's disgusting for falling for it and for even thinking I'd do something like that to you—to anyone, or even you, I mean." He makes a disgusted gagging sound. "Jordan will also be useful, because if Advangen calls the police and if they run his license plate, I could bet they'll look at street surveillance. They'll find his black Camaro heading out of town, and while they follow him, we get away with the RV in the other direction."

I shake my head. "You're an evil genius, Gabe."

A small smile tugs at the corners of his lips. "I have my moments."

He pulls into the same parking spot we stood in a mere twenty-four hours ago and kills the engine. Interesting how nauseous an empty stomach can be. I suck in a big breath. "Ready?"

"As ready as can be." Gabe un-clicks his seat belt and reaches for a bag behind my passenger seat. "Here. One for you, one for me." He hands me a small, rectangular action cam snapped into a chest belt.

I sneak my arms through the loops and position it in the center of my sternum. I'd call this our insurance policy. Or stupidity, because it's not only going to record the way Cris is held but also our moderately illegal breaking and entering.

Oh, well.

We both get ready in silence.

Once we're good to go, we pull our beanies lower, exit the car and use the tree to scale the wall to the Advangen parking lot. Been there, done that.

Everything's quiet. Good. Nobody's here, nobody's suspecting anything. Even better.

Gabe's breathing is harsh as he follows me down the same route and into the elevator. I get it. Yesterday was nothing. Well, we thought. Today we know what's at stake, besides Cris' freedom: Ours, possibly.

I give a quick look over at Gabe before I scan Dad's ID in the elevator.

He nods. "Do it."

Beep!

The doors close, and the elevator whisks us down. My blood pressure drops with every meter we descend. Shouldn't be nervous, and yet I can't stand still, can't focus. I feel bad. Like, something's-about-to-happen-bad, which is ridiculous. We're fine. *Fine.*

But then, it's not as if Gabe was doing much better. He fidgets with his cuticles, and he's not fidgety at all. Usually, at least.

The doors hiss apart and we sprint into the non-functioning air lock. Time matters.

Fifteen seconds later, we're in Cris' hallway. Last time I called out his name, this time I don't dare to. Maybe because the situation feels more serious, maybe because I'm not sure if they have somebody here or they're watching, but we both stay quiet, by—

harr, harr—wordless agreement.

I dash down the hallway toward his bedroom. The dimmed lights suit us well.

I knock on his door and open it at the same time.

Rustling of a blanket, movement— "What the—!"

"Cris, it's us. Nya and Gabe." With two steps, I'm in front of him while he all but jumps out of bed. The only light comes from his alarm clock, a faint green glow throwing the slightest shadow onto his face.

"What are you doing here?" His gaze darts from me to Gabe and back, eyes wide, brows pulled down into a V.

"We're getting you out." Gabe grabs a shirt from the chair next to the door and throws it at him. "Get dressed. Now. We don't know if their surveillance is better today, but we don't wanna risk it."

Cris catches the shirt and slides into it. "I appreciate the thought, but the alarm—"

"We'll take care of it. Get dressed." Gabe throws over a pair of pants, and only now do I realize Cris was sleeping in his boxer briefs. Well, modesty went out the window with our attempt to break him free, and it's not as if I hadn't seen his chest before, courtesy of our introduction.

As soon as he slides into his pants, I kneel. "Give me your ankle."

"What are you doing?"

"Assuming that the bracelet works with RFID technology. I'm trying to block it from reaching the reader that's probably integrated into the air lock's entrance. Once we're out, we're gonna cut it off, but we can't risk a feedback in case a disrupted signal is triggering an alarm."

"My ID bracelet? But that's only a good luck—"

"Nope. Has a small chip embedded into the charm."

Cris groans. "Awesome. I'm really losing my trust in everybody right about now."

Gabe kicks over Cris' shoes. "We're kinda working on gaining yours."

"Present company excluded, obviously."

I wrap one more layer of aluminum foil around the charm. Too many *ifs* in our hypothesis. *If* the tag is RFID or radio frequency. *If* aluminum blocks it, and not only tunes it down. *If* the reader gets fooled by the weaker signal.

Extra-thick aluminum, here comes another layer. "There, done. Socks, shoes, off we go." And if we're lucky and we're right, it won't trigger the alarm. If it does… well. Let's hope it won't.

Cris is ready within two seconds. Okay, maybe ten.

"Do you need to take anything?"

"Wouldn't know what."

"Okay." Gabe holds the door open. "Clock's ticking, guys."

We run back to the airlock. "Gabe, your turn!"

Gabriel darts into the airlock and hits the button. Fifteen seconds, counting down.

"What about us?" Cris whispers, both arms wrapped around his upper body as if he needed to hold himself together.

"We go next." I gently rock into him, playfully. "I wanted him to get the elevator ready. If there is an alarm, we want to have the elevator down here to enter it right away, not have it bring down security."

"Good idea." The apple in his throat moves up and down once.

Ten seconds later, Gabe exits the air lock and pushes the elevator button, then turns around and gives us a thumbs up.

I blow out a puff of air. "Here goes nothing." I go in first and give the door a slight shove for Cris to catch.

Only one way to find out if our theory was right.

And if it doesn't work…

Yeah, I'd rather not think about it.

Five layers of aluminum. *Thick* aluminum. Must be enough to weaken the signal. The reader won't pick up on it. Won't.

Like last night, Cris takes a deep breath. Another one. He bites his lower lip—

And steps into the airlock.

Silence.

"Geez." I blow out a puff of air.

Both guys laugh out loud, Cris next to me and Gabe on the other side of the airlock. His comment sounds muffled. "Nice, man. Welcome to freedom."

Gosh! Way to go jinxing us! Turning toward the other door, I ready myself to burst out as soon as possible. I love it went well so far. I hate it went well so far. Feels like I'm missing something.

During the fifteen longest seconds of my life, the elevator arrives and Gabe holds the doors open until finally Cris and I burst out of the most unnecessary airlock in the history of airlocks.

All three of us hurry into the elevator, and Gabe punches the button for the first floor.

That's when those premonitions finally take over. "Nope." I slam Dad's ID in front of the reader, pushing and holding the button for the second floor, overriding Gabe's choice.

"Second floor? Nya, we need the ground—"

"It doesn't feel right." Best explanation ever, I know.

"It doesn't feel right." Gabe keeps his tone neutral. Barely so.

"Too easy." I suck in my lip. "It was too easy. All of it. I mean, Dad was weird tonight. And I felt like I was missing something, and… I don't know. Can't we just play it safe? Humor me. We go to the second floor, no video surveillance there, we take the east stairs down and sneak out the back. Fine?"

Gabe rolls his eyes. "Fine."

"Thank you, oh big leader," I grumble.

The doors open onto the second floor, and I run ahead. "Come on, guys follow me." I don't care if I'm being ridiculous. I'd rather be safe than sorry.

We jog down the hallway toward the stairs.

Ping!

Adrenaline shoots through my arteries. "The other elevator!" The doors are opening—shit, shit, shit! Nobody's supposed to be here, and security—

Some male voice yells: "Hey! You there! Stop! Stop!"

"Crap," Gabe curses.

Crap indeed—I'd have loved to be wrong on this one! "Faster, guys," I call out, dragging Cris with me by his sleeve, as our jog becomes a full-on run fueled by adrenaline.

Hectic, fast steps follow us down the hallway, coming from at least two people, I'd say, but I'm not about to stop and count.

"We have them! Second floor, running toward the east stairs! Get people there *now*!"

Oh, no! The east stairs! They're cutting off our way out!

"Nya," Gabe hisses between two heavy breaths as he's sprinting down the hallway. "What now?"

Now? My breath turns into wheezes and I think my heart stops beating, like, completely. My brain, on the other hand, is doing a surprisingly focused job staying on top of things.

Yes!

I've got an idea. A ten-year-old idea, to be precise. "Follow me!"

Gabe sighs in annoyance, but does as he's told, just like Cris. We sprint around a corner, the boys so close behind me, they're bumping into me when I stop dead without a warning.

I grunt from the impact. "Guys! Here!" I open the door to room L2-23, otherwise called Mr. Yannic's office. "Quiet!"

We squeeze through the door, close it fast and silently, and lock it. "Let them think we went ahead to the stairs," I whisper, while speed-walking to the window. "Come here." I turn the handle and swing the window open.

"You're kidding me," Gabe whisper-groans. "Another tree?"

"It's that or security and their buddies." And I really would prefer to not get caught in the act. Or at all.

Gabe wipes his palms on his thighs. "Tree it is."

Glad we agree.

Cris holds his head tilted to the side, eyes darting over the tree, taking up most of the view from the window. His breath is coming out fast, choppy and with a little wheeze when he swallows hard. "The outside," he whispers. "It's really not dead."

Gabe and I exchange a glance. Yeah, we're not getting caught. We're getting Cris out and a life he deserves. Not sure how, but we're going to get that done, which means: We're not. Gonna. Get. Caught.

I lay a cold, sweaty hand on his forearm. "Cris. Focus. Watch me. You wanna jump off well, keep your balance, rather go slow, okay? It's foggy tonight. The bark could be slippery. Always have a good grip before you move on. Gabe will watch out for you from behind. Do you think you can do that?" Tree-climbing one-oh-one in a nutshell, crash-course version.

He nods, face serious. "Yes. I sometimes get dizzy, but I should be fine."

Heck, not if he gets dizzy up there. Still, I smile what I think is my most encouraging smile. "You'll be fine. I sometimes get dizzy, too. We'll just slow down if that happens, okay?"

Or we'll fall. Alas, no time to worry about that, in addition to everything else. I turn and hoist myself up onto the windowsill, reaching for the first branches. Obviously, it's been a while since I fed squirrels from here. The tree has grown, and what would have supported kiddo-me does now support teenage-me. Quite convenient. As a demonstration for Cris, I climb into the tree, holding on as well as I can. I'm strong. I got this.

And so does Cris. He's behind me in no time. "I like this," he whispers. "It smells good."

Banging against the door, the knob rattling. "Open! We know you're in there! Open!"

"Oh, hell." Gabe scrambles to follow, and he's the only one having a harder time. Never been a climber, that one, plus the added pressure... yeah.

I lead the way through the tree and across another branch that extends over the wall to the parking lot, like the one we used to get in here.

Voices come from around the corner, and with them shouts, yells, and a couple of chopped-off beams from several flashlights.

We're gonna make it. We *are* gonna make it.

My heart hammers at an unhealthy pace as I climb ahead as fast as I can, the boys following stat. Once we're over the wall, I jump and land in a stable crouch. So does Cris, with no traces of dizziness. He looks from left to right and back. "Wow," he breathes. "Just... wow."

Unfortunately for us, security has caught on. "Behind the wall! They're over the wall!"

With a thud, Gabe lands, not as graceful as Cris and I, more like a bag of wet cement. "Run, peeps." He scrambles into a run and darts ahead.

"Cris!" Dude's too mesmerized. I grab him by the hand and drag him with me.

Gabe unlocks the car and jumps behind the wheel. I tear open the passenger door, lift the seat and all but squish Cris inside the back, sliding in next to him, ignoring I'm ending up half on his lap when he isn't fast enough.

Gabe floors it, and the Camaro takes off with squealing tires.

"Whoa!" Cris holds on to my hand with his right, and the door with his left. "This is *fast*! Is it supposed to be— I mean, it doesn't look that fast on TV!"

I squeeze his hand and slide down into my seat. "It's okay, Cris. He's not really going that fast." Although he is. Gabe is definitely breaking the speed limit. Crushing it. He forces the Camaro into a right turn off the premises—

"Shit!" He swerves to the side, barely missing the person—

Bang! Bang!

I scream out. "They're shooting at us! What the absolute fuck! Go, Gabe, *go*! Floor it!"

Bang! Bang!

Sparks fly from the right part of the Camaro's hood. Another two guys run into the street as Gabe speeds toward them. Both seem older. One man gesticulates wildly with the other one, a white-haired—

Gabe curses. "That's Dr. Sherman—"

The white-haired CEO of Advangen jumps back, rips a gun from a holster mounted on his hip, and shoots.

Bang! Bang! Bang!

We all scream as Gabe spins the wheel to the right and forces the car into a tight curve, exposing our rear end instead of ourselves.

As we drift past the other man, his wide and panicked gaze locks with mine.

Dad.

For that one moment, time stands still as the world as I knew it changes into a much, much scarier place.

Then we hurl past him, the connection gone.

Oh, shit.

CHAPTER FOURTEEN

"**S**ee you later, man." Gabe closes the door and winks at Jordan. How he can pull off the calm voice and fake story, I have no clue, because I'm about to either throw up or faint.

Dr. Sherman.

Dad.

Sherman shot at us—and had the others shoot at us—and Dad didn't stop him.

My next breath comes in wheezy.

You don't just shoot at people. You also don't lock a teen into the basement. Or design his genome.

And yet he did it. All of it.

My *dad.*

And Dr. Sherman.

I really, really can't wrap my head around it.

As Jordan speeds off, Gabe gives him another thumbs up, then turns to us. "Fast now." The urgency missing in his voice before is back, and clearly so. "I want to make sure they didn't follow us. Or that Jordan sees the bullet holes in his car and turns around. Or… whatever Murphy's Law can come up with." He power-walks ahead through the little alleyway between the club and the three-story apartment building next to it. It smells of urine, and normally I wouldn't go through here if I got paid to do so, but today is different.

Because today Advangen shot at us.

Everything is different.

Cris cranes his neck to look left and right. To him, this alley must be the epitome of interesting thanks to his skewed frame of reference. I reach back and take his hand. "Come on," I whisper. "You ain't seen nothing yet."

At the other end of the alley, Gabriel unlocks the RV. It's parked under the trees of this small, residential area and looks a tad out of place. Too big.

"Get in, stay down low," Gabe hisses through his teeth.

"Got it." Not that it needed specific mentioning.

As soon as we're in, Gabe starts the engine and backs us out of the parking spot. Slowly. Screeching tires and skid marks are the fastest way to attract unwanted attention.

"Cris, sit on the couch, bend forward, stay low." Part two of freeing Cris starts now. I reach for the lead bucket Gabe found somewhere in his grandpa's tool shed. Here's to good preparation, because it's already filled with water. "Get your shoes off and put your foot in here."

Cris cocks his head. "You're thinking this is going to block the signal?" He rolls up his pants.

"Well, I hope so. The aluminum foil around it, together with the water and the bucket, should dampen some, if not all, of the charm's radio signal. These things are weak to begin with, and since yours only alarmed when you stepped right through the doors, I'm thinking it's not one of the stronger chips, or the alarm would've gone off a couple of meters sooner." I *think*. But no matter what, we can't leave the tag on him. Who knows if it has a GPS device in it or sends out an alarm when tampered with? Doubt it, but I'd rather play it safe. Hence, the bucket, etc.

Gabe throws a quick glance over his shoulder into the back of the RV. "Status, guys—you got it off?"

"Almost." I'm fumbling around with the trauma shears, trying to cut off the bracelet. I press harder, harder—and it snaps. "Got it!" I blow out a puff of air while Cris lifts his foot up and out of the water, leaving the bracelet in the bucket.

Gabe slows down and pulls over. "Then get rid of it."

My pleasure. I grab the bucket, sneak out of the RV, and hide it between some bushes in somebody's front yard. Sorry, guys. With three big steps, I hurry back inside. "Done!" And doesn't it feel good? I mean, besides the nauseating flutters churning inside my gut. Those I can't control, and the more I replay the last couple of minutes, the worse it gets.

They shot at us.

I expected our break-out to possibly not go smoothly, but I didn't expect *that*. Maybe I should've, but I didn't. At all. Can you just shoot at people? Can you?

Gabe speeds up—well, as much as this ginormous RV can speed up—and gets us going. I sit down on the floor with my back leaned into the couch and tap the area next to me. "Come on down." We should stay out of view as much as possible, despite the darkness and tinted windows.

Cris slides down on my right side. For a while, silence hovers. I pull my knees in and wrap my arms around them. The next few minutes are critical. Once we're out of town, we have a good shot at escaping for real, but for that to happen, we've got to keep our fingers crossed—and adhere to the speed limit. My chest squeezes tight. If they caught us now, would they shoot again? They wouldn't dare, out in the open. Or would they?

Cris presses his palm onto the floor. "It vibrates," he whispers.

I nod. "From the engine."

He chuckles once. "It's funny. I mean, I watched so much TV. Granted, I thought it was all make-believe and CGI, and turns out it's all true—"

"Actually, not all is." Judging by the posters hanging in his hallway, he might need a little reality-check. "No vampires. No starships. No superheroes—"

His face drops. "What? Are you kidding me?"

The look of disappointment on him is epic. Like I was the Grinch and just stole Christmas from him. Maybe I could've softened that blow a bit. I mean, I know he hasn't been out before.

I cringe. "You know, well, they like to exaggerate on TV, and—"

Cris bursts out laughing. "Relax, Nya. I know. They taught me to read, remember? I might've fallen for the Atomic Wars-storyline—at least for a while—but that doesn't mean I'm completely naïve." He chuckles and rocks his shoulder into mine.

Oh. Okay. "Well, whatever," I grumble under my breath.

The RV speeds up. "Hitting the freeway." Gabriel gives us a thumbs up. "By the time the sun rises, we should be nicely hidden and safe."

Safe.

Without people shooting at us. Without *my dad* having people shooting at us. I let my head sink down onto my knees.

Safe.

Honestly, at this point, I don't quite know anymore what that means.

That moment when our gazes locked and Dad recognized me and I recognized him… I knew it before I stole his ID, but now my premonition rings way more true: No matter how this ends, I don't think our relationship is ever going to be the same again. How could it? *My Dad* kept Cris captive in the basement. *My Dad* experimented on him, or at least used him for his stem cells. *My Dad* violated about a million ethical standards, and I'm sure I only know half of it, if at all.

My. Dad.

Who knows if it was all on Sherman's order or not, and would it even matter? Dad didn't do the right thing, that's what counts.

Yes, we've had our issues, but to think he could keep a person hidden away and lying to me? Do I even know the real him? What else do I not know? Should I've picked up on something—anything—sooner? Maybe I could've saved Cris years of captivity. But what should I have picked up on? There were no signs, no red flags, no nothing. Dad was my normal dad, who just didn't want me near a lab, I—

When Gabe asked if I was willing to break with Dad to help Cris, I said yes, and I still stand to it, but… Yeah. I guess the break with Dad is happening, but it's ragged and messy.

It hurts.

I rub my shaking palm across my eyes and exhale as slowly as I can. In control. I'm in control. I can deal with it.

For the next close to five hours of the drive, I focus on my breathing, and it helps. Once we hit our camping spot, I feel somewhat on top of my emotions.

Somewhat.

"We made it." Gabe turns off the engine and lets his head fall against the backrest. "Ugh. That was long."

I peel myself out of the couch and stretch. At least I'm not as wobbly as I felt a mere few hours ago. "We could've at least stopped once to give you a break."

Gabe shakes his head. "Not taking the risk. We didn't stop,

but we also didn't *get* stopped. I have no problem with sore muscles if it means I can feel better with every mile we put between them and us."

I nod. Same here. "*Better* as in more sure that at least for now we're good, as long as we're one step ahead."

"Exactly." Judging by the sounds coming from the front, Gabe is getting up and coming over to us in the back. It's still dark, although the sun should be out in a few more minutes. We haven't turned the lights on at all, and we won't for now, at least not until we've seen who else is on this campsite.

"Wanna stretch your legs?" Gabriel opens the door.

I rub my eyes. "I'd love—"

"Wanna stretch your legs, *Cris*?" Gabe holds the door wider.

Oh. I see. Our truce only holds up so long, apparently.

Cris' head whips up. "Do I? Of course." He's over at the door in no time. A breeze of fresh air comes in, smelling of lake, trees, and dirt. The boys jump down the three steps, and I follow stat—barely avoiding running into Cris.

"Whoa, Cris—"

Gabriel lays a hand on my shoulder and shakes his head, giving a pointed glance at Cris.

The pale moonlight illuminates enough of his face that I can see the wonder in his gaze as it darts from left to right, jumps from tree to tree, over to the lake and the hills in the distance. The apple in his throat bobs up and down. He takes a small step forward. Another one. Squats down, and touches the ground, raking his fingers through the grass. "I've always wondered what it felt like," he whispers. "So soft. And cool." He stands back up and turns around on his axis. "This is beautiful. And it's *real*."

Emotion clogs my throat and makes it difficult to breathe. Yes, we're in deep doo-doo with Advangen out for us and apparently willing to kill to keep their secret—but *this* is why it's worth it.

Cris walks over to a tree, hesitating for a moment before he touches the bark. "Rougher than the other one." A small laugh bubbles from his chest. "And it smells good." He bends closer and… well, sniffs the tree.

Somewhere out on the lake, a couple of birds make noises and fly up. Cris jerks and whips his gaze over in that direction. A strangled breath leaves his throat and, as if pulled by a magnet, he tiptoes ahead, checking every step before putting his foot down. He stops right at the shoreline. In the distance, the upcoming sun bathes the mountains in a mesmerizing reddish hue. Cris' outline is clearly visible as he looks out onto the lake. For a moment, this could be a photograph or a still picture—but then Cris' shoulders shake. He squats down, then falls back on his butt and buries his face in his hands. Drowned sobs break from his throat, each and every one piercing my heart.

I dart forward. "Cris—"

Gabe gets me by the sleeve. "Wait. Let me." He passes me by and sits down next to Cris, legs crossed. I'm waiting for him to hug him, to talk to him, but he doesn't. And yet his presence seems to calm Cris down. The sobs become less violent and less frequent, until they stop, and when they do, Gabe reaches around Cris' shoulders and squeezes him once. Then he lets go, and both of them look out onto the lake and into the rising sun in silence.

Tears prick my eyes as I watch them sitting there, at the dawn of a new day, and the first day of a new life for Cris.

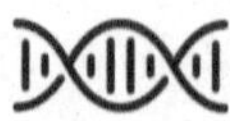

"He's gonna be here in a minute or two." Gabriel closes the app and lays the phone down. There's an advantage to having a rich daddy. Did I mention that already? Not only does Joel Hargrove have an awesome RV, he also has enough money that he won't even notice Gabe bought all three of us new iPhones, because *we ain't getting tracked,* and ours stayed at home.

Cris jumps up and down, shaking out his hands like a boxer before a fight. "Okay. Anything specific I need to do? Shake hands, I can do that. Be nice. I always am. Then—"

"Relax." I reach for his hand and hold him down. That bouncing makes me all antsy. "We'll lead you through the interview. All he needs to hear is the truth. Your story." Cris' story, our insurance.

"Okay. No biggie. Only the third new person I meet within as many days." He falls onto the couch next to me and blows out a big puff of air.

"I know it's strange, but you got us, okay?" I reach for his hand and weave my fingers in-between his. "We're going to win this. You're not going back."

Cris drops his gaze onto our entwined hands, then shoots another quick glance from under his lashes at Gabe before he withdraws his hand. "Uh, I'll take your word for it."

A car pulls up to the campground. "It's him." Gabe peeks out of the rear window. "And he's alone."

Good. One reporter feels weird enough, two… I don't know. Gabriel said he trusted this one, and I really, really hope his trust is well-placed.

A knock comes from the door, and Gabe opens it. "Duncan. Thanks for coming." He steps aside to let the reporter in.

"No, thank you for calling. Gotta say I'm curious what kind of story you have, secrecy and all." Duncan comes up the steps and into the RV. "Oh. Hello there."

Gabe points first at me, then at Cris. "Duncan, these are my friends Nya and Cris."

"Nice to meet you." I lift a hand in greeting, while Cris only nods. The two of us stay on the couch, while Gabe and Duncan take a seat at the table across from us. Well, Duncan has to squish himself behind that table, since he's a good head taller than Gabe. Bit lanky, too. He's not that old, maybe late twenties. With his blond hair in a shaggy bob he could pass for a surfer dude, only he'd look ridiculous on a board, given his height.

"Nice ride, Gabe." Duncan takes a good appreciative look around, and right he is. Joel Hargrove, being the famous sports star he is, doesn't just have any RV standing around in case the urge for recreation hit him—he has a *stylish* RV standing around, unused, for exactly that purpose. Black exterior, black interior with chrome accents. Not the usual beige and brown, but sparkling accents instead.

"Thanks. Includes a well-stocked fridge. Coke? Water? Anything?"

"A water, please." Duncan unpacks a pad, pen, and a little recorder from his messenger bag. "Do you mind if I record our conversation?"

We all exchange a glance. "No." Gabe is the one to answer as he hands Duncan his water. "Okay, so… I guess I'll just start." He clears his throat. "It's going to sound crazy, but please bear with me, okay? So, Cris here… Nya and I broke Cris out of Advangen's basement."

Duncan shakes his head. "Broke him out? Like, did the door fall shut behind him?"

Gabe shakes his head. "No. *Broke out* as in, he was born down there and has never left the facility."

That has Duncan's eyebrows shoot up to his hairline. "Okay. You're not kidding me, I assume?"

"Nope."

"Okay. Didn't expect you would, but you know, it does sound weird. Tell me more."

So, we do. We tell him the entire story, how I got suspicious and eventually snuck down there, meeting Cris for the first time. How I watched him being tasered. How we broke him out a mere ten hours ago.

Duncan watches the video on my cell, the one that still brings tears to my eyes. He watches the footage our action cams recorded of our flight with Cris away from Advangen. In none of them we captured Sherman, but in mine, my dad is clearly recognizable.

That image, it hurts.

When he's done, he turns the cams off. "You've never left that basement."

Cris lips press into a thin line. "Never. Atomic Wars. Surface uninhabitable."

"They did… *that* to you." Duncan points at his chest, and Cris lifts his shirt as a response, then pulls up the legs of his pants, exposing his shins, and lastly shoving up the sleeves of his shirt, pointing to the same round, dark scars marking the area on his shoulder as they marked all other sites.

He draws a finger over the ones on his upper arm. "They did that since I can remember."

Duncan huffs. "But why? Why would a world-renowned company like Advangen keep a teen prisoner and use you for a guinea pig and ever-present stem cell-donor?"

Cris crosses his arms in front of his chest. "I don't know."

Gabe meets my eye. We do. My cheeks heat. We know, but we haven't even had time yet to tell Cris he's… a mutant. Designer baby. Part Neanderthal, if our assumptions are correct.

Duncan takes a sip of his water. "There must be something.

I'm not that much into science, but I know that stem cells can be grown and multiplied. What's so special about you they need to do *that* to you over and over again? No offense."

"None taken, but I still don't know. It was all to monitor my health, because, *radiation*." Cris uses air quotes. He likes those.

"But—"

"Actually, we think we have the answer." Gabe reaches into the side pocket of his cargo pants and pulls out a copy of the papers I found in my dad's drawer. "Nya, do you want to…?"

I scoot forward and turn slightly, so I can have a good look at Cris and the guys at the table at the same time. "So, here's the thing. I searched my dad's desk at home, and… and I found this in a hidden compartment in his drawer." I reach for the papers Gabe is handing me. "You're welcome to look at it—both of you, obviously—but what matters is this." I flip the pages to the last one, showing the two sets of chromosomes and circled areas.

"Genes?" Cris takes the papers. "There's something in my genes?"

"Yes." I say the word as gentle as I can and take the papers back. "We think they changed your genes, Cris. They designed your genome and inserted new genes in place of old ones."

He blinks. "So?"

I sigh and turn the page to Dad's research. "And we're pretty sure they gave you special genes. If I'm not mistaken, you're the first chimera, the first cross, between a human and… and a Neanderthal. They gave you Neanderthal genes, Cris."

Cris blinks again. "What?"

I show him the papers. "It looks like they gave you some Neanderthal genes," I repeat.

"I'm not a Neanderthal. What the actual—" He lifts his hands in front of his face and looks at them, as if he could see the makeup of his genes, then raises his gaze to mine. "I'm a normal human. What makes you think that's really what they did?"

Gabe unlocks his phone and turns the screen so that Cris can see it. "Because it would make sense. Those papers make sense. And then, when I look at you…" He points at the screen.

I lean closer. Gabe has pulled up a picture of a Neanderthal. "No offense, but there's a certain resemblance," he says.

"Resemblance," Cris repeats.

"Well, take, for example, your hair—"

Cris throws his hands up. "Just because I have some red streaks in my hair, you think I'm part Neanderthal?"

"Well—"

"This is insane!" His breath comes out fast. "I mean, really? Just because of my hair? It's…" Leaning forward, he buries his face in his hands.

Gabe works a hand through his hair. "Look, you have some… phenotypic features that could go along with a Neanderthal genome. The reddish hair—sorry. The bridge of your nose is wider. Your stature."

"My nose? And what exactly about my stature? Geez." Cris jumps out of his seat and paces back and forth. "Anything else about me that automatically makes me a mutant?"

I lay a hand on his shoulder. "You're right. None of that makes you automatically a mutant, and red hair doesn't automatically mean Neanderthal. Human, right here." I give Gabe a pointed glance and jab a finger at my hair. *Give that boy a break, dude.*

For one teeny-tiny split second *something* flashes across Gabe's face, and even though I haven't spent much time with him in the recent years, I know that look.

"Gabriel Hargrove," I hiss at him. "You're not really thinking what you're thinking, are you?"

Gabe grimaces. "No. Nope. Am not."

"You better not," I grumble. Dad may not be the man he thought he was, but I am the human I know I am. *I'm* not the one locked away being experimented on.

Duncan clears his throat and taps a finger on the papers. "Cris, I'm sorry to say so, but it makes sense. Advangen altering your genome, I mean. It would fit right into their business scheme."

Cris groans and continues his pacing.

I scoot forward in my seat. "And that's why *you*'re worth so much to them, Cris. Something in your genetic makeup must be marketable. Neanderthals had a stronger immune system, so maybe that's what they need *your* stem cells for." I shoot Gabe a pointed glance. His. Not mine.

Duncan facepalms himself and lets himself fall back onto the couch. "Better immune system. I mean—and I'm just speculating here, this is not my area of expertise—could they use that to design a vaccine against something like, I don't even know, Ebola? HIV? The common cold? Or one against COVID that needs no boosters?"

"Sure." Gabe shrugs. "Anything goes. I would think though that we'd need Cris to have actual antibodies to any of those, so they could see if his immune system keeps the memory of the virus—but for that he would have to be out of the basement, amongst people, and gotten infected. And that didn't happen, so who knows what they're using his super-special stem cells for? Right now, we can only speculate."

Cris stops dead in his tracks, then works a jittery hand through his hair. "Exposure… You know, one time, maybe three or four years ago, they brought a new staff member. He looked like crap and was obviously sick. They said he needed protection from radiation, and let him stay with me for two or three days. Once he started looking terrible, like gasping for air, they took him away again. No clue what happened to him, but after that, they came more often." He points at his breastbone.

"Oh gosh." I bury my face in my hands. The list of wrongdoings by Advangen—and potentially my dad—is growing by the minute. "They exposed you on purpose, to who knows what, possibly Ebola or COVID, to see if you'd develop antibodies—"

"Which he probably has," Gabe adds. "Otherwise, he'd have been sick—"

"Which I wasn't," Cris says.

"Which he wasn't, and also, they wouldn't have needed his stem cells more frequently unless something changed. All of this story should cause an uproar, and not only in the scientific community, but everywhere! Jesus, Advangen clearly violated about a dozen ethical conduct standards!" Gabe slams a palm onto the table.

Duncan leans forward again, hands folded, thumbs twiddling. "You're right. So I'm thinking, this story could be Advangen's death blow. Right?" He looks from Gabe to me. "You both know this stuff better than me, but besides the clearly unethical conduct, isn't it forbidden to mix genes of different species?" He takes the papers and flips through them again.

"Inter-species breeding, altering the human genome on a whim? Yeah, pretty much. Keeping somebody in a basement and drawing bone marrow against their will? Pretty sure that counts as well, human rights and all." Gabriel glowers at the papers as if they were responsible for Cris' fate.

A harsh blow of air leaves Cris' throat. "Excuse me, I … I need some air." He walks to the RV's door seemingly in a trance, leaving the door ajar behind him.

For a moment silence hovers, the heavy kind, only broken by the drumming of Gabe's fingers on the table.

"That went well." He sighs. "Not. So, what's going to happen, Duncan? They kept him in the freaking basement. Ignored his rights. The boy needs our help. Your help. Alone, we can't do squat. No papers, nothing. We have to go public or else… I mean, I doubt they're gonna kill us if they can avoid it, but I wouldn't bet on it. And you're right. Exposing Cris is their death blow, and it's also the only thing that can grant him freedom. You in?" He holds out a hand to the other man.

Duncan takes it without hesitation. "You kidding me? Of course I'm in! Even if I didn't feel bad for Cris, which I do, just FYI, even then it'd be a story too good to pass on. I'll see what else I can find out through back channels, and then—"

"You'll publish it?" I lean forward.

"Yes. I would like to wait a day or two, but I fear you don't have the time. It'll be in the paper tomorrow. I promise."

The weight of the world drops off my shoulders. We're not alone. As soon as our story is out, we have protection.

Cris has protection.

Right now, the future doesn't look too bad.

CHAPTER FIFTEEN

Once Duncan backs out of the small dirt way and his car has vanished behind trees, Gabe lowers the curtain in front of the window. "One problem taken care of, about a million remaining."

I prefer the optimistic point of view. "True, but I like the one we've tackled today. Ranked pretty high on my list of priorities. But speaking of…" I point over my shoulder into the general direction of where Cris is sitting at the lake. Where he has been sitting for the last thirty minutes. I would know. Every ten seconds, I glanced out of the window. "I'm going to check on him."

A shadow falls over Gabe's face, gone so quickly I might've imagined it. "Sure. I'll upload the videos to the cloud." Because while Duncan has a copy, we need to play it safe.

I leave the RV and walk over to Cris. Gotta give it to Gabe. He picked a beautiful spot—beautiful and empty. We're at the very back of the campsite, hidden by trees, and there is literally nobody else but us. Yosemite isn't too far from here, so most people probably go there for the better social media-posts rather than enjoying nature farther up north without the option for spectacular status updates.

Cris sits on a log close to the water, playing with some little twig in his hands, taking it apart one strand at a time. The amount of shredded foliage in front of him suggests he's been at it for a while.

"Hey." I sit down next to him. "You okay? I mean, all things considered?"

"Mh." He grunts and rips another piece off the dead twig. "Yes. Kind of. It doesn't really matter, you know?"

"Wait—what doesn't matter? How you're doing?"

"No. Yes. Ugh, I don't know." He throws the twig down and rubs both hands across his eyes. "I'm out, Nya. First time in my freakin' life I'm out of that basement. I should be happy, and don't get me wrong, I am, but hearing what they did... what I am—" The next word is swallowed by a wheezy breath.

Pity hits hard. "I know, Cris. Well, rather, I don't know. It's cruel."

Cris makes a choking sound and leans forward.

Well, he's right. "Actually, it's beyond cruel, true. They—"

A strangulated gasp, like half a choke and half a cough, breaks from his throat, and he falls forward. Flat. *Boom.* No bracing his fall, no catching his weight. Just *boom*, straight into the grass.

"Cris!"

Like he had stuck a fork into a power outlet, Cris' body convulses. His legs jerk, his arms twitch and shake. Every breath is short and harsh, sucked in through clenched jaws and grinding teeth. His eyes stare straight up into the sky, not seeing a thing.

Holy cow—

"Gabe!" I don't yell it, I scream it at the top of my lungs. "Gabe! Come! Gabe!" I fall down on my knees next to Cris. What do I do? How can I help him? Is he breathing? He's grunting, so he *is* breathing. Right? Right? "Cris! *Cris!* I'm here. It's all going to be fine, it's all going to be fine—"

"Fuck!" That's Gabe, out of breath, kneeling down next to me. "Seizure. How long?"

"Thirty seconds." I try to hold on to Cris' shaking arms, but no use. He's way too strong. He shakes me instead of me stabilizing him.

"Don't hold him, it can hurt him!" Gabe shoves my hands away. "Let him ride it out, and if it takes too long, we'll have to call 911." His eyes are wide as he stares down at Cris convulsing in front of us. Both our breathing is as harsh as Cris'. Never in my life have I seen anything more scary. A chill snakes around my inside and burrows itself deep into my heart, because this... this doesn't look good.

"Cris, hey." I brush over his hair that shines with the purest red in-between those brown locks. "It's gonna be fine. It's gonna be fine. You hear me? It's gonna be over soon."

Gabe uses his foot to kick bigger rocks and branches away from Cris. "One minute."

"Shh, Cris, it's gonna be okay, it's gonna be okay..." It's a mantra of helplessness, but all I can do. I give his hair one more brush as his neck overextends and his body writhes in the dirt—and then, like somebody turned down the volume, the shaking dies down.

His arms stop twitching.

His legs.

His body relaxes, all tension leaving, like air from a popped balloon.

And yet he doesn't wake up.

Gabe feels Cris' pulse, eyes as wide as mine. He lets go of a big puff of air. "Steady. It's probably going to be awhile until he's back to normal."

But at least he isn't seizing anymore. I scoot forward on my knees, never minding the dirt. With shaking hands, I cradle his head in my lap and swipe those sweaty strands of red-brown hair out of his face. "Shh. Relax. You're fine. It's all over. It's all over." I caress his head, murmuring the same soft words again and again and again, because there's nothing else to do as he transitions out of his seizure and into a deep sleep.

Gabe watches me, his chest rising and falling out of rhythm, an odd twist to his lips.

Then he swallows hard. "I'll be in the RV. Holler if you need me, but seems like you're doing pretty well on your own." He gets up and all but stomps back to the RV.

Cris twitches once, and the fear of another seizure shoots through me, but no. Just a simple twitch, nothing else. I keep brushing over his hair. *Brush, brush, talk, talk. Brush, brush, talk, talk.*

Once in a while, I see the curtains in the RV move out of the corner of my eye, but I don't care.

I don't care what Gabe thinks.

I don't care.

All that counts is Cris, so I ignore Gabe checking on us, and keep talking to Cris, senseless stories, but at least I'm doing something.

After what feels like an eternity but probably wasn't much over ten or fifteen minutes, Cris wakes up. First, he grimaces, then blinks, then opens his eyes.

"Hey." I smile down at him. "Quite the scene you made here."

He blinks again, long lashes fanning his cheeks. "What—"

"Seizure, I guess." Scary as hell.

Cris groans. "Sh't. Shorry." His speech is slurred, like he just woke up, which, technically, he did.

"No worries, at least it's over."

"Uh-huh." He grunts and works himself up to sitting. I scramble out from under him. Ow. My legs have fallen asleep. Little by little, I help Cris up and over to the RV. Gabriel opens the door from the inside and supports him from under his arms on his way in.

"Dude. That was scary. What was that?" He avoids my eyes as he helps Cris to the couch.

"Dunno." This word at least comes out clearer. "Been happening a lot lately."

"A lot?" I ask at the same time Gabe asks, "Lately?"

"Yeah." Cris falls back onto the couch and groans. "Makes me feel like crap. Started with headaches and stuff, now this. *They* say it's from the radiation, which obviously only means either they don't know, or they don't care, but I'm not getting any meds for it, if that's your next question, so it can't be that bad."

"Would've been my next question, and yay, no meds." I sit down on the floor in front of him. No meds are good, it means it's not serious. Right? But why-oh-why then does the pit of my stomach feel heavy, as if it's filled with lead? Because no meds also could mean they just don't care enough to treat him?

Gabe opens the fridge, rummages around and comes up with a bottle of water. "Do you know what started it?"

"Nah. Just happened one day." Cris rubs a palm over his forehead. "I'm having them more often lately, so that sucks."

"No kidding. But did you ever get checked out—?"

"Steve says I'm fine."

Steve—my dad. He looked at Cris. That's… good, right? I give him a reassuring smile. "Well, he's a worrywart and freaks out with every little headache or whatnot I have, so I assume—and hope— that means there isn't a reason to be concerned, if he isn't." I neglect the glaring issue that there might be a world of a difference between Dad's intentions for me versus Cris, like how he freaked out when I lied I had a headache, but I'm ignoring that. I'm thinking positive, dammit! "Not wanting to excuse anything he did to you, but he's good at medical stuff, considering he isn't an MD. He's been taking care of me my whole life." The only reason we went to the pediatrician was to get the routine vaccines. The rest Dad took care of—still is, he's checking my blood every six months, same routine as a doctor would.

Gabe, of course, is equally skeptical. He blows a raspberry. "Please excuse me if I reserve judgement about that, given recent developments about your father."

Grr. "Okay, yes, I see your point, but those are two different things—"

"All I'm saying is that right now, I trust nothing your dad says, period."

If my eyes could shoot arrows at him, he'd be turned into a kebob right about now. "Neither do I, but for now we know Cris is fine, and that's all we need." *Hint-hint*, let it rest, Gabe!

He opens his mouth, then shuts it again. One-Mississippi, two-Mississippi— "Yeah. Of course." He says it like he means it but sticks out his tongue at me when Cris doesn't look. So mature.

I roll my eyes and reach up to lay a hand on Cris' clammy forehead. "No fever."

He moves his head from under my touch. "Never had a fever in my life. Besides this, I'm healthy."

Gabriel hands him the bottle of water. "Which makes sense, because you've never been exposed—"

"Besides when they threw those sick people into the basement with him," I say, because that's unethical on so many levels. I guess we'll add it to the list.

"—to *regular* everyday viruses, I was going to say, before I was so rudely interrupted." Gabe rolls his eyes, then bows theatrically. "Either way, welcome to the outside. I expect your first cold to hit you hard in T minus two days or something." He winks, but I know him too well. I see the worry-crinkles around his eyes. I know the tone in his voice. It matches my own.

"Mh." Cris sits up and cracks the bottle open. "Keep your germs to yourself, thank you very much. And even if you don't, I'm a mutant with a supercharged immune system. Your germs will die." He takes a sip of water and closes his eyes. "If you don't mind, I'm going to take a quick nap." And with that, he curls up on the couch. His breathing turns regular, and I could bet not even ten seconds later, he's fast asleep.

Gabriel scratches his neck. "I don't like it." Our eyes connect and he shakes his head. "I don't like it a single bit."

The lead in my stomach gains another pound. "Do you think... do you think something's wrong with him?" I whisper. Obviously something is, but there's wrong, and there's wrong-wrong.

Gabe lowers himself into the chair next to the table, never taking his eyes off Cris. "Don't know. I'd say Advangen has an excellent incentive to keep him healthy, since they're profiting from him, but..." He rakes a hand through his hair. "But it doesn't feel right."

I look at Cris, face relaxed, dark circles under his eyes, a bit of stubble showing on his cheeks. "No," I whisper. "It doesn't feel right at all."

The next morning, an annoying, repetitive pinging sound wakes me.

Ping. PingPing. Ping.

Ugh. Not my alarm sound.

PingPing. Ping. Ping.

I pull my pillow from under my head and bury my face in it.

PingPingPingPing.

Aww, man. I drop the pillow. "Gabe. That's you."

Only indistinguishable grunting comes from the bed across from me. Grr. Screw you. I swing my legs out of bed, never minding the cool floors. I'm good with the cold. While tiptoeing over to the table where all our cells are charging, my gaze drifts over the boys.

Gabe and Cris are sharing the double bed across from mine, and they're both still far, far away in la-la-land. Gabe's on his back, one arm slung across his face, shielding his eyes, a naked, well-defined chest peeking through from under the covers. He's squished all the way against the wall of the RV, because Cris… Cris is using quite a bit more than quote-unquote *his* half. Apparently, he's a tummy-sleeper, and one who sprawls out. A small chuckle bubbles up. Well, he never had to share his bed with anybody, while Gabe—

Yeah. Know what? I don't want to think about Gabe and his flavor of the day sharing a bed.

Whatever.

I pick up Gabe's phone and five messages pop up on the screen: all from Duncan. "Whoa. Gabe! Wake up, Duncan is texting you!" That's good news, right? Is the story live?

The only response I'm getting is more grunting.

Ugh. Guys. "Gabe, seriously!" I strut over and yank his blanket away. "Wake up and unlock this thing so we know what's going on, dammit!"

A high-pitched squeak leaves his throat, followed by a sit-up faster than a trap would snap shut and a tug on his blanket to cover himself. "Nya! Some privacy, please?" He glowers at me, but hey, at least he's awake.

"Privacy went out the window when we decided to share an RV. One of you snores."

"Not me," Cris mumbles without opening his eyes. "Nobody ever told me."

"Harr, harr." Gabe shoves him in the shoulder in good humor, then finally—finally—turns his attention toward me. "So, what's going on this early in the morning?"

I throw the phone onto the bed next to him. "Duncan is. Check it."

He rolls his eyes. "Yes, ma'am." One click later, his eyes pop wide. "Holy—"

"Holy what?" I clamber onto the bed, dropping into a cross-legged sitting position in-between the guys' legs. This better be a good holy, like *holy cow*, not a bad one, like *holy shit*.

Cris sits up and draws his legs in, leaning over to Gabriel to see. "That's a lot of texts."

"Yeah." Gabe's voice is nothing more than a whisper. "And there's a reason for it." He looks up from the screen and swallows. "The story's been out for a few hours online. It's out in print as well, but it's so early, not much reaction is to be expected yet. But anyway, Duncan has over one thousand emails, comments, or messages regarding us. And that's only within a few hours."

"Holy cow." One thousand comments! "What do they say?"

Gabe scans over the texts. "Most are outraged at what Advangen did, it appears. Some are calling us crazy for releasing an—" His mouth snaps shut.

I cock my head. "A what?"

His lips thin. "For releasing an *abomination* from a secured facility."

Cris flinches. "Ow. That hurt."

"People are idiots, Cris."

"So I've noticed. TV got that one right."

Gabe mumbles to himself as his thumbs fly over the screen, typing. "Any response from Advangen? Sent."

Not even two seconds later, the response pops up: *Nope.*

I smooth out my PJs. "Guess the ball is in their corner now."

And we can only hope they want to play.

CHAPTER SIXTEEN

For the next few hours, we keep rechecking the comment section under Duncan's article, waiting for each and every update like addicts for their next fix. Most people are with us, which is great, but there are some that scare me, the ones that call Cris a *thing* or *an abomination, something unnatural, a freak.*

Those comments are the ones that make me nauseous and Gabe turn off the phone, at least until the urge to recheck becomes too strong.

Duncan also texts us updates.

Police have contacted me, investigating.

DA collecting evidence for legal actions against Advangen.

Highest number of comments in last thirteen months.

International press is picking up the story, we're going global!

Overall, it's great and what we wanted, but… I drum my fingers onto my thigh. "I don't trust that silence."

"Whose?" Gabe throws a little pebble out into the lake. We've been sitting out here in the shade of the trees for the last two or three hours. Feels like a mini-vaycay, if it wasn't for the tense waiting, or the nervous twitching every time we thought we heard a car or people. Thank goodness it's empty here. I'd have otherwise already had a nervous breakdown.

"Advangen's." I mimic him and throw a twig past his pebble. "I mean, the accusations are out there, and they're big, like, stock market-dropping big. Right now, Mr. Sherman must be panicking."

"I'm sure they're working on an appropriate response." Gabe's voice holds some snide in it. "Lawyers, PR, their marketing—" His phone buzzes.

"Duncan?" I lean closer to see, and even Cris, who's been lying stretched out in the grass, asleep as I thought, lifts his head.

Gabe unlocks the phone. "Yup. Duncan. He—" His eyes pop wide. "Crap," he groans. "Crap, crap, crap."

"What?" Cris and I are next to him in the blink of an eye.

Gabe presses his lips into a hard line. "Careful what you wish for. Advangen has made their move."

"And?" I reach for his cell, but he turns it away.

"And I don't know if you want to read it. Especially you, dude." He gives Cris a pointed glance.

"Me? Why?" Cris shakes his head. "I don't care what they say. They've ruined my life already. What else can they do?"

"Own you," Gabe says and turns the phone around for me.

One look at the screen, and I all but rip the phone from Gabe's hand. "What the what? They can't mean that, they—" My eyes fly over the text, absorbing every word as fast as I can.

And it makes me nauseous.

"Holy crap." I swallow the bile rising in my throat. "Cris, they…"

"They *what*? Will you please talk to me? Because this is really not helping right now." His eyes are wide as saucers, his face even paler than usual.

How do I say it? How can I explain something of this

magnitude? *This* is a game changer. The bile rises again, bringing a bitter taste to my mouth. "They didn't go through Duncan or the press to respond. They went straight to their lawyer."

"To be expected, though. That part. Damage control." Gabe holds up a finger.

"Yes, that part was to be expected." But I didn't expect *this*. I swallow hard. "Cris, Advangen says… they… dang it, here, see for yourself." I turn the phone so he can see the screen.

No Human Rights for the Non-Human Boy. Human-Neanderthal Hybrid Claimed Property of Advangen. Charges Against Stealing Teenagers Filed.

They regard Cris as their property. Their *property*!

We thought we were in deep before. We didn't have a clue.

The apple in Cris' throat bobs up and down. "Shit. No. That's not possible. I'm human. I'm me, I'm…" He shakes his head and rakes a hand through his hair. "Can… can they do that? Legally? I'm a *person*, I'm *human*, who cares about a few genes—"

"They can." Gabe takes his phone back, thumb scrolling down the article. "According to their argumentation, only full humans are given human rights—no other animals on this planet have anything close to it." He cringes with those words.

"I'm not an animal—"

"Duh. We know. But they say, since your genome is not entirely human, human rights don't apply to you. They didn't break the law by keeping you locked up, or else *'every laboratory working with lab animals would need to be sued as well'*." He lowers the phone. "Bastards."

I close my eyes. How dare they. How dare they deny Cris his basic rights—he has more humanity than any of those Advangen-idiots, my dad included, it seems! How. Dare. They.

I huff. "The audacity to call freeing you *stealing*. Not kidnapping, not abduction, not *freeing you*. Nope. *Stealing*. Like we took something that belonged to them."

"And that's how they're going to play it in court, I can tell you." Gabe clicks his phone off. "Legally, I'm pretty sure they have a case this way. They'll look at the definition of humanity, then at Cris' genome, and *boom*, we've lost. Shortest trial ever."

I stare at him, wide-eyed. "You can't think that's how it'll go."

A muscle in his jaw ticks. "Not *thinking*. I *know* it will go that way. The law isn't prepared to deal with something like this, and until it is, Cris will be back with Advangen. Now, granted, at some point, the law might change, depending on the ruckus we make to support him, but I doubt we'd walk out of that courtroom a winner if we went there right now. Seriously doubt it."

Silence falls after his last words, and it weighs heavily. Once in a while, a duck quacks, or a bird tweets, or leaves rustle, but I doubt either of us feels any of the peace radiating from this beautiful scenery. Inside my heart, it feels like I've stepped into a war zone. Out of the corner of my eye, I see Cris wipe at his eyes, and only because of Gabe's intervention yesterday do I not acknowledge it and wrap an arm around him. I want to, though. I hurt for him, and I can't imagine how bad it must be being in his shoes. How terrifying it must be to feel absolutely helpless, to have no ground to stand on—and all after uncovering a lie so big, it's already unfathomable.

Advangen and my dad screwed Cris over. Majorly.

I ball my hands into fists. Thank whomever Dad isn't here right now. Those moments when I thought I'd grown up and had more self-control? Surprise, they're gone, together with said self-control. Hitting something—or rather, somebody, namely my dad—would feel really, really, *really* good right about now.

Gabe's phone alerts and we all twitch. Guess our nerves aren't the strongest right now. "Check it," I whisper, and pretend I'm not seeing him roll his eyes at my comment. Usually, I'd get a snarky one-liner back in response, and that I'm not shows how Duncan's news affected him.

Gabe reads over the text and sighs. "Duncan says he has lawyered up, and the Times have instructed the lawyer to cover us as well. He still recommends staying hidden for now until a couple of things are clarified."

A couple of things? "Such as?"

"He doesn't say."

Cris draws in his legs, wraps his arms around them and lowers his forehead onto his knees. "So that's what my life is going to be? Hide, or be locked up?"

Determination springs to life in my heart and in my soul. "No. No way, Cris. This is a temporary setback. Nothing more. Duncan has a lawyer for us, and we have us."

Gabe gives me a curious glance. "What's that supposed to mean?"

I shake out my fingers and curl them back into fists. Heck no, I'm not just going to sit this out and wait for others to decide Cris' fate—and ours as well. Let's be honest, them declaring Cris is the property of Advangen equals us being guilty for theft. No idea what punishment comes with that sentence, but I doubt I'm going to like it. But Gabe's and my involvement and potential punishment are secondary to what may happen to Cris if Advangen gets what they want, and that means they simply cannot get what-slash-whom they want.

Pushing my chin up and forward, I look at Gabe. "Easy. We have two moderately smart scientists here." I point to him and myself. "And we have the subject here." I point at Cris. "Between the three of us, we have enough brainpower and proof to come up with something in Cris' defense. Let's look at human rights, let's look at his genome. Figure out how much is mutated and Neanderthal, and compare to the natural rate of mutation in the human genome. Is the percentages of genes mutated more than in a genetic disease? Or in any genetic aberration? While we wait, we can do things. We will find a solution. We will."

Gabe whistles through his teeth. "That's actually only half bad, Nya." Respect swings in his voice, which is why I also hold back my automatic snarky response, born from years of conditioning to take everything and anything he says as an invitation for verbal sparring.

"Is it?" Cris asks. "No offense, but what, you're saying everybody is a mutant?"

Gabe grins. "Kind of, only not the cool kind like you. The human genome isn't perfect, and yes, mutations are in every single one of us. Often, we don't know about them and they're not clinically significant, meaning they don't show. And sometimes those mutations become evolution and they stick. Like—" He smacks his lips, thinking. "Like elephants in Africa now being born without tusks in response to hunters killing the ones with tusks for their ivory."

"Jesus," Cris says. "I liked the world better when I didn't know that fact. That's sad."

"And survival of the fittest," Gabe adds. "But my point is, Nya is right and we might have a defense strategy. We just need a lab, then we could start with our own genome and look for the rate of mutations for us, as a comparison to yours."

"Like building trust with the public. *Hey, look at us Joe and Jane Shmoe here. Even we got mutations,* and then normalize it." I rub my palms together, then wrap an arm around Cris' shoulders. "This could *so* work. We'll get access to a lab somehow and some when. Maybe with Duncan's help, but the point is, there's always hope. We won't let you down." I pull him closer, willing him to understand we got his back.

And while I wasn't lying and I do feel that spark of hope, I can't help the creeping sensation that we haven't even touched the surface of the trouble we're in.

I can't say the mood was splendid throughout the rest of the day, not that anybody would expect that, but still. At one point, Gabe and I get to making dinner, although that's actually overstating it. We open a couple of canned ravioli and nuke them in the microwave. Boom, done. Neither of us has eaten much today, and yet we're merely picking at our food. Well. Gabe and I are. Cris' appetite doesn't seem to be affected.

"You guys are the epitome of entertaining tonight," Cris says, bringing his spoon with another heaping load of food to his mouth.

"Sorry," I say and drop my spoon, then rub my eyes. "It's just… I dunno. Everything?"

"Apt description." Gabe leans back in his chair. "Truth be told, I don't know which of the events over the last days freaks me out the most. Cris, just FYI, it's not normal for our society to hold somebody against their will."

Rolling his eyes, Cris answers through his mouthful of ravioli. "Duh. I might be new to freedom, but I figured as much. And maybe that was why they told me the lies, so I'd comply and stay put."

"Would make sense. And all that is of course a biggie I have a hard time getting over. Under our very eyes. In freaking America, not some third-world country, and no offense to any of those. Then, what they did to you, I mean…" Gabe shakes his head, lifting and dropping his hands. "Playing God? That's just not okay."

"Which part? Where Steve kept me locked up? Or where they dictated my every move?" Cris asks.

I cringe when he mentions my dad, but Gabe ignores it. "Well, yeah, that too, but mainly that they used you to their own benefit. That's already despicable, but I can't get over the fact that they did genetic experiments of this magnitude. The implications are mind-boggling, seriously. They opened Pandora's Box, and honestly, I'm sure not we'll be able to close it."

Cris freezes, spoon hovering halfway to his mouth. "And that means…?"

I sigh. I get what Gabe is going for. Can't say it hadn't crossed my mind. "It means that we've crossed a line. We've altered what Mother Nature gave us, and now, what's next? Where do we start? Where do we stop with genetic editing? What do we change? Just illnesses and weaknesses? Somebody's near sightedness? What about their eye color? Intelligence? Athletic abilities? Oh, of course somebody is going to come up with a super soldier. I mean, you've all watched Star Trek, right? Eugenic wars, super strong mutated humans?"

"Khaaaaan!" Cris whisper-yells, drawing a chuckle, the first in a while, from Gabe and me.

"Happy to see at least your TV education was on point, mate." Gave gives Cris the Vulcan salute, making a V between the middle- and ring fingers of his right hand. "Nya is right, though. Humans aren't ready for this kind of responsibility. Instead of using it for medical purposes, we'll be designing babies in no time like we order cars." He huffs. "Not too long ago, some scientist in China used CRISPR to modify embryos and make them resistant against HIV. It caused an outcry in the medical and scientific community. Didn't take the American Society of Human Genetics and other global organizations long to recommend against genome editing that leads to a viable fetus being carried to term until those techniques were studied and debated further. Boy, did we feel like the future had arrived. But boy, were we late to the game." His gaze drifts over Cris. "You were already in your teens at that point and nobody knew you even existed."

"And I bet Advangen would've liked to keep it that way." How inconvenient of us to spill their secret. "We—"

Gabe's phone beeps again. Fair to say we all twitch at the same time.

Cris groans. "I don't want to hear it."

"Neither do I, but I don't think we have much of a choice when Duncan texts at 9:00 P.M." Gabe swallows and wipes his hands on his thighs before reaching for his phone.

I pat Cris' shoulder. "I'm sure it's good news. Duncan's on it, and so is their lawyer. Once we text him what we came up with, he's—"

"Holy sh—" Gabe jumps up from his seat, tipping over his glass of water.

"What?" I'm up just the same, heart racing. Gabe's eyes are wide, his mouth open as he's staring on the screen, then looking at me, at Cris, blinking… "What, Gabe? You're scaring me. *What?*"

He shakes his head and darts for the driver cabin up front. "Seat belts, now! We've gotta go!"

"Wha—"

"Freakin' seatbelts, Nya! Now!" He jumps into the driver's seat and rips his seatbelt over his shoulder, missing the buckle like three times before he gets it to click in place.

Whatever it is, it's bad.

I dash forward into the passenger seat, hitting my shoulder on the door frame and my ankle on the seat on the way there. "What. Is. It?"

Gabe has turned the engine on and backs out of our parking space, and not too gently so. When he breaks hard, a drowned-out *oomph* comes from the back, together with the sound of a body falling against something.

"*Sit*, Cris! Seriously!" Gabe yells over his shoulder, spinning the wheel like crazy and maneuvering through the narrow dirt path. As soon as the first straight bit is ahead of him, he throws his unlocked phone over. "Here."

I catch and read the text.

Gt out NoW! Advangen knows where u r.
Don't know how. mUST leave NOW!

I read it again.

And again.

And—

The phone sinks down into my lap, my hands shaking. "Gabe, that—"

"That's yet another game changer?" He breaks hard and turns onto the main road, accelerating with all this thing's got, because he's right. This is a freakin' game changer, and we need to get out of here!

"Okay, guys, what the heck is going on?" Cris yells from the back. "Some information, please?"

Gabe and I exchange a quick glance under the passing lights illuminating the campground before his focus is back on the road. Guess I'll be the bearer of bad news. "Advangen knows where we are. They're coming for us."

Even through the noise of the engine, I hear his shocked intake of air. "Crap."

That says it all.

"Why didn't he call?" It's so easy to overhear a text. Calling would've been safer.

"There are tons of typos—so I assume he was in a hurry? Maybe he was typing blindly? Couldn't talk? Who knows? Important part is, we got the message and we're putting distance between us and them."

I turn toward him. "Where are we going?"

"I don't know. Away from here, like I said, put distance between us and that park, and then—"

"Gabe." I point to the front. Not that he could see that in the dark. "Gabe. Traffic." There, in the far distance, not just one set of lights travels toward us, but several. "What if that's—"

"Them?"

"Yeah."

"Say no more." He fumbles for the light switch and—*click!*— we're driving in the dark. Gabe slows us down, which I appreciate, because while I don't want to be captured by Advangen, I also don't want to be smeared against a tree.

Funny how the darkness makes everything else louder. I could swear I hear Cris panting in the back, could hear Gabe's heart hammer in his chest, could hear the sweat tickle down my neck. "What's our next mov—ugh!" I get thrown into the seatbelt as Gabe floors the brake.

He punches in the reverse gear, backs us up and turns us right, off the main road and into a tiny narrow small dirt path that barely fits our RV. Twigs and branches screech along the hull on either side, probably leaving scratch marks, but who cares.

Once we've reached a bend that hides us from the road, Gabe stops and turns off the engine.

"I can't turn off the lights completely otherwise," he whispers, each breath coming in with a bit of a wheeze. "Rear window, let's go." To check on the incoming cars. To check if they saw us, or if they're passing us by.

I hear him un-click his seat belt and move to the back. With one quick push, I unbuckle myself and feel my way through the darkness after him, Cris joining the club on our way there.

Like three schoolchildren peeking out of the bathroom window into freedom, we look out the rear window and to the right.

"Any time now…" Gabe taps the window. "Any time…"

Swoosh!

One car.

Swoosh.

A second.

Swoosh.

Swoosh.

Swoosh.

Swoosh.

"Six cars in a row," he whispers. "All looking like fat SUVs of the same type. Can't tell me that's regular traffic. Nothing for miles, and then six cars, same model? That's them until proven otherwise."

Hard to argue against. "How'd they find us? Cris, any other trackers you know about—"

"No." Cris turns away from the window and lets himself fall into the couch we're kneeling on. "Nothing else. At least nothing I know about. And wouldn't they have been faster, if they knew all along where I was?"

"True, but—"

Gabe slides onto the couch. "I think we need to lose the RV."

"Why lose the RV? It's our only way to get away from them." Cris doesn't sound exactly happy, and I second his opinion.

"Gabe, it's *your* RV. No way they can track it. We're off any big roads with camera surveillance, and even if they found out we took it—"

"At this point, I'm pretty sure they do, Nya. I'm really thinking that's how they found us. Satellite search. This thing is huge, custom, and easy to see from space, no matter the surrounding trees. We have new cell phones, so no way they found out through those, no implanted trackers we know of, at least—plus, Cris is right with the timeline—so all that's left is the RV."

Like the guys, I slide down onto the couch right in-between them, more feeling my way down than seeing anything in this pitch-black dark. "Crap. When you say it like that… I hate to say it, but you might be right."

Even though I can't see Gabe's smile, I hear it. "Words I never thought I'd hear from you. Hallelujah." He elbows me in the side, but gently. More a light bump than anything else.

"Oh, shut up," I mumble and aim a slap for his thigh—a *gentle* slap, as well.

Gabe chuckles and catches my hand before I can pull it back. He knows me too well. "Always so violent, Nya. So, people, here's the plan: we ditch the RV, as sad as it makes me, and we continue on as mere pedestrians. We have a few hours until the sun comes up and they can search for the RV, so let's pack and make the best out of those few hours." He keeps on holding my hand, like he had forgotten it was there. He must have, because he's stroking over the back of my hand with his fingertip, and no way Gabriel would do that if he wasn't completely distracted and his mind somewhere else. And pathetic as it is, that brief touch shoots right into my core, like via superconductor. Super *pathetic* response, by the way, Nya—because he isn't even doing it on purpose.

Still, I'm not withdrawing my hand. Not scooting away. Not telling him off or calling him out.

That's... my maturity. Look at that. Maturity.

Gabe continues his motion across the back of my hand. "I'll start packing food. The two of you pack the backpacks with the sleeping bags and whatever else we need. We'll have to hike for a few miles, then see if we can get a car or some other means of transportation or hide somewhere close by. They might not expect us to do that, but to do what we initially wanted, to put distance between us and them." He gives my hand a squeeze before he lets go and gets up, leaving my hand and my side strangely cold. My brain really must be malfunctioning or something.

Three seconds later, the fridge opens, illuminating Gabe in front of it and half of the RV's interior. He looks back at Cris and me, still frozen on the RV's rear couch. "Hop, hop, party people, speed it up! I don't want to be here in case they turn around and start looking for us." He sticks his nose deeper into the fridge. "Oh, and I hope y'all like jerky and protein pouches."

CHAPTER SEVENTEEN

Six hours later, we're not a bunch of happy campers. Fair to say we all have bruises, scrapes, and scratches from running into trees and stumbling into things, and none of us are happy about the time, temperature, our situation, our outlook, or Advangen going all gung-ho on us.

"When exactly did my summer internship turn into an action movie?" Gabe asks as he scrambles up from the ground and wipes off his butt. Little hills and dips in the terrain are tricky in the dark, it turns out.

"Probably when my summer turned into *Free Willy*," Cris gives back and helps him up.

Bits and pieces are visible thanks to the moonlight, but more often than not, we get blindsided between all those dark, tall trees, bushes, and whatnot. Well, Gabe is. Cris and I are doing better, but I'm not about to point that out. All it's going to do is put him in a bad mood. He doesn't like it when I criticize him, and, well, considering it's all I've been doing for the last few years, maybe he has a point.

Plus, the last thing I need is to open the door for more of Gabe's wild theories, because I vividly remember the look on his face when we talked about how obvious or not obvious Cris'

Neanderthal-genes were. Buzzwords red hair and freckles. Now I can see better than him at night? I must be Neanderthal.

So, I roll my eyes because it makes me feel better even if Gabe can't see it, and say nothing. Oh, and enjoy him walking into the obstacles Mother Nature provides so plentiful.

Annoyingly though, while Gabe might have a lack of night-time vision to deal with, I got an uncooperative body to handle. It's killing me tonight. My head hurts like crazy, and my body is sore from the heavy backpack. Maybe I should've practiced with the cheerleaders after all.

I sigh as I bend over and support my weight on my knees. "How much longer?" Usually I'm better than this, more stamina, but today is not my day. Blame it on emotional distress.

"Tough to say." Gabe opens the compass and angles it so that the bit of moonlight shining through the tops of the trees illuminates the dial. "The direction's good, in broad daylight and with a straightforward path to walk on. We should've been there already, but obviously we're not."

Cris takes a peek at the compass. "But do we really want to go to those caves? They're going to find the RV, eventually. Don't you think they're going to check shelter within a certain walking distance? And you said it's moderately touristy, so others might be there. I say we stay here for now and get some shuteye." He plops his butt down onto a mossy area, sitting criss-cross-applesauce.

"I like the way you think." I drop to the ground as well, swiping some twigs and forest debris off the soft surface. "This works. Gabe?"

Gabe groans. "It's freezing here. The caves will at least offer some protection."

Gotta side with Cris. "From the cold. Not from discovery. We're safer in the middle of nowhere." I.e., here. I pat the ground next to me. "Come on, Gabe. It's nice and soft. We have the inflatable yoga-mattress-things, sleeping bags, and we're dead tired. It'll be fine. We need to rest and think about our next steps with a clear head, which means staying here. It's like three in the morning. We need sleep."

He groans again, but it's the kind of groan that announces defeat. "All right. Whatever. Yes, you have a point. But it's so cold, dang it."

"I don't mind," Cris says.

"Me neither," I add and stick out my tongue at Gabe. Playfully, of course.

He lets his head hang. "Weirdos," he whispers. Also in a loving way, of course.

Over the next ten minutes, we set up our campsite and settle into our sleep sacks. Coincidence helped us tremendously for once, because this is as good as it gets, I'd say: soft moss over an area large enough to accommodate one short me, one medium Cris, and one tall Gabe. Nicely protected from all sides, including overhang from the trees above us. Not too windy. Me likey.

I cuddle deeper into my sleep sack, and within a minute or two, Cris' breathing on my left becomes regular. Asleep in no time.

Me, on the other hand… I want to sleep, I really do. My body demands I shut my eyes and let it rest, but my brain is fresh out of compliance. As if Advangen coming after us had ripped open that carefully locked drawer where I stored all the traumatizing thoughts of the last days, I can't shut out the image of Dad anymore. Or rather, of Dad next to Mr. Sherman firing at us as we sped past him with Cris in the back of our borrowed car. I can't get past that, even though we have more pressing problems. Call it a breach of trust when your father's people shoot at you.

I suck in a sharp breath.

"What?" Gabe's sleep sack rustles as he sits up, hyperalert. "What's going on? Everything okay? Nya?"

I squeeze my eyelids shut against the sudden rush of emotions. "Yeah." I force the word out through clenched teeth. "Yeah. Sorry, I... I just... had a moment."

"Oh." Gabe lays back down, but rolls on his side, facing me. "What kind of moment?" His voice has lost the edge of instant-alertness, but he doesn't sound sleepy at all.

I chew on my lower lip. "Just... You know how Dad never supported me going into anything science related? I'm thinking he was trying to avoid exactly what happened, me finding out about Cris."

Gabe whistles softly. "Actually, you might be onto something there. I always thought it was so odd for him to be so excited whenever I talked to him about anything science, but as soon as you even said Bunsen burner, he threw a knitting class at you or something."

A small chuckle breaks free. "That actually happened." A year ago. I was thrilled, obvs.

"I know."

I lift my head. "How do you know that? That was when—"

"When we weren't talking, yup. Doesn't mean I wasn't listening. I... I kept my ear close to the ground." He clears his throat and pulls the sleep sack tighter around him, while I... I stare at him through the darkness.

For Gabe to have heard about the knitting class, he must've either spoken to Dad or talked to the few people I hang with at school. Either way, neither is something I imagined him doing. Not when he purposefully looked the other direction whenever we walked past each other in school. Not when he clearly couldn't be bothered with me. Not when we weren't *we* anymore, because we were too busy out-snarling each other.

And yet… And yet he listened and kept tabs on me. Not sure what to do with that information, really, but I'm not about to ask. There's definitely an elephant in the room—or rather, the forest right now—but asking would mean acknowledging it. Not going to happen. Our truce might not survive if we did.

Gabe sneaks his hands out of his sleep sack and blows on them. "If your dad tried to keep you away to avoid you finding out about Cris, his behavior would make a bit more sense. That being said, Advangen has how many employees? Over three hundred in that location alone, right? And he's not worried about them? They can't all know. I'm sure the circle of trust is small. Him, the guys who drew his marrow. Sherman, of course."

I consider his reasoning. "True. And who knows what Dad's been thinking, I can't say I understand that man anymore." Bitterness creeps into my voice. I thought we were a team, despite our differences. I thought I knew my dad. Obviously, I was wrong, and that thought, it stings. "But you know what also is really, really crappy?"

The noise coming from Gabe sounds like he is rubbing his arms inside his sleeping bag. "Wh-what?" He sniffles.

"If I had been more attentive, maybe I would've found out about Cris sooner. Maybe I could've spared him years of marrow aspirations. Years of torture." Torture by *my dad*, just once again for emphasis.

Gabe snaps his mouth shut, the clattering of his teeth stopping for a moment or two. "Nya… No. You can't think like that. N-none of what he did is your f-fault."

I ball my hands into fists. "Intellectually I know that, but still… I can't stop thinking it. Blaming myself is stupid, and yet I feel there should've been something I could've picked up on.

Maybe I was too wrapped up in my own little world. Maybe there were telltale signs. Maybe I missed something and—"

"Seriously, n-no. Like I s-said, Advangen has over th-three hundred employees. If that sh-shoe fits for anybody, it's them. They were in that building, they could've n-noticed something. It took you how many days to b-become suspicious? And how long to find him? They c-could've picked up on something, but if they did, they d-didn't act upon it. You d-did. If anything, pat yourself on the sh-shoulder, not feel bad because you were quote-unquote l-late." He shudders, teeth clattering once more. Actually, all I'm hearing is the friction of his shivering body in the sleep sack and— not exaggerating—the percussion concert of his clattering teeth. He sounds like he is trying to eat corn on the cob, without the corn on the cob.

"Sheesh, Gabe!" I whisper at him. "You can't possibly be *that* cold."

"Apparently, I c-can. It's b-barely above f-f-freezing."

If at all, but the sleep sacks are super cozy. I mean, mine is, and they're the same brand. "Are you getting sick? Cris and I are fine. You want my jacket?" The last thing we need is another man down, really.

"N-no. I'm f-fine." I hear him turn onto his back, and for a while he works on suppressing his shaking.

For a while, like, about five seconds.

Then, it's back to jackhammer-categories, and it flips a switch inside me, one I haven't used in a while, and one I don't want to look too closely at. I sit up and unzip my sleeping sack, and fish for the zipper on his.

Gabe squeals when the cold air enters his sleep sack. "Nya! What the—"

"Shut it, Gabe." I fumble for the bottom of his zipper and mine to connect, which is not an easy feat in the dark, then pull it up and around me.

Gabe stops shivering. "Uh, what are you doing?"

I feel my cheeks flush. Good thing it's dark. "Coupling your sleeping bag to mine."

"Coupling—"

"Gabe, you're freezing. I'm not. Coupling the sleep sacks makes them bigger. You can warm up." I'm not stupid enough to say or imply that *I'm* going to warm him up. He'd jump away faster and farther than an electrocuted squirrel. All I'm doing is offering warmth. Question is, is he willing to take the offer? Just because we talked and it was nice, doesn't mean we're at that level of companionship.

When we were young, we camped together in his backyard in the summer. His dad put up a tent for us. We started the night in it, but then took all the gear outside once it was dark and slept under the stars. I was what, ten? Best nights of my life, hands down.

These days, though, I doubt Gabe was up for anything even remotely similar. But then, I've just taken the choice from him.

And it's about warmth, nothing else.

For a moment I think he's going to make me un-zip my work, but then he scoots deeper into the bag. "Th-thanks, Nya."

Oh. That came as a surprise. "Sure thing, Gabe." I cuddle into the comfy material and take a deep breath.

Mistake.

What before was a clear serving of fresh forest air holds now the unmistakable scent of Gabriel Hargrove. A touch of spice, a touch of musk, and a whole lot of *him*. Every shiver and shake brings over a fresh assault for my olfactory nerves. Since I'm reminiscing anyway, it reminds me of the time when Gabe was my number two person, right after Dad. That scent, that special Gabe-scent, would be enough to light up my world and bring out all those endorphins.

Ah, good ol' times.

Now, of course, there's no way he affects me anymore. I'm over that. Over him.

Still, I can't deny my heart's speeding up. But that's probably because I'm exhausted.

I'm also breathing faster. But really, that's recovery from our trek.

The sensation of something coiling in my stomach—

Hunger, I'd say.

Yup. Hunger. *Period.*

"Nya?" Gabe's voice is nothing but a hoarse whisper.

"Yeah?" Look at that. Mine doesn't sound much better.

"M-may I?"

"Wha—"

Gabe scoots closer to me, pressing his front against my right side.

Oh, holy hell. This isn't happening. Parallel universe? Alternate reality?

He pauses for a second—then moves his right leg over mine and drapes his arm over me. His breath dances down my neck, tickling down my spine in a series of shivers, or maybe it's my reaction, who knows. My brain has kind of short-circuited when Gabe decided to use me as an oversized stuffed animal.

"W-why are you always so warm, and I'm n-not?"

I use my hand that's not trapped by Gabe to pull the sleep sack tighter around us. Last thing I need is him thinking I'm affected by him. Temporal lapse in sanity. That's all this is. I clear my throat. "I'm just hot."

One-Mississippi.

Two-Mississippi.

Three—

We both burst out giggling.

"Not what I meant," I whisper-laugh. "I meant, I don't mind cold, you know that." We were like that during our summer campouts already. More often than not, Gabe got my sleep sack on top of his.

Gabe still shakes from keeping his laugh quiet. His whole body rocks, which means mine rocks, too. His chest rubs over my side, his leg over mine, his arm… well, that one lies under my boobs.

Deep breath, Nya, deep breath.

I suck in another lungful of Gabe-scent. Man, I can't win this today.

Slowly, our laughter dies down until both our breathing becomes more regular and Gabe's shivering dies down, like those weird coiling sensations in my tummy.

At one point, just before I'm about to doze off completely, I think I hear him say something. I think—a slight whisper, a breath of air spoken against my skin: "You're always hot, Nya."

Commotion.

Rustling.

Grunting.

Snorting.

Wha—

My eyes fly open.

Dark.

I blink.

Stars. Trees. Oh, okay—the forest. *Camping.*

Something heavy half on top of me—Gabe.

More rustling, accompanied by a grunt sounding like a choke. Shit!

"Cris!" I jerk up to sitting, effectively pushing Gabe off my body. Only peripherally do I register we were way more tangled into each other than when we fell asleep. Way more, as in, I was totally cuddled into him, just as he was into me.

But my lack of judgement is not important right now. Cris is.

I scramble to reach for the flashlight with my right hand, the left feeling for Cris. "Cris! Cris!"

A shoulder, that's a shoulder—a twitching shoulder.

Gabe sits up. "Seizure?" He sounds a hundred percent awake, like me.

"Think so." I fumble to turn on the flashlight and shine it at Cris. As my beam of light pierces the darkness, Gabe sucks in a harsh breath.

"Oh, crap."

Oh crap, indeed. Cris looks way worse than last time, and last time was scary already. His eyes have rolled back so that only the whites are visible, his teeth clenched and bared, his body rigid, then twitching, then rigid, then twitching.

And we can't do a thing.

"Shit." Gabe scrambles up to more of a sitting position behind me. "This one's bad." He reaches over me to touch Cris, his upper body pressing into my back. "Hey. Cris. We're here. We're watching out for you, okay?" He withdraws his hand to my shoulder and squeezes it. "That's two within a day."

"And that's not good." No matter what's causing the seizures, I doubt it's good. It feels like things are gliding away from us— mainly control. Or maybe control was an illusion, but either way, right in this moment, in the middle of the forest, with Cris seizing again, it feels like we've turned into the losing party.

I brush the hair off of his sweaty forehead. "You're going to feel better soon. Not much longer, okay?" I keep caressing his hair, and my heart goes out for him. Gabe's hand never leaves my shoulder as we watch Cris seize for what feels like an eternity. It's definitely longer than the last, and when he finally calms down, he doesn't wake up. He goes from seizing straight to sleeping, and seeing him so still…

It scares me even more.

When I'm sure he's in deep sleep and totally not seizing anymore, I turn toward Gabriel. "We have to do something, Gabe."

He lets go of a frustrated grunt. "You're right with that. I just don't see much we actually *can* do, Nya. We're stuck here, in the middle of the night, in the middle of the freakin' forest with Advangen hunting us and no proper backup. It's not leaving us many options to choose from."

I click off the flashlight. For a moment, everything's dark and pitch-black, but after a few seconds, my eyes adjust to the little bit of moonlight shining through the trees. "The seizures scare me. What if something is seriously wrong with him?"

"And with *seriously* you mean wrong-er than having seizures? Because I'd already call that not a good thing."

"You really have a way with words, Gabe. So motivating. Ever so optimistic."

He huffs once. "And you're too optimistic. What are we supposed to do? We can't really walk into the nearest ER and have his head scanned." Pulling the sleep sack higher to his chest, he sighs. "Maybe… maybe we should quit running and hiding and instead get out in the open."

"What?" My body twitches like after a punch in the gut. "You can't mean that! Once we're out, the police are going to snatch us, and that's it! Following Advangen's argumentation, we *stole* Cris from them, and you can't tell me they won't give him back to his *owner*!" I can't believe he said that! All we went through, all we let Cris hope for, only to hand him back on a silver platter? Not going to happen.

"That's not what I'm saying! But hiding and running won't get Cris any of the help he needs! And…" He lays himself onto his side, propped up on one elbow, facing me. "And I think something's up with him. I think he's getting worse. He looked bad all day. Dark circles under his eyes, slow on foot… and that guy is muscular. It's not as if he was a couch potato."

I swallow hard against the tightness in my throat. "You're right," I whisper. Cris didn't look good. I thought it was because of, well, everything, but more like the psychological impact rather than something physical. Now, I'm not so sure.

Gabe pokes a finger into my ribs. "You said it again. That I'm right."

"I wouldn't get used to it if I were you." I lay down, mirroring his position and facing him. With the bit of light, all I see is a white face with two dark areas where his eyes are. "So how do we help him, then?"

"The situation has changed, and we need to adapt. And that might mean we can't hide anymore—we have to settle things enough to get Cris to a neurologist or something."

Ugh. Stupidest idea ever! "The moment we're visible to Advangen, they're going to snatch him out from right under our eyes, Gabe! It's like you handing him back. Should we wrap a bow around him maybe, too?"

Gabe grunts. "I'm not saying to hand him back, I'm saying to reevaluate our options, Nya!"

I fall onto my back and cross my arms in front of my chest. "Then we'll reevaluate them and find a suitable solution that does *not* involve handing Cris back." Not. Going. To. Happen.

"Sounds great. When you think of a way to figure out what's wrong with him without going to a doctor, let me know, because right now, I don't see what else we can do."

"Well, maybe then you need glasses." I turn away from him and face Cris, steaming on the inside. Gone is that peaceful sensation from before. Gone are those coils, or rather, they totally and completely uncoiled, poking my insides to the point of hurting. That's how mad I am.

Gabe doesn't move for a minute or two, then sighs and lays down next to me, keeping his distance.

I wish I never coupled our sleeping bags.

But as I'm learning these days, no good deed ever goes unpunished.

The next morning Cris sleeps, and sleeps, and sleeps. Twice we try to wake him up, but nothing. He's zonked out completely, but at least breathing regularly and moving in his sleep. That's… good. Right?

Gabe and I are packed already for an early start, before Advangen comes looking for us. All that's missing is Cris' sleeping bag and -pad, but it's not as if we'd pull it out from under him, pack it, and then shoulder him like a bag of potatoes and hike on.

The sun is up already in the morning when Gabe checks on him again with a gentle shake on his shoulder. "Cris? Hey, Cris? Wanna wake up? We kind of have to move on." He doesn't say to what or where, and it's not as if we knew. Both of us have avoided that topic this morning, and it doesn't make for a good mood. At all.

When Cris doesn't react, Gabe stands up, shaking his head. "When I said he was getting worse last night… definitely the case. This is way longer than last time."

"Uh-huh." I keep my back to him and continue carving patterns into the branch I broke off. It's called channeling your frustration. Granted, Gabe got pale when I got that knife out, but hey, so far, it's only carving into the branch.

So far.

With two quick steps, he's next to me. "What, Nya? Why are you so pissed? Is it because, for once, somebody is not agreeing with you on everything? As it is, I also want Cris to get better, and this here—"

I whirl around, the knife tight inside my fist. "Exactly! You know exactly what we have to do! We're both ignoring the obvious, Gabe!" I throw my branch down and stomp my foot.

"Really? And what would that be?" He glares at me.

"Very easy! We have a genetically altered human. Said human has something wrong with him. So how can we say it's not from the mutation?"

Gabe crosses his arms in front of his chest. "How can we say it is?"

There we go, exactly what I'm going for! "We can't either way! But my point is, we have to get him checked, and we have to find somebody who has the means to do so and knows what they're doing!" Hint-hint.

He stares at me, blinking twice. "And when you say *knows what they're doing*, you really mean with CRISPR and genetic modifications."

I cross my arms just like him. "Yes, because remember, we also wanted to check the percentage of mutated genes in him.”

“Oh, I remember.” He smacks his lips. “And you probably aren’t talking about your dad.”

“Nope.” Any time now, he’ll figure it out. Any ti—

And he does. It’s clear in his deflated puff of air, in the way his shoulders slump forwards and he rolls his eyes. “Aww, come on, Nya! Seriously? WissenSCHAFFT? They’re dealing with *plants*!”

“And the basics are still the same! CRISPR is CRISPR, PCR is PCR! It’s our best bet, Gabe!” You don’t just change science, period.

He rolls his eyes. “And you think they’ll have the knowledge and supplies, oh, and the willingness to help us.”

“Yes!” I barely refrain from stomping my foot. “It’s our best chance.” I feel like I said that before, but apparently, he needs to hear it repeatedly.

Gabe harrumphs and crosses his arms in front of his chest. “Okay. Sure. And how are we supposed to pull that one off?”

“Again, easy.” I zip open the backpack and grab the folder of documents I found in Dad’s desk. “Somewhere here… and there we go.” I hand him the *Congrats, you’re having a baby*-card.

Congrats, Jessica! Please let me know where you’re registered! +49-555-8181409
Love, Johanna

Gabe’s protest gets stuck in his throat and turns into another deflated sigh and a much calmer tone of voice. “Okay. Okay. You’ve got her phone number. But what then? I see why it’s tempting to call. But in all honesty, Nya, what do you expect from her? You’ve never met her, right?”

Can’t say I have. “Nope. She was supposed to be my godmother. I would like to think that if Dad hadn’t been completely overwhelmed and against anything—and anybody, including myself—who reminded him of Mom, she would've stayed in contact with me. But no, never met her." If growing up without a mom is hard, growing up without even being able to mention or talk about her is harder. Having a Johanna in my life would've made a difference. Thanks, Dad. I'll add it to the list of things to tell my future shrink about.

Gabe points at the card. "And if she remembers who you are—*if,* that is—what do you think she's going to do to help us? How do you know she won't call the police or Advangen?"

I zip the backpack up again. "Leap of faith. She was my mom's best friend, so I'm taking that as a proof of character. And what I'm hoping for…" I shrug. "I can't really say."

He rolls his eyes. "Now, that's making me want to call her real bad."

I shove Gabe in the shoulder. "Shut up. All I'm saying is that we're stuck, and that Johanna is one of the few people who could bring some motion into this. If she's not on our side, for whatever reason, what can she do from Germany? Until she gets to the appropriate people, we can be long gone, and it's not as if I'm going to tell her where we are. I doubt she's going to triangulate our call." Now I roll my eyes at him. There you go. I can stoop to the same level of maturity.

Gabe still doesn't like it, if his frown is any indication. "So now I know why it's not the biggest risk calling, but what is there to gain? You said it yourself, she's in Germany. Do you want her to fly over seizure meds for Cris? How long's that supposed to take? Or is she supposed to fly us over to Germany to her lab? Sorry, I happen to have left my passport at home. So, what else can she do? Diagnose him via phone?"

I draw my phone from my back pocket and unlock it, thumb

hovering above the phone-icon. "I get what you're saying, but…" I sigh. "Johanna is the only other person we know—well, kind of—who's involved in any research even remotely similar to what Advangen did to Cris. I guess I'm hoping for… support. Bouncing off ideas. If nothing else we can use, then at least support and somebody telling us we're doing the right thing." I shove my backpack into Gabe's hands, and he sets it down.

"Then let's hope your need for a pat on the shoulder won't get us deeper into trouble," he says, and takes the card from me, opening it up. "Ready? That's plus-forty-nine—what?" He blinks twice when I don't dial.

Heat invades my cheeks. "Nothing. Just thinking it's… *nice* you're going with my decision." Because over the last years I've gotten used to *antagonizing Gabe*, not *supportive Gabe* or at least *neutral Gabe*. I said, I've done my fair share of antagonizing too, but I've always seen that as payback.

Gabe looks at me, and that look, it carries *something* that pierces down to my soul, something warm and fuzzy, not cold and spiteful. The deep gray of his eyes shifts by degrees, their intensity pulling on my core like a magnet.

Which I need to ignore.

Nothing good will ever come from that, as we have seen last night.

Still, for a moment, I feel connected to Gabe. A shiver runs down my spine, accompanied by a confusing skip of my heart, when I notice the way his gaze bounces between my eyes and my lips, and how his throat bobs with a hard swallow. It draws me in—*he* draws me in—to a degree I didn't expect.

He steps closer, so close, our arms brush together, and that tiny touch brings the hair on my skin to rise and my heart to a stumble.

Unacceptable, Bennison.

I step back and drop my gaze to the phone, away from the eyes that for a moment made me feel special. *Special* is a dangerous, slippery slope. "Anyway. The number?"

Awkward silence hovers.

Well, I'm the one who put it there.

I clear my throat. "Hello? The number? So we can help Cris?" These few seconds were nothing but a temporary lapse in my sanity. I need to keep a clear focus on what's important, and me fan-girling over Gabriel Hargrove like one of his groupies is not part of that. Here's hoping he has no idea how close I came to actually liking him again.

Yuck.

Focus, Bennison.

Out of the corner of my eye, I see him go rigid. "Then get it over with," he growls under his breath. "Plus forty-nine. *Dial,* Nya." He makes an impatient hand motion.

Ah, wonderful. Snarky. Normality has been re-instated. That's what I wanted. Right?

I dial the numbers he dictates, but to my dismay, my fingers shake.

That hollow feeling in my stomach?

Worry about Cris. That's all.

That's all.

The phone rings and it sounds different from in the States. Maybe the key is different in Europe? After the fourth ring, a female picks up and my heart skips a nervous beat.

"Johanna here. Hello?" English—thank God. My German is non-existent. Must've seen the international number.

I clear my throat. "Uh, hi. This is Nya. Nya Bennison. I'm Jessica Bennison's daughter? From California? My Dad's name is—"

"Steve," she says. "His name is Steve."

She remembers! A smile breaks free and releases some of the weight wrapped around my soul. "Yes, that's my dad. I know we've never met, but… I was wondering if there was a way… I don't know, that you could maybe help me?" Gabe cringes and rolls his eyes, so I jab him in the side with my free hand. Not very eloquent, I got it, but come on, what am I supposed to say? *Hi, I'm Nya, I think my friend has Neanderthal genes edited into his genome and now he is really sick?* That's going to go well.

Surprise colors Johanna's voice. "Sure. What can I do for you?" She only has a very slight German accent, from what I can tell so far.

I close my eyes and take a deep breath. She's a scientist. She's going to see there is a possibility I'm saying the truth. So, I go with it. "I think my friend has Neanderthal genes edited into his genome, and now he's having seizures and we don't know what to do. We're right now in the middle of—"

"Stop."

I snap my mouth shut, gaze darting up to meet Gabe's. He's scooted much closer and leaned forward to listen in, pulse jumping in his throat, brows pulled down into a V. He catches my glance and shrugs.

On the other end of the line, I hear Johanna take two long, heavy breaths. "Are you being serious?"

"Unfortunately, yes."

Pause.

"Why are you calling me? Your father is one of the leading experts in human genome modification— Oh." I hear her swallow. Yeah, she figured it out.

"Yup," I say. "So that's why we have a problem."

"We?"

"My two friends and I. It's complicated. We're on the run and hiding—"

"Stop, please," Johanna says again. "I'm assuming nobody is listening in, but I can't be sure. Genetics are a hot topic at the moment." She pauses, and it sounds like she was pacing on hardwood floors in heels. "I'm in California right now. We're opening up a satellite lab for WissenSCHAFFT. California City. Can you make it there?"

OMG, she is in the States? California, to top it off, and moderately close? Gabe gives me a thumbs up—California City is doable! Hope springs to life, carried by enthusiasm.

"Yes, we can! We'll be there in a few hours."

"I'll be awaiting you." And without another word, she has hung up.

I let the phone sink down and click it off. It took all but two minutes, but our situation has changed completely. Gabe nods to himself twice.

"That was good," he whispers.

"Yeah," I whisper back, because now there's hope.

For once, there's hope.

CHAPTER EIGHTEEN

Cris loosens his death grip on my hand after about thirty minutes on the freeway. Ever since he woke up ten minutes after our call to Johanna, he's been more on the quiet side—especially once we started our drive to California City in a car organized by Duncan. Without him, we'd have had a much harder time finding a ride, since renting wasn't an option. Staying out of sight was.

I squeeze his hand once. "How are you feeling?"

He shrugs, keeping his eyes glued straight ahead from the rear middle seat. Took us less than five miles to figure out speed and Cris alone in the back didn't work well, not unless we were willing to risk some throwing up on his part, which we weren't. Having him ride shotgun wasn't a great idea either, since the whole speed aspect still freaked him out, meaning he needs the rear middle seat and somebody to hold on to. Somehow, I was the more suitable candidate compared to Gabe.

I rock my shoulder into him. "Bit better? Gabe's driving like a kid who just got his license." Right at the speed limit, signaling, everything. Smooth.

Cris frowns. "Yes. Better. But I really wish I'd had an idea what speed actually meant. I mean, it looks impressive in the movies, but experiencing it myself…" He shrugs. "Different."

Gabe looks into the rearview mirror. "We're going to be there in less than fifteen minutes." And still before noon. Ah, the advantages of an early start.

"I'll be fine." Cris looks straight out the front window, still pale around his nose.

"You will. You are." Gabe nods with both sentences, as if he really wanted to make sure Cris understood. Not sure though if he meant now or in general, because in general… I'm not sure. I want to be optimistic, and heck, this was my idea, but we're in so deep, I honestly can't say in which direction this disaster will go. Sorry. This is the first time I basically freed a genetically mutated hostage from my dad's company and ran with him.

Yikes.

Gabe taps his fingers onto the steering wheel. "And speaking of fifteen minutes until we're there, you really trust Johanna, Nya?"

I nod. "Yes. The little I know of her is all good. Not that Dad told many stories, but the few he shared made her seem like a good person. Plus, she was my mom's friend, so I'm hoping she'll be partial to her, and then by proxy, me, and be on our side."

"Okay. I sure hope you're right. We could use somebody on our side."

"And a lab."

Gabe chuckles. "We could always use a lab."

"You guys," Cris says, rolling his eyes and mock-sighing. "The entire world is open to you and you want to work indoors?"

That definitely stops the smile on Gabe's face. His gaze darts to mine in the rear-view mirror, then to somewhere behind me on the road, eyes narrowing. "I guess we've had the luxury of making our own choices for all our lives, so yes."

"Because you know you can get out at any time." Cris says it completely matter-of-factly, yet it carries the echo of his lifelong imprisonment.

I swallow hard, then nudge him with my shoulder. "What would you do?"

"If I could do anything?"

"Assume that at one point you can, and you will, please. But yes." Steel laces Gabe's voice. Just like me, he wants Cris to get through this and have the freedom and life he deserves.

A faint smile graces Cris' lips. "I always wanted to try out sailing. Or be on a boat. The idea of only water around you, nothing else… It fascinates me. I've never seen the ocean in person. Obviously." He sighs. "And I can't even swim, but… I don't know. I want to be on a ship, and if I could work there…" He drops his gaze to his lap, then shrugs. "Well, whatever. It's not like—"

Gabe's phone rings, and all three of us jerk.

Yeah. At this point we're all PTSD'ed by that sound.

Gabe throws a glance at me in the rear-view mirror. "Pick up for me?"

I nod, reaching between the seats for the phone in the cupholder. "Duncan, if anybody was wondering." I tap the accept button and then turn on the speaker. "Duncan, hi, this is Nya, you're on speaker."

Static fills the air before Duncan's voice fills in. *"—to hear the car worked out. You're on the road, I assume?"*

"Yes, we are," Gabe says, raising his voice. "Thanks for getting us this ride, much appreciated."

"Least I can do. No matter what I do with the rest of my life, you're already the biggest story I can ever publish."

"Yikes," I whisper.

"Is that good or bad?" Gabe asks.

"Let me put it this way: every major news outlet across the world has picked up on your story. It's out there. People know about you, about what Advangen did."

"Why does it sound like there's a but coming?" It totally did.

"Because there was. But it doesn't necessary help us."

I close my eyes for a second. "Are people on Advangen's side?"

"Not in general, but of those who are, their voices are loud. Very loud. Mutant, a crime against God and His creation—"

A muscle in Gabe's jaw tics. "What happened to being pro-life?"

Duncan huffs out a dry laugh. *"Do I really need to spell it out for you? Cris isn't human life, or at least they don't consider him that. I hope that we're going to get different feedback from the EU. They've been more progressive when it comes to—apologies—animal rights and personhood, so I would think they're more progressive in accepting life other than a hundred percent human. Either way, this thing has blown up. I have the lawyer ready for you, by the way. Chelsea Hunt. Call me when you're there and we—"*

"Whoa!" Cris slams a hand onto my thigh to keep himself from falling into me as inertia shoves him into me when Gabe swerves over to the other lane, narrowly avoiding a large truck. The side of my head hits the window and I yelp.

Straightening myself and rubbing my aching temple, I glare at the back of Gabe's head. "Geez, Gabe! I just praised you for driving—"

"We're being followed."

That extinguishes my annoyance and lights a different emotion, one that comes with bile rising in my throat. "Followed?"

"Followed?"

He nods. "A black SUV, similar to the ones that passed us when we were hiding last night."

I turn in my seat, heart hammering. "Where?" Who is it?

Advangen? They can't have found us. How would they have? Plus, sorry, following us—that's again movie material, not reality. Maybe Gabe's just overreacting.

Duncan curses. *"There must be a leak somewhere. The car rental, who knows. Can you—"*

Gabe nods his chin to the right. "Three cars behind us, very right lane."

Finding the car takes no effort. "I see them. Why do you think they're following us?"

"Because like you said, I've been driving like a student with their instructor in the passenger seat," Gabe says. "Everybody has overtaken me, besides these guys. They've been behind me for the last twenty minutes."

"That's not normal?" Cris asks. "I mean, I'm nauseous in this car, so maybe somebody else is too?"

"Possible." Gabe gives him a smile in the mirror. "But every time I switch lanes, they stay at an angle so they can see me. About five minutes ago I dropped to like 40 mph, and they still didn't go past me."

That bile rises higher. "Crap." Nobody's that patient to stay behind a car crawling on the freeway. "You're right, we're being followed."

"Advangen?" Cris looks out of the back window once more, as if he was checking for an Advangen-ad on the car.

"Could be reporters," Duncan says. *"My kind can be very dedicated and committed to reporting our stories."*

Gabe takes a deep breath in. "In this kind of car, my money is on Advangen. And I'd also assume they're here to catch you as soon as you step out of this car, Cris."

I ball my hands into fists. "Then we won't let them do that."

Gabe opens his mouth, then closes it, then tries again. "I love that you're proactive, Nya, but last time they had guns."

Shit. Point taken. "What do we do then?"

"For one, we don't stop until we reach WissenSCHAFFT. Cris gets out of this car, and all bets are off. I have no idea how they found us or if they know where we're going, but—"

A shadow falls over the car as another big, black SUV pulls up on our right.

And another one on our left.

"Uh-oh," Cris says as Gabe curses.

"Yeah, no doubt. It's them, and they brought backup."

"What happened?" Duncan's voice sounds anxious.

I can't see through their tinted windows, but no doubt it's *them,* agreed. I can feel the evil stares directed at us.

Sweat breaks out and trickles down my neck. "How much longer, Gabe?"

"We just hit the city limits. Two turns, per Apple Maps."

I wet my lips and swallow hard. "If they have guns on us right now…" Not sure what I'm saying or implying. That they would shoot at us? Would they dare?

Gabe meets my gaze in the rear mirror, eyes wide. "Say no more. I'm with you. Duncan, we're gonna have to call you back. You two, hold on!"

We barely have time to reach for each other's hands before Gabe floors it. I yelp out and hang up the phone as the car lurches forward with an angry howl of the engine. Gabe swerves over to the left, putting one of the SUVs behind us.

And the game is *on.*

As if we had all played a role until now, all pretense falls away the moment they realize we finally figured it out. We become the fugitives we've been since we freed Cris, they turn into the head-hunters they surely are.

With screeching tires, the SUV speeds up, but Gabe won't have it. He weaves through the freeway traffic like a pro, trying to outmaneuver them. People honk at us, somebody we're passing shoves their middle finger against the window, face distorted in anger, but Gabe keeps it up. We're flying down the main road, the train tracks to our left and nothing besides desert behind them, and some fast-food restaurants and stores on our right.

One of the SUVs speeds past us and cuts into our lane, break-checking us.

"Shit!" Gabe curses and I yelp as he hits the brakes and pulls us over to the right onto dirt and gravel. The car fishtails, once, twice—and Gabe gets it back onto the blacktop.

"I think I'm going to be sick," Cris groans. "I—"

"Red light!" I yell, jabbing my index finger in the general direction of the traffic light we're coming up to. "Red light!"

"I see it, Nya!" Gabe yells, fingers clamped around the wheel so tightly, his knuckles turn white. Yet, he doesn't slow down. Nope. He speeds up.

"What the heck are you doing? The light's red—"

"And if we're stopping. They box us in and that's it! We—"

"And if we get t-boned, we're dead, that's it as well! Dammit, Gabe—"

"Trust me, I got this!"

Cris groans, pressing one hand onto his stomach as Gabe cuts into the intersection and barely pulls around a large truck. The trunk honks as tires screech—and that would be the SUV, or all of them. With the eighteen-wheeler between them and us, it buys us a few seconds.

Exhaling loudly, Gabe glides his shaking fingers through his hair. "It's to the right over there, then left. Then we should be at their new research center," he says, voice rough and shaky. "Guys, when we're there, I'll pull to the entrance as close as I can, and then we all gotta run into that building."

"Like we're looking for refuge in an embassy," Cris mumbles, eyes closed, hands still pressed into his stomach. "Forgot which movie that was, but I liked it."

"Kind of." Gabe's gaze darts to the mirror, and a muscle in his jaw hardens. "And they're back. But at least we're in the lead." He turns sharply into a street on the right, the car barely withstanding the pull to tip over.

"Geez, Gabe!" I grab whatever I can to hold on.

"One-weekend crash-course of stunt driving. Dad knows this Ryan-guy who teaches that for movies and—"

"We're not in a movie!" I yell, as Gabe turns us hard into a street on the left. "We don't get second takes!"

"I got this, Nya!" Gabe white-knuckles the steering wheel as he races down the street, the howling of the SUVs' engines behind us and closing in. About two hundred yards ahead, in the middle of this industrial-looking area, a big, at least five-story all-white building pops out like it's illuminated, WissenSCHAFFT's logo on its front and side.

We're close, but so are the SUVs.

"They're trying to cut us off from entering their property!" Gabe throws a frantic glance into the right-side mirror and the approaching SUV, a black menace on our heels. "Hell no!" He cranks the wheel to the right, the high-pitched squeal of breaking tires following stat.

"Uh, guys…?" Cris yanks on my sleeve. "Guys?"

I look to the left— "Gabe! Incoming!"

Gabe checks the left side— And the SUV rams into us, sideways. Sparks fly, metal screeches, we all scream out, as Gabe tries to control the car and keep it from hitting one of the trees lining the street.

"Holy crap, that's attempted murder!" I yell. "Who in the name of all that's holy does something like that? What the—"

"People with guns who hold teens hostage, Nya! And screw this!" A determined look settles on Gabe's face. He hits the brakes so hard, we all get thrown forward into our seats. The SUV that glued itself to our side shoots forward and away, tires screech behind us— And Gabe takes a sharp right turn through the hip-high hedge on our right and onto WissenSCHAFFT's property. Branches scratch over the car, surely leaving more than just a little damage. We get thrown from left to right as the car bounces off first the curb, then bursts through the hedge, and then over one of those parking spot bumpers. Cris makes a gagging noise, one very suspicious of actual vomit coming up, but at this moment nobody cares.

"There!" I point to about two o'clock from us. "The main entrance!" Only what, a hundred yards, and we're there! We can make it! "Don't hit any cars!" Because, well, there aren't a lot of cars, but definitely enough to potentially be a problem.

"No shit, Sherlock!" Gabe yells, speed-weaving our way through scattered parked cars in the shortest way to the entrance.

The sound of metal hitting asphalt comes from behind us. I twist in my seat, blood swooshing in my ears, heart pumping like I was physically pushing this car to its speed instead of sitting in it. "They're behind us! One of them drove through the hedge as well!" Unbelievable. Everything is unbelievable. This is too much action movie and too little how real life works, or so I thought.

"Get ready," Gabe yells and keeps the speed up, up, *up*—until he hits the brakes about fifty meters before the main entrance. I get thrown into my seatbelt with a grunt and Cris with a retching, gagging sound. No idea how he pulled it off after one weekend of stunt-driving, but Gabe drifts the car sideways right up to the main doors. A security guard jumps back, a panicked expression on his face.

With one final rocking motion, the car comes to a standstill.

"Out!" I yell, unbuckling myself, then helping Cris. "Come on, come on!" I shove the door open, scramble out, one hand holding on to Cris, the other waving at the security man. "Johanna Friedrichs is expecting us! We need to get inside, like, fast!"

The security guy's eyes widen as he sees three SUVs barge at us. No idea if that's what's powering his decisions, if it's that we're all three young, or that I mentioned Johanna, but he opens the doors for us.

We burst through the glass doors and keep on running past the empty bellboy desk to the elevators. Gabe hammer fists the elevator button so hard, I worry it cracked either the button or his hand. "Which floor?" I yell back at the guard.

Momentarily distracted by several men, all dressed in black, pouring out of the SUVs, he takes a second to respond. "Uh, third floor! She's on the third!"

Six men are storming toward the entrance doors, none of them looking friendly. One isn't wearing a jacket and his holster shows—with a gun in it.

"Crap, crap, crap," I breathe. We're sitting ducks in the lobby here. We don't stand a chance against six Brock Lesnar types.

The security guard must've thought the same thing. He reaches for his back and grabs the keys hanging from a carabiner. In one quick motion, he locks the door from the inside—and not a moment too soon.

The goons crash into the door, rattling on it and slamming their palms into the glass. One of them pulls their gun—

"Jesus Christ!" The security guard pulls his as well and steps into a combat-ready stance. "What the hell is wrong with you people?" He yells loud enough I'm sure they can hear it all the way through the safety glass. "And we have y'all recorded! Don't be stupid!" Shaking his head and nods his chin to the upper left corner of the lobby, toward the camera.

While I can't hear them, I can clearly read the f-bombs off the six men's lips. Gun-dude holsters his weapon, and as they all glare through the doors at us, the elevator arrives and we step in.

Gabe presses the button for the third floor, and the doors close, shutting us off from the craziness outside and wrapping us in a cocoon of blissful quiet.

For a moment, terse silence hovers.

As if we rehearsed, we all exhale at the same time.

A small chuckle breaks from Gabe's throat. "Holy shit," he whispers, raking his hand through his hair. "We actually made it."

I take the hand he drops from his hair and weave my fingers through them. "Because of you, Gabe. Somebody needs a thank-you card. Your dad or that instructor. One weekend of stunt driving, holy cow. That was… beyond impressive." How he kept his cool and maneuvered us through. Without him, we wouldn't be here. We'd be either in a car wreck or Cris would've been taken. Maybe even both.

"You think so?" Pride and disbelief shine in his voice.

"Absolutely," I say at the same time as Cris says, "Heck, yeah."

"Well then." Gabe keeps his fingers entwined with mine, opening both arms wide. "Group hug, people." He pulls me close, Cris following stat, sandwiching me between the guys and smashing my cheek smack into Gabe's muscular chest. And to my complete and utter surprise, after a wild car chase and narrow escape, with too many problems to count on our hands, for this one moment, I'm at peace.

CHAPTER NINETEEN

Luckily for us, the elevator takes its sweet time. Once it comes to a standstill, we pull apart, but it's not even awkward or weird. Guess a near-death experience or two changes one's perspective.

The doors open to a white, sterile looking hallway and a blonde, moderately tall woman in her early fifties leaning against the wall across from the elevator. If Google image search didn't lie, this must be Johanna. She has her hair twisted on top of her head, and the black turtleneck sweater together with her black glasses gives her a professional yet casual vibe. She holds her phone in one hand and has one finger pressed into a wireless ear bud inserted into her left ear.

"… got it, Keith. They're here. Thank you. Keep me posted, please, and yes, call shift one back in and double security. Talk to you later." She ends the call, takes the ear bud out and slides it into her black jeans pocket, together with the phone. Her gaze glides over us, eyes widening when she sees me.

Yup. I'm my mom's daughter, for sure.

Taking the initiative, I step forward and hold out a hand. "Johanna? I'm Nya, and these are Gabriel and Cris. It's very nice—"

Johanna ignores my outstretched hand and pulls me into a hug. "I'm happy you made it here safe and in one piece," she says, then releases me, holding me at arm's length by the shoulders. "You look so much like your mom." She looks me up and down, then narrows her eyes. "Did she— Never mind." She lets go of me and waves a hand. "All in due time. It's very nice to meet all three of you. I'm very much intrigued to hear the entire story. Come on. I got my conference room ready. Let's talk."

As she leads the way, Gabe catches up with me and taps me on the shoulder, giving me an excited nod and a thumbs up. "You were right," he whispers. "We like her. I mean, you're the most awkward hugger in the existence of huggers, but Johanna is cool."

I shoot him a shut-up glance from under my lashes. "I don't do well with unexpected hugs, okay? And yes, she's cool," I reply, then pointedly look away from Gabe, who clears his throat before he speaks up.

"Johanna—by the way, sorry about the chaos in your parking lot. We had—"

"You had some followers, Keith says. My security guard." She gives Gabe a smile over her shoulder. "He's taking care of it. Luckily, we're not running at full capacity yet, so the lot is mostly empty. And we've been there, done that, and have had our fair share of attempted industrial espionage, protestors, or saboteurs over the years and in all our locations."

"Yikes." Gabe's eyes widen. "Over genetic editing on plants?"

Johanna throws him a knowing glance. "We get that more than companies like Advangen. After all, they cure illnesses—which is good, while we change our food—which apparently is bad." She sighs. "It's a complex topic, and I understand people's opinions. But when climate change kicks in even more, they all still want to eat, so…" She raises her palms to the ceiling, then drops them. "In any case, this isn't the first time Keith has been dealing with *unruly* guests."

"Nicely phrased," Gabe mumbles as Johanna leads the way into a large conference room with floor-to-ceiling windows across from the door.

"Have a seat, please." She motions at the large glass table in the middle of the room, and while it's big enough to seat at least twenty people, the three of us choose our seats next to each other and across from her. I kind of like she didn't take the seat at the head of the table. I always felt people who did that needed to prove a point or satisfy their ego.

"So," Johanna says, scooting forward in her seat and resting both forearms on the table, "so far, I heard a couple of buzzwords that included Neanderthal genes and seizures, but please, tell me—"

Somebody knocks on the door.

"Come in," Johanna calls out, followed by the door opening to a young guy in his early twenties.

"Sorry to interrupt, but I've got the venipuncture supplies you requested." He holds up a tray with needles, tourniquets, and some vials.

I raise an eyebrow. Venipuncture set. Is she thinking what we're thinking?

"Wonderful. Please draw the samples and then get me the chromosomal analysis as fast as possible." She points at Cris. "Sorry to jump ahead, but we'd need a full analysis of your genome to see what they changed and what could be responsible for your problems."

Cris glances at me, and I nod. "That's what Gabe and I wanted to do anyway," I say. It'll also help us see what percentage of his genome is altered, so we can start working on our defense. And that being said, sometimes fate just drops a little help into your lap:

"Would you mind running Gabe's and my genome as well? One of our defense strategies—and I'm sure we're going to talk about that in a minute—is to show everybody has mutated parts in their DNA, not just Cris. Might as well start with ours." I tap the vein in the hollow of my elbow.

Johanna's gaze darts over to Gabe, and when he nods, so does she. "No problem. Torin, if you wouldn't mind…?"

"Not at all, ma'am. One poke at a time." He walks over to Cris, kneels next to him and takes his arm in his hands. "Sir, if that's okay with you?"

Cris huffs. "Please. First, you're actually asking me and two, it's only a blood draw. Knock yourself out."

Johanna raises a questioning eyebrow, but stays quiet until the blood is drawn from all three of us and Torin has closed the door behind him. "Back to the matters at hand. Please, Nya, tell me what's been going on besides what I've been reading in the L.A. Times."

"Okay." I take a deep breath and spill the whole story: how I found out about Cris, what they did to him, how we got him out of Advangen and how they chased us here. I show her the documents and the ultrasound I found in Dad's drawer, and her mouth drops open. Yeah. That was me too, right there. But the more I talk, the more Johanna's brows crunch down into a V and the more her mouth tightens. Once I'm done, a good thirty or forty minutes later, she shakes her head.

"I didn't know Advangen was this advanced in genetic modifications that long ago. You're how old? Eighteen?"

Cris nods, and Johana takes that as her cue to continue. "Eighteen-nineteen years ago then. Quite impressive. We're using CRISPR to repair genetic defects in embryos, even in adults, but to create a new species… that's as fascinating as it is irresponsible, no offense."

"None taken, I think," Cris mumbles. "Ouch for the *irresponsible*."

She gives him an apologetic smile. "Sorry. But you can't tell me they really knew what they were doing at that point in the game, or what effects the changes would have. I'm sure they had an idea, but in vitro differs from in vivo. Theory and reality don't always align. So, no, I don't think they knew what any of these manipulations meant in the long run, and here we are, with you possibly carrying the burden. It's unethical, really."

"Point taken," Cris says after a hard swallow.

I lean forward. "So, you think Cris' seizures could be from that? Or does he quote-unquote *just* have seizures? I mean, un-mutated humans also have those." Right? I give her a questioning glance.

"Either or is possible. I'll have to wait for his genome to come back, which shouldn't take too long. We should also get a neurologist involved. I'm sure an EEG would be helpful. That being said, I'm curious to see which Neanderthal genes exactly they inserted besides the ones already in his genome." When she sees Cris' questioning expression, she adds. "We know there has been some crossbreeding between Homo sapiens and Neanderthals. Most people have a certain amount of genes that can be traced back to the Neanderthals."

Now we're talking. That's good news for us and our strategy. "Is there data? Like I said earlier, we're looking into how to best defend Cris, and making him seem more normal and less mutant seems like a good idea. So if we can quantify the amount of mutations *and* Neanderthal genes in a regular, good ol' Joe Shmoe and then compare it to Cris' percentage of Neanderthal genes, it'll hopefully show the difference isn't such a big deal." I hope. I really hope. What percentage could they even change into Neanderthal genes without risking a non-viable embryo, aka one that died? How did they know what was safe and what wasn't? Or, holy cow, that thought is scary: were there others? How many embryos didn't survive until Cris did? I want to believe none, but what kind of scientific experiment works out on the first try?

Nausea rises.

Few do, which means… which means Advangen most likely caused the death of some human-Neanderthal hybrid embryos.

I close my eyes and shake my head once. Can't go there right now. Just can't.

Johanna reaches for a water bottle on the table. "Good strategy. Well, depending on the study, we're talking an average of one-point-eight to two-point-six percent of Neanderthal DNA, depending on origin."

Cris chuckles. "That's oddly precise."

"That's science," Johanna replies with a smile and winks at him. "And that Neanderthal DNA also seems to influence genes related to cholesterol, vitamin D, eating disorders, fat accumulation, even response to antipsychotic drugs. And we think their genes gave us a good boost of our immune system, for example."

Cris grins and wiggles his eyebrows. "Never been sick. Told you I'm special."

I pat his thigh. "We know, we know. But I'm also never sick, so don't get too excited about your superpowers, right?" Especially if their downside is seizures.

Johanna's eyes widen for a split second before she fixes a smile on her face. "Superpowers, maybe, but we're still discovering new functions caused by those genes. And messing with something you don't understand…" She gives us a pointed glance. "Could lead to problems down the line. That's why I said unethical, no offense to you, Cris."

"None taken. It's not like it was my fault."

"Definitely not, even though you're dealing with the impact of the mutations." Johanna presses her lips together and shakes her head. "What were they thinking—?"

Her phone rings, and with a sigh she pulls it out of her pocket, frowning when she sees the number. "Who—" Her gaze snaps up to mine. "Is three-ten a local area code?"

I furrow my brows. "Yeah, that's L.A. Why?"

She holds up the phone and wiggles it. "Because this is my private phone. Nobody has this number, and yet I'm being called from Los Angeles, apparently."

Oh.

The three of us exchange a worried look. Reporters? Advangen?

"Well," Johanna says, "now I'm curious." She accepts the call. "Hello?" A second later, her eyes widen. She opens and closes her mouth before she holds up a hand. "Wait a second. Hold on. Let me go somewhere more private." Placing one finger against her lips in the international sign for *don't say a word,* she lays the phone onto the table, display side up, and activates the speaker. "This is better. Can you hear me?"

"Loud and clear. Thank you for taking my call."

I suck in a sharp breath. Dad! "That's Dad," I whisper to Gabe and Cris. Both roll their eyes at me like, duh, we know. Okay. Right, yes, they know him too, it's just… Every new involvement of Dad is still a shock to the system.

"To be honest, I wasn't sure who was calling me. I didn't even know you still had my number. It's been not quite twenty years, but close."

"And to be honest myself, I had deleted your number, but Jessica had some, uh, documents, with it on it, so here we go."

Hearing him say Mom's name is so surreal. I can't remember him ever calling her Jessica, only *your mom*. How little do I know about this man? And by the way, Mom had *some documents*? I bet he means the same ones I found, the ultrasound and congrats card from Johanna. I fish down in my back pocket for the copy I took and slide both the card and the infamous ultrasound picture over to Johanna.

"This is how he got your number," I whisper.

Johanna's mouth forms a tiny *o* when she sees the ultrasound. She picks it up, chewing on her lower lip, then closes her eyes and exhales slowly.

"Johanna?"

"I'm here. Sorry. So now I know how you're calling me, but that leaves me curious for the why."

"First, I would like you to know that I'm calling privately, and not as an employee of Advangen's. And second, I… I was wondering if Nya was with you."

I hear my dad swallow hard.

She lays the ultrasound and card on the table, aligning it parallel to the edge. "You know I haven't met Nya in all those years. Why would she be with me, of all people?"

Silence hovers until Dad sighs. *"You've read the news?"*

"I flew into the US a few days ago, but even in Germany we're getting news, especially the kind Advangen is finding itself in the middle of. Not sure what to call what you did. Ballsy?"

"Desperate?" Dad coughs out a harsh, dry laugh. *"But either way, knowing my daughter, she will want access to a lab. And our security- and loss-prevention services tell me they tracked her to California City and, lo-and-behold, your facility. So, is Nya with you?"*

Johanna looks up at me, one eyebrow raised. She tilts her head and lifts both palms to the ceiling. Cat's out of the bag. What do you want to do?

Gabe elbows me in the side, then leans in and whispers into my ear. "If he knows we're here, Advangen might know as well, and that means the police could know. Let's play nice and bide for time?"

I smack my lips quietly. He's got a point. Nodding at Johanna, I hold up my finger. My turn.

"I'm here, Dad."

Dad inhales sharply. *"Nya. Hi. "*

"Hi."

"Can we talk privately?"

Nu-uh. Everybody needs to hear what he has to say. "This is as private as it gets." I cross my arms in front of my chest. My heart's beating like crazy, like it was adrenalized beyond belief, which is even crazier, since we're talking about Dad and nothing about him should make me nervous, but alas, one abduction and car chase later, here we are.

"Fair enough, " he says. *"Can I meet you and talk in person, then? Some things are difficult to discuss over the phone."*

Oh, really? "What things, Dad? Like how you kept Cris locked in the basement? Or maybe the reason why you did that? Like some genetic experimentation? Is that what's easier to discuss in person?" I lean forward, arms resting on the table and fingers crunched into fists, mad on so many levels and for so, so many reasons.

He keeps his voice level, but I know it costs him. *"Yes. That and... other things."*

"Other things?" I throw my hands up, a mad, sarcastic laugh breaking from my throat. "Sure, there's more. Of course there is. But you know what? I don't want to hear it."

"Nya—"

"No, Dad! Not going to happen! I'm sorry, but I don't know how to handle you right now. At all!"

"Nya—"

"Hard, no, Dad."

He takes a breath and holds it, before releasing it with an oomph-sound. *"Johanna. Let's reason."*

"You heard your daughter, Steve. I'm not going against her decision."

"But you might understand the bigger picture here, unlike the children in your presence. Let me be frank. Advangen knows where you three are. Right now I could convince Mr. Sherman to let me try to solve this in a less public manner, but if you don't hand over Cris—"

"You mean, if we don't hand over *your property*," I call out. Their property! I can't even!

"—if you don't hand over Cris, Advangen will get a judge to rule in their favor and the police to take him from WissenSCHAFFT's building. Advangen will get him back. But it will make waves, much more so than it already has. And, Nya, believe me, you don't want that. Johanna, back me up on this. You understand." The way he says it, like he and she were the only sane ones in this conversation, makes me see red.

I stand up so fast my chair would've fallen over if it wasn't for Cris' fast reaction and catching it. "Dad—"

"Give me a second," Johanna says and presses a button on the phone. "We're muted." She drums her fingers onto the table. "What do you think?"

What I think? That's easy. "Dad can go and—"

"Wait a sec, Nya." Gabe holds up and hand scoots in his seat to face me. "Dealing with your dad might be better than dealing with Advangen."

I narrow my eyes at him. "Are you suggesting we meet and hear him out? We give him what he wants? Isn't there like this thing that we don't negotiate with terrorists?"

He raises an eyebrow. "We as in the US? So, we here are the States, and he's the terrorist?"

"Basically, yes." I cross my eyes and plop my butt back down.

"Look." He pauses. "I see why this is hard for you, but he might have a point."

I harrumph, but when I say nothing else, Gabe continues. "Right now, your dad is the lesser of two evils. We need time to work on our strategies. Wait for Cris' genome analysis to come back. And maybe with him we can come up with a solution better than with Advangen's lawyers."

I take in a slow, deliberate breath before trusting myself to speak. "A solution. With Dad. Like what?"

"Well, for starters, we need Cris' freedom guaranteed. He can't go back to that basement or any other form of confinement. Is that in your best interest, Cris?"

"Definitely." Cris gives us a thumbs up. "I'd prefer that. A lot."

"Okay. But would you be willing to maybe work with Advangen? Under certain circumstances?"

"Work with them? Doing what?"

Oh, I know what Gabe's going for. A growl breaks from my throat. "Giving them your bone marrow. That's what he means." And it's stupid. Working with the people who tortured him? Robbed him of his freedom? Denied him basic human rights? That's a big, fat no for me, dawg.

"Huh." Cris scratches his neck. "I dunno. It depends, I guess? I would want to have a say in it, like when, how often, and where they draw." He rubs a hand over his sternum. "But if that's buying me freedom, I'd be willing to do that."

"You'd—" I snap my mouth closed when I see the sincerity in

his eyes, and it drives one point home: I've been spoiled my whole life. Nobody ever restricted me, and even if I compare Dad's attempts to get me out of science and into whatever, homemaking, to what happened to Cris, I can't complain.

So, I swallow my outburst and instead nod. "That's... big of you, Cris."

He shrugs. "Meh. A compromise. Making everybody equally happy or unhappy."

Gabe lays a hand on my knee. "We've got to work with them if we want the best for Cris. Can you get your dad here and buy us time?" He looks over at Johanna. "We haven't even talked about any of this, but can we stay here? You have security downstairs, which feels like it's a plus at this point."

"Of course you can," Johanna says, then points a finger up. "We have rooms for our employees upstairs. You can stay as long as you need. And, Nya..."

"Yeah?"

"Talk to him," she says, keeping her gaze on the phone. "I... I have a feeling it'll be necessary."

I don't know why, but a shiver runs down my back, leaving goosebumps in its wake. It feels like I'm missing something, but what? I don't think I am, but...

I shake off that annoying sensation and, for the umpteenth time, take a deep breath in to keep myself leveled. "Okay. Okay. Let's get Dad here, and I'll see what I can do." I'll have to face the music at one point anyway—and so does he.

Might as well do it now, where it hopefully serves another purpose.

CHAPTER TWENTY

After Dad agrees to drive in to California City, Johanna takes us to the top floor. When she said they had rooms for their employees, she didn't do our accommodation justice: This is an apartment. A penthouse. Two bed, two bath, a living room with an open kitchen and dining area, and large glass sliding doors leading out to a terrace on the roof.

As Johanna closes the door behind her on her way out, Gabe lets himself fall into one of the thick-cushioned couches. "When I'm all grown up, I want to be important enough to be invited to a company like WissenSCHAFFT and hosted in their penthouse while I do my groundbreaking research." He slides out of his shoes and props his feet up on the table. "This is nice."

"I liked the RV more. Even the sleep sack." Cris opens a cabinet in the kitchen. "Wow, there's tons of stuff in here. What is—? Oh. Peanut butter? Nutella?" He reaches for the second shelf, brings out a tall jar with a white lid, and looks at it skeptically.

"Good stuff," I say. "Careful though, once you get started, it's tough to stop."

"Huh." Cris shrugs and puts the Nutella back before he closes the cabinet. He nods his chin toward the window and toward the mountains in the distance. "Although this view is nice. But it's what I've had forever, rooms, rooms, rooms. Trees and sand and the lake… not."

Gabe picks up a throw pillow and throws it at Cris. "I know, but count your blessings. Nobody is trying to push us off the road."

Cris catches the cushion, grinning. "Because they know already exactly where we are." He throws the pillow back at Gabe.

"Which doesn't bother us, because we're using that to our advantage." *Swoosh*, the cushion goes back to Cris.

"Which means," he throws it back with a good amount of *oomph* behind it, "we need our plan A and Plan B ready."

"And of course, we're gonna work on—"

I grab the pillow before Gabe can throw it again. Guys. I roll my eyes. "Yes, we're going to work on it, but that's much easier without you throwing things back and forth." I sit down in the chair across from Gabe, keeping that pillow on my lap.

"Spoilsport." Gabe sticks out his tongue. "But okay then. Plans. Easy. I have one."

"Then speak, oh grand master." I roll my eyes again, because, boys.

He shoots me a cautious glance from under his lashes. "We need to involve the public more. Duncan's articles are great, but even with other news outlets picking up on it, they don't reach as many people as we should and not in the way we want to."

I pull my legs under me, criss-cross-applesauce. "Do you want to give interviews now?"

He looks at a spot somewhere behind me. "Not really. Rather something more intimate, yet more distanced. Everybody has a social media account. Old-school Facebook, X, Insta, TikTok, TeenVoice, you name it."

Social media. Of course. I swallow down the rush of old hurt and insecurity. I'm the bigger person.

"Yeah," I croak. "You're right. Basically, everybody has an account. We want to get our point of view out there." I rub the bridge of my nose, unable to stop the next sentence from bursting out. "That's your specialty, after all."

Gabe stills. "It's not my specialty. I just know about the power of social media."

I shoot him the same glance he cut me a moment ago. "And I don't?" Clearly I'm not the bigger person, because not only do I remember, very, very clearly so but also I don't seem to have forgiven. Seven hundred and fifty-three likes for a wet t-shirt picture isn't quite going viral, but it's enough to bring a fourteen-year-old to tears. For several weeks on end, I might add. Especially if it comes with the loss of her best friend, because clearly a best friend would never do something so idiotic.

Well. Mine did.

The apple in his throat moves up and down as he scoots up and swings his legs off the table. "Nya, I…" He looks down onto his folded hands, chewing on his lower lip, then meets my gaze again, chin held high. "I was an absolute idiot. An asshole. A bully. What I did was not okay, I know that, and I knew that then, but…" He drops his gaze again and shakes his head.

A wave of dizziness hits me. Did he— Did he just apologize? Call himself an asshole and bully? Did I hear that or did my mind make that up? Just wondering, because I've been waiting for those words for years. "But?" I repeat his last word, my voice rough.

He looks back at me, his expression open and vulnerable. The apple in his throat bobs up and down with a swallow. "But Brodi Corrington was asking you to help him with bio, this Kevin idiot started to always sit with you at lunch, and Alex Khorramian had asked you to Spring Ball before I could even ask you, and I… I… I didn't know how to handle any of it. Obviously." He huffs out a harsh laugh and shoves a hand through his hair. "And when talking bad about you didn't keep them away and Corrington was putting the moves on you, I saw red. That's not an excuse, but I didn't make a conscious decision to throw that water at you. It just happened. I… I just wanted that moment to stop, to get you away from him. And once Jason sent me that picture and said I should post it—and I'm not saying that to blame Jason, *I* posted it, that's on me—I put it up, because… Hell, I don't even know why I did it. Something didn't work right in here." He rams his index finger against his temple, "I wasn't *thinking*, I was just… *acting*. It was stupid and so not okay, I know that. But when I wanted to apologize…"

Gabe exhales sharply and leans forward for a moment, supporting his forehead with both palms. Then he sits up straight, hands clasped together between his knees. "When I wanted to apologize, you told me to fuck off, rightfully so, and again, I'm not saying that to blame you or use it as an excuse. I'm just saying it to explain that I was hurt. I was an idiot who didn't understand what he'd done, and I felt rejected. So, I did what most fifteen-year-old boys would do—"

"You pretended like it didn't bother you and continued the war," I whisper. Because that's what I did. I was so raw and wounded after that post, so violated that I couldn't *not* snap at him when he tried to apologize. But that didn't mean I hadn't hoped he'd come back, that he'd try again. In fact, I was banking on it. Yet, he never did. Instead, we were suddenly on two different sides, when before we'd always been a united front. Suddenly we were working against each other, both of us trying to come out on top in a fight apparently neither of us wanted.

All that hurt…

He lowers his lashes, and when they flutter open again, one

emotion overpowers all the others reflecting on his face: Regret. "I should've said this the moment I did it. Hell, I should never have done it, but I'm sorry, Nya. For everything."

For everything.

As if somebody had snapped the chain around my soul, a light, warm feeling spreads in my chest, which is ridiculous, because obviously I've *so* been over this whole thing, but… maybe not. Maybe I've been grieving the loss of my best friend since the day it happened. Maybe I never moved on, which is also quite pathetic, to be honest, yet here we are.

My heart pitter-patters. It shouldn't matter that Gabe's apologizing now. We've broken the law together, got chased, had to go into hiding—we're still not where we used to be, but close, like we ignored the last years and carried on. So, it shouldn't matter, but it makes all the difference. It puts a spotlight on the elephant in the room, and maybe it helps to shove it out the door.

But for that, *I* need to help to push it, too.

"Thank you," I whisper. "That… felt surprisingly good to hear. And, you know… I'm sor—"

"Please don't say you're sorry." Gabe holds up a hand. "Everything you did, you did because of my initial action. You have nothing to be sorry—"

"Uh, guys?" Cris steps closer to the sliding doors and fumbles with their lock. "Guys? I know you're having a moment, but you should have a look at this. Like, really."

The alarm in his voice takes only a split-second to tear Gabe and me out of our, uh, *moment.* We jump off the couch and both come to a dead stop when we catch up to Cris.

"Holy cow," I whisper as I follow where Cris is pointing, not that I'd have needed that literal pointer. "That's…" I don't have words. For the last two days, my life has been surreal, and I can't say it's getting better.

"How many news vans is that?" Gabe asks, incredulous. "Two, four, six, seven… eight? Eight news vans?"

"Nine, actually." Cris points to the right. "One just went around the corner. Maybe they're covering the back exit, who knows."

Nine news vans. Nine news vans, all with their big antenna-pole-things up in the air and at least two or three people busying themselves around their vans. Oh, and competing for the best spot in-between the few parked cars, it appears. At least two ladies in business suits seem to go toe to toe down there.

"Well." Gabe crosses his arms and shakes his head. "At least Advangen won't try to break in and take us with force while the eyes of the world are watching."

I chuckle and cut him a glance. "You might be overselling the local Fox and CNN branches, but I get what you're saying."

"Bet Duncan is happy he knows me, now that the cat is out of the bag." He flexes his muscles in his left arm, Arnold-style. And sue me, it feels lighter than *before*. Guess the elephant has really left the room.

Anyway. "We should probably talk to Duncan and update him. See what else he has for us," I say, wrinkling my nose. "The lawyer sounded like a good idea, for Cris and for us." We need them more for Cris though. No idea if our quote-unquote crime equals stealing a Snickers bar or more like grand theft auto, and it's our primary concern at the moment.

"Agreed. And that drives my previous point home." Gabe clears his throat and wraps his arm around my shoulders, squeezing once. "We need to shift public opinion. No, not shift: form. Shifting means it's too late, and I don't think that's the case. We need people to form an opinion based on what they see of us." He holds me tight, as if he feared the elephant would come back in and charge at me.

Turning away from the window, Cris pulls one brow up. "Social media, right? It's all over TV. Always thought it was a bit of a stretch the way people seem to use it, but apparently, it's real." He shrugs and rolls his eyes. "I'll add it to the list of things I didn't know about."

"It's real for sure, and I don't think whatever you saw was exaggerated. Social media is everywhere and big." Not that I'm the expert, despite—or maybe because—of what happened between Gabe and me. Do I have an Insta account? Yes. TikTok? Yes. TeenVoice? Sure. Do I use them? Not really. My last Insta-post might've been several months ago, and I only check my feed every once in a while, when I'm really bored. "That being said, Gabe's idea was good. We need to humanize you, Cris. Literally. We need more people to know about you and like you. The more do, the better you're protected."

Gabe nods, keeping his gaze glued on the reporters in the parking lot. "Exactly. We need outrage and support. Not only in L.A., or in California, but in the whole States. Worldwide." He pulls his phone from his pocket. "So, let's start. Bring it in."

I stiffen under the weight of his arm, mentally cursing at myself the moment I do it. Get a grip, Nya. This isn't seventh grade, and he just apologized. Posting a picture now is so different, it's in a different universe compared to the last post of Gabe that featured me. Guess old habits die hard, though.

Gabe's hold on my shoulders loosens, although he keeps the arm around me as he looks down at me. Understanding flashes across his face, followed by a hard swallow. "I'm sorry," he mouths. His gaze meets mine, open, soft, and… I don't know, filled with *something* that I'm going to blame for my temporary lapse in sanity and why I sneak my arm around his waist and bump my side closer into his.

"Let's do this," I say. Elephant, stay out of the room. We're done here.

"Thank you," Gabe whispers the moment my side bumps into his, then louder, "Cris, come on in."

"In what?" Cris lifts his palms. "I'm already inside."

Gabe chuckles and points his phone to the spot next to him. "Come in here, it's selfie-time."

"Selfie— Oh!" He smacks his forehead. "Right. I got it." He comes over to us and angles himself so that he's half in front of Gabe. "What do I need to do?"

"Nothing besides look like the nicest, most handsome mutated abomination the world has ever see— Hey!" Gabe twitches when I pinch him in the side. "I meant that in a nice way!"

"Yup." I beam up at him and brush a palm over the ribs I hit. "The urge to pinch you just really overwhelmed me." I need to counter-balance all his sweetness, or that sugar-rush is going to my head even more than it already has.

Gabe looks down at me, mouth open, before he reads me and a smile graces his lips. "Okay then. Get it out of your system." He clears his throat and holds out the phone. "Ready? Three, two, one—say *genes*!"

Our picture flashes once on the screen and I grunt. "Ugh. All you see are my million freckles." I roll my eyes. Annoying.

Giving my shoulder one more squeeze, Gabe lets go to type with both hands on the phone. "Fifteen."

"Huh?" I throw him a confused glance.

"Not a million. Fifteen."

An odd sense of familiarity washes over me. I swallow it down and cross my arms in front of my chest. "Fourteen and a half freckles, I will have you know. If we're being precise, I mean."

Gabe looks up from the phone. "And a half? Why a half?"

"Because this one doesn't count." I point to a tiny freckle on my left temple. "That one is much smaller than the rest, so, because it occupies less body surface area, it also counts only as half."

Slowly, Gabe raises an eyebrow, then shakes his head and drops his gaze back to the phone. "I disagree. That one looks like a tiny heart, so it counts for full. A for effort. Fifteen, I stand by it."

Before I can analyze that warm feeling in the pit of my stomach, Cris points at the phone and asks, "And now? How long does that take?"

I let myself fall into the same chair I sat in before and clear my throat, hoping my mind will clear with it. *Fifteen.* "Not long. Gabe will set up an account in twenty seconds."

"You honor me, but I might need a full minute." He types fast, using mostly his thumbs. "Insta with my spam mail account, check. Shall I?" He keeps his thumb hovering above the screen.

"What did you write?" I ask.

"Besides using a million hash tags? I kept it simple. *Hi from Gabe, Nya, and Cris.* I don't want to start with something too political or sarcastic. Good?"

I nod. "Cris?"

"I'm fine with it. Not that I know what else we should be doing."

"Okay then. Here we go, project getting the public to love Cris, take one."

For the next few hours, Gabe works on our social media presence, while Cris and I make suggestions. Tbh, it's all Gabe though. Cris and I are useless. Mostly, at least, and I'm woman enough to admit to myself I'm not the best person for a cool one liner and posts. Even Cris, new to the game, is doing better than me.

The guys have taken the couch, while I'm sideways in the comfy chair on the other side of the coffee table, legs draped over the armrest. Cris looks at the picture Gabe took of him earlier today out on the balcony, looking past the assembled press into the distance. It's so full of melancholy, especially in the way Gabe edited it in black and white, it delivers a powerful statement.

"*The second free day of my life.* Post that. And use the hashtag *bornasprisoner*. It feels appropriate." Cris hands the phone back to Gabe.

"Will do. Considering we just started a few hours ago, we've got a good amount of content. And a good amount of followers."

I take a sip of my tea and set the mug back down on the coffee table. Ah, the joys of a fully stocked penthouse suite. "Speaking of. How many followers do we have at this point?"

"And the next picture posted." Gabe taps the screen with his thumb. "Which platform do you want to know?"

"All of them?" We posted—I'm sorry, we *created content*—for the last three or four hours, sometimes with videos and screenshots we took on our action cams when we broke out Cris, some from the lake and the RV, and some without pictures. I would hope we got a couple of followers out of our efforts, although what do I know? It's still only been a few hours.

Gabe nods and swipes through his apps. "Okay. Got the numbers. What do you think we got so far?" He draws in his legs and scoots a tad away from Cris as he crosses them on the soft couch.

"Huh. Tough to say. I mean, I have about thirty followers on either platform, but I know I don't count." Not with my lack of engagement on either social media. "That being said, I would hope we'd see a couple of thousand followers. We're somewhat high-profile, right? Maybe that's reaching high, but we're on four different platforms with all kinds of up-to-date hashtags, and given the hype about Cris' story—"

"—and that Duncan also used our hashtags and linked to us," Gabe adds.

"Yes, given that, I would hope we have at least… ten-k followers?" I cross my fingers and squeeze my eyes shut. "Tell me it's working. Tell me it's working!"

Gabe chuckles. "Relax, Nya. Take a deep breath. Don't pop an artery. The numbers look good."

I blow out a puff of air. "Phew. Okay. And that means what, exactly?"

"It means that this mutant here," he smacks Cris over the back of his head, lightly, "is now known to a hundred thousand people on X, eighty-nine-K on Insta, eighty-seven on Facebook, and a whopping hundred and freakin' twenty-K on TeenVoice. You asked, I deliver. You're welcome."

"A hundred and—" I snap my mouth shut. That's… whoa. "Does that qualify as going viral?"

"Considering we got millions of views? Yup. A hundred and twenty K, and counting." Gabe gives me a thumbs up.

I snap my gaze at him. "Have you read the comments?" Because followers mean nothing. If we're followed by a hundred and twenty thousand trolls and haters, it won't do us any good.

"Not all of them, obvs. I would say the majority is positive toward Cris, but skeptical toward the genetic modifications. Many are appalled by what Advangen has done, but that counts for both sides, the ones who are still pro-Cris, and the ones who aren't. Like, there are obviously haters and preachers out there. They're the most vocal about his mutations."

"Boo," mumbles Cris, then furrows his brows as he snaps his gaze toward the windows. "Huh." He shakes his head in dismissal, then sighs. "But I'll take the outrage either way, because they're right. Can't say I enjoy being designed as an unlimited source for stem cells and without the option of living my life."

"Or possibly being left with a mutation that gives you seizures," I add. Luckily, he has had none in the last hours, but according to him, there's no method to the madness. Sometimes they come in close order, sometimes spaced out over days. Let's hope for the latter.

A whistle blows outside, a faint sound amidst some other noise, like a few yells, I think. Like Cris, I furrow my brows and look toward the floor-to-ceiling windows.

Gabe opens both palms to the ceiling. "Okay, what is it? Are you two hearing something I'm not? Those glances make me nervous. And I feel like I'm missing something."

"Possible," Cris says and slides off the couch. "There's some weird noise." With three large strides, he's at the terrace door and opens it. As soon as he does, the noises crank it up and Gabe's eyes widen.

"Oh. Whistles and yells? What the…?" Like me, he jumps up and follows Cris outside.

It only takes us a few seconds to cross the three meters to the belly-high concrete wall at the end, the wooden floorboards warm under our feet. At this point I have a sinking feeling in my stomach, because that noise… it reminds me of things I've seen on TV.

The first to look down, Gabe jerks back, then leans forward again. "Holy shit!"

"What?" Cris is as fast as me catching up with Gabe. We lean forward—

—and all air punches out of my lungs. Down there, on the

ground, the parking lot in front of WissenSCHAFFT, hundreds of people crowd the area, many of them holding up signs, many others blowing into whistles, yet others yelling or screaming words I can't all understand.

The ones I can, I wish I didn't.

Lock him up! Kill the mutant! Abomination! Devil! Lock him up! Monster!

A pretty big group close to the building chants the same words over and over. *"No right to live! No right to live! No right to—"*

A few signs seem to be nicer, like *Science FTW* or *genetic research cures cancer.* Some others are plain weird, like the bright yellow one I can barely read: *Welcome, new species.* It's a lot. A *lot.*

"Holy shit," Gabe whispers, the words barely audible over the cacophony below us. "That's… unexpected. I can barely see the news vans anymore."

He's right. The vans are more or less swallowed by the crowd. If it weren't for their antennas and our height advantage, I wouldn't see them.

Cris stares down at the masses below us, mouth slightly agape, blinking. The apple in his throat moves up and down as he slowly shakes his head in slow motion. "They—"

Yells get louder as the parts of the crowd move forward, toward the building, and point up. *"There! There he is!"*

"Monster!"

"Lock him up! Lock him up!"

"No right to live! No right to live!"

The people who spotted us point up, and within seconds everybody is looking at us, pointing at us, yelling at us. The calls morph into one blanket of unintelligible screams and yells, deafening and scary.

A loud bang pieces the chaos, followed by a cracking sound

behind us. What the—

Somebody screams down there, differently, with a bit of panic, then others join—

Another: *BANG! Crack!*

Gabe's eyes pop open wide. "Holy shit!" He grabs me by the arm, Cris too, and yanks us back. "Down! Get inside! Go, go, *go*, dammit!"

"What—" Cris stumbles back, barely catching himself before falling.

Then, it clicks for me. Adrenaline shoots through my bloodstream because I get it. Oh, I get it. "They're shooting at us! Run!" I grab Cris and yank on him, as Gabe lets go of our sleeves and whips out his phone from his pocket.

"Cris, Nya, inside," he yells as he presses the record button and drops low, crouching behind the wall but holding his hand with the phone up, camera pointing down.

BANG! Crack!

Plaster flies from the bullet's impact into the wall somewhere behind us. I scream out and pull Cris down. "Go! Go, go!" I shove him forward, then reach back to grab Gabe. All I get is the sleeve of his shirt, but I don't care. I ball up the fabric in my hand and pull with all my might. "Gabe!"

He grunts as he falls on his butt, bracing his fall with one hand, while keeping the phone up and aimed toward the parking lot. "Geez, Nya, I'm recording—"

"Who the fuck cares? They're shooting at us and that wall is plaster, you idiot! Move!"

I yank again, as another *BANG! Crack!* thunders through the air, this one hitting the wall close to the terrace doors.

"Shit!" Cris yells and leaps inside like a frog, and maybe it's the terror in his voice, maybe the bullet's impact closer than before, maybe the panicked screams in the parking lot, or maybe me pulling like crazy, but something akin to understanding lights up in Gabe's eyes. He tugs his phone in and scrambles on all fours, following me on my mad crawling dash to safety.

We make it through the opening at the same time, falling all over each other, Gabe on his side, me like a weighted blanket on top of him. Cris rams the door shut behind us and drops to the floor again, hands above his head, protecting himself. Not that it'd help much against a bullet, but reflex is reflex.

Cut off from the masses' noise, silence hovers, only interrupted by our heavy breathing. They *shot* at us. They freakin' *shot* at us! And instead of getting to safety, Gabe took out his phone? What the absolute—

I hit his shoulder with my fist. "What is wrong with you, idiot?"

He twitches. "Hey—"

"You could've gotten shot!" I hit him again, this time with more feeling.

"I—"

"They could've freakin' killed you!" *Punch, punch.* They could've *shot* him! He could be lying there right now, bleeding to death! "Do you think you're invincible or something? What. The. Heck. Is. Wrong. With. You?" I emphasize every word with another hammer fist to his shoulder or back.

Gabe brings up his arms, covering. "Nya—! Nya, I—" My fist shuts up whatever he wanted to say.

He grunts and rolls himself onto his back, grabbing on to both my wrists. "Nya! Stop! Please stop! Nothing happened!"

I struggle against his hold. "You could've been shot! You can't bank on nothing happening! This isn't a movie where the heroes always survive! You could've been killed!" I twist my body to loosen his grip— And freeze.

Yes, I was lying sprawled over his side when we burst through the door.

Yes, he turned onto his back when I punched him.

No, I didn't realize that meant we were belly to belly with that move.

Until now, that is.

Awareness creeps in, of our flush bodies, connected in all the interesting places, of his hands around my wrists, their hold strong, but gentle. Of his gaze on me, wide, lips slightly parted.

For a moment, time could've stopped. There's only the feeling of Gabe's body under mine, his chest lifting and falling with each breath, his heart hammering so hard I feel it all the way in my chest. His scent, the typical Gabe-scent I've known since we were little, invades my senses and wraps itself around my limbic system. The green specks in his gray eyes seem to glow from the inside, his gaze intense and mesmerizing.

"Nya," he whispers, and brushes his right thumb across my wrist.

Holy cow.

Sparks fly, traveling up my arm all the way to my core, all from this little touch. A gasp parts my lips, one I couldn't have held in, even if I wanted to. The world narrows down to only him and me. Nothing else exists. My heart skips a beat, unsure whether to stop or gallop at a racing pace.

Gabe draws his thumb across my wrist again, slower this time, even more gentle. He swallows hard, then lifts his head off the ground ever so slowly, gaze dropping to my mouth.

I would have ample time to move away, yet I don't. I stay right where I am, body taut with anticipation and—

The door to our suite bursts open.

"Are you okay?" Johanna storms into the room, and Gabe and I vault apart like repelling magnets. I scramble back, sorting my limbs in some sort of crab walk, while Gabe scoots up and back until he hits the side of a chair.

Cris looks from one of us to the other, mouth agape, then to Johanna. "Yeah. I guess so. More or less, at least."

Johanna blows out a harsh burst of air. "Jesus. That aged me by about ten years." She waves a hand over her shoulder. "Check the windows, check the walls. We should be fine, but I won't take any risks."

Three security guards enter the room from behind her. "Yes, ma'am," one of them says as they stride in with wide steps, all business, checking the wall facing the parking lot and the windows.

"Everything's holding, as expected," the same guard says after about half a minute. "That stuff is tough."

"And worth every penny," Johanna says. "Thank you. Please monitor the situation on the ground and let me know if the police need to speak to me."

"Will do."

All three men leave the suite, closing the door behind them.

Johanna waves her hands. "You can get up. The entire wall is bullet proof, glass and all."

"It is?" My voice cracks, which I blame completely on my temporary lapse in sanity when it comes to Gabe. What was I thinking? Or was I even thinking?

"It is. Most of the building is. Believe it or not, but research isn't always peaceful. Apart from espionage, we've been the target of political splinter groups before. Sometimes people are afraid of what they don't understand, and I prefer to protect my people rather than wipe their blood off the floor." She shrugs, like it wasn't a major big deal that WissenSCHAFFT's building had to be a freakin' fortress for the safety of their employees.

Gabe is the first to get his legs under him. He all but jumps up, straightening his shirt and working one hand through his blonde mane. "That's good to know. Scary, but reassuring. And the police have been called?"

"Even before the first shot was fired. Oppositional opinions in crowds like this tend to have an explosive potential here in the States."

"True, unfortunately," Gabe says, "and if they need more evidence, I took a video." He holds up the phone.

Johanna blinks slowly. "You took a video?"

"Well, I thought we might need evidence—"

"Johanna, is the terrace wall also bullet proof?" I raise my eyebrow at her.

She shakes her head. "No. Only the walls and windows."

"Uh-huh," I say, leveling Gabe with a glance.

Gabe drops the phone onto the table with shaking hands. "I got it, okay? It wasn't the best idea, but I figured it might help us…" He blows out a puff of air. "But yes, you're right. I behaved stupidly."

Our gazes connect, and for a moment that same flutter from before is there, the one that makes me feel like my insides lighten.

"Stop being stupid, Gabe," I whisper, watching his face light up with an easy smile.

"I can't promise anything, as I've been known to act like an idiot here and there, but I'll try."

"Cool." I drop my gaze and suck in my lower lip. That was… intense.

Johanna clears her throat. "I know it's a lot, and I'm sorry, but I'm going to pile on even more." She holds up an iPad. "The lab results are in."

CHAPTER TWENTY-ONE

*T*he lab results are in.

That shuts us right up and plops our butts into the couch, Gabe on the right, Cris the left, me the middle, all of us facing Johanna like we were school kids called in to the principal's office.

Cris leans forward, forearms on his knees, then lets himself fall back into the cushions, rubbing his palms over his thighs. "Okay. Tell me. How bad is it?"

Johanna shakes her head. "Not bad at all, from my point of view. After running the sequencing scan on your genes and having a cursory look at your genome, I've got to say Advangen did well."

Cris grimaces. "Thank you, I guess."

Johana's face falls. "Don't thank me too early, because while they did well, they also did this work almost twenty years ago, when CRISPR was in its infancy, and with it, our knowledge about it."

My heart skips a beat. That doesn't sound good. Johanna is right. Twenty years ago, we had barely figured things out, and *barely figuring things out* and *genetic engineering* don't fit well together into one sentence.

Cris harrumphs. "Okay. You're saying I'm a lemon, cool, I get that, but I'd rather see myself as a contribution to groundbreaking science. Matter of perspective."

"Good point." Johanna takes a sip of water from one of the bottles draped in a basket on the coffee table. "And no, you're not a lemon. You're a marvelous creation."

"My ego likes to hear that." Cris chuckles, and for the first time in the last minutes since we were freakin' shot at his voice sounds somewhat light.

I pat his knee, impatient. "While I like every chance to help your ego out, let's talk numbers and get to the point. Johanna, how much is he a Neanderthal? Does Advangen have a case?" Because that's what this really is about. How can we spin the story? Is Cris a Neanderthal-Neanderthal, or does he happen to only have a few more Neanderthal genes than most humans carry anywhere? Or is his mutation rate at least similar to us plain humans? The devil lies in the detail for sure.

Setting the bottle back onto the table, Johanna nods. "Numbers, yes. Let me put it this way. For him to be a full Neanderthal, they would have had to alter about 30k genes. They didn't. They altered about 300, which is a lot, let me tell you, but still only 0.01% of his genome. And here's the good news for your strategy: every time human DNA is passed on to the next generation, it accumulates hundred to two-hundred new mutations."

"Hundred to two-hundred versus three hundred," I whisper, the weight of a boulder falling off my shoulders. "We can work with that, right? That's good news!"

Gabe reaches past my back to clap Cris' shoulder. "Guess I should cancel that order for those Neanderthal FTW-shirts I placed, huh? You don't even count as a Neanderthal."

Cris huffs dry. "I wish Advangen had seen it the same way.

Apparently, those three hundred genes still gave them what they wanted." Leaning forward, he picks up a water bottle and presses it against his forehead. "And I know I'm new to living with a whole real world out there, but something tells me those people, like the ones in the parking lot, won't care whether it's three hundred or three thousand genes. I'm still going to be the mutant."

Anger shoots through my veins, not at Cris, but at those idiots down there and all those trolls on the web who disillusioned Cris within two freaking days of him realizing there was a society beyond the walls of his prison. "Maybe. But we don't care about them. At all, you hear me? Our job is to convince a judge you're no different from Gabe or me, and that you belong to nobody else but yourself. That human rights apply to you, and with them, the freedom to live your life. And for that, we now have the ammo. This is good news, okay?" I smack him lightly over the back of the head, a total Gabe-move, but hey, when he does it, it works.

And it does for me, too. Cris grins and swats at my hand. "Okay, okay. Yes, I got it. Can't fault me, though, for freaking out a bit here and there."

"Won't. But I reserve the right to smack some sense into you when you do." I lift my hand and swing it in a smacking motion. Once we have a quiet moment—good one—I'll have to look into human rights and definitions. Or have Duncan's lawyer do that. Point is, somebody has to.

Johanna lifts a finger. "Not to rain on your parade, but there's one more thing you'll have to take into consideration when dealing with the general public."

I narrow my eyes. "What are we missing?" How much worse can it get, really?"

"Not saying you're missing it, just saying that you're not considering all aspects of the mutation." She points her thumb over her shoulder toward the parking lot. "What do you think will happen when the public understands that all changes to his genome are permanent and are passed on to his children? You procreate with a human—since we're, uh, somewhat short on Neanderthals—pass your genes on, and boom, suddenly we have new genes entering the pool, which could be beneficial, for example, considering your immunity, could be bad—"

"Considering my seizures," Chris whispers.

"Yes. That's why pre-natal experimenting in genetic engineering is so tricky. If I have a sick adult and I'm trying to repair their issue, it's different. They understand the risks, they might not have other options, and they can consent. You couldn't, and your risks are far more reaching. I'm still very much surprised Advangen threw all ethics out the window, considering the potential consequences."

I huff. "Are you really? I mean, we're talking about an organization that held Cris captive and violated him for years. I, unfortunately, can't say I'm surprised they thought about their own gain and not about potential consequences." That sentence brings a little sting to my heart. What I said, I basically said about Dad, and that's so not him. At least that's what I thought, but alas, you live, you learn.

Cris clears his throat. "Since you mentioned consequences, do the genes at least show why I have seizures?"

"And can we fix it?" Gabe adds.

Turning her iPad over, Johanna points at the karyogram on the screen, the twenty-three pairs of chromosomes neatly lined up, some with little red circles marking specific areas. "I'm not one hundred percent sure yet. This gene here"—she points to chromosome twenty—"is a Neanderthal-gene in a sensitive location. It might—might—be responsible for your seizures, but

I'm still waiting for the neurologist and some more results."

She turns the iPad over for her to see the screen. For a moment, she lets her gaze drift over the image on the screen before she shrugs one shoulder and sighs. "You know, I shouldn't be as impressed with Advangen as I am. I should be more shocked at what they did, but considering what little information they were working with… They did really well overall, or else you, as a boy, wouldn't even have been born."

I exchange a look with Gabe, knowing his train of thought mirrors my own: Who knows how many attempts at success came before Cris? Every single one being one too many, of course.

Cris picks up on another part of what Johanna said. "What does being a boy have to do with why they did or didn't do well?"

Johanna makes a gesture in front of her stomach, as if she was pregnant. "There was a study in the American Journal of Human Genetics once that suggested humans wouldn't have been able to carry a male half-Neanderthal fetus to term, since some of their genes found on the Y-chromosome trigger an immune response in humans, meaning they'd be triggering a miscarriage."

Scrunching up his face, Cris rubs a finger over his temple. "And meaning, I shouldn't have been born, but miscarried?"

"Meaning, it looks like the very modifications they applied to your genome helped to avoid rejection by the maternal immune system and therefore miscarriage of the fetus, i.e., you. As I said, they did well. I am reluctantly impressed." She drops her gaze to her iPad, her fingers fidgeting with a part of its case. "But… I need to talk to you about something else. It's… personal." She looks me straight in the eye, yet it takes me two or three seconds before it clicks.

"Me?" I point at myself.

"Yes. The results from your blood work came back as well."

I shrug. "Go ahead. It's fine." How personal can it be? It's not like I've a risk of STIs, since no exposure means negative results by default. And what else could there be? I don't mind the guys hearing I'm borderline anemic or that my cholesterol is high—a total possibility, given my body type, by the way. I don't consider that sensitive personal information, au contraire to doctors. For them, everything is personal, even when it's no biggie.

Johanna gives me a long look, so long, I wonder what I'm missing. Eventually she sighs and unlocks her iPad. "Okay. Remember this picture and the ultrasound?" She opens the photos app and first shows us the two sets of chromosomes with certain areas encircled, then the ultrasound picture I copied from Dad's desk and Johanna photographed off me when we first arrived.

"Yeah, of course." I narrow my eyes. Not where I expected the conversation to go. "What does it have to do with my blood work, and what's wrong with the picture?"

"Nothing is wrong with it, just with your guys' read. It's a typical error. This here"—she points to the small, yet defining body part between the baby's legs—"is not a penis. It's part of the umbilical cord."

Oh.

"Oops," Gabe and I say simultaneously, then both smile, and dang him if it didn't light up his face. Dang me if it didn't release some butterflies inside my stomach that have absolutely no business in fluttering around. None. And maybe that little high Gabe's smile brought me is responsible for me being slow on the uptake.

"So wait, if that's the cord, then this isn't a boy. This isn't Cris."

Johanna shakes her head and looks at me like somebody kicked her puppy. "No, Nya, it's a girl, and I would assume the female genome in this other image is hers."

Gabe stiffens and sucks in a harsh breath, and yeah, agreed. That's a biggie. It's a big biggie, because that means Gabe and I were right and we're missing something—or rather, somebody. "If that isn't Cris, we have to look more into Advangen's history. If there were others—"

Without a word, Gabe takes my hand and weaves his fingers through mine. I throw a confused glance at him, but he's not even looking at me. Sitting ramrod straight, he's staring at that ultrasound picture, jaw so tight, I'm worried he might crack a molar.

I pull on my hand, but he keeps it locked with his. O-kay… Whatever. Apparently, we're doing this. I shake my head to focus. "Anyway. I was thinking, we might need to check then what happened to the embryos before Cris—"

"Not before. After." Johanna smiles at me, but the smile doesn't look quite right. "I know this handwriting. It's your mom's." She's looking at me, like she just gave me a huge chunk of information and was waiting for me to do the math, but what math is there to do?

Gabe squeezes the living daylights out of my hand, and the way he exhales, with a gasp he tries to suppress— I whip my head around to look at him. He's pale, and even Cris stares at me like he'd seen a ghost. I wrinkle my forehead. "What? What am I miss—"

And then it clicks.

It clicks with a deafening clap of thunder.

Gabe looking at me with that *expression on his face: red hair. Freckles.*

My mom's handwriting.

It's a girl

Our little CRISPR.

Right idea, wrong person.

"It's not Cris," I whisper. "That's me." *I'm* their CRISPR. That baby in the ultrasound, it's *me.* Blood swooshes in my ears. The air doesn't seem to hold any oxygen, no matter how much of it I suck in. Dizzy. I think I'm dizzy. And I'm probably wrong. Right? I'm wrong. Wrong conclusion, because it's ridiculous to think that I—

Johanna nods, and my world crumbles down. "It's you. Your genome is mutated. Like Cris, you are part Neanderthal, Nya."

"No," I whisper. "No. That can't be, I—" I don't know what to say. "There must be an error—"

Johanna's voice is soft when she answers, full of empathy. "There's no mistake, Nya. We re-ran the sequence just to make sure."

I close my eyes and let her words sink in. As a scientist, I understand them. As a human being—crap, as a *half*-human being, I'm having a hard time processing them.

I'm part Neanderthal.

A mutant, like Cris.

An *abomination.*

But… but it doesn't make any sense. "Why… Why would my dad modify my genome?"

Johanna gives me a soft, sad smile. "I can't answer that, Nya. I can only tell you that the results are unequivocal. And… well, I can also tell you that you seem to have one hundred more mutated genes than Cris."

"A hundred more?" Gabe leans forward, never letting go of my hand in his. "Jesus, that's—" He lets himself fall back into the couch and rakes his other hand through his hair. "Irresponsible."

"Yeah," I whisper, my heart fluttering more than beating. Irresponsible. I didn't know. I didn't even have a suspicion something could've been off with me. How can I have lived my life so blissfully unaware of such a ginormous fact about myself? Shouldn't I have known I was born part Neanderthal?

I jerk when the next gears click into place. "Oh God," I moan. "Oh, God." Pulling my hand from Gabe's, I lean forward and drop my head between my legs, folding my hands on top of it. Air. I need air. Can't breathe. Can't—

"Nya. Hey." Gabe rubs his palm over my back. "It's not that bad. It's still only twice the rate of normal mutation. And you're doing well. It—"

"That's not it." My last word ends in a wheeze. "My mom… When I was born—" Gosh, I never had problems saying those words. After all, it wasn't my fault. Still isn't. But…

Gabe keeps on rubbing my back. "Your mom died when you were born. I know."

I nod, then release my clamped hands from behind my hand and sit up. Worry fills Gabe's face. "She died because my enormous head got stuck in the birth canal, Gabe."

"I know. But— Oh." His eyes widen. "Larger heads. A Neanderthal trait."

Blinking several times to keep the tears at bay, I nod. "I'm sane enough to know it still wasn't my fault, but I know whose fault it was."

"Your dad's," Gabe whispers. "Because you're saying he modified your genes."

"Yeah. Dad modified my genes, and Mom paid the price." All that misery—why? Dad loved Mom with all his heart. It's obvious in the way he suffers without her. Her death threw his life in disarray, and mine by proxy, too. There's always been this disconnect between us, even before I went into science against his wishes. I always thought it was because I lived while Mom died. That he blamed me for it. But maybe I was wrong, maybe… maybe he blamed himself.

"Hey, Nya?" Johanna taps the iPad and opens the picture of the ultrasound again. "That's your mom's handwriting. I'm not presuming I know what happened, but I can tell you she was in on it. She knew what he was doing. And I remember she was beyond excited to be pregnant with you."

Only she died before she could even hold me in her arms. I swallow hard, then snap my gaze to Cris when the next gears grind into place. "You said you don't know who your parents are, right?"

His brows pull down into a V and then jump up his forehead. "Yes, I said that. Are you thinking that you and I…?"

That's exactly what I'm thinking. "Are we? Johanna?"

Johanna tilts her head. "Are you asking if you guys are… siblings?"

"Yeah," Cris and I say in unison. It would make sense: Both genetically engineered by the same person, within the same-ish time frame. For Heaven's sake, Gabe called it, he has freckles, just like me! My hands shake, so I slide them under my thighs.

Not even checking her iPad, Johanna shakes her head. "You're not siblings. You both have different parents."

An odd feeling snakes around my insides, one I can't quite interpret. It's not relief, although that's part of it. Some sadness, because even within this short time, I feel connected to Cris in a way I'm not accustomed to, and differently so than with Gabe, or others. But maybe that's from the Neanderthal genes calling to each other.

A knock at the door draws us to attention a half-second before one of the security guards opens it and steps through. "Boss? Two things. One, I have the police in the lobby regarding the shooters. They're asking to speak to you."

Nodding, Johanna gets out of the chair. "On my way. Radio Doug downstairs, I don't want them anywhere besides the lobby and conference room on the ground floor. To come up here, they'd need a warrant." She throws a glance at Cris—and me.

Oh. Right.

Because most likely I'm now also Advangen's property. The shaking of my hands increases, no matter I'm sitting on them. The floor has vanished under my feet, and the couch, too. Feels like I'm floating in a sea of panic, complete with waves of anxiety, and without a life vest.

"Two, the neurologist you requested is here. Waiting in Conference Room three." The guard nods his chin to the left and down.

"Faster than expected, good." Johanna turns toward Cris. "Do you mind coming with me? Dr. Lionsmane can have a look at you and see what we can do to control the seizures."

Cris all but jumps off the couch. "Oh heck, yeah. Tell me where to go and I'll be there."

Chuckling, Johanna points at the guard. "Just go with Rey. He'll get you there and back. And you two, please stay up here. I'll keep you informed of what's going on, but I feel it's best if everybody stayed out of sight as much as possible."

"We will," Gabe says. I hear him swallow hard.

"Thank you." With one last concerned smile at us, Johanna follows Cris and the guard, then closes the suite's door behind her.

For a moment, silence hovers.

"Nya?" Gabe gently rocks into me. "Hey."

"Hey," I whisper back.

"How ya doing?"

"I dunno." My voice gives out on the last syllable. "Feels a bit like I've been hit by a steam train."

Gabe sighs and lays an arm around my shoulders. "Fair to say the last days didn't go as we expected them."

I huff. "You think? I still can't wrap my head around any of it."

"You've had like five minutes, so I'm not surprised," he deadpans.

"But you called it. You knew." And I didn't want to hear it. No, not true. I didn't even consider it. Dad altering my genome was so in the realm of that-doesn't-happen-to-me I couldn't even see the signs. And I consider myself a scientist. Disgraceful.

"I didn't know. But I guess some things are easier to see—or to suspect—from the outside."

No kidding. I lower my gaze to the ground. "Yeah, right? And so many small things make more sense now. Like, why I'm sometimes so aggressive. My fourteen and a—"

"Fifteen," he whispers, giving me a small smile and wink.

I swallow hard. "My fifteen freckles. Or why I never got sick."

Gabe grunts. "Right. Same as Cris. Better immunity."

"Makes me feel special in a whole new way, believe me. Makes sense now, too, why Dad took care of most of my health needs—" I groan.

"What?" Gabe looks alert. "What is it?"

"Nothing." I sigh. "I'm just thinking Cris and I are both genetically altered, and guess what? Cris has seizures." I give him a pointed glance.

"Yeah, that doesn't mean you're going to get them. We don't even know what's causing them. People get seizures for all kinds of reasons."

And it's also something I can't worry about now. Only one

major revelation at a time, please. I've been healthy all my life, so let's hope that continues. I take a long, slow breath in. "Okay. But what I wanted to say before I started doomsday-thinking is that Dad didn't only take care of my health because he's a protective dad who knows best, but because he didn't want anybody to become suspicious." Guess when you have a secret bigger than the Eiffel Tower, you become a wee bit paranoid.

"Or why he didn't want you in science, especially at Advangen."

I look up at him. "Not just because I could've found Cris?"

"No, because you could've sequenced your own genome at one point. And you would've found out his-slash-your secret." Gabe brushes his thumb over my shoulder, and only now I notice now how close we are. How his side is pressed into mine, and how he brings a whole motherlode of Gabe-scent.

Warmth blasts my cheeks.

"Look," he says, keeping up that maddening brush of his thumb, "I can't say I understand what's been going through your dad's mind. At all. I've always respected him as a man and scientist, so I'm willing to cut him some slack, but—"

"I don't know if I am." The moment I say those words, I know they're true. We're talking about my dad, the only family I've left, but I'm still not sure if I can forgive him, or even move on from this betrayal. It cuts deep, so deep, it severs a heart string or two.

And damn if that realization didn't tear down the last barrier I barely kept up around my heart and soul.

Tears rush to my eyes, too fast for me to blink away. I turn my head away from Gabe when the first one falls, but too late.

He stops the movement of his thumb and holds his breath for a second. Then he exhales and tugs on my shoulder. "Come here." Drawing his left leg up onto the cushion, he scoots back until he hits the arm rest of the couch, all but dragging me with him.

"Gabe—"

"Shut it, Nya." He says it in a gentle, soothing tone, while pulling me into his chest. "Come on." He nudges my legs with his until I swing them up and stretch them out onto the couch next to his.

"Better," he says, reaching for my head and guiding it toward his chest.

Old Me would've thrown a fit. She would've hammer fisted him in the face, or at least punched him in the groin for even daring to come so close. But this New Me... She remembers how we used to be. She sees so much of that old Gabe in this one right here and now, and she... she just doesn't want to fight anymore.

With a choked-off sigh, I nestle myself against his chest, on my side, my ear pressed against his left pec. Gabe wraps both arms around me and lowers his chin onto the top of my head. His left leg is sandwiched between the couch's backrest and my body and he brings his right one up and drapes it over my curled up ones. There wouldn't be room to fit a sheet of paper between our two bodies. I feel every breath he takes, every beat of his heart, as if they were my own. The analytical part of my brain notices how fast his heart beats, way too fast for a normal resting heart rate, but it doesn't really register. Too much of Gabe is invading my senses, adding to the emotional overload of the last few days, and especially the last few minutes.

"I got you. You know that, right? I got you," he whispers and... and kisses the top of my head.

As if a bomb had struck and shattered my defenses, the last bit of my thinning restraint crumbles. I dig my fingers into his shirt and all myself closer, inhaling his Gabe-scent and willing it to make me feel like everything will be okay.

Gabe's next inhale stutters. He pulls me even closer, even tighter. "I got you. Always, Nya. *Always*."

And then, I cry.

CHAPTER TWENTY-TWO

Cris comes back about an hour later, and not in a good mood.

"What did the neurologist say?" Gabe asks and points to the chair across from the couch he and I occupy. After I calmed down, I untangled myself from Gabe, a move not nearly as awkward as I feared. He booped my nose and stuck out his tongue at me, then handed me a tissue. And he completely ignored how much I soaked his shirt.

I really appreciate that.

Anyway, since I recovered from my meltdown, we've been sitting on the couch like an old couple, our backs against the armrests, feet stretched out and meeting in the middle. And maybe the most remarkable thing about that is that we've tangled our legs together, like we used to.

Oh, and… that I'm loving it. Gabe grounds me and keeps me from going into that panicky space inside my mind, just by sitting here with me. He's on his phone, preparing posts and using some app to schedule them in advance, and I'm just reading a book on Kindle.

Considering the amount of crap that has happened today, I'm somewhat even-keeled. Surprisingly. Or rather, thanks to Gabe.

Cris blows a raspberry and lets himself fall into the chair. "Well. This gentleman says he can give me meds—"

"That's good, right? Help you control the seizures?"

"I guess." He shrugs and drapes his legs over the armrest. I don't think either of us have sat in that chair in the way it was intended to. Oh, well.

"Then why the long face?"

"I don't know. I just felt like… like he was holding something back. By the way he looked at me, you know?"

Gabe narrows his eyes. "You mean because of your mutations? Like, he's discriminating against you?"

Cris waves his hand dismissively. "I dunno, okay? It was just a weird feeling, so never mind. It was probably nothing."

Chewing on his lower lip, Gabe nods. "Okay then."

"So, what's been happening here? What did I miss?"

Gabe's gaze flickers to mine, and I swear he blushes. "Nothing, really. I've, uh, been setting up some more content for our Project Humanize Cris, but uh, that's it."

"Right." Cris glances from Gabe to me and back. "Okay. So—"

A knock comes from the door.

"Come in," Gabe calls out, swinging his legs off the couch and turning to face the door.

The same security guard as before comes in, Rey. "Johanna wanted me to let you know that Dr. Bennison just arrived."

My stomach drops, yet still pushes bile up my throat. Dad. Dad is here. "That was fast," I croak out. Way too fast. I haven't even come up with a game plan. Haven't mentally prepared myself for what I may hear, or even for seeing him.

Gabe lays a hand on my lower leg. "But that doesn't mean you have to go to him right now. Let him wait." The heat of his skin seeps through my pants and infuses my body.

I shake my head. "No. If I wait, I'll either get furious—"

"Sounds appropriate," Cris mumbles under his breath.

"—or I'll chicken out. I'm going." Like Gabe, I swing my legs off the couch.

Rey opens the door wider. "I'll bring you down. Johanna has him waiting in the conference room."

"I'm coming with you." Gabe stands up. "No need to do that alone."

"Me, too." Cris pops out of the chair. "Haven't seen Steve in a while. It'll be like a family reunion."

That thought makes me laugh. "A very dysfunctional family reunion."

Cris grins. "We're the Addams family of family reunions."

Rey guides us down the hallway to the elevators, then to the third floor and down another hallway. At the very end, he halts in front of a door labeled Conference 03.

"Johanna is in there already, and so is Dr. Bennison." He nods at us, then turns crisply and leaves us alone.

I shake out my arms and crank my neck. "Show time." Yes, I'm going to walk in there and own that room. No, I won't let all these stupid emotions affect me, at least not so that Dad realizes how he hurt me. Yes, I'll talk to him like an adult, matter-of-factly, and see what info he can give me.

Easy-peasy.

Reaching out for the door, I ignore the slight shake to my hands. Nerves. Without knocking, I open it and enter.

The first person I see is Dad, sitting at a large, black, oval conference table with at least ten chairs around it. He whips his head toward the door the moment it opens, and when he recognizes me, a myriad of emotions skates across his face, all gone too fast for me to identify.

He pushes the chair back with his legs and stands up, the chair rolling away from him. "Nya," he says, not at all in his usual Dad-voice. It's missing the confidence, the authority, and if I'm not mistaken, there's a shake to it.

I step to the side to make room for—

"Cris." This time I'm positive Dad's voice is shaking. And since I'm giving him the nth degree with my glare at him, I notice how his face loses color.

No change when Gabe comes in.

"And Gabe." Dad swallows audibly. "You're all here."

I cross my arms in front of my chest. "What did you expect? We had to find safety somewhere after we almost got pushed off the road."

"And shot at," Gabe adds.

Dad flinches. "You were intruding on our property and breaking and entering. I didn't know Dr. Sherman was going to—"

That excuse doesn't count. "Welcome to the club, Dad. There are a lot of things I didn't know that I do know now." I strut toward the right side of the table, away from Dad and closer to Johanna. Gabe and Cris follow me and take a seat to my side, as always, Gabe on the right, Cris on the left. It gives me an immense sense of belonging to know that this is what we do. This is us. The dysfunctional Addams family functioning.

I glare at him, my arms crossed in front of my chest. "And I meant that, by the way, Dad. I *really* know."

Dad's chest freezes mid-inhale. "Know what?"

With maturity beyond what I expect of myself, I hold back my snarky response, push down the anger rising and threatening to break free. Instead, I keep my voice even. "You gave me Neanderthal genes."

Whatever color was left in his cheeks, vanishes in an instant. "I did." Dad's voice is hoarse. "This is not how I wanted you to find out. I should've told you earlier, but… But it's a difficult topic to start."

I smack one palm onto the table. "No shit, Sherlock! I'm mad, Dad! About so many things, the list is too long to go over! But what I'm most mad about are two biggies: One, obviously, Cris. And we'll get to him in a second. Two, me: How could you do that to me? You made me a non-human! You had no idea what the changes would modify! And how did you want to play it when I got older? Tell me I have a rare genetic disease and I shouldn't have kids? Hope I don't get my genome tested anywhere else? I can't even!" I ball my hands into fists under the table. I'm so, so mad. Gone is the shock, the sadness I first felt, all replaced by hot, burning anger.

Dad exhales slowly through purses lips. "It's complicated."

"Well, try me. I'm here all day. And the night. And potentially longer."

He flinches, then flattens his palm onto the table, as if he needed to ground himself. "What you said, that I didn't know what I was doing, that's wrong. I knew what would work and what wouldn't."

"A magic eight ball?" Gabe's voice drips with sarcasm.

"No. A trial-and-error-run." Dad lifts his gaze and looks straight at Cris.

"Oh," Cris says. "Me. Great."

"He was your… your trial-and-error run? What is wrong with you?" Disbelief floods me. A trial-and-error-run? What in the name…!

Lowering his gaze back to his hand, Dad shakes his head. "Cris isn't *my* trial-and-error run. He's Brian's."

"Dr. Sherman's?" I shouldn't sound surprised, but for the last days I've so gotten used to seeing Dad as the bad guy I had completely forgotten it's Sherman's company and Sherman's basement where Cris was kept.

"I'm not saying that to give myself absolution, not at all. I'm not proud of what I've done. Believe me when I say I never intended for anything to go as far as it did. I…" He inhales sharply and holds his breath for a second, before releasing it in one burst. "I made an error in judgement twenty years ago, and one step led to another. And here we are."

"You'll have to be a bit more detailed than that, Dad." As in, a lot.

A muscle in his jaw thrums. "I know. I know. When I was just beginning at Advangen, we were already cutting edge in genetic research. We worked with CRISPR before it became mainstream, not long after it was discovered in E. Coli. One day we had excess human embryos—and yes, I know how that sounds, but they were barely zygotes, heaps of a few cells. They'd been left over from a cancer research we did and were supposed to be destroyed."

I know where this is going. "But they weren't."

He lowers his head even more. "No, they weren't. I didn't know that, or rather, I didn't know in the beginning. One day, though, Brian took me aside, after hours. Everybody else had left. I knew it was about something good when he lowered the blinds and locked the door to the lab. I just didn't expect it to be… well, a blastocyst with a genome modified with Neanderthal genes."

"On first try?" Johanna asks, and dad pales.

"No," he whispers. "The first thirty fertilized eggs didn't even reach a stage where they could've been transplanted into a womb."

Jesus. Exactly what I feared. I want to be shocked, but at this point I'm not. Just… horrified. "But there are regulations…" Lots of them. Especially when working with human tissue and human eggs or sperms, let alone embryos.

Johanna raises an eyebrow. "At that time, I don't think there were many regulations besides one's conscience. Nowadays, yes, germ line editing is outlawed in many countries. We simply don't know enough about the risks, although the risks we know about are plentiful."

Dad fidgets with his wedding band. "Hindsight is twenty-twenty. When Brian showed me what he had done, I had a choice. I could've reported what he did, but… I was young and fascinated. Implanting those genes using CRISPR wasn't just cutting edge, it was cutting edge of cutting edge. So, I jumped on the bandwagon, so to speak. I signed his NDA, beyond excited he trusted me with his research, that he wanted me to work on it with him."

For a moment, a small, wistful smile crosses his face. "I should've known better, but I was blinded by what success Brian had had already. Despite that, we never expected the cells to keep dividing and reaching a stage ready for transfer into a human womb. But once they did, we needed to see what happened next. We couldn't just stop there. So, we used a surrogate to carry the embryo, hopefully to term, but even if not, we were going to learn an unbelievable amount from its development."

Cris is so still next to me, I wonder if he's frozen in horror, just like I am.

"Did the surrogate know what—I'm sorry, Cris—whom she was carrying?" Johanna presses her lips into a thin line. Her cheeks are red, like two angry circles on each side of her face.

"No." Dad shakes his head. "She knew we were trying to fix a genetic illness—that's what our official research was for. And we really didn't expect the pregnancy to last more than a few days—you know how it is. Usually we implant several fertilized eggs and only one or two will take—but then it worked. Days turned into weeks, into months, and then into a full-term birth. And then you were there."

"Right. And because I was such a good lab baby, you turned me into your lab rat." Cris' voice is so low, I wonder how Dad can hear him. He sounds beaten. Hopeless.

"That wasn't the plan. In fact, we didn't have much of a plan. We always knew you weren't perfect, no offense. Parts of your genome were faulty. We… we never expected you to survive as long as you did."

"Ouch," Cris flinches.

"Oh my god," Gabe rasps. "What you did is wrong on so many levels. You designed a human being fully expecting him to *die*? I can't even unpack how cruel that is."

"I know," Dad simply says. "If I could go back in time, I'd make a different decision and keep Brian from tinkering with those Neanderthal genes. But, as always and as I said before, hindsight is twenty-twenty. And once you were there, Cris, things became complicated."

"Oh, complicated. Cry me a river." I give my dad the same look he gave me a million times when I messed something up or did something he didn't approve of.

Dad averts his eyes. "Suddenly, we had a child without parents, a genetically modified child. Who was, against all our expectations, thriving and growing despite some obvious health problems thanks to some unintended off-target alterations." He pauses and tilts his head. "Speaking of: How are you doing, Cris?"

"Still having seizures." Cris shrugs. "But you know that. Don't know if you couldn't fix them or didn't want to, but they're still there. Johanna got me a neurologist."

Dad's gaze flicks over to Johanna, worry in his gaze. Or maybe I read that wrong. "And—"

"Dad." I tap my fingers onto the table. Patience is a virtue I can't call mine today. "Please continue."

He gives Johanna one more look that could mean sorry, or TTYL, but at least he has the decency to carry on. "Yes. All right. As I said, we had prepared for an experiment, but we got a baby, a baby that needed care. Eventually, we set up the basement for you. Neither of us was willing to deal with the questions where you had come from, and again, it was supposed to be short term until you—"

"Until I died. Gotcha."

"But you didn't. And when you got older and asked questions… we had to come up with a cover story. You were too strong to fight every time we needed your cooperation, so… we invented reasons and a purpose for you, so you would be… content and adhering to what we needed you to do." At least Dad has the decency to look ashamed.

"A purpose," Chris huffs. "I was pushing buttons for nothing, reading fake memos to convince me I was safest where I was. My very own *Truman Show*."

Dad's response is barely a whisper. "It seemed… the least cruel thing to do."

They kept him from realizing he was a prisoner, and yes, it probably improved his cooperation—but he was still a prisoner. Worse, one operating under false assumptions.

"Oh, great, now we're talking grades of cruelty," I throw at Dad. "Almost merciful considering you didn't even freaking numb him for the marrow draws!"

"Of course we numbed him, we're not—" Dad snaps his mouth close when his gaze falls on Cris. The apple in his throat moves up and down. "What… what happened?" His voice sounds raspy.

Cris shrugs, as if it was no biggie. "Couple of months ago, I started fighting the draws, and I guess a quick shot with a taser and drilling into my bones without numbing is less of an effort."

"They—" Dad opens and closes his mouth, a fish out of water. "That can't— I never knew— Brian must've—"

Any other time I might feel pity for Dad. He looks genuinely shocked. But right now, in this very moment, I'm fresh out of pity—or other things—to give. "Add it to the list, Dad."

"What about the surrogate?" Johanna draws a pregnant belly with her hands.

"A woman from Romania, here on a tourist visa. Delivery happened at Advangen, off the records. She got paid well for her participation."

I grab a water bottle and wrap my fingers around it, squeezing. If I didn't do that, I might lose my temper. Even more, I mean. "What happened then?"

Dad lifts his head and looks at Cris, remorse shining in his eyes. "Then, as you were overcoming whatever obstacles we had unwillingly programmed into your genetic code, Brian wasn't happy with only observing you anymore. He saw you as his property, Cris. After all, he designed you with Advangen materials and Advangen money. At this point, we both still assumed you'd not get very old, that what we did would catch up with you, and Sherman wanted to get from you what he could before that happened."

Cris rubs his sternum. "Meaning, he wanted my stem cells."

"Yes."

My jaw drops. "And you let him? You knew what he was planning, and you let him *use* Cris?"

"I wished nothing more than to get Cris out of there, but my options were limited—"

"Limited? You could've gone against Sherman—"

"No, I couldn't."

"Of course you could've!" I throw my arms up. "Screw whatever NDA your signed! Legal problems versus throwing Cris to the wolves. That should be an easy decision to make! Cris was a baby! Sherman wants to abuse Cris, you tell him you go public!" I've paid attention, I know how that works. "Yes, you're going to take the fall with him, but Sherman had more to lose! He owned Advangen already! You could've done the right thing, Dad!"

Dad's gaze rests on mine, infuriatingly calm. "No, I could *not*."

Ugh! "Then please enlighten me, oh wise one, why you couldn't."

Closing his eyes, Dad swallows. "Because your mother was pregnant. With you."

I don't get it. "So what—" And then it clicks, and with it so much becomes clear all at once. Like my brain received a mega-information dump. "Sherman didn't know you modified my genes as well. He didn't know." And boy, does that explain a lot.

"He *doesn't* know." Dad whispers that sentence. "I went behind his back. He couldn't know. I saw how he was with Cris. He treated him like a thing. I was the one taking care of him many hours a day in that basement, me and a nanny. You took your first steps with me. Your first word was ball. I was there for all of it." A wistful smile crosses his face for the shortest moment, before it gets wiped right off his face again. "Brian's sole focus was on finding ways to utilize Cris' stem cells. How we could use the knowledge we could gain from his Neanderthal-heritage. If Brian knew what I had done, he wouldn't have hesitated to do the same to my baby. I needed to keep you away from him."

I blink rapidly. "That's why you were so mad when I got that internship? Because I'd be at Advangen, and right under Mr. Sherman's nose?" Wait—that's it? All that fuss over... over not meeting his boss? WTF?

"Yes. When I saw you standing there backstage with Brian, it was my worst nightmare coming true. There you were, about to join Advangen and risk everything I'd worked to protect, and yet I couldn't protest too much, or it would've piqued Brian's curiosity. The only saving grace was that you were in a good disguise and that Brian had planned his Europe trip already, therefore reducing the odds of you running into him at work."

I face-palm myself and engage my sarcastic mode. "Oh, right. I could've accidentally told him I was part-Neanderthal—oh wait, I didn't know! But then, maybe he could've read it off the tattoo on my forehead saying *Neanderthal-halfling*."

Dad closes his eyes and exhales slowly, as he does when trying to summon patience. "He would've taken one look at you and known, Nya."

"Bull shit!" I spit out the words. "Guess what? That tattoo I mentioned? I don't have it!"

Dad huffs out a harsh laugh. "No need for that, it's obvious."

Anger rises—no, actually, anger peaks. It's been there for a while. "That's such a bull—"

"I knew." Johanna's calm voice cuts through my anger like a warm knife through butter.

"You… knew?" I ask.

"Our field of genetics might differ from Advangen's, but I knew you had Neanderthal genes in you the moment I saw you." She holds my gaze, nodding at the words. "Just like with Cris."

"You— How?" I snap my mouth shut and tame my anger down. Nobody ever said anything. I went through life as me, Nya, a normal human with a touch of dorkism and nerdism, but not as part-Neanderthal!

She smiles and shrugs her left shoulder. "Let's put it this way:

I know your father is a genetic researcher. We were talking about a genetically modified human with Neanderthal-genes," she nods at Cris, "so I knew the moment you stepped out of that elevator. You have certain phenotypic features I would expect." Johanna gestures to her face, hair, and moves her hands in a way that suggests she's talking about my body type.

I blink again, as if that could help clear matters up. "It's that obvious?" I feel like somebody should've told me, should've said something. It's like I'd been talking to people with spinach between my teeth, yet nobody called me out on it.

Johanna nods. "It's that obvious if you know what you're looking for. You're built in a more… robust way. I bet you're strong, right?"

"Yeah," I whisper and nod. I'm not the slim and slender type, I know. And I've always been strong and in shape, especially considering I don't work out.

Johanna taps her nose. "Widened nasal bridge. Stronger brow area. The reddish tone of your hair. The freckles."

I close my eyes. When she lists all my tells like that it *screams* Neanderthal-genes. Only it had never clicked for me, because who would look at themselves in the mirror and think, *oh gee, I wonder if I have Neanderthal-genes in me?*

I swallow hard. But now I understand her reaction when Dad called her. "That's why you wanted me to meet with Dad." He made it sound like she knew more than we did—*you might understand the bigger picture here, unlike the children in your presence*—and she did. She had understood the moment she saw me. Oh, and coming to think about it and doing the math: I bet that's why we didn't stay in touch with Johanna—Mom's *best* friend—after her death. Maybe it was too painful for Dad, as he claimed, or maybe he just didn't want to risk her realizing what he'd done.

Actually, I'd bet on the latter.

Johanna nods. "I figured that's what he wanted to talk to you about. But it felt unfair to keep the lab results from you until he could tell you, and I didn't even know if he planned to. Steve, apologies for the direct question, but I take it Brian didn't know about yours and Jessica's carrier status?"

Carrier status? I shoot a questioning glance over at Gabe, but he's on his phone, scrolling through something with his lips set tight and his brows pulled into a V. No help there, so I tip my head at Johanna instead. "Carrier status?" As in *genetic carriers* for something?

Johanna points at Dad, who sighs, lips set tight. "Yes. Carrier status."

Oh. What else do I not know about our family? "Okay, could you please explain? Dad?" I make an impatient hand gesture. "This isn't pulling teeth."

Dad ignores my jibe. Guess we've moved past the point of adhering to parental goals. "Johanna, to answer your question, no, Brian didn't know about that. Despite being genetic researchers, we never talked about that. It was... private, between me and Jessica." He looks me in the eye. "Your mom and I both are carriers for a disease called SCID. It's an acronym for Severe Combined Immunodeficiency. There are many variants with many genetic mutations causing them, but the combination of our genes would've brought on a severe form in our offspring. No T-cells in your immune system to fight off viruses or bacteria. No B-cells to remember the infections your body went through and provide antibodies when exposed again. Your immune system would've been overwhelmed by a simple cold, and usually..." He sucks in and holds a breath before releasing it in one puff. "Usually, patients affected by this variation die within weeks after birth."

Silence hovers.

"Oh," I say again, but this time it comes out as a squeak.

Gabe turns off his phone. He looks pale as he glances from Johanna to Dad. "Isn't there… I mean, can't you treat it? Not that I'm an expert, but I think I read about stem cell transplants?"

Dad huffs. "We didn't consider it an option. The rate of success, of surviving the transplant and all the potentially deadly side effects and limitations on a patient's life *if* it succeeds… We didn't want that for our child. Not if we had other options we considered better."

Johanna lowers her chin in a small nod, as if she understood completely where Dad was coming from. "So, you decided to fix the genes instead and improve on what could be done with gene therapy at that time."

"Yes. When I saw what Brian had achieved with Cris and how Cris was thriving… I was and still am the better geneticist. I knew I could make improvements to what he did and give us a chance to have a child of our own. A healthy child."

Dropping his gaze to his hands, he swallows hard. "But when your mom was pregnant and as Cris was getting older, we knew Dr. Sherman would realize what I'd done to your genome. We were naïve thinking nobody would notice, because Cris… Cris showed more and more phenotypical signs of his Neanderthal heritage, and so would you, since we did most of the same modifications on you, and then some. He would've taken one look at you, and he would've known. I had no choice. I kept you away from Advangen as best as I could, and Dr. Sherman was happy and busy with Cris in the basement, even though he let others do the dirty work. Stepping out of line would've risked your discovery."

Silence hovers, the shocked kind.

I work on a dry swallow but can't get my throat to work. "You sacrificed Cris to Sherman so that I... that I..."

"So that you were safe. I needed to stay under the radar for your safety. I couldn't have Brian turn you into a lab specimen."

I don't know what to think. What to feel. Dad protected me, but at what cost? It's because of me Cris was thrown to the wolves. Because of me, he spent a lifetime locked away. Because of me they tortured him with bone marrow aspirations.

All because of me.

Logically, I know it's nothing I did, but all Dr. Sherman and Dad's doing, but emotionally I can't say it feels great knowing that I grew up free and unbothered while Cris paid the price. In fact, it feels pretty darn awful.

Johanna drums her fingers onto the table. "Nya is your biological child. I don't think Dr. Sherman would've been able to just take her, Steve."

"That wasn't the only problem I was trying to avoid." He pauses. "Bryan and I had one big fight, shortly after Cris was born. I had offered to take him in, raise him. After all, Jessica and me were starting a family, but Brian wanted Cris closer—such a hypocrisy considering he never took care of him. I disagreed. Cris needed a home, not a lab. We got into that huge fight, and in the end... In the end, Brian threatened to inform the public. So many of the logged codes during the work process were mine. He easily had enough material to make me a persona non grata in the scientific world. That's what he used against me."

I can't have heard that right. Ice runs through my veins. "*Excuse me?*" Dad condemned Cris to a miserable life because he could've lost his job? Does he have no decency at all?

"It would've discredited you. Your career would've been non-existent after. But so would his." Johanna holds on to her bottle of water. "Also, I understand that's not a pleasant prospect, but why—"

Dad holds up a hand. "I didn't say that was the reason, but what Brian used against me. It worked, but not because I was worried about myself. I always knew what I'd done would one day catch up with me and cost me my job or more, and I would have accepted it then as I do now. But the danger to you, Nya, was real. Sherman goes public at any point, maybe because I don't hand over Cris, or maybe because I don't hand *you* over, or maybe because I break the NDA, and yes, my career would've been gone. I might even have been punished by law, but can you imagine what would've happened to you? Look outside, because at this point I guess you do, if what I saw when I drove up onto WissenSCHAFFT's parking lot is any indication. Is it so hard to understand I didn't want that for you? That I wanted you to grow up as normal as you could? I couldn't risk Brian seeing you, Nya. Ever."

My stomach untwists by half a turn, but the nausea stays as strong as before from these ups and downs of what I'm feeling. I'm mad at Dad, but I… I understand. It's twisted and wrong and will take me years to come to terms with, but I understand. Doesn't mean I like it, but I can understand why Dad did what he did.

He lowers his voice. "I just wanted you to be safe. And Advangen wasn't that for you. That's why I restricted your access to your research level—"

I grimace. "Yeah, nice try." Despite that my name bought me an ID with full access. "And I told you I did run into Dr. Sherman." On the day I was trying to show off my all-access to the then-very-annoying Gabriel.

Dad closes his eyes and shakes his head. "Oh, I remember you telling me. That fear that he discovered your secret… The night after you told me I was lying awake, trying to convince myself your phenotypical Neanderthal traits weren't that pronounced after all, but—"

Realization strikes like a viper when I remember that odd interaction with Dr. Sherman. "But he knew," I whisper hoarsely. Blood swooshes in my ears. "He knew, Dad. He looked at me like he was trying to figure me out, and…" I close my eyes. Ugh. So, so obvious in retrospect. "And he asked me whether I had fun at Advangen already, if I'd maybe sequenced my genome. And then he invited me to do that with him, and… geez. Well. He wanted me to join him right away to do that, and when I declined, we settled on next week. And… and he asked me to not tell you about it." Now I know why. Hindsight is twenty-twenty. To think I was so eager, so eager to meet with Sherman. I was a fool, and he played me—and played me well.

Dad turns white as the wall. "Fuck." He scoots back, rests his forearms on his knees, and lets his head hang forward. For a good ten or twelve seconds, we hear him drag in rough breaths before he slowly sits himself up again, the dark circles under his eyes even more pronounced. "I'm not sure what his next step will be, but I can tell you he knows. This isn't a battle about Cris anymore. It's a war over the both of you."

CHAPTER TWENTY-THREE

The advantage of being in a penthouse suite all by yourselves is privacy. It's only the three of us, Cris, Gabe, and me, seated at the large, probably mahogany dining table and having a late dinner together.

The disadvantage of being in a penthouse suite all by yourselves is also exactly that, privacy.

Since we left the conference room and Dad, my brain hasn't been able to shut up. What I would benefit from right now is distraction, and I'm not getting that here. Not with all of us in the same funky mood. Food had been up here already when we came back, Thai food stored in an insulated carrier to stay warm. Like the very much functional, dysfunctional family that we are, we took over tasks. Gabe got the food, I set the table, and Cris got us drinks from the fridge, all without a single word being said.

Once the food was out, Gabe took a selfie of us to post later, but nobody smiled. We all looked like we needed about a months' worth of rest and some good news, stat.

And now… now everything's so quiet, I can hear my thoughts screaming at me. Maybe even the guys' thoughts, if I listen closely enough. Although that being said, mine yell at a deafening level, so maybe that's a no for hearing anybody else's. Can't say that's surprising given what we just learned—or rather, what we all have been through in the last few days, but two highlights make it to the top of the list:

Dad secretly designed me at Advangen.

Cris had to pay the price for my freedom.

My whole life still feels so… unreal. I shove my veggies from left to right.

Veggies.

Right.

Have I been preferring veggies over meat all my life because of my Neanderthal genes, or just because I like veggies? Dad is the opposite of me, a meat lover extraordinaire, so who knows, might be my altered genome. Is there anything about me I cannot double-guess? Anything I can't trace to my Neanderthal heritage? So many little peculiarities make sense now, and it makes me sick.

As if on command, nausea churns in my stomach, and the headache cranks it up to the nth degree. Tonight it's out to punish me, apparently. Again, no wonder my brain is writhing in agony given what it had to digest. We're stuck in a crappy situation, having to play with cards just as crappy we didn't even choose—and that's applying to all of us. Obviously, Cris had it the worst, but the recent revelations concerning me are also quite newsworthy. And Gabe, currently typing away on his phone in-between bites, Gabe is stuck with us, literally, but as the only one from our trio he at least got to make a decision about—

I freeze, the hand with a loaded fork of veggies half-way to my mouth.

"Nya?" Gabe asks, looking up from his phone. "You okay?"

"Yeah." It comes out croaky. "I… I just had an idea."

Cris reaches over and gently pushes onto my hand until I let it sink down. It doesn't even register, because the idea I've just had could be a game-changer to our advantage. My mind races, finally freed of the numbing quicksand it's been stuck in for the last half hour.

"I like you had an idea, but you're scaring me a bit. I thought you stroked out on me." Gabe points his fork at his own temple, then resumes typing frantically on his phone again.

"Harr harr," I say, rolling my eyes, then drop my fork next to my plate. "I was just momentarily amazed by myself. Sometimes my genius creates gravity. That's all."

Cris snorts, while Gabe doesn't even move a single facial muscle. He's completely immersed in what he's typing. And at this very moment, it annoys me. "Gabe! Dude! Stop selling your soul online and be present, if you don't mind?"

As if I hit him, Gabe jerks. His eyes pop open wide. "What?" He squeaks it out more than anything.

Ugh. I wave my hand. "I get what you're doing is important, and I appreciate that you're on top of all the social media stuff." Because Lord knows, I'm not. "But I just made a great joke, and I need you to at least acknowledge it, because I'm losing it as it is, and I need us all to be there for each other." Needy much? Yes. But I think I have good enough reasons for it.

Gabe lowers the phone and clicks it off, then puts a smile on his face so fake even somebody knowing him way less than I do would've noticed. "I'm sorry, it's just…" He works a hand through his hair in his typical Gabe-move. "A lot."

Duh. But I get it. I sigh. "I know. But I had a good idea, which is why I said I'm amazed by myself." I pat my shoulder for emphasis.

Now Gabe chuckles, and the smile turns real. "Okay, then let us be amazed at you as well. I mean, more than we already are.

What's your idea?"

I cut him a questioning look from under my lashes, because, did he really just say that, but his focus is on loading his fork with another bite of his tofu-dish. At least not the phone. So, I clear my throat. "Okay, bear with me. We're trying to convince the public Cris is a friendly little mutant. But at this point we have not only *one* friendly little mutant," I point at Cris, "we have *two*." I point at myself. "And guess what? One of those mutants has been living smack in their middle for seventeen long years."

"That's so *Among Us*," Cris says.

"Jesus," Gabe shakes his head. "Is there anything pop culture you don't know?"

"Not sure, but with the world gone to shit thanks to the atomic wars, watching movies and playing video games is kind of all you can do. I thought that's what everybody did."

"Point taken." Gabe frowns. "But let's hope our storyline is more peaceful than *Among Us*."

"I'm all for it."

Right. "And I have no idea what you're talking about. If I may continue?" I cross my arms in front of my chest. Guys. "My point was, I've been a normal member of society, going to school, avoiding PE, like everybody, hobbies… The usual. That's our chance to normalize Cris!" I look from one guy to the other, waiting for their reaction, my heart pounding, because this idea is good! Better than good!

"You're saying we're using you as an example that Neanderthal-mutated humans aren't dangerous and just as normal as literally the girl next door?" Gabe doesn't sound nearly as thrilled as I was expecting.

"Yes." I nod like a bobble-head figurine. "What works better to normalize Cris than to show everybody how harmless *this* mutant is? How boringly normal my life was? So far, at least. Before this whole thing started."

Gabe blinks slowly. "I like the idea—"

"But?"

"But that would mean you would have to come out and tell people you have the same mutations as Cris—and more."

"Exactly." That's kind of the basis of my plan.

Gabe's chest lifts with a slow inhale. "But you saw what happened out there." He points toward the terrace door. "You read some comments under our posts. You were there when they *shot* at us."

I cringe. Won't forget that one anytime soon.

Gabe carries on. "I understand what you're trying to do, but you're opening yourself up to all of that. Cris had no choice, but you—"

"I have one, I know. And I'm choosing to let people know. On my terms." It's what made the lightbulb go *ping* above my head: I can make it my choice. "You know what's going to happen. Dr. Sherman most likely knows already, like Dad said. What's his next move going to be? Either he blackmails us, à la *hand over Cris or I'll tell everybody Nya is a mutant*, or he's going to spill the beans anyway and make it look like Dad is Frankenstein and I'm the monster he created. That's not going to make us look good at all."

Gabe smacks his lips, then sets the loaded fork down onto his plate. The way he looks at me, all serious, with a hint of something else in his eyes…

I raise a brow. "What?"

A hesitant smile curves his lips. "I like the way you think. I just don't like that we'll have to worry about your safety the same as about Cris'."

Cris tilts his head left to right, a pensive expression on his face.

"But is it really such a big difference? Nya and you got shot at already, just like me. Almost pushed off the road—again, just like me. And why? Because you were with me. You're in danger by proxy, quite literally."

Gabe sighs. "You're probably right. Nya, just know that your life will never be the same if you go public."

My heart hammers and skips a beat, and my head answers with another pang of pain. Hearing Gabe say out loud what I've been thinking makes it seem more real. More irrefutable.

"I know. But listen, it's going to happen anyway, and this way I get to send cool pictures of us with it, or pics from when I was younger and in the middle of doing something completely mundane *human* instead of being demonized by Sherman. I can't say I love the idea of informing the whole wide world about my genetic status, but I don't think I have a choice. I mean, I do: *I* want to call the shots." I cringe and rub my aching temple. "Bad phrasing. Sorry."

For one long moment, Gabe stays quiet. "Okay," he says. "Then we'll do it that way. It makes sense, you're right. In fact, why don't we start with this here..." He unlocks his phone and scrolls through something. "Ah, got it. Gotta love cloud storage. Here. Let's post this right now and title it Throwback-Thursday. What do you think?" He hands me the phone, the screen facing me.

First, I don't recognize what I'm seeing, but once I do the picture shoots straight into my heart, like an arrow, burrowing deep. "That's us," I whisper. Us—when I was like five years old, in the tree house in Gabe's backyard. It's one of my favorite pictures of when we were young. The picture is taken from below, although not from that far below, since Gabe's dad is really tall, but still. Gabe and I are lying in the entrance of the tree house, shoulder to shoulder, on our tummies, each of us holding an ice cream cone. I've got ice cream around my mouth, Gabe's has dripped onto his hand, but we're both grinning into the camera with the purest, happiest smiles ever.

Something pulses inside my heart, something warm and wholesome that spreads through my veins, heating my body and soul.

I have to clear my throat or else I don't trust myself to speak. "You found that real fast in the cloud..."

"Yeah. Well organized." He says it like it's no big deal, like *yeah, sure, whatever.* But the pink splotches appearing on his cheeks and the way he focuses on shoving his food onto his fork, like it was the most difficult task known to man, sell him out. He knew exactly where it was.

Cris takes the phone from me and chuckles when he sees the picture. "People really build tree houses, huh?"

"My dad did," Gabe says. "Actually, he had somebody build it for him, somebody who knew what they were doing. That's why we had two benches, a table, and shelves up there. All built to last. That thing is still there, by the way."

"It is?" Cris rubs his hands together. "I'm calling dibs on climbing up first. Whenever we get to do that, I mean. Oh, and whenever *I* get to do that. If I do. Well, you know what I mean." A frown pulls on his lips as he slides the phone back to Gabe.

"The goal is for you to live a normal life, man. That's why we're doing all of this." Gabe taps something on the screen and types. "Hence, Operation Normalize Nya is starting right now. I'll add some more pics to schedule for a later post... You don't mind if I use some of the old elementary school pics, or middle school? Science Day? Dress like a teacher day?" He looks up at me, one questioning eyebrow raised.

I open my mouth, close it, and open it again, feeling… I dunno, somewhat flabbergasted, if that sensation comes with a warm and wholesome churning in my core: He has all those pictures of me. Of us. "S-sure. Go ahead."

"Cool." Gabe nods, and swipes and types some more. "And here we go… Picture one, posted, pictures two to five… scheduled. Now, we wait."

But I don't need to just wait. I don't want to, either. "You know what? Let me copy a page from your playbook. I have this one picture of Dad and me from Thanksgiving a few years ago; it's basically us and a mountain of food."

Gabe gives me a thumbs up. "Nothing says normal more clearly than a table loaded with mashed sweet potatoes and a turkey on Thanksgiving. Plus, it shows your *creator*"—he makes air quotes—"saw you as a normal person too."

"Exactly. Now, if only I can remember my cloud password." I rub my temple, staring at my phone. Given how fast Advangen found us, we could've kept our old phones and not bothered leaving them and getting new ones. Would've made my job easier right now.

What's my password again? The letters on the screen blur, and I blink.

Blink again.

What did I want to do?

Ah, look up pictures in the—

Geez. That's really hard to read.

I shake my head, then press my palm against my temple. That hurt.

"*A-ck?*" Gabe asks.

I lift my head. It weighs a ton. "Wha—?" What did he say?

His mouth moves, but no sound comes out. I think.

The phone drops from my hand, although I could've sworn I held it tight. Turning my head to where it fell only works in slow motion. And is hard.

Gabe gets up, fast.

I want to reach for my phone, but can't move my arm.

Why—

Blood swooshes in my ears. Something is off. I suck in one breath—

And everything turns black.

As if somebody turned the volume up, voices break through the silence.

"Everybody! She's waking up!"

"About damn time. That was too damn long."

"Was it the same for me? When I—?"

"You were out for a while, but I can't freakin' *think*—"

"Calm down, everybody. That's completely normal after a seizure."

A seizure? Johanna?

"Nothing is normal with this seizure, absolutely nothing."

Dad?

I try to open my eyes, but all I manage is wrinkling my forehead.

There's a sigh of relief. "She's really waking up!"

Gabe! That's Gabe.

Somebody squeezes my right hand.

"About damn time," Dad repeats with his usual level of grumpiness, although it holds an undertone of something else, something I'm not used to from him.

I try again to force my eyelids open, and this time it works. Uber-bright light blinds me, but once my eyes adjust, I can make out my surroundings and the surrounding people.

Couch. I'm on the couch. And everybody is here. Gabe, kneeling in front of the couch, Dad behind him, Cris and Johanna on the other side of the sofa, behind its backrest.

It's a party, apparently.

"Hi," I croak.

"Hi, honey." Dad looks at me with worry shining from his eyes, no matter the smile trying to convey otherwise. "You gave us a little scare there."

"Huh?"

"You had a seizure, honey."

Great. I guess this time I called it. "A seishure." Oh, man… My tongue isn't doing what it's supposed to.

Gabe still understands me and all that I'm not saying, judging by his intonation. "Yes, a seizure. You seemed out of it the last few seconds before you fell to the floor. I caught you somewhat, so at least you didn't hurt your noggin." He gently knocks onto my head with two of his knuckles. "We called Johanna, who came up lightning fast, your dad in tow. You seized for a good three minutes and then slept a bit."

"About twenty minutes," Cris says. "I hope you're feeling better now. For me, once I wake up, it's like nothing happens. The headache is gone, the dizziness. Like a cleansing thunderstorm in my brain."

Dad flinches, then fixes that smile on his face. "Do you want to drink something?"

Now that he mentions it, my throat is parched. "Yes, please." There you go. That sounded better.

Gabe slides his left hand under my shoulders and gently pushes me up, using his hold on my other hand to pull. Has he been holding my hand this whole time? I think so?

I grunt when I'm up, but generally speaking, Cris was right. I do feel better.

Dad hands me an opened bottle of water, then rubs his palm over my shoulder. "You scared me there, Nya," he whispers.

I take the bottle with my free hand and put it to my lips. The cool liquid washes down my throat, taking the last bit of haze with it. I had a seizure. Great.

I swallow, then put the bottle down, testing out my tongue. To my utter relief, talking is way easier now. "Well, it's not like I'm thrilled to have had a seizure. Where did that come from? Stress?" Seizures aren't contagious, so just because Cris has them, doesn't mean I'm going to get them.

Dad takes a seat in the chair Cris usually hangs out in. "We should… we should talk about what just happened here." He clears his throat. "If you're all up for it, that is."

Something in his tone has the hair in the nape of my neck stand up and my stomach twist some more. The water tastes sour all of a sudden.

"Yeah." Gabe stretches the word as he moves up to sit next to me on the couch, still holding on to my hand. "And now I'm not sure I want to hear what you have to say."

Dad blows out a harsh, brief chuckle. "Believe me, you don't. But I don't think there's another option anymore."

"Let me guess: It's genetic." Johanna takes a seat in one of the chairs from the dining table she dragged over. "It would make sense." She nods her chin at Cris.

Dad opens his mouth, then snaps it closed, muscles in his temple twitching. The apple in his throat bobs with a hard swallow. "Correct."

"Genetic?" I look from Dad to Cris and back. "We have the same thing?"

"Yes." Dad's voice is barely a whisper. "Unfortunately, it appears that way. I wasn't sure the mutation would be clinically significant in you, after all, you hadn't shown any symptoms… I mean, when you started with headaches, it definitely freaked me out, but it wasn't like it was with Cris, so I hoped… But this seizure… it confirms it." The way he sits, fingers digging into the chair's armrest, his focus is on somewhere on the floor in front of him.

"Excuse me. Am I to understand you knew this was going to happen?" Gabe's voice is soft when he speaks, but it carries an edge, a barely contained one.

"I didn't know, but I always worried it would. Cris showed symptoms much earlier, and Nya didn't. I hoped the alterations to your genome would've worked. It seems they only delayed the onset. I—"

"You knew this could happen to Nya and you did nothing about it?" Like a whip, Gabe's angry words cut through my Dad's. "You just *gambled* everything would be fine?"

Dad jerks back, eyes wide. "No! I didn't gamble! Not with Nya, never! I… I checked her blood every couple of months, and I found the markers, but she wasn't showing any clinical symptoms, not like Cris was."

I subconsciously rub the pit of my elbow. That explains that, it appears. So much for quote-unquote routine blood work.

"What markers?" Johanna asks, her brows narrowed. "I saw something on chromosome twenty—"

"It's not that chromosome. That's what I thought first, but I couldn't prove it. The work Brian did on Cris' genome is… is very well done, as much as I despise the man. But one mutation had an off-target effect—"

"A change somewhere else that wasn't intended," Johanna says to Cris.

"And that's what's causing the seizures." Dad pulls his phone from his pocket, unlocks it, and taps on something. Then, he throws it to Johanna. "Here. This is the last screenshot I could take before Advangen's IT kicked me out and killed my access codes. Maybe you can make more sense out of it. Because I clearly have failed so far."

He sounds so beaten and hopeless, my heart goes out to him, despite everything. I know he's always been worried about my health—

Wait a second. I tilt my head. "Is that why you've always been so hyper-worried whenever I had anything? Because you thought—"

"Because I thought you might go down the same route as Cris, yes. His symptoms started years ago though, and I can't—" He gulps in a deep breath, then holds it.

"And you can't what?" Cris asks. "Don't be shy. I find it stimulating to find out new details about my life every few hours. Makes the first eighteen years of my life seem even more boring in comparison."

Dad chews on the inside of his lip, gaze still glued to that one apparently mega-fascinating spot on the ground. "And I can't fix it," he whispers. "I've tried to replace the gene in vitro, but it just… won't take. Cas9 protein binds to the DNA at the cut site, and—"

"And blocks the DNA repair enzymes from cutting," I say. Cas9 is supposed to make a cut for the new, edited gene. But if the area is busy, that won't work.

Cris looks over at me, brows crunched together, a questioning look on his face. I shake my head. I don't understand Dad either.

"So, you're saying we're going to have seizures. Okay. Can't say I'm thrilled, but there are meds." We can control them, right? I can still get my driver's license. Seizures don't have to rule my life. "Right?"

Closing his eyes, Dad shakes his head. "I wish." Those two words, spoken so softly I barely hear them, give me the creeps. Goosebumps explode and run down my spine, bringing a shiver of awareness: something is off here, and it's not just us having seizures. Something is *very* off here.

"Dad?" I ask. "What. Is. It?" My throat feels tight, my breathing raspy. Why does it feel like impending doom all of a sudden?

Ever so slowly, Dad looks up. First at Cris, then at me. "The off-target effects are the problem. I thought I had prevented them in you, Nya, but turns out..." He huffs out a dry laugh. "Turns out I'm not Mother Nature, and she doesn't like to be messed with. The seizures... they're affecting your brain. And they are progressive. There's no way to prevent them, no miracle cure. Whatever I tried, it failed. And that means for both of you that..." He closes his eyes and releases a slow, measured breath. "The condition is fatal, and... at this point, any seizure could be your last. You both will die from this."

For a good five seconds, absolute silence hovers.

Then, Gabe jumps up, both hands balled into fists, glaring at my Dad. "Are you fucking kidding me? You're saying they're going to fucking *die* from these fucking seizures? You know that for a fucking fact?" Like an avenging angel, he stands in front of me, in a wide stance, as if he expected my dad to do... I don't know, something I needed protection from.

But apparently that ship has long sailed, since it seems I would've needed protection when I was nothing more than a heap of cells.

One should think some words are pretty clear cut and easy to understand: *you will die from this.*

It's binary. Either you do, or you don't. On or off. Yay or nay. Not a hard concept to grasp, at least in general. Right now, I can't say I get it. That sentence is more like the Schroedinger's Cat of sentences: Am I as good as dead already? Am I not? Is there wiggle room? What does my death depend upon?

"Do you have any evidence for that… that *theory* of yours? You drew her blood, and that's all? *That's* how you claim to know Nya's going to fucking *die?*" Gabe spits out the last words.

"It's enough to know," Dad says, face contorted into a mask of pain. "There are markers. We've been tracking them in Cris and I've been looking for them in Nya. Her levels were minimal last time I checked, and are now much higher than I ever cared to see. And Cris' markers are through the roof, according to Johanna's blood work." For a long two seconds, he closes his eyes and inhales slowly. "We know what to expect. Cris went through all the tests until we knew the seizures were progressive and every single one had the potential to fry his brain from the inside, to put it crudely. After he had the first one, we were amazed he was still alive. And then another one, and another—"

"So maybe there is hope it's chronic, but not fatal." Johanna raises an eyebrow at Dad.

"No," he rasps hoarsely. "If I correlate Nya's lab work and her clinical symptoms and relate it to Cris' progress, Nya is deteriorating at a much faster pace. At this rate of increase, I expect her to survive maybe two or three seizures more than Cris, but

Cris…" Dad kneads his hands, knuckles white. "Cris might survive another seizure, maybe two, but I'm close to certain not three seizures."

Three seizures max… I choke on a wheeze. One to three seizures for Cris and what, four to six for me and that's it?

That's it?

Cris has had *two* since we met him, within a few days, so—

The ground opens beneath my feet. We have no time. I don't have much, apparently, and Cris has even less.

"… and that there was nothing we could do about it, unless we fixed the responsible gene. And for that… I just wasn't smart enough." Dad stares at his hands, folded in his lap.

"And you never thought to tell me anything? Maybe I would've liked to know any moment could be my last, or was my life that unworthy of living I didn't even deserve to know when I was dying?" Cris folds his arms across his chest, and while he's glaring at Dad in a similar way to Gabe, I catch the flicker of fear in his eyes.

It matches my own.

I close my eyes and hold my breath. I just had one seizure. One. And that seizure means my brain is on its way out, and so is Cris'? *That's it?* We're going to die with potentially the very next seizure, as it fries our brains?

My heart flutters more than it beats. Maybe it's gotten the memo before I did and is already declining, who knows?

I blink. Gabe is yelling at Dad—has been yelling at Dad—and I appreciate that. I can't summon the energy to yell, even though my thoughts are screaming at me. The rest of my body is numb. Disconnected from my brain. Foggy.

"—don't get it!" Dad jumps up to his feet, jutting one arm out, pointing toward the window. "Everything I did since Cris started with symptoms was to look for a way to fix what went wrong! Everything!"

"Oh, please, don't pretend it was because you cared about Cris! You were worried about Nya!"

Fire spits from Dad's eyes. "Hell yes I was! Of course I was! But don't you ever insinuate I wasn't worried about Cris! He might not be my son, but I was the closest thing to a father he had for most his life!"

"And yet you knew I was going to die before I even got to live a day." Not sure if it's the words themselves or the calm, monotone way Cris said them, but Dad jerks back as if slapped. Hurt skates across his features, followed by regret and something akin to sadness, before he has himself under control again.

"I know we failed you, Cris. *I* did. You, too, Nya, although differently. I hoped the more we experimented with Cris' bone marrow, the more likely we were going to find a solution for you. If we could have found a way to prevent the same decline in you—"

That breaks through my numbness. I jump off the couch and step out from behind Gabe, knees wobbly. "Are you saying you put Cris through all these… these *assaults* because of me? Because you were looking to fix *me?*"

Dad snaps his mouth close, and I know the answer. I whip my gaze over to Cris. "You said they drew more bone marrow recently, right?"

Cris nods.

"So, when did you find out I had the same problem Cris had? Probably when you started forcing Cris to give his bone marrow, am I right?" I'm swaying a bit, but Gabe takes my hand and tugs, keeping me stable.

"Nya, it's complicated. I needed to find—"

I should be focusing on the words that pulled the rug from

under my feet, but knowing that I was the indirect cause for Cris' suffering just breaks another piece off my soul, it breaks a part of *me*. I stomp my foot. "No, it's not complicated, Dad! Have you seen what they did to Cris to get the bone marrow? They fucking tasered him, so he'd hold still! I've been there, I've seen it, and I can't believe you ordered somebody to do this to Cris—and in my name! Once you feared for me, you used him—" I suck in a short, cut off breath when the next set of puzzle pieces fall into place. "Oh my god," I whisper. "You'd given up on him already. You thought he was going to die anyway, but whatever, you all expected that since he was born, but when I got sick, you used Cris to find a cure for me. Not him. For me." I think I'm going to be sick. Nobody prepared me for how to handle the overwhelming force of what has been thrown at me, and it engulfs every system of my body like a tsunami wave that just won't stop.

Tears well in Dad's eyes. "Nya—"

"No." I shake my head and slide my hand out of Gabe's. "I can't even. I can't." With three large steps, I've cut past Gabe and Cris. My knees still feel like Jello, my breath still comes out too short, but I won't stumble. Once there, I rip the terrace door open and step outside.

Cool night air assaults me, bringing the scent of a few drops of rain that must've fallen a while ago. Somebody yells unintelligible angry words down in the parking lot, and more angry voices chime in. The noise makes me stop a few steps onto the balcony: maybe going up to the railing isn't a good idea, given that we were shot at the last time we did.

I close my eyes.

Because yeah, that happened too amidst all the other crap that's been raining down on us lately: we were shot at. They could've killed us.

A desperate, cold laugh breaks from my throat. Apparently, it would've only shaved a few days or maybe weeks off Cris' and my life expectancy. No biggie then, like everything else in my life currently.

Like the reason for Dad freaking out about my headaches: just some deadly seizures.

Right.

No wonder he reacted so strange when I mentioned headaches. But what did he want to do then? Just *hope* I'd be okay? And if I wasn't? If I hadn't discovered Cris, where would we be now? What would he have told me?

Somebody closes the door behind me and steps closer.

"Hey." Cris bumps his shoulder into mine.

"Hey," I rasp.

"Are you out here looking for a vampire? Cause I've watched enough *Twilight* to have hope for eternal life, vampire-edition."

A small smile tugs at the corners of my lips. "I'd pay money to see you sparkle."

He chuckles. "I'd so rock it and you know it."

For a moment, silence hovers, or as much silence as there can be with who knows how many people a few floors below us. Several cars have their engines running. Once in a while, somebody honks. People shout and talk, but overall, the loud chants are gone. No more *Kill the Mutant* or any of that crap. Even hate needs sleep, it seems.

Cris turns toward me. "I knew I was going to die, by the way."

What the— I whip my gaze over to meet his. "You did? Why? How?"

He shoves his hands into his pockets and shrugs. "Just a feeling. A couple of off-hand comments. The way they told me the radiation was getting to me when I said I wasn't feeling well. That they kept pushing when I was allowed upstairs further and further, as if they were waiting for the problem—i.e., me—to solve itself."

I stare at him. The hits just keep on coming with him. Whenever I think I understand the horrors he's been through, some new revelation adds another level of cruelty.

"I'm sorry, Cris. I'm sorry for everything, and especially for everything my dad did to you, from the moment you were born to now. Had I known he did *that* to you," I flatten my palm against his sternum, "because of me, I—"

"It's okay." He covers my hand with his, and my eyes widen.

"No, it's not okay, not even remotely!"

He squeezes my hand. "Look, had they told me they needed my marrow to help somebody else, I would've done it, and with pleasure. That they didn't put me through the draws just for some weird shit, but to help you makes it better, in retrospective."

I blink. "You're too nice, Cris. Why are you so nice? You should rage against what they did, what my dad did—"

"But it won't help me, will it? Maybe I'm a bit like Loki—the one from the TV series, you know?—and I've realized I don't want to be alone, and I don't want to waste my time angry. I want my life to mean something, and if that's helping you, then that's a price I'm willing to pay."

I swallow hard. "But I don't know if I'd be willing to accept you paying that price. Not the way they treated you."

"Granted, they could've handled that better."

"Ya think?"

The door opens and closes with a slight creak. Neither of us looks back, but judging by the sound of the steps, it's Gabe.

"Hello, my favorite mutants." He wraps one arm around Cris' and one around my shoulders.

Cris shakes his head. "I prefer Zombie at this point. We're half-dead anyway, it seems."

One-Mississippi. Two-Mississippi. Three—

We all snort out laughing.

"You suck!" I laugh and box Cris onto his side.

"Ow! So brutal. You wanna kill me faster?" He flicks his fingers at my earlobe. "Take that! Payback's a bitch, I heard."

Smacking his hand away, I grin as Gabe gives an exaggerated sigh.

"Children, children, can I never leave you alone?" He pulls us closer by the shoulders, tighter. "And that means vice versa you shouldn't leave me alone either, because I was *this* close to clocking your dad, Nya."

"He's had it coming for a while now," I mutter. "Go right ahead."

"I can report it's very satisfying," Cris adds. "Although it didn't solve any of my problems when I hit him. Sadly."

"I wish it had." Gabe keeps us anchored close to him, as if he feared we'd run if he let go. Or die. Who knows these days? "Boy, do I wish it had."

I lean my head against his shoulder, and not a second later, Gabe rests his head against mine. Down in the parking lot, somebody honks like crazy and gets some angry yells in return, and while a mere hour ago it would've given me the creeps to know there were people out there hating Cris—and me—without knowing us, it feels like the smaller problem at this point.

Cris and I have a fatal mutation.

That really changes one's perspective on things.

Tears well in my eyes. My walls are non-existent at this point. Every new piece of information chopped at them until nothing but a few crumbled bricks remained, and even those Dad pulverized with his latest revelation.

I really don't want to die. Not yet. Not this young. Not at this shitty, crappy junction in my life, at odds with Dad, myself, and the freaking world.

I want to live. I want to make the world a better place, as cheesy as it sounds. I want Cris to live, to experience, to grow outside of his prison at Advangen.

Yeah.

I close my eyes and the first tears fall. Silently. I don't sniffle, I don't sob, I just let them fall, but Gabe must have some kind of built-in radar. His arm tenses around me before he pulls me into his chest and Cris equally close. I sneak one arm around him, the other around Cris, who does the same to us, then leans his head on Gabe's shoulder, just like me.

And so we stand, leaning on Gabe, silent, until our hearts stop bleeding and our souls have found the strength to carry on.

For now, at least.

CHAPTER TWENTY-FOUR

When I wake up, I have a blissful ten or fifteen seconds before I remember why my eyes feel so puffy and my head so heavy.

Yeah.

I've had better mornings for sure, and I'm saying that not even a minute into this one. When people say something is weighing them down—I never got that. Now I do. It feels like there's another stupid elephant sitting on my chest, making it hard to breathe, to move, to think. Sun is shining through the gaps of the blinds, but how can it be a regular day out there, when everything has changed in here?

Yesterday I was a normal teen, dorky, but normal. Yesterday I helped a friend. Now I'm a Neanderthal-mutant who needs help herself.

Oh, and apparently, I'm falling apart.

I rub my palm over my stinging eyes.

Yesterday I was healthy.

Now I'm going to die when my brain gets fried by the next seizure or the one after, or the one after that. Life's a game of Bingo, apparently.

To be honest, that part is the most scary of it all. Having to die is horrible and terrifying, and I want to curl into a ball and not think about it, but not even having a remote idea when it might happen?

I cringe. Yes, okay, that's the way it is with death. Most people don't know when they're going to die, but to be fair, it's not on the menu for most people until they're way older or sicker. It shouldn't be on the menu for neither Cris nor me, and it freaks me out that every moment could be my very last one, and I wouldn't know.

The way I felt before the seizure hit, this slow confusion before I faded to black… Would I have the time to realize what's happening? Would I have the time to know that I might die, to say goodbye?

I slide my palm over to my temple and press against it. The stinging of unshed tears burns in my eyes. I squeeze my eyelids shut, so hard, stars dance in front of them. After what feels like an eternity, the stinging eases up, but the pressure around my chest doesn't. I take it back. It's not an elephant sitting on me, it's a gray straitjacket of fear and sadness strapped around my chest, strangulating my heart and soul.

So poetic.

Blaring TV-noise comes through the closed door. The boys must be up. I probably should get dressed too, but getting up means facing reality, and I… I'm not sure I'm ready.

I slam my hand into the mattress. "Dammit," I whisper. We got a hard blow delivered yesterday. Nobody expects me to just carry on as if nothing happened, but I want to. I want everything to be the way it was before yesterday, and I—

I know that's not going to happen.

But I need to function today. Dying is not a reason to give up—harr harr. We still have to fight for Cris to at least spend the last days, weeks, or hopefully months of his life on his terms. Me, too.

We still have work to do.

Spreading out my fingers over the cool cotton sheets, I close my eyes. I can compartmentalize. Deal with the emotions, the frustrations, the fear, later. Push all that crap away and tackle the day one problem at a time, one minute at a time.

I can do that.

Even so, getting out of bed, taking a shower, making the effort to wash and blow dry my hair, getting dressed… it all feels like pushing through quicksand. Heavy. Unnecessary.

But, I do it.

Eventually, I step out of my bedroom into the open-spaced living room. As I thought, the guys are already awake and in front of the TV, Cris with a bowl and a spoon in his hands, gaze fixated on the screen.

"…is your opinion as a man of faith?"

"Now, Clarice, the first thing you have to understand is that man is made in God's image, and I would like you to really think about what I said: We are made in His image. God created mankind, and what has been done to this poor soul has removed him further from God. Somebody has tried to assume a power only He should hold. They decided they were bigger than Him and could do better—a preposterous idea. Science—"

"Minister, sorry to interrupt, but the Vatican said, in 2002, I believe, that germ line editing with a therapeutic goal in man would be acceptable, and I'm paraphrasing here."

I step around to get a better look at the large flat-screen TV. Ah, look at that: that's WissenSCHAFFT's building in the background, complete with protesters in front of it. Actually… I strain my ears. Yup. Hear them. The windows might be bullet proof, but they surely ain't soundproof.

The reporter, a lady in her thirties with probably a whole

canister of hairspray in her hairdo, shoves the microphone at the man in his sixties, dressed in a black suit with the Roman collar of a catholic priest.

"Well, Clarice, you said it yourself: The Vatican talked about therapy. Restoring a genome to a healthier condition brings us closer to the Creation's original condition. But, Clarice, no such thing has happened here. In fact, this genetically engineered being is a danger to God's creation. I might even go as far and say—"

Gabe grunts and switches the channel. "Heard 'nuff, thanks, Clarice."

I clear my throat. "Morning, gentlemen." I plop my butt down next to Gabe. Gravity feels stronger in these necks of the wood today, pulling me down. A whiff of shower gel and something very much Gabe-like hits my nose and shoots through the gray straitjacket surrounding my soul, releasing some kind of weird flutter inside my core. It's like a lightning strike of color infusing my gray world.

Swallowing hard, I blink three or four times. Can't go down that path. Can't open myself up to any emotion, or they'll all come spilling out like a dam just broke.

A bitter sting of sorrow pierces my soul, so I cut that thought off and fix a smile on my face. "I see you're checking the news?"

"Checking the news," Gabe confirms. "We're pretty high up there. Opinions vary, depending on the network and whom they ask. CNN tried Advangen for a statement, but all they got is getting kicked out by security."

Yikes. "I bet that looked good on TV."

"I'll take anything that makes them look like the bad guys, not us."

Us.

I like that he's saying *us* and including himself, but Gabe is the only one who'll come out of this in one piece—oh, and alive.

There's that.

I clear my throat. "What else has been going on?"

"A lot, actually," Cris says, pointing his spoon at the TV. This morning, he has circles under his eyes I swear weren't there yesterday. Looks like I'm not the only one having a hard time dealing with things.

Milk drips from Cris' spoon onto the carpet, but he doesn't notice. "Today I learned some people consider dogs people, so *I* should also be considered people. Others aren't so much in favor of that. After all, where do we stop? Is Rex then allowed to vote as well? You should've heard it. It was quite ridiculous."

"I'm fine with you not having heard it, Nya. Neander— Huh." Gabe crunches his brows together and turns to look at me in a weird, evaluating way.

"What? Do I smell?" What's that look for?

He grins. "Let me check." He dives in and sniffs my neck. "Nope, you're fine. Fruity."

A laugh bursts from my throat, powered by Gabe's ridiculousness. I push him off. "Go away, weirdo. I know I smell good. I just showered. So what was that look for?"

Gabe straightens his shirt. "Well, I just realized your dad's genius only applies to his work, though right now that jury is still out after the recent developments. But that being said, I bet you he felt so smart naming you and Cris."

"Why? Because he used CRISPR to name Cris Parr?" Something I should've seen the moment I read his name on the sign in Advangen's basement.

"Yes, that. And that you, *Nya...*" He stretches my name to *Neeeeee-uuh*. "... have *Neeeeanderthal* genes."

My mouth drops open.

I blink.

Blink again.

"Dammit," I whisper, incredulous. "He really named me after his work."

"Welcome to the club." Cris reaches past Gabe and pats my leg. "Membership fees are due every first of the month."

I facepalm myself. "So obvious in retrospect, and yet it never clicked for me." The way he got mad when somebody mispronounced my name to *Ni-ah* wasn't something I paid much attention to, and why would I have?

Cris slurps some milk from his bowl, then swallows. "If we get any pseudo-siblings, the next one is gonna be called Cas."

"After the genetic scissor Cas9?" Gabe chuckles. "I see you've been paying attention and learning the ways of science. You're my favorite little mutant, even though Nya isn't bad either." He rocks his shoulder into me, and it makes me realize how things between us have changed in the last few days. How walls have crumbled down and bridges have been rebuilt. It's almost as if those last few years of mutual hurt didn't happen.

Gabe's phone buzzes on the table, and within half a second, he has snatched it up and unlocked it.

"What's going on?" I sit up straighter. "Makes me nervous when you're nervous."

"I'm not nervous—"

"Sure, you aren't," I mumble, then ignore the glance he shoots me.

"Seems to me you are a tad on the edge today," Gabe says. "Not that I don't get that." He waits for a reply, but when I don't give one, he sighs and lays his phone on the couch before he pushes himself out of the soft cushions. "Let me make you tea. Something to warm your soul. What would you like?"

He's making me tea? My soul already feels warmer, like a fire had been kindled by his small act of kindness. I peek up at him. "You know the answer, don't you? Tea—"

"Earl Grey."

"Hot," I add, holding up one finger, and Gabe breaks out in the widest, purest grin. Dang it if that doesn't add fuel to said fire in my soul.

"Aye, Captain!" He fake-salutes and walks over to the kitchen area.

Cris slurps some milk from his spoon, then nods at me. "Nice. I got that."

"Didn't doubt you would. You're somewhat scary with your knowledge of pop culture references. You know more than I do."

He snickers. "You know nothing, Nya Bennison. Get that one?"

I roll my eyes. "Didn't watch it, but that's everywhere. *Game of Thrones.*"

Gabe's phone buzzes and lights up with another text message in the open thread, drawing my gaze to it.

Cris points his spoon at the TV. "Didn't watch it either. Started it, but it took me only a few minutes to figure out I better stick to—"

The rest of his words fade into the background. That message. I— Am I reading this right?

—need is your statement Cris and Nya are mentally unstable. You discredit them publicly and keep that up, and the money is yours.

—okay, got it.

I blink rapidly, but the message stays the same. My heart doesn't beat, it only makes weird seizing twitches, which is so ironic, given my situation. Dizziness swamps me. Publicly discredit us? The screen dims, but before the phone can turn off, I snatch it up and scroll up, up, up, all the way to the top—and my seizing heart stops.

I know that number, have known it since forever, since before voice control, when Dad had me dial and put his phone on speaker when his hands were deep in meatball dough or otherwise occupied and work had yet another urgent matter to attend.

Nausea rises.

Gabe is messaging with Dr. Sherman.

Why is Gabe messaging with Dr. Sherman? It can't be what I think is going on, it just can't.

I scroll back down, eyes darting over snippets of a conversation I wish I didn't know about.

—thank you for your response—

—you deserve better than to ruin your life because of them—

—what do you want me to do—

—enough money to not worry in life—

—how much more can you offer—

"Here you go." Gabe sets a steaming mug with tea on the table in front of me. "Tea, Earl Grey—" He halts as his gaze meets my wide one and then drops to the phone in my hand. With half a second, all color drains from his face. "Nya—" He reaches for the phone, but I scoot back and keep it out of reach.

"You're selling us out?" My voice is low, gravelly, and way stronger than I feel. If I had to stand now, I couldn't. My knees are pudding, my stomach a mess, my heart still doesn't pump any oxygen to *freaking anywhere* in my body.

Gabe flinches and raises both palms. "No! God, no, I'm not—"

Right. "Oh sure, you're not selling us out. There must be another reason Dr. Sherman is offering you more and more money to discredit Cris and me." Anger pours into every cell of my body. Gabe hasn't changed. I thought we were on the same team, but clearly we're not. How stupid was I? I even started to be okay with him, to *like* him! What he said to me, how he held me—

I inhale through my nose. Don't trust myself to open my mouth or I'll scream.

"What the what?" Cris looks up from his bowl. "Gabe's doing what?"

The ultimate breach in trust, that's what Gabe is doing.

Gritting my teeth, I grunt out the words, each of them ripping off the band-aid that had started to heal years of snarky comments from Gabe. "Sherman is buying him behind our backs. Gabe's getting rich off of us."

Confusion fills Cris' voice. "I don't get—"

"Nya." Gabe drops down to both his knees in front of me, reaching for my hand. He winces when I snatch it away. "Let me explain—"

There's nothing to explain. Nothing! "I think everything is pretty clear." I wiggle the phone.

"Actually, it's not."

I huff out a sarcastic laugh. "Sure. Of course it isn't." Without warning, the little vault for all my fears surrounding Gabe bursts open and spills all my thoughts straight into my speech motor area. "I should've known it. It was too good to be true, but oh, benefit of the doubt, right? So, are you playing a long con? When did you decide we weren't a team, huh? Right from the start, when I knocked on your door and asked for your help? When we ran from those black SUVs? Sure, let's play Nya, what a fun way to get back at her—"

"I'd never—" Gabe shakes his head so fast, his features turn blurry, but I'm on a roll. Hurt and disappointment spur me on. I throw my hands in the air and keep talking over him, because I freaking won't give him the time of day anymore!

"—how we can make life worse for Nya—"

"That's not what—"

"—beyond disgusting to sell us out—"

"Nya!" Gabe slams his palm onto the couch cushion, and I snap my mouth close, startled. He closes his eyes and takes one long, deep breath in. "Exit that app. Open SecretText, which is a red icon with a snake on it. First home screen."

"I'm not—"

"Just do it, Nya." Cris sits up straight and nods at the phone.

Okay, whatever. I do as he says and find that snake-icon.

"When you open it, there's only one conversation. Tap it."

The moment I do, the conversation opens up, and with it, at least ten screenshots.

"Look through the screenshots. See they're the convo with Dr. Sherman?"

I pinch and zoom in. They seem to be what I just quickly glanced over in the other app: the same disgusting offer to sell us out, the same disgusting questions how much more money Gabe could get for it. "Oh, yeah. All that crap is here." I give him a challenging look, keeping my lips pinched together. Try me. I'm in a rip-your-head-off mood.

Gabe doesn't take the bait. "Okay. Then please check whom I've been sending these to." He regards me with quiet intensity, which… I dunno, makes me antsy rather than angry. Like I was missing something.

I scroll farther until I find the profile picture in the top right corn—

Air punches out of my lungs, taking my anger with it. "That's—"

"Who? Who is it?" Cris sits up straighter and leans forward.

"Duncan," I whisper, then swallow hard as my brain adds one

and one. "You texted the screenshots to Duncan.. You... you *goaded* Sherman into this?"

"I did." Gabe nods, then reaches for the phone and hesitates. "May I?"

The fact that he asks, that he isn't gloating at how he was right and I was wrong... I nod and hand him the phone.

Our fingertips touch as he takes it, and Gabe's eyes widen as my heart gets kick-started back into somewhat of a normal rhythm.

He clears his throat. "Sherman contacted me a couple of hours after our first post, via DM. It was under a false name. My first mistake was reading the message, but it was so early in the game, I... I wanted to read the comments and messages. He identified himself and that's where my second mistake lies: engaging with him. Should've blocked him, but once I responded, he got straight to the point. And you know what bothers me most?" He drops his gaze and chews on the inside of his cheek. "That for a moment, I considered his offer. I considered walking away, getting a shit-ton of money out of it and keeping my reputation intact, while ruining yours."

Silence hovers.

If I'm really honest with myself, I can't blame him. I wouldn't have been mad at him had he left us to our own devices, given that Gabe is the only one who isn't affected by any of Advangen's actions. Had he been open with us and told us he wanted out, I would've felt abandoned, but I would've understood. Finding what looked like a conspiracy against Cris and me on Gabe's phone on the other hand... yeah. That ruffled my feathers differently.

Still, I get it.

"How long did you consider his offer for?" Cris asks.

The corners of Gabe's lips twitch. "Zero-point-six-eight seconds. For an—"

"—android, that's nearly an eternity," Cris finishes the sentence and grins. "Sherman is the Borg Queen?"

"He's evil enough." Gabe shrugs. "But to be serious, I considered his offer for a very miserable day. Kept going through scenarios how the rest of my life is going to play out, but in the end, I knew I couldn't live with myself if I accepted his offer. So, I decided to play him like he tried to play me. I got him to verify his identity and then to dig his own grave with his offer. Duncan is going to run this in the Times tomorrow, and I'm sure it's not going to reflect well on Sherman or Advangen. I'm just embarrassed it took me so long to figure out where my loyalties lie. Maybe I'm not as good a person as I thought I was." Regret radiates from his body and rolls over in palpable waves.

Well. That shoe fits both of us. I scoot forward, looking him straight in the eye. "Maybe I'm not as good a person as I thought I was either," I say, and I mean it. My chest feels lighter with the next breaths, as if my lungs and heart had grown wings and didn't care about gravity anymore. Gabe didn't betray us. He didn't sell us out. It sounds ridiculous I even thought he did, but years of not trusting Gabe have left their mark on me. "I should've asked for details before I jumped right at accusing you," I say and offer a small, hesitant smile. "Instead, I jumped right to what seemed like the obvious conclusion, so…I'm sorry, Gabe."

He waves his hand. "No, I get it. It looked bad, I know. But I didn't want you to think what you ultimately thought when you saw the messages. Should've just told you and been open about it, but you live, you learn." He regards me from under his lashes. "Are we good?"

I reach for his hand and pull him off his knees and onto the couch until he's sitting next to me. Then I rock my shoulder into him. "If you forgive and forget my idiocy jumping to conclusions,

I'll do the same for you hiding your texts with Sherman."

A lopsided grin appears on his face. He wraps one arm around my shoulders and pulls me into him. "Forgiven and forgotten then."

We stay on the couch and in front of the TV for a good thirty minutes before Gabe picks up his phone again, hesitating before he unlocks it.

"Do you want me to take the phone off FaceID so you can check it whenever you want?"

I don't miss a beat. "No. Your phone is yours and private. We've all learned our lessons today, and mine has to do with trusting you." I pat his knee. That whole thing… embarrassing. But also reassuring somehow. I mean, Gabe had a pretty perfect out offered by Sherman, and yet he stayed. Didn't throw us under the bus to save himself. That's proof of character, right there. No matter it took him a while to get there.

I wonder if that was why he seemed off here and there over the last day or so, him making up his mind. To know he decided for us, to support us… A little shiver runs down my spine, causing a confusing skip of my heart I ignore, just like I ignore the next skip when Gabe's thick lashes fan down before his lips curl up. He has beautiful lips, that man. Very kiss—

I shake my head. Change of topic. I clear my throat. "Uh, I am curious, though. Whatcha doing? New post?"

"Actually, no. I'm merely checking if Duncan is ready for us."

Oh. "Duncan is here?"

"Was supposed to arrive about an hour ago. He's bringing a film crew for us. Right now, he should be talking to Johanna as the expert other than your father, but I think the goal is to get him to talk as well."

"Wait, Dad is still here?" I didn't expect that. I figured he'd sneak out of here as soon as he could, back to Advangen, tail between his legs.

"Refused to leave. Johanna put him in another room, albeit a much smaller one than ours." Satisfaction shines through with his last sentence. "Anyway. Duncan loved our strategy and wanted to shoot a video of us and get our take on things. Show our personalities. It can only help us. Social media-wise we're up to millions of followers. We're being tagged by I don't know how many new people coming out in our defense, and, well, a few who're coming out against us."

"I personally like the Mutant Mutiny account," Cris says. "If you don't know whether they're for or against us, that's the beauty and how they lure you in. They're all sarcastic though, like the Onion?" He looks at Gabe, then carries on when Gabe nods. "Like the Onion. *Shortage of razors after neanderthal-man tries to appease humans by adhering to their beauty standards* and stuff like that. It's quite funny."

I snort out another laugh, and man, it feels good. "It actually is funny. I don't mind that kind of reporting."

Gabe hits a button on the remote. "This guy here's been quite busy apparently as well. Seems to be the resident scientist for CNN. We like him, right, Cris?"

"Yes, we do."

I direct my attention to the screen, showing the news anchor spiffy in his gray suit and the picture-in-picture of another man in yet another gray suit.

The anchor is in the middle of a sentence when the sound kicks in. "*...can you tell us why Advangen never published their success? A* *discovery like this—sequencing the whole Neanderthal genome and successfully transferring genes to a human—should have been big news."*

"It would have been Nobel-prize worthy," the scientist—I'm sorry, John F. Rondeau, PhD, clinical geneticist—says. *"When the first Neanderthal DNA was extracted—well, we thought it was the first—it was an amazing milestone and achievement. We gave Svante Pääbo the Nobel prize for it, back in 2022. Even as a scientist who's been working in this field for over twenty years, I cannot wrap my head around how successful Advangen was this early in the game."*

"I understand that, but why would they never have shared their findings? Especially if it was Nobel-prize worthy?"

The PhD shrugs. *"Fetal gene therapy has such an enormous potential… My only thought would be to monopolize what they could do. To be the only one with this kind of success and access to those altered stem cells… It seems to me, but mind you, I don't know the whole story, that Advangen kept their success hidden to be ahead of their competitors, which they certainly are."*

"And that is considered normal in the scientific world?"

Rondeau jerks back, then shakes his head vigorously. *"No. Not at all. In fact, it is appalling behavior. Every aspect. Unethical, to top it off. And as much as I am in awe of what they have achieved, as much do I condemn how they did it. Keeping that young man—"*

Gabe mutes him. "Honestly, I feel like the pendulum is at fifty-fifty, or maybe fifty-one to forty-nine for us. That's not too bad. I think we're making progress."

I nod my chin at his phone. "What about social media?" Millions of followers don't equal automatic success.

"Project Normalize Nya is going well. Really well. We're getting more and more positive comments, likes, shares. We're pretty big right now."

"Exactly what I always wanted," I mutter. "Be big on social

media."

Gabe chuckles. "It comes in handy sometimes." He turns serious a second later. "Have you decided how and when you want to break the news?"

The news.

I let my head fall back against the cushion. Feels so unreal that *the* news is about me having Neanderthal-genes as well. That's *old* news, because the true newsworthy piece of information is about Cris' and my impending demise.

Yikes.

I yank my head upright and clear my throat. "Well. Yes and no. I want to do it today, because I don't trust Sherman to hold back. Information is power, and depending on how they or we play it, one of us is going to win some points, the other will lose. I don't want to be the one to lose." I grimace, because let's be honest, I've lost already, and so has Cris.

Gabe must be thinking something similar, if the flash of sadness crossing his face is any indication. "Gotcha. Instead of posting it on our social media, do you… want to maybe do it during the interview with Duncan?"

"On live television?" My eyes pop wide. "I don't know if I have the cool to pull that off." I might start bawling. That's a distinct possibility, given that my emotions are close to overpowering my internal containment fields.

"It won't be live," Gabe says, "but it would be perfect. People like you, we know that. And if they saw you tell them you have Neanderthal genes, and you grew up *normal*…" He puts the last word into air quotes. "It would make it more personal."

"I get it." Chewing on my lower lip, I throw Gabe a sideways glance. "How much do I tell them? Everything?"

Gabe doesn't need me to specify. He gets it. "I don't know.

That's up to you two to decide. You might want to start with your genome and see what the reaction is before you move to… to what your dad said yesterday."

That we are going to die.

It's hard to say, I get it. Speaking the words makes it more real, more tangible, and that's the last thing I want.

"I don't care either way," Cris chimes in. "Do what works best."

As if I knew what worked best. Tactical thinking about influencing public perception—that's Gabe's specialty, not mine. I can only say what I'm comfortable with, that I know. And no, I'm not comfortable discussing being marked for death while a TV camera is aimed at me. "I don't want to talk about the… the seizure-death-and-decay-part."

Gabe flinches. "You have such a lovely way with words."

I shoot him a look. "And that's one of the reasons I don't want to talk about it."

His gaze softens. "I know. And—"

Gabe's phone rings.

"Video call?" He turns the screen and gives it a critical glance. "Ah, that's our lawyer. Duncan—"

"The one he mentioned the Times got us?"

"That's her. She's really good, supposedly. Duncan gave me a heads-up. She wants to talk to us. Come on closer, both of you." He gestures for Cris and me to lean in. Once we're cuddled together, he accepts the call.

Not even half a second later, the image of a woman pops up on the screen. *"Good morning."* The woman nods. All I can see of her is her head and part of her upper body. She must be what, mid-forties or so, judging by her short brown hair with a few gray streaks in it. Overall, I'd consider her surprisingly stylish, but maybe that's because I had expected somebody in another boring gray suit. Not this lady though: blue-rimmed glasses frame her equally blue eyes, and even though she is wearing a dress blouse, it's bright pink and decorated with a Gordian Knot-look alike pin.

"Good morning," we all reply in unison, Gabe and mine drilled through years of school, and Cris… well, Cris is a fast learner, as we all know.

"So…" She smiles into the camera. *"Duncan has obviously told me everything. Which of you is the one with Neanderthal-genes?"*

"Well…" Gabe draws out the word. "I'm Gabriel Hargrove, call me Gabe."

"I'm Chelsea Hunt. You can call me Chelsea. Nice to meet you, Gabe." She smiles, and it seems genuine. *"So that means the scientific surprise must be you."* She looks more to her right, where Cris is sitting.

"Kind of," Cris says, cutting me a glance.

I elbow Gabe into the side, gently so, then lean closer and whisper into his ear. "She needs to know, right?" Because she's our lawyer. She can only defend us—defend me—if she knows what's going on.

Gabe nods. "This is a secure call?" he asks.

"Of course. This isn't my first rodeo." Ms. Hunt points behind her to the wall decorated with too many diplomas to count.

Gabe and I exchange a look, and I nod. Then let's do it.

"Gotcha," Gabe says. "Well, you're the first to hear that we're not just having one person with Neanderthal-genes in their genome," he points at Cris, "but two." He points at me.

"Excuse me?" Ms. Hunt's eyebrows shoot up to right under her hairline, her gaze darting from left to right. *"Cris and Nya?"*

I nod. "Yes. Turns out Cris was my dad's boss' creation, and then my dad designed my genome, since my dad and mom had a genetic abnormality that prevented them from having healthy children."

Within a minute, we've given her the rundown of what happened to Cris and me and explained our plan of Project Normalize Nya.

Eventually, Chelsea nods. *"Good. I like it. You're working the right angle. Advangen is claiming you, Cris, as their property, but I agree with your assessment that, once everything's out in the open, the same will hold true for you, Nya. The contract and NDA your father signed make all his inventions, results, discoveries, ideas, etc, etc, while under contract with the company, the property of Advangen. So, to paraphrase in vernacular, everything your father cooked up while employed belongs to Advangen, and that would include the alteration of your genome. That's a normal contract, by the way, it's just playing out to their advantage right now."*

I blow out a soft puff of air. "Oh, great." It's one thing expecting the worst, another getting it confirmed.

"I know that doesn't sound good, but I feel we have something to work with." She shuffles through some documents on her desk, then picks up a folder and opens it. *"Your approach to proving Cris, and therefore, you as well, Nya, are human, is the right attempt. My goal is to have the court understand you are human, but even granting legal personhood would make a difference."*

"Ruff ruff," Cris barks under his breath, and I elbow him in the side.

"Personhood, as in we're saying we aren't human, but we're granted human rights?"

"Not human rights, but certain protection from cruelty and the right to live your life. Honestly, the personhood laws need a closer look, and have needed one for years. No matter the outcome of our adventure here—which I intend to win, by the way—it will start a new discussion about whom to grant personhood. We're very ambiguous

about it. Animals with higher cognitive skills—great apes, dolphins, elephants—are one thing, but we're not even considering pigs, cows, or other nonhuman animals we use and, unfortunately, also abuse. Doing so would mean we'd have to change our way of life, and we're not ready for that. No American court to date has been willing to include nonhuman animals within the meaning of legal personhood. I also intend to change that."

Gabe whistles through his teeth. "You've done your homework."

"Always. A topic dear to my heart." She winks. *"You might be the catalyst case that shifts the animal personhood argument from the metaphysical to the mainstream. But, going back to business. Advangen has filed their complaint, as expected. Gabe and Nya, you are charged with breaking and entering, and grand theft."*

"Grand theft, look at that, Cris. You're worth more than… what is it… a thousand bucks to them!" Gabe gives Cris a thumbs up.

"Nine hundred and fifty in California, correct. I'm assuming once the trial begins, the charges will be changed to burglary, which includes breaking and entering with the intent to commit a theft of property of over nine hundred and fifty dollars."

"Yikes." I cringe. "That sounds bad." Am I surprised they're taking legal actions? No. After all, we did break in, to a degree. We had a badge, but it wasn't ours and we had no permission to enter. Does it still sound wrong to hear my name next to a charge? Oh, heck it does.

"It is quite bad." Chelsea takes a sip of coffee from a clear glass mug. *"If you're found guilty, you could be in prison for over six years."*

Over six—!

Dread forms in the pit of my stomach, heavy and sour. Six years, that's— I'd be twenty-three when I got out. At that age, I wanted to be in grad school, working on my thesis, not a convicted felon.

A spike of fear shoots through my core before reality brings up a shield and deflects it. What a quote-unquote lucky coincidence I won't have to worry about spending time behind bars. Rumor has it, I'll probably be dead before I'll ever have to face my punishment.

The game is different for Gabe though. I lean more into the camera's view. "But prison time isn't going to happen, right?"

"Not if I can prevent it. I'm close to finishing our answer, but I needed to make sure we are all on the same page, which it seems we are. Now, while I deal with the legal aspects, I would like you to continue your angle. You need to be visible and as human as possible for us to gain traction."

"On it," Gabe says, giving her a thumbs up.

"I know you are. I'm one of your followers." She holds up her phone. *"Now, regarding the timeline. I'm assuming we're going to have to move fast. Advangen's lawyers aren't stupid either. They know that the longer they wait and the longer they give you free rein, the more likely public opinion is going to sway. To be honest, I'm expecting a few days to the first hearing or even a gag order to keep you from spilling further details about your time at Advangen."*

I grimace. "That would be bad." It would mean our only weapon got neutralized.

"It would be most unfortunate, but if that happens, we'll deal with it. For now, post as much as you can. Be as human and engaging and non-threatening as possible. I don't want to be overly dramatic, but your freedom depends on it."

CHAPTER TWENTY-FIVE

Half an hour later, all three of us enter the same conference room I've spent way too much time in already. Wouldn't say it makes me feel all warm and fuzzy, but at least I'm not the only one.

"This is giving me PTSD," Cris mutters as we enter.

"Yup," I say and squeeze through the half-open door. This room hasn't exactly been a happy place for us.

"I like what they did with the place though," Cris tags on when he enters after me. And right he is, the video crew changes the room completely, or rather, the four uber-bright lights around the table, large video screen, and camera on a tripod, do.

Trepidation creeps up my spine. I'm about to give up my status quo, my untouchable-status as a full human. Voluntarily. Nothing will be the same—

I huff. Right. As if *anything* was still the same. And if I don't want to end up in the basement at Advangen together with Cris or in freaking prison until we both die, I better take the first step and set the tone right.

As we enter, Duncan and Johanna are getting up from their chairs, shaking hands. My dad is nowhere to be seen, not that I'm surprised. Two people adjust the lights, while a third person fumbles with the video camera, and a fourth—geez, Duncan really brought an entire team—checks some footage on that nice, big screen secured on some kind of cart.

All in all, it looks very busy and very professional.

And it makes my heart beat double-time.

Duncan looks over his shoulder, a big smile popping up on his face when he sees us. "There you are. Thank you for making the time." With four large strides, he's come around the table, hand extended.

Gabe shakes it first. "It's not as if we had much else to do. We're kind of in limbo here."

"And locked in. Took me a while to get through the masses in the parking lot," Duncan says, shaking my hand next, then Cris'.

"And our security a good while to keep everybody else besides your crew out." Johanna rolls her eyes and shakes her head. "We're approaching Taylor-Swift concert vibes here."

If only they were all as excited to see us. "If I can get all those people out there to cheer for us and not plot against us, I'll gladly stay in here some longer."

"Working on that, aren't we? I got some good screenshots from Gabe, and once they go out into the world, I'm sure people are going to find Advangen's actions disgusting." Duncan lays a hand on Cris' shoulder. "And how are you doing with all of this?" He gives him an evaluating glance, because, right, he doesn't know about my new Neanderthal-status yet.

"Pretty well, all things considered. I mean, I'm not in my basement anymore. That's something, right?"

A shadow falls over Duncan's face. "Yes. And I'd prefer we'd keep it that way. When did you speak to Chelsea? The lawyer?"

"Earlier today," Gabe says. "She seemed nice and on top of

things."

Duncan nods and chews on the inside of his cheek. "Yes to both, but she's unfortunately a lone good soldier fighting the good fight against an army. Make no mistakes. We're in the middle of a war." Funny he should say that, echoing Dad. "I spoke to her maybe an hour ago, and…" He smacks his lips. "We're out-lawyered. Advangen is throwing everything and everybody they have into this case, because for them *everything* depends on it. If the charge of grand theft against you is dismissed, it means Cris is not a thing—duh—but a person. And that in return would mean they held a *person* in their basement, arguably against their will. That's a whole new Pandora's Box being opened, especially for Mr. Sherman and your dad, Nya. Taking somebody's liberty and freedom is not something you walk away from with a slap to your wrist. We're talking prison time, Chelsea said."

Prison time. My first thought is *good, serves them right*, but then I realize it would mean the same for Dad. Dad could be sent to prison for what he did. While I can't say that thought hadn't crossed my mind, I definitely pushed it away, for many reasons, one of them being that I would've had a hand in getting him imprisoned. I was the catalyst. *I* found Cris. *I* brought everything to light. You can draw a straight line from what I did to what could happen to him. On the other hand, you can also draw a straight line from what he did, keeping Cris hidden, to what I did, breaking him out.

Guess we're even, although I don't think the shoe really fits on either foot. None of us are responsible for the actions of the other, or if so, he of mine, to a degree. Still doesn't feel good to be the catalyst that gets your father into prison, no matter how strained our relationship currently is and no matter how appropriate the sentence might be.

I shake my head to snap out of this train of thought and catch the last part of Duncan's sentence.

"… and the risk is highest for Dr. Sherman. It's an entire list of charges Chelsea rattled off, I forgot half of it, but then of course there's also the bodily harm every time they drew bone marrow from you when you didn't want that to be done to you. That's another reason Advangen's lawyers are kicking so hard to keep us down. They need to win, or else Advangen and Mr. Sherman are going to lose big."

Gabe crosses his arms in front of his chest. "Not as big as we will if we lose. All our freedom is on the line."

"Yeah, about that…" Cris shoves both hands into his pockets and looks down. "I'm sorry you guys are in so much trouble because of me. I—"

I hold up a hand. "Stop right there. Even if we're found guilty and go to prison—or, well, one of us does," given that my chances to make it to prison alive seem to be slim, "leaving you there was never an option. We knew the risks." Somewhat, at least.

"Exactly." Gabe raises a balled fist. "We'll give them a fight to cause them nightmares."

Duncan grins. "That's the spirit, and that's what we're going for. I was thinking for today's interview with you we keep on focusing on humanizing Cris. Most of the charges against either Advagen or you hinge on whether or not he's human. So, let's make that easier for the judge and jury. They also need to see—" He pauses. "Have you seen the latest MailDrop post yet? Nya?"

"No." I shake my head. "We're focusing on social media, not so much on any of the newspapers." Be that print or online. Gabe has enough to do with all our posts, and as we have established, I'm not the one of our group to be on top of anything media-related. "Why?"

Cringing, Duncan tilts his head from left to right. "Well. You might not want to look at it, but in the interest of full disclosure and so that you know what hinges on this interview…" He unlocks his phone, taps round, and shows me the screen, the typical MailDrop-logo on top and a picture of me—well, of me as Cassidy Sibagatullin in all my two thousand sweaters, on the stage at Advangen, accepting the Advangen Junior Scientist Award:

Cheating her way into Advangen
Nya Bennison (17), who has been making headlines together with Gabriel Hargrove and Neanderthal-mutant Cris Parr, appears to have been cheating her way into the internship that allowed her to work at Advangen. According to—

What the—! Pressure builds inside my chest. I'm reading that wrong. I'm not looking at an article calling me a cheater. Advangen didn't sell me out like that!

But I am, and they did.

A rush of hot betrayal sweeps over me. I blink rapidly. "That's all wrong. I won, because my work in epigenetics was worth the win. They said I was bringing new ideas to the field of genetic engineering, and—"

Gabe lays his arm around me and squeezes once before he lets go. Then he blows out a puff of harsh air through pursed lips. "They're fighting unfair."

"Yeah. They do." Duncan clicks off his phone and pockets it. "Discrediting you is part of their strategy, Nya," he says softly. "But it shows us they're desperate. They know they can only lose, no matter how the court decides. And even if they win and Cris has to return to them as their property, the fact that they violated countless ethics standards will get Dr. Sherman and your dad restricted from ever working in genetics again, I can almost promise you that. And what that means for Advangen…" He shrugs. "I bet you can guess how much that would affect their business."

I huff. Yeah. They're called AdvanGEN for a reason.

"So yes, they're fighting with all they got. But, so are we. You running the screenshots I sent you?" Gabe crosses his arms in front of his chest, a look of steely determination on his face. That stance and look… They make the Gabe-proof wall I erected around my heart all these years ago crumble down some more.

"Heck, yeah, I'm running them." Duncan grins. "It'll come out of left field and hit them smack where it hurts the most."

"Wonderful," Cris says. "I hear payback is a bitch. And if I'm going down, I'd like to take them with me as much as I can."

Gabe lays a hand on Cris' shoulder. "That's why we're here."

Right they are. Advangen bringing up my Cassidy-stint isn't the worst of what has happened to me over the last days, nor will it be the worst of what's yet to come. So, I swallow all the hurt pride and nod. "Yeah. And I'm with Cris. Payback is a bitch." I might've chosen to not dwell on it, but calling me a cheater on a freaking worldwide accessible and well-known online news site is not something I'm going to forget anytime soon either. Or, ever.

Duncan tips an imaginary hat. "Good. Then let's change perception back to where it should be, on Cris being the victim, and the two of you being the good guys." He points to the set up behind us. "Business: For the interview, I'd like you three to have a seat at the table, back toward the windows. With the angle in here, we can still catch the crowd in the parking lot, which makes for more of an impressive backdrop." He motions for us to follow and leads us toward three chairs somebody already pulled out for us.

By force of habit, we sit down in our usual order, indeed the very much functional, dysfunctional family. For one brief moment, discomfort washes over me sitting with my back to the window, but then I remember the windows are bulletproof.

Never had to worry about that before this week. Go figure.

Somebody directs the lights at us, and I swear it gets instantly hotter in here. A woman in her early twenties with pink hair tips attaches small microphones to our shirts, all the while Duncan keeps on talking. "This isn't such a big deal. Ignore the camera and people, rather think of it as a normal discussion, similar to when I met you guys in the RV."

Normal discussion. Right. With cameras, etc.

My glance drifts over the crew, the cameras, the screen facing us—and bounces right back to my image on it, recognition smacking me right in the face. Holy cow. How could I never have seen it? How could I never have thought I resembled a Neanderthal?

Seeing myself displayed on that screen makes it so obvious it hurts. Or, maybe Johanna was right: If you know what you're looking for, it's obvious.

It should've clicked for me: I'm pale, yet have never been anemic. I'm just the white-as-the-wall kind of gal. I got freckles, and I'm a redhead. There was something I read once about a mutation in Neanderthal genes that made melanin less effective. Less melanin to pigment skin and hair, and voila, you look like me and Cris. Even our noses are similar, wider, even though, from what we're being told, we're not related. Cris' brows are stronger, more pronounced than mine, though, but maybe that's the effect of testosterone, who knows? In the end, it doesn't matter. We both look like Neanderthals, if you know what you're looking for.

I drop my gaze to my lap.

"Nya?" Duncan waves a hand in front of my face.

"Huh?" I jerk my gaze up to his.

"Gabe said you maybe wanted to talk about something?"

I open my mouth, close it, and swallow. "Yes. I'll… I'll see how it goes. Is that okay?" I wipe my sweaty palms over my thighs.

"Of course. We'll wing it. If there's anything you didn't like, we can cut it out. I'm not throwing you to the wolves, you know? I'm the nice kind of reporter." He winks, then takes a seat in the chair positioned at an angle to us and claps his hands. "All right, team, let's get started."

"On it," somebody says. No idea who. I cannot see anything with those lights directed at us. "Recording, take it away."

Duncan crosses his legs. "I'm here at WissenSCHAFFT with three young adults who've been at the center of our attention for the last couple of days. Welcome Cris, Gabe, and Nya."

We all give a small nod. I hope I don't look like the deer caught in the headlights that I feel I am.

"Now, obviously, we have read all your posts, seen all your pictures and the videos—the videos! I must say, the one where you get tasered, Cris, that one really was horrific. Is that something that happened frequently?"

Cris swallows once. "Recently it has been. When I was younger, they used different sites to draw marrow, like my shin, and while that hurt, I could handle it. But the sternum…" He rubs a hand over it, absentminded. "It really hurts. Sometimes the old wounds didn't even have time to heal, and they drew more marrow again."

"When you say marrow, you mean they had to drill into your *bone*?" Duncan adds an extra layer of horror into his voice.

"Yes, they drill into my bone until they break into the marrow."

"But they numb the area?"

"I wish they did."

Duncan blows out a puff of air and leans back. "So understandable you were not looking forward to those draws."

"Not at all. They told me it was in my best interest—because radiation polluted the world, right? Which is why I wasn't allowed anywhere else but the basement—"

For the next five minutes, Duncan does a fantastic job talking with Cris about his time at Advangen, how he felt growing up (lonely), where he's learned human interaction (mostly TV), or what he did all day (read, work out, watch TV). After the first few back-and-forth comments, they fall into an easy conversational style, and while it makes me feel a bit more at ease, I'm still melting under the heat of the lights and the pressure of having to get this right.

I'm sure they're going to come up with new endearing nicknames for me, besides cheater.

Alas, I've never shied away from pressure. When I won the Advangen symposium, I didn't mind the attention then, the eyes on me, the lights. Oh, and screw Advangen for trying to take that from me. I won't let them. And I hope they're bracing for impact, because just like it was then, this today is *my* game. *I'm* in control.

I got this.

"… been a real life-changing event when Nya told you her discovery, Gabe?"

"Indeed, Duncan." Gabe huffs. "Life-changing, because I never in my wildest dreams would have believed people could do any of what we just talked about to another person, but it was also close to life-ending. Did you know they shot at us?"

"Excuse me?" Duncan sits up straighter.

"Yup." Gabe points a thumb over his shoulder. "The first

time—and yes, there were several instances—when we freed Cris from Advangen. Advangen's security—oh, and Dr. Sherman—fired several rounds at us. We're lucky we came out unharmed."

Duncan whistles through his teeth. "Security *and* Dr. Sherman? The CEO of Advangen?"

"The very same." Oh, how I wish we had that on video.

Duncan shakes his head in disbelief. "No matter who shoots at you: That must've been scary."

"Horrifying, actually. Just like the second incident, here at WissenSCHAFFT. We were outside on the balcony and, well, somebody took that opportunity to shoot at us. We could hear the bullets whip past us and hit the wall behind us and the haters scream for our death downstairs. I don't think I've ever been that afraid in my life."

"That I believe without a doubt," Duncan says, directing his attention to me. "How did you feel when you realized somebody wanted to kill Cris?"

The answer comes without the slightest bit of nerves. "Angry," I say. "Scared, too, of course, but mainly angry. Cris hasn't even been able to live, and now somebody is trying to kill him? For a few genes that are different in him? Shame on them. I'd like to see nothing more than Cris find his place in society, and in return I wouldn't mind locking up the person shooting at us. Both would be beneficial for society."

Duncan chuckles. "Well spoken. Now, your father is the COO at Advangen, Nya. Has he ever hinted or given you reason to believe they had Cris hidden in their basement?"

"No, never." I shake my head. "My dad and I... have a complicated relationship."

"In which regard?"

My heart skips two beats ahead. This is my opening. I

straighten my spine. "My dad kept me as far away from Advangen as possible, even though I wanted nothing more than to do research, like him."

"Meaning, he preferred a different career for you?"

Deep breath in. "Yes, but the main reason was that… that he didn't want Dr. Sherman to see me."

Duncan furrows his brows. "Why would that be?"

"He was worried Dr. Sherman would do to me what he has done to Cris."

Confusion scates across Duncan's face. "I don't understand. Why was that a concern?"

I smile, then point at Cris, then at me. "Do you notice something? The red in Cris' hair?" I tug on mine, then point at my face. "Freckles. Nose. We have some similarities, right?"

"Yes?" Duncan tilts his head.

"And that would be because Cris has Neanderthal genes Dr. Sherman gave him. I have Neanderthal genes my dad gave me."

Pause.

Duncan blinks, then shakes his head. "Are you saying that you also have Neanderthal genes?"

"I do."

"But… did you know this?"

I shake my head, opening and closing my hands on my thighs. "Not at all. We found out a day ago, by accident, when we checked Cris' genome and ours as well here at WissenSCHAFFT. We wanted to see how different his was from ours, and turns out his and mine are pretty similar. Similar genes, very much different upbringing." I give him *the* look, *hint-hint*.

Something lights up in Duncan's eyes. He's catching on. "Because you lived a normal life, up to now at least."

Thank you, Duncan. Exactly what we're going for.

I let a small smile show. "That I did. Everything you consider American and normal, I've done it, from 4ᵗʰ of July fireworks to Thanksgiving dinners." Okay, that might be a bit thick, but I'm trying to appeal to the more right-leaning, conservative audience, so maybe this will work.

For the next couple of minutes, Duncan and I chat about my normal life as an unknowing mutant, and it's strangely relaxing. Duncan is a pro. Everything he asks me or the guys plays into our strategy, and it feels more like a real-life conversation than an interview.

"…so you've never really gotten sick because of that extra immune boost?"

"Exactly. I had to fake being sick if I wanted to stay home from school, but I'm sure I'm not the only one who's ever done that." I point a thumb to my right and hide the next word with a cough: "Gabe."

Gabe feigns indignation. "Excuse me? You're selling me out on national TV? I'm sure my dad is watching—"

"And probably his entire team," I add, grinning, shooting another metaphorical ball into his court. It helps Gabe's dad is somewhat famous. He's the real-deal, all-American kid I'm trying to appear as.

He throws up his hands, then waves. "And probably his entire team, there you go! Hi, Dad, please beat the Northern Knights this weekend! Anyway, Nya, thank you. Seems that's what I get for faking stomach pain in sixth grade so we could watch movies together, because your school had a student-free day and mine didn't?"

I wave him off with a grin. "I don't think you need to worry. The statute of limitations has expired on this. But I very much appreciated it."

Gabe narrows his eyes and purses his lips. "You better. I endured hours of Brave, Moana—"

"Endured? You loved it!" My soul gives a little happy squeak. I can't believe he still remembers what we watched.

Duncan holds up both hands, laughing. "Peace, peace. I get the point. Nya's immune system is so strong, she'll probably outlive us all."

Well.

That shuts us up and wipes the smile from all our faces.

And Duncan notices.

"What did I say?" he asks.

I snap my mouth close and drop my gaze. The easiest way out would be to smile and say it's nothing, then ask him to cut this part out later. But...

Gabe reaches for my hand and weaves his fingers with mine.

Maybe it's that feeling of security, with Gabe and Cris next to me and Duncan being so clear on our side, that I make a decision.

Pushing my chin up, I look straight at Duncan. "Actually, I won't. And neither will Cris."

He must've caught something in my expression, or rather, in the way we all shut down, because he doesn't ask, he doesn't push. He just waits, concern shining from his eyes.

I wipe the palm not connected to Gabe across my thigh again. The fabric is damp already. Guess I've been doing this a bit for the last minutes. "When we got those Neanderthal-genes, there were unintended side effects, and..." My heart slams against my chest. Only one way to say it. "And that means we're going to die, sooner rather than later. The mutation is killing us."

"No," Duncan whispers, and that sadness in his voice... it nearly undoes me, but I stay strong.

"Unfortunately, yes," I say with a sad smile on my face.

Duncan closes his eyes for a good two seconds. "Explain, please."

So, I do, as hard as it is.

I do, until twenty minutes later somebody calls *cut*, and somebody else turns off those blinding lights and hands me a steaming mug of tea. "Thank you," I mutter and wrap my shaking fingers around it. I feel drained, and I'm not sure whether that's from the interview itself or the topic.

Who am I kidding? It's the topic that did me in, pun intended.

I held it together. Didn't cry, although my voice broke twice. And yes, I got teary, but the tears didn't fall. Cris was quiet and tense, and Gabe… Gabe was angry. So, so angry, not at me or Cris, why would he, but at my dad. At fate.

Duncan pulls over one chair from the conference table, turns it around, and sits on it, supporting his weight with his arms on the chair's backrest.

"Riker-style," Cris murmurs, then blows on the hot tea he's holding onto equally desperate as me.

Gabe chuffs. "Favorite mutant," he whispers under his breath, and holds his fist out for a bump Cris hits.

For a moment Duncan stays quiet, gaze drifting from one of us to the next and back. Then he sighs. "I can't believe you might die with your next seizure. That there's no way to prevent it."

"I wouldn't say we've really come to terms with it, either." I give him yet another sad smile, a current specialty of mine, then take a sip of my tea.

"And your father…?"

A sting shoots through my heart, but I keep my voice level. "According to him, he's been looking for a solution since Cris started with symptoms, but failing." I shrug, like it's not a big deal, any of it. "I believe him. He's one of the leading experts in the field of genetic engineering, so he would definitely know more than I—or we—do."

"And you understand what he's talking about because that's also what the two of you have been doing during your internship at Advangen, right?" Duncan points at Gabe and me.

"Yes, but not really," I say. "I'm more interested in epigenetics, Gabe, in applied medical. It's similar in the grand scheme of things, but what Dad does is look at the genes themselves, how to change them and put new information into them. Epigenetics means I look at what turns those genes on and—"

I stiffen at the same time as Gabe chokes on his tea.

"Off?" Duncan supplies.

"Yeah," Gabe wheezes, then spins in his chair to look at me, eyes wide. "Are you thinking—"

"Yes." Of course I'm thinking the same. That was an epiphany of epic proportions! I stare at him, heart thumping triple-time. "What if we looked at it the wrong way? Maybe Dad is right and we can't fix the genes themselves, but maybe we can fix how our bodies react to the mutated and faulty DNA!" Holy cow, holy cow, holy cow…! It's a chance! It's our *best* chance. It could work!

Gabe sits up straight, as if somebody shot a rod through his spine. "Epigenetics," he whispers. "We're changing the way the information in your DNA is read!"

I nod so fast, a wave of dizziness hits me. Or, maybe that's because my heart's beating too fast to pump much blood, courtesy of the boost of adrenaline shooting through my bloodstream. "Exactly! If we can't repair the DNA to keep our bodies from seizing, then let's hide the switch that causes everything!"

"Uh," Cris says. "That's all good, right? We're happy?"

"We're very happy, Cris!" I grin at him, feeling about a giga-ton lighter than a mere minute before.

"Because…?"

"Because we potentially can silence the gene that causes all the seizures. We'll basically put a lock in front of it so it can't be read!" Excitement surges. I hold up one finger: "And if it can't be read—"

Gabe lifts two fingers. "It can't cause seizures—"

Cris supplies the third finger. "—and we won't die, I get it!"

A wide grin splits my face. We won't die. We probably won't be cured either, whatever damage the seizures might have done is already there, will stay there, but we *won't die.*

We won't freakin' *die.*

CHAPTER TWENTY-SIX

Gabe and I burst into the fourth-floor lab at WissenSCHAFFT, Johanna hot on our heels.

"—the supplies are labeled, you know the hygiene and—"

"We do." I rip a fresh white coat from the cubby and slip into it. No time to lose. "Can we use whatever we need?"

"Of course you can. The lab is yours, you just have to share it with—"

"Nya?" Dad looks up from a lab table, a pipette in one hand, a vial in the other. The safety goggles on his nose make him look like the absolute uber-dork, or maybe that's courtesy of the protective bouffant cap on his head. "What are you doing here?"

I hand one of those to Gabe and don mine. "Bringing new ideas to the field of genetic engineering," I repeat the words that brought me my Advangen internship-win in another lifetime. "You said you can't exchange the broken gene because Cas9 gets stuck and blocks the cut. Okay, so why don't we use that to our advantage, and instead of trying to cut the gene out, we silence it? We might be able to block the transcription of the faulty gene by putting up a roadblock. Methylation."

"Epigenetics to the rescue," Gabe says, sliding into size L

gloves.

Dad's eyes widen. "That is... a phenomenal idea."

One he wouldn't come up with, I know. Dad is an old-fashioned genetic engineer. It's all about cutting and replacing. Epigenetics are the softer skills, but equally valuable.

In any case: "What are you doing here, Dad?" I crank my neck and look around.

Dad swallows hard and lets the pipette sink down. "Betting on the wrong horse, I guess." He clears his throat. "Tell me what you got."

Gabe and I look at each other. Two minds are great, three are better…

"Okay," I say. "Here's what we got."

By the time we leave the lab, it's two in the morning, and we're drunk with success and somewhat delirious from sleep deprivation.

I lean against the wall of the elevator whisking us up to the penthouse level, a ridiculous happiness surging through me, one that comes with a high bigger than any I've ever experienced, goody-two-shoes that I am. Grinning, I lightly bang my head back against the wall. "We're almost there, and it's only been half a day. Almost. Soooo close." I giggle. OMG, it went so well, I feel like I'm on top of the world. "Viral-mediated gene-transfer for the win! *Boom*, gene identified. *Boom*, road block designed. And tomorrow, *boom*, replacing the virus' genome with our creation and *boom, boom, boom*, we have a serum! Who are the best interns Advangen has ever had? Who? Who?" I point my thumb at Gabe, then me. "*We* are the best interns Advangen has ever had!" *Whoop whoop!*

"And potentially the last ones." Gabe grins as wide as me, then makes a fake serious face and drops his voice an octave deeper. "After encountering problems with professionalism in the last batch of interns, we have decided to discontinue this program. We sincerely regret this step, but cannot risk other interns finding more hidden ethical violations and ruining our reputation. We apologize for the inconvenience."

I burst out laughing, holding my stomach. "Oh my god, that was so good! You nailed it! Problems with professionalism, *hee*!" I snort, not very lady-like, but who cares, and push off the wall when the elevator doors open right across the door to our penthouse suite.

Gabe still grins like an imbecile and flexes his biceps as he opens our door with the other hand. "Thank you. I'll be here all day."

"And tomorrow."

"And probably the day after."

We look at each other—and burst out laughing again as we step into our dark living room area, only the moon and some remote light from the ground bringing a bit of illumination.

"I dunno why this is so funny," I wheeze out in-between two laughs. "It's not, it's absolutely not, but... *tee-hee*!" I snort again, louder.

"Oh, shit! Cris is sleeping!" Gabe bursts forward and covers my mouth with his hand. "It's like two or something, we're gonna wake—" He freezes in mid-sentence, pupils dilating, despite the low light.

For one moment I don't get it, but half a second later, as if my nervous system was delayed, I feel a tug in my stomach, followed by a flutter. A strange heat invades my body as awareness creeps into the room.

No, sorry. It doesn't creep. It hits us full-frontal smack in the face.

As if somebody had put a filter on reality, everything narrows down to Gabe: his hand on my mouth, the scent of a bit of what must be his aftershave still clinging to his skin. How close he is, so close, I feel the warmth of his body; I hear the shaky breath he takes in, and I let it all fill me up and push away the bad stuff.

Gabe's lips curve into a soft smile. "Have I ever told you how amazing you are?" he whispers. "Like, you get this death sentence, and not only does it not break you, but you come up with a plan to beat it. You're absolutely amazing." He brushes his thumb over my skin, then moves his hand to cup my cheek, and I…

I'm lost in him.

The way he looks at me—he's never looked at me like this, all open and vulnerable, and… and like he wants me. Like I'm the next best thing since sliced bread—

I giggle.

"Why are you laughing?" He brushes his thumb across my cheek, and oh gee, I melt. I melt into a puddle.

"Because I thought you thought I might be the best thing since sliced bread—"

He chuckles, the sound so deep it reverberates through my chest. "Actually, I do."

I grin up at him, like an imbecile, but it doesn't bother me. "Did you know being sleep deprived is like drinking alcohol? We're having like zero-point-one—"

"If you're implying I don't know what I'm doing, I hate to burst that bubble. I know exactly what I'm doing." He cups my right cheek with his other hand, cradling my face. "And even if I was acting under the or any influence, I can promise you I would do the very same thing after twelve hours of sleep and completely sober."

And with that, he lowers his mouth to mine.

The moment our lips touch— Holy everything, a firework breaks loose inside my stomach. It's the softest contact, yet it hits me *hard*. A gasp breaks free, but that's good, because that means I'm still breathing. Can't really be sure. My whole being, *everything,* is focused on Gabe.

I lift my hands up and touch his cheeks like he's doing to me. *Stubble.* Manly stubble. I wondered what it would feel like. He's so different from when we were young, but he's still my Gabe. A smile tugs at my lips.

Gabe pulls away, but leans his forehead against mine. "You're doing it again," he whispers. "You're smiling."

Said smile widens. "I just realized I like touching you."

"Mhh." He makes a deep, rumbling sound. "And I've known for a while I want you to touch me."

Before I can digest that sentence completely, Gabe's lips are on mine again, and no idea what gives me the courage, but I unlock a new level: I let go of his face and press my palms against his chest, then slide them down his stomach and up his side, to his back and down again until I cup his butt. Out of the two of us, Gabe's definitely gotten the better luck with his genes. Guess a sports star dad overrules a geneticist dad, because Gabe has an athlete's body with a nerdy mind, the absolute perfect combination.

A moan breaks from his throat when I squeeze his butt, and that moan, it shoots right to my core. Goosebumps erupt down my spine, bringing tingles all over my body.

"Nya, I—" He sucks in a harsh breath when I circle my hands around his glutes and press him against me. "I like where this is going. Hold on."

Hold—

In one smooth movement, Gabe's picked me up. All I can do is wrap my legs around his mid-section and my arms around his neck as he carries me to my bedroom. I pull out the hair tie keeping his Thor-like mane under control, then dive my hands into his hair. Since I'm already here, might as well enjoy myself. "I always wanted to do that," I murmur. So soft. Gabe has magnificent hair, better than mine, for sure.

"I would've been all for it," he says as he lays me down on my bed. "But as we have already established, I was an idiot." He raises a challenging eyebrow at me when I keep my legs locked around him. "But I hope you're not holding that against me anymore." He pushes his hips forward into mine, and now it's my turn to suck in a breath. I feel him against me, his hardest part against my softest, and bite down on my lip to restrain a moan. My body moves on its own account and arches up and into him.

Gabe hisses as he gives me resistance. "Nya—"

"More," I whisper. "I want more of you."

A throaty groan leaves his lips as he dives to kiss me, never breaking contact with our lower halves. His weight feels delicious on top of me, not heavy, not suffocating, just right. Sliding one hand under my butt, he lifts me up while circling his hips against me and sparks shoot across my skin and through my soul.

I reach over his shoulders and tug on his shirt, breaking the kiss only long enough to get one word out: "Off."

And Gabe obliges. As if he used magic, the shirt is gone within two seconds, maybe three, and I get to look at all the glorious skin and muscle. I don't know where to look. Gabe is beautiful when he's dressed, but now... Now he's pure seduction. Those well-defined pecs, the biceps, the muscles along his sides... Definitely not the cliché scientist. Definitely a real-life version of Thor.

He keeps himself propped up and lets me look my fill, never stopping that maddening circling and pushing of his hips. I trace the outline of his pecs, then the line leading to his bellybutton and lower. Gabe closes his eyes as his lips part.

So damn beautiful.

I tug on the waistband of his pants. "Off," I repeat my earlier command, and Gabe's eyes pop open.

He swallows hard. "Are you… are you sure?"

Heck, I've never been more sure of anything in my life. "A hundred percent."

"Counts." Lightning fast, he jumps up and drops his pants, leaving him in black boxer briefs. Tented black boxer briefs.

I suck my lower lip between my teeth. My mouth is dry, must be from all that adrenaline, or oxytocin, or— Who cares? It's oddly thrilling to really see Gabe, the man he has become, with freaking chiseled abs and heat in his stare as he looks at me, the same heat that's thrumming through my veins and making me itch for his touch. I reach for my shirt—

He darts forward between my legs. "Oh no, that's for me to take off." He takes my hands and lays them above my head, keeping his fingers entwined with mine as he uses his other hand to push my shirt up, just to below my bra. He lowers his head and kisses my stomach and I rear off the mattress. Holy crap, that's an armada of butterflies lifting off at the same time!

Gabe looks at me from under his lashes as he kisses his way up my stomach, never letting go of my hands. My breath comes out in quick puffs. I have an almost-naked Gabe between my legs, and he's kissing my stomach and—

He trails his fingers up my side and over to the front, halting just under the wire of my bra, waiting.

I nod, because, oh God, please don't stop now, please don't—

He doesn't.

Gabe drags one finger over the cup of my bra and I swear I feel it like it sliced all the way through the lacey material and into my soul. It *burns.*

In a totally exciting, awesome, life-affirming way, of course.

"So beautiful," he whispers.

All those butterflies speed it up to racing speed inside my stomach. "That's my line," I whisper back.

"Sharing is caring." He keeps his gaze trained on me as he kisses his way around the lace of my bra. My eyes roll back as I buck up and into him. I want to feel more of him, feel him closer. It's like my body had waited so long for him, that denying it the closeness it craves is torture.

And speaking of: Gabe is definitely out to torture me. Holy everything…! He keeps my hands pinned above my head as he trails kisses from the swell of my breasts to my neck and back, and that alone would be enough to seriously overload my systems, but to top it off, he slides his unoccupied hand down my stomach, dragging his nails across my skin.

I haven't heard of anybody exploding from making out, but I might just become the first recorded case.

Gabe proves his fine motor skills by popping those jeans buttons open before he flattens his palm against my lower belly and slides it under my pants and between my legs.

A breathy sound escapes me as my senses become hyperaware of his touch around my very center. "Gabe," I whisper, pushing up and into him. "More. There's too much fabric." I'm needy, and I want him, and I've waited too damn long. Reaching one hand down, I yank on my pants, then kick my legs until they come off, leaving me in my undies. "The rest is for you."

But instead of pulling down that last bothersome piece of fabric, Gabe gives my neck one more peck, then rests his forehead against mine, dragging in deep breaths. "We won't have sex tonight."

We won't? A weird mixture of regret, missing out, and relief wash over me. "But what if I want to?"

He groans. "Then I will still do my very best to stay a gentleman. I mean, to some degree." He drags his fingernails up my flank until I gasp. "But we're not sleeping together tonight. We'll build our relationship slowly, brick by brick, and when we're both ready, *then* we'll have the most amazing sex of man- and mutant-kind."

I giggle like I was on some kind of natural high. Actually, I am. I'm high on Gabe, and how could I not be with him almost-naked, on top of almost-naked me? My heartbeat pulsates between my legs, surging together with desire. I want Gabe, all of him, and stopping now—

A tiny bit of awareness rears its head: Slowing down makes sense, even though I'm a tad disappointed. But then, no, actually, I'm not. I think I'm falling a little more for Gabe just for putting the brakes on.

He cares.

Gabe-who-cares lifts his head and looks me straight in the eye, a mischievous expression on his face. "But you know what? That shouldn't stop us. It should make us adventurous."

And before I've digested what he just said, he's rocking his hips into mine.

Holy—!

Holy *everything!*

It's like he pressed a button of pleasure right *there*. Lightning zips through my veins, igniting every single cell and every freakin' strand of DNA in my body. Is that sensation normal? How can it be? It's shortening my fuse, burning me out—

Gabe circles his hips again, pressing in against me, and all conscious thought stops. All that matters is him and me.

I reach up and dive my fingers into his hair, keeping his head low, forehead against forehead, as I push my hips against his.

"Gabe," I whisper. It's more a moan than a word, a plea to continue, to please not stop.

Gabe makes a deep, throaty sound as he continues his motion, and we both forget about the past and become lost in the now, lost in each other.

CHAPTER TWENTY-SEVEN

When I wake up in the morning, I'm wrapped in a wholesome, all-encompassing mix of feelings: Warmth. Security. Closeness. Comfort. Trust. Protection. Maybe even lo—

"Good morning," Gabe whispers, presses a kiss to the top of my head and pulls me tighter against him. Which, by the way, is basically impossible: like two very needy octopuses, we're cuddled into each other, front to front, my face buried into his chest, his chin resting on top of my head, and arms and legs entangled and wrapped around each other.

A bit as if we were afraid to let go when we fell asleep.

Happiness surges. "Good morning," I whisper against his skin. "I like waking up like this."

"Me, too." Gabe rubs his palm over my back, and I'm a wee bit disappointed we did at one point last night put some clothing on. The touch of his skin on mine... addictive.

"I've been awake for a while," he says, voice low and soft, "enjoying holding you."

A face-splitting grin pops up on my face. "Laying it on thick, are we?" But please, keep doing it. It charges up my batteries and soul.

"Just learning that the truth is the better way to go."

Aww.

I place a kiss against his gloriously naked chest. At least *he* didn't put on a shirt. Would've been a waste, considering Gabe's toned abs and soft skin.

The muffled sound of dishes being handled comes through the door.

"Cris got up a few minutes ago," Gabe says. "And as much as I want to stay right here, I guess we need to get back to business."

Dang it. That diminishes the happiness-upload into my batteries and soul. He's right though.

I nod. "I'm mentally putting a pin into this very situation to come back to later tonight." I nuzzle his pec with my nose one more time, then untangle myself from him and swing my legs out of the bed and get up.

I push a button on the wall, and the automated windows lose their tint and let in the faint, reddish light of the rising sun. As I turn around to go to the bathroom, my gaze falls onto Gabe.

The same armada of butterflies from last night takes up flight and goes through a series of aerial maneuvers at the sight of him in my bed.

He's propped himself up on his side, head resting on his palm. His blond, wavy mane of hair is tousled thanks to me repeatedly grabbing it last night. Some more stubble shows on his face, making him look even more manly, as if the very defined pecs and abs didn't already do a fantastic job with that. The sheet has pooled around his lower hips and legs, but I can still see the band of his boxer briefs before the rest of the goodies are hidden from view. Add the reddish glow from the rising sun…

Yeah.

All of a sudden I understand why the old master painters

during the roman or Greek empire or whenever liked to draw women in those poses: it's a damn turn-on.

I must say, it gives me a whole new appreciation of art.

A mischievous, indulgent smile grows on Gabe's face. "Like what you see?"

Now, there were times where I'd been embarrassed caught staring, and I would've denied everything, no matter how obvious it was. Not today, though. Not anymore, and not with Gabe.

I learned my lesson, too.

"Yeah," I whisper, letting my gaze drift over his body. "Definitely enjoying the view."

His smile widens to a grin and he wiggles his eyebrows at me. "Please, don't hold back." Pushing off the blanket, he gets up, which gives me a superb view of his toned butt. He lifts his hands to the band of his boxer briefs—

—and yanks them to under his glutes as he shakes his booty. "One last look until later."

I laugh out loud as he pulls the pants back up, turns around and beams at me.

"Glad my butt is making you laugh." He grabs his pants and shirt and slips into them, then takes his phone off the charger and holds out a hand for me. "Breakfast?"

"Yes, please." Quickly, I slide into my pants, then take his hand. Gabe opens the door, and together we walk out of my room into the combined living- and kitchen area.

As Gabe predicted, Cris is up and in front of the TV, like yesterday, a bowl of cereal in his hands.

"Morning," Gabe says.

"Morning," Cris replies with his mouth full, only sparing us a quick glance before he swallows. "Ah," he says, "is this what's referred to as the walk of shame?" He licks the milk off the spoon, sets the bowl onto the table and reaches for the jar of Nutella. Looks like he's branching out.

Gabe grins. "There ain't no shame in this walk, my friend." He wraps his arm around me and kisses my temple. "Ever."

Aww. My face heats, but it's nothing against the warmth enveloping my soul. Guess those batteries can keep on charging.

"And here I was thinking I read you both wrong and TV wasn't a good education on real-life human interaction." Cris shrugs and opens the Nutella.

I take out two mugs from the cupboard. "Were we that easy to read?" I ask Gabe under my breath. Because I sure didn't— Well. I take it back. I was in denial, and in retrospect I might've given off some me-like-Gabe-vibes.

"I probably was." He shrugs as he fills the electric kettle with water. "But Cris is family, so all is well."

The truth of what he just said strikes me right into my chest. He's right. Cris is family. He's the brother I never had, somebody I love, although differently than Ga—

I clear my throat.

Nope. Not going there.

Not yet.

Busying myself with the loose tea leaves and tea bags, I pretend I didn't just try to name my feelings for Gabe in a whole new and scary way.

Lalala, didn't happen.

"By the way, I've been monitoring the news." Cris points the spoon at the TV.

Oh, right. Neanderthal-genes. Seizures. Death.

I clear my throat and give a shake of my head. Not going there. This here, this morning, is the upwards slope of our story. We'll continue our work, prevent the seizures, and Gabe and I… Heat rushes my face, and boy, if it didn't make me bite on my lower lip, I'd look like an imbecile grinning: Gabe and I.

Squee!

"The news. And?" Gabe turns away from the electric kettle and leans against the countertop.

"Lots of jolly news about us. I mean it, some actually is good for us. Like, the highlight of my morning was to hear Advangen's stock has plummeted and is predicted to drop even lower. Shareholders aren't happy with what they've done, and apparently they're especially unhappy with Dr. Sherman. Yes, Duncan has published those screenshots, Gabe. And also yes, they seem to have cost Advangen a nice chunk of supporters."

"Duncan, my man," Gabe pumps a fist, then shakes his head. "So this is where people draw the line with ethics? Editing somebody's genome, experimenting on them—whatever, but man, paying somebody to lie, that's not okay."

Cris lifts the hand holding the spoon and waves it. "Don't ask me. I'm slowly losing my faith in common sense." Cris sighs and rolls his eyes. "Also, because now we're into semantics if what you did is theft or kidnapping. That then basically became yet another discussion of whether or not I'm a thing. To stick with their favorite example, which is getting so old, by the way, a dog would be stolen from its owner, and so would a chimpanzee from the zoo. They wouldn't call it kidnapping."

"Jesus," Gabe mutters, arms crossed in front of his chest, legs crossed at the ankles, staring at the TV. "What are they saying about… the other stuff?"

I.e., me being in the same boat as Cris and our… predicament.

Cris takes a moment to lick some Nutella off his spoon. The moment he does, his eyes widen. Turning the jar in his hand, he smacks his lips. "Oh. That's… unexpectedly good, considering the color." He scoops up another heaping load of the brown, sugary goodness onto his spoon. "Anyway. It seems people have realized we're the victims here, now that the mutation became a death sentence. There was a poll, taken before yesterday's news and then after, and it showed that eighty percent of people now say we should be allowed to live our life the way we want to."

I huff. Sure. "One, never trust an analysis you didn't falsify yourself—old math proverb my math teacher used to say—and I'm with him. That survey means nothing. Two, of course they're now okay to have us live our life, because we're going to die soon anyway."

"Yeah. That." Cris drops his gaze, then sniffs once and points his loaded spoon at the TV. "But on the fun side, did you know Earth is being taken over by mutants? First there were none, then one, now there's two—but how many are there really, and how is the government hiding them? What's their ultimate plan?"

"Ah," Gabe says. "Fox News?"

"Yup."

"Of course." Gabe shakes his head in mock despair, then unlocks his phone and scrolls through something, an intense look of concentration on his face that doesn't change when I gently nudge him aside to get to the kettle with the now boiling water.

I pour both of us our tea and grab both mugs. "Gabe? You know that this look and silence make me nervous, right?"

"Huh?" He snaps his gaze to mine, seeing through me for a moment, before his eyes focus on me. "Yes. Social media. Sorry. Just annoyed by the world, or at least by the people who don't condemn Sherman's attempt at buying my loyalty. And..." He smacks his lips. "And maybe a tad surprised by the amount of hate aimed at me for not screwing you guys over and looking out for myself instead. It's... impressive."

I grimace. Crap. Of course we all have gotten our fair share of hate-comments, but seeing Gabe so exposed to them… It makes my heart ache for him. It's so unnecessary—and he's the one who's choosing to be here. "You sure you don't want to rethink leaving—"

"Don't even finish that sentence." He steps closer and rubs both hands over my upper arms. "The saying goes, in for a penny, in for a pound. It doesn't mention getting out for a million dollars anywhere in there. And I know you're only saying that because you like me—"

"What? Me?" I squeak. "Why would you think—"

He shuts me up with a kiss, and OMG, will those butterflies please take it down a notch? They all flutter up at the same time, making me feel weightless.

"That's why," Gabe whispers against my lips when he breaks the kiss. "And no, thank you, but I made my bed. I'm gonna sleep in it now. Preferably with you next to me."

Aww. My cheeks heat. "I wouldn't mind that either."

"Then we stick to that plan." He winks at me and kisses my nose, then pockets his phone. "And all my timed posts have gone live as scheduled, by the way. So, welcome to a life of full disclosure in every type of media. No matter what people read or listen to, they all now know."

Gabe takes a cup from me and follows me to the couch. I sit down next to Cris as Gabe falls into the cushions on my other side, miraculously not spilling any tea. Having him sit next to me, his side touching mine, is such a disconnect from everything crappy in my life.

And thanks to Gabe, I didn't think about any of that crap for many, many hours.

Yesterday, those genes were the most important thing on my mind, but this morning… not. This morning, Gabe was important. Gabe and I. *We* were important. And last night, not a single thought had crossed my mind that I wasn't human. I didn't feel self-conscious or weird when we made out, because what was happening between us was exactly that: between us. Between Gabe and Nya, not between a human and a mutant. And not between a boy who'll live, and a girl who'll die.

Having set the Nutella on the table, Cris wipes his mouth with the back of his hand and gives the suspiciously empty-looking jar a longing glance before he sighs and turns his attention to Gabe. "You added the seizures and death sentence as well, right? Because I feel full disclosure is a thing, and I want people to know the whole story. If they call me a thing and I return to Advangen, I will die in that basement. And I really don't—"

"Easy there, Cris." Gabe reaches past me and slaps the back of Cris' head. "Nya and I are working hard to have neither of you die."

Cris perks up. "You got something?" Hope swings in his words.

"We do." I nod. "I mean, we're not there yet, but, to sound super vague, it looks promising."

"Just wondering, what else did you expect when this dynamic duo is doing the research?" Gabe turns his phone around for Cris and me to see.

I burst out laughing. "You posted this?"

"Highest number of likes so far: *#fixingwhatswrong* and *#hopetosurvive* have been surging after this went live."

Whistling through my teeth, I pat his shoulder. "Impressed, Gabe. Impressed." He did well, the picture is a magnet for likes: us, in the lab, in our white coats, protective goggles on, holding up a pipette—me—or a beaker—Gabe—and grinning into the camera as the embodiment of go-getter attitude and optimism.

"Aww." Cris makes puppy dog eyes at the picture. "What a

dorky dynamic duo."

Gabe levels him with a gaze. "Master of alliterations, you forgot delightful. And the dorky-part don't hurt, we know that and we own that."

I snort out a laugh. "That we do." Always have. "So, anyway. We'll get to work in a minute or two, because today we'll have to—"

A knock comes from the door. We exchange a glance. Johanna, maybe?

"Come in," Gabe calls out.

The door opens, admitting my dad.

A weird mix of feelings rises at the sight of him, like a sixth sense of foreboding.

"Good morning, sorry to come by so early, but…" He closes the door, then shoves his hands into his pockets, and boy, does he look like crap: dark circles under his eyes, hair all over the place, and stubble on his face. Are those the same clothes he wore last night? I narrow my eyes and shake my head once, trying to get rid of that annoying sense of doom Dad brought into the room.

"Can I… Can I sit?"

Wordlessly, Gabe points to that chair.

Dad shuffles over, a far cry from his usual uber-on-top-of-it persona.

And it makes what's left of my somewhat good mood go *poof* in absolutely no time. "What's going on?" I wrap my fingers around my mug, all business. "Did you even sleep?"

"Not really." He suppresses a yawn and rubs a palm over his eyes. Geez, he looks like crap. But the worst part is that he looks… beaten. Like fate did him one over after he thought he tricked her.

I swallow hard. "What's the problem?" Because there is one. There might be a chasm between us deeper than the Grand Canyon, but I know Dad. A sickening feeling rises in my gut. Not good. So not good.

Dad leans forward, bracing his elbows on his knees. He lets his head hang forward, and I don't need premonition to know in which direction this is going.

"It's the vector," I say, sorrow wrapping around my heart. It's the only step that can throw a wrench into our progress at this point, the only pitfall courtesy of working with WissenSCHAFFT instead of Advangen.

"Yes," Dad whispers, a look of soul-crushing sorrow on his face. "WissenSCHAFFT doesn't have the virus vector we need. The plasmids they use for plants won't work, for obvious reasons, since they're, well, for plants, and the few gamma-retroviruses they use... They won't cross the blood-brain barrier. And if it doesn't get into the brain—"

"It won't stop the seizures. Even I get that." The finger Cris uses to tap his temple shakes.

"No, it won't. We can start the design anew, but it will take us weeks to produce enough for even one dose."

"Fuck," Gabe hisses and lets himself fall back into the cushions.

Fuck, indeed. We don't have weeks. We have days, maybe a single week, if Cris' rate of seizures is any sign. The floors open beneath me. My road block is great, but it's nothing without a delivery vehicle to the brain.

Nausea rises, pushing bile up my throat.

Dad kneads his hands together. "The absolute vexing thing is that I have a serum we can use at Advangen. It would only need a simple alteration and it would be good to go. I have it. I just can't access it."

"Advangen?" Gabe asks, voice hoarse. "That doesn't sound good."

"It's not. But the serum I have been working on—"

I narrow my eyes. "Serum." There's that word again, and it rings a bell. "Like the one that kept you late at work the last few months?" Before things went downhill, when he was the epitome of a distracted scientist during dinner?

Dad nods. "Yes. Exactly that serum, actually. My serum plus your approach *can* work. We—"

I tilt my head to the side, remembering how stressed he was about that serum. And remembering the details. "You said the patient was going to die if you didn't get it done."

"Well." Dad gives a pointed look at Cris. "Yes. Thanks for rubbing it in, Nya."

I snap my gaze to Cris, then back to Dad, adding one and one and surprisingly arriving at two. "The serum was... for Cris? It can't have been for me, because when you started working on it, you thought I was healthy." I only started showing symptoms later, markers and headaches. And that can only mean... "You were trying to fix Cris."

Dad doesn't even have enough energy to sound insulted by the incredulity in my voice. "Of course I was. Cris may have been Brian's creation, but he was always under my care. I always felt responsible, I still do."

That epiphany rushing over me, it's eye opening. It explains so much. The late hours for the serum—to help Cris. The way Dad insisted patients would come to harm if he left Advangen—because Cris wouldn't be under his care anymore.

Everything about my dad and Advangen is convoluted and complicated, but... but I don't think he's a bad guy.

Dad locks his gaze with Cris'. "I wish... I wish things had been different. I wish I could've taken you home and made you part of our family."

No, Dad isn't a bad guy. Just a guy who made poor decisions.

The apple in Cris' throat bobs with a hard swallow as he lowers his head in a slow nod. "Yeah. Me, too." He drops his gaze and exhales steadily through pursed lips.

"Okay." Gabe slaps his thighs, then rubs his hands together. "Love the bonding moment, but what about that serum? What is it?"

"A stable lenti-viral vector I altered and designed specifically for Cris's case. It doesn't cause immune reactions in the host, crosses the blood-brain barrier, and integrates into the host's DNA, meaning the changes are permanent. The cure would be permanent. The only reason I couldn't use it with Cris was that my approach to fixing the gene was not the best, as I now know." He gives me an acknowledging nod. "What we have here at WissenSCHAFFT is great for what they do, but not what we need. In a very cruel twist of fate, we need the serum I designed, which of course is stored at Advangen." Dad lets his head hang lower, shoulders slumped forward.

"And you have nobody on the inside, nobody?" I swallow, but my throat is too dry. It feels like I jumped out of a plane, happy to have a parachute, only to realize it had a gaping hole in it. Oh, and the ground was racing to meet me.

"Even if I did, you'd need a constant, stable temperature for transport. It's not like somebody could just drop it in their pocket and bring it over. Plus, Advangen isn't stupid. They will have everything that is—was—mine under constant surveillance. They like to hold on to their secrets, and right now, I'm their biggest liability."

"And that means we're this close to a solution, but the detour will take too long, since the next seizure still might kill me. Or, Nya." Cris looks from one person to the next. "Correct?"

"Unfortunately, yes."

Oh boy, does that make me angry. Which, let's be honest, is better than bawling my eyes out, which is still option number two I'm considering.

I ball my hands to fists. "We need the serum Advangen has."

Dad shoots me a glance, like, *you don't say*. "I've been texting Brian. Begging him to give me only the amount I need, but he hasn't responded. I doubt he will. He's lawyered up to the teeth, and I probably shouldn't have texted him, but… I needed to try every avenue available."

I close my eyes. There's always something. Always. We get Cris out of the basement—and get chased from our hiding place by Advangen. We find shelter at WissenSCHAFFT, and we find out I'm also part Neanderthal. We adapt our strategy, and then it turns out Cris and I have a deadly genetic mutation that'll kill us. Okay, so we adapt again, but now fate just *had* to throw in another roadblock.

Is she freakin' kidding me?

Silence hovers, and it's heavy and oppressive.

Gabe wraps an arm around me, pulls me closer and kisses my temple, which prompts Dad to do a little jerk. He opens his mouth, then snaps it shut and sighs.

Thank you. I don't need comments on my love life in general, but especially not at this very moment.

Gabe smacks his lips. "What if we—"

"Yes." I cut Gabe off, jump off the couch and hold out a hand for him. "Let's."

His eyes narrow. "You don't even know what I was about to say."

But I do. I've known Gabe forever. I know how his mind works. "You wanted to get back to work and *make it work*." Which is exactly what I need to do. I can't sit here and wallow, because that won't help me. Won't help Cris. There must be a way to attach our Trojan Horse to a delivery vehicle. There *must*. We just have to look hard enough, try enough routes, and one will lead to the destination.

"Well." Gabe takes my hand and gets up. "You got me there."

I lift my chin. "Dad, we'll be in the lab. I'm not giving up, and… your input would be appreciated." That's the only olive branch I'm willing to extend for now. I squeeze Gabe's hand. "Let's work on a miracle."

Eight long, frustrating, and disappointing hours later, I push back from the lab table and stumble back against the concrete wall in the lab. Everything feels surreal.

I blink, but that feeling of disconnection from reality stays. I'm here, physically, I know that. The wall feels hard and cold behind me. Cold sweat is running down my spine, droplet after droplet, leaving goosebumps in their wake, and my hands are shaking. I feel all that, but my mind is detached from my body. On a different plane of existence, one where we didn't just run out of options, where we didn't fail.

My knees can't hold me up anymore. I let them buckle and slide down the wall until my butt hits the equally cold floor.

It didn't work.

Only a day ago, we were so ecstatic, so optimistic, rightfully so. My idea was good. Really good. Once-in-a-lifetime-good. It should've been a piece of cake, considering how difficult genetic engineering can be. It should've been perfect: my idea, plus Dad's serum, both designed for exactly the same purpose, to fix Cris' and my mutation.

It should've been so many things, yet was and is none of them.

Dad's perfect serum is out of reach, and without it, my perfect idea is worth nothing anymore.

To make it worse, we don't have enough time. There's no shortcut, no matter how hard I look. We can't conjure another magic potion out of thin air, even though I know what that potion should be. We just can't get it manufactured fast enough. Thinking it up is easy. Production is not.

We're out of options.

I draw my legs in, wrap my arms around them and rest my forehead on my knees.

We're done for.

Steps approach from my right. *Gabe.*

I hear him suck in a breath, then whisper my name with such a sadness in his voice, I know he knows as well.

He comes closer but stops when somebody else's steps reach him. *Dad.*

"Let me," Dad says under his breath. "Please."

"I don't think you're the right—" Gabe's phone rings, and he curses. "Dammit, I'll have to take this, but make no mistake, I *will* keep an eye on you." The threat in his voice in unmistaken.

"Don't worry, I… I have no intentions of being difficult."

I don't think Gabe replies, but the sound of his soft steps announces his leaving.

For a moment, silence fills the room before Dad comes closer and sits down next to me. "Nya?" he whispers.

"Yeah?" It comes out broken, *wrong*, like that wasn't my voice, but somebody else's.

"I won't give up. We'll get that serum somehow."

I sniffle. "You're just saying that to make me feel better."

"No." Determination hardens the word. "I will get my serum,

and if I have to break into Advangen—"

A choked off laugh breaks from my throat. "See? Sometimes you have to break the law to fix things." Like Gabe and me, getting Cris out of this damn basement.

Dad stays silent for a good thirty seconds before he draws his legs up and scoots closer until his left side is pressed into mine. "You know… I'm very proud of you for what you did. For freeing Cris."

I lift my head. Did I hear that right? "You are?"

A small smile plays on his lips. "I am. It's quite odd, because I want to be mad at you for uncovering all my secrets, but… you deserved to know the truth, even though I wish it were a different truth."

"Yeah." It comes out hoarse. Don't we all.

"But even in the mess I made, you just… shine. Cris was a well-kept secret for close to twenty years. You figured out about him within days." He huffs, but it sounds more incredulous than anything else. "And then you don't turn a blind eye, but do the right thing… Again, besides the part that got me in trouble, which also, I expected to happen eventually; it's exactly what I raised you to do. *You did the right thing.* I really am proud of you."

Dad is proud of me. I didn't expect that—neither those words, nor to hear them now, of all times. Dad and I always had a complicated relationship, at least since I started my way into science, and now I understand why. But those years when I felt I *wasn't* doing the right thing, when I felt his disapproval in every cell of my body, they hurt. So, hearing him say he's proud of me… it lays the foundation for the hole in my heart to be filled. Eventually. If I don't die before that happens. Emotion clogs my throat, and it comes with a load of tears blurring my vision. "Th-thanks, Dad."

His smile turns sad and tears shine in his eyes, just like in mine. "And even now that all my goodwill to do good, to have you born healthy and stay healthy, has proven to be worthless, even now you use that fantastic brain of yours and come up with ideas my senior scientists would never think of. You have so much spirit, and so much of it from your mom. It rips my heart wide open to see you like this."

"Dad," I croak-whisper. Not sure if I can hold back those tears pricking at my eyes.

"I'm sorry, Nya," he whispers, voice cracking. "I'm so, so sorry for everything. I wanted to make things right, and I messed them up instead. I'm so, so, sorry." The raw vulnerability on his face and in his voice break the last bit of restraint I had barely held up.

The first tear falls from my eye as I suck in my lower lip and bite on hit, hard.

Dad swallows loudly, then reaches up to my face, wiping away the tear with his finger. "I'm so, so sorry."

Maybe it's his gentle touch, the sorrow in his gaze, the hoarseness in his voice, or just every-freaking-thing combined, but it does me in. Tears spill down my face as I cry with big, ugly sobs, and—

Dad wraps his arm around me and pulls me into him, pressing my head against his chest with his other hand. He holds me so tight; I feel his body shake like mine, wrecked by the same sobs. I sneak my arm out and hold on to him, like I used to when I was younger. He smells of Dad and home and safety, and boy, does that make me cry even harder. Dad's tears fall onto my head, and so we sit and hold on to each other for dear life.

After a good two or three minutes, the door to the lab opens and closes softly, followed by Gabe's soft steps coming closer. I can tell when he sees us, because he stops and takes a moment before he clears his throat.

"I'm sorry to interrupt, but… We have a situation."

"Oh, great," I mumble into Dad's chest. "'Cause we haven't had one yet."

I straighten up and wipe my nose, then notice how soaked Dad's shirt is where I cried. I wince. "Sorry," I say, wiping at the fabric.

Dad catches my hand. "Never be." He holds on to it and covers it with his other one. I must say… it feels nice. More normal. Less like we're on different sides. Maybe crying together helped, not that we'd look like it did us any good: if I look anything like him, red and puffy eyes, wild hair, we must be a sight to behold.

Gabe slides down the lab island across from us, the one I worked on before… well, before. He draws up his legs and rests his forearms on them. "I just spoke to Chelsea. The lawyer," he adds for Dad's benefit.

My ears perk up. "And?" Because that could be good or bad, but given the last couple of days and the way Gabe looks, I'd go with bad.

Nausea churns, but it's been my constant companion for a while now, so it's not like I didn't have time to get used to it.

A muscle in Gabe's jaw ticks. "Well. Chelsea has already been contacted by Advangen's lawyers. I'm sure your lawyer is going to inform you as well, Steve, but here we go. I'll deliver the message: They would like for you to refrain from contacting Mr. Sherman, but that's not our biggest problem. That would be…" He holds his breath for a second before slowly releasing it and smacking his lips. "Well. No easy way to say it. Advangen won't budge. They hold all cards in their hands, and they know it. To spell it out, they claim proprietary reasons and *do not* intend to give us the serum you requested. Unless—"

I suck in a sharp breath while Dad growls. He actually *growls*. "These fuck—"

"I did voice a similar opinion, especially when I heard the second part."

A groan leaves my throat. "I don't think I want to hear it."

"No, you really don't." Gabe's voice is clipped. Hard. "Dr. Sherman notified Chelsea that the only way he'd consider giving us the serum was if we handed back his property. He gets Cris, we get the serum."

He gets— "No." I shake my head so hard I get dizzy. "Not going to happen. Never. Not in a million years."

"That's also what I said." He gives me the smallest smile and wink, then holds up his phone and wiggles it. "In the end, *this* is the game that's being played. And we've started playing it before they did. We're leading it, I hope. So, we all better come up with content, y'all." His gaze meets mine, full of so many emotions, all of them warm and wholesome, patching the hole in my soul and holding it together. "Because this fight isn't over. Not by a long shot."

CHAPTER TWENTY-EIGHT

As most of the time since we moved into Johanna's penthouse, the TV is on and blaring news crap about us I'd rather not hear. I find it difficult to comprehend why the boys continue to turn on that stuff, but I assume it's crucial for us to be aware of what's happening around us.

I find it bearable only because Gabe and I cuddle together on the couch, with my head resting against his shoulder and his head leaned against mine. Hearing and feeling his heartbeat is an unbelievably exciting yet calming sensation.

And I need calming today.

While yesterday was a day loaded with fear, frustration, and failure, today was more about overcoming—or rather, ignoring—those obstacles and upping our game. We picked ourselves off the ground, literally, in my case, and went to work. We've posted, we've updated, we're doing well, but Advangen hasn't made a single move. They're silent. And it's making me antsy beyond belief. Everything we do gets some kind of reaction. People comment, like, share, and view our content—Gabe has a table of responses sorted by platform, so yes, people see us. We aren't loved by everybody, but we're seen. The noise we make is loud.

Only Advangen seems to be deaf.

One should think the damage to their reputation was already big enough, but maybe that's the problem. Maybe it's at such a level, it can't get much worse. Nobody likes them right now, either because they altered our genes, or because they altered our genes in secret, or because they won't fix what they broke. No matter what people fight about, that they can agree upon: Advangen messed up.

The ethicist currently on some kind of news show agrees with me.

"—several ethical red flags. Foremost, there appears to be a clear lack of informed consent and a violation of basic human rights—"

Ya think?

"—subjected to invasive medical procedures without his knowledge or consent. This is a fundamental breach of the principles of autonomy and self-determination—"

I throw my head back against the couch's cushion. Patience is a virtue I don't possess today. "How long are we supposed to wait Advangen out? I mean, it's been a whole day. Twenty-four hours since they refused to give us Dad's serum. None of us had a seizure, which is wonderful, but that could change any second, and then Cris could die! Sorry," I tag on, throwing an apologetic glance at Cris in the comfy chair off to the side.

He only shrugs. "Oh no, please, don't hold back. Say it as it is. When one only has a few days to live, reminders to enjoy every minute are appreciated. And I'm not even kidding." He wiggles his spoon and then dives it deep into his jar of Nutella, a look of pure joy on his face when he digs out a heaped serving.

Gabe, as always the last two days so close to me I can hardly tell where his body ends and mine starts, toys with the hem of my sleeve. "Don't want to sound too negative, but according to Chelsea, the legal system can take forever." He fishes for his phone on the side table next to him and unlocks it. "So, she says she's throwing everything at them she has, and that includes two civil lawsuits—"

"Two? One for me, one for Cris?"

"Actually, then four. Two per person, one malpractice, because the unapproved genetic engineering resulted in harm to you both, and one wrongful life suit, which is saying that you wouldn't have chosen to be born with the genetic modifications had you been given the choice."

"Debatable," Cris says. "I still don't hate the life I had. Could've been worse."

"Well, if you want to win your case, please don't say that out loud in court," Gabe comments drily.

"No worries. I've watched enough reality court TV to know how the legal system works." He grins and licks some Nutella off his lips.

Gabe drops the phone onto the pillow to the right. "So, to answer your question how long it can take… A very, very long time. I mean, even if they speed it up, because, public outrage, etc, I can't imagine it will be under a few months. Even getting a neutral and unprejudiced jury is…" He shakes his head. "Challenging."

Months. I close my eyes. We don't have freaking months. I let out a frustrated growl. "There must be something else. How can we increase the pressure on Advangen? What do other people do when there's nothing you can do? Like…" I wrack my brain and slap my temple, to help it along. "Like… Oh! I know! Injustice— people go on hunger strikes! We could—"

"Hard no." Cris holds the spoon filled with about a pound of Nutella halfway to his mouth, lips set in a thin line. "Seriously. Hard no. I just discovered there's a world beyond broccoli, kale, and dry chicken breast. I'm not going to give up the one thing I actually have to bring me joy—for an unclear outcome."

"But—" I snap my mouth shut, then deflate. "Okay. You're right." We're already unleashing as much public pressure on Advangen as we can. More than many, many other people have amounted to with their hunger strikes. What difference will it make besides making us miserable until we die?

Yeah.

Fun times, for sure.

Cris lets go of a little relieved Nutella-happy sigh. Watching him with that stuff is like seeing somebody going through a religious out-of-body-experience or something like it: His eyes are closed, lips turned up in a soft smile as he sucks the last bit of the hazelnut spread off the spoon. Some of it sticks to his knuckles, meaning this jar is probably more empty than full if he had to dig that deep for his fix.

No, I can't take that from him.

Neither I—nor anybody, really—should take *anything* from him. He just got his first taste of a tiny bit of freedom, a freedom people like me, who grew up with real freedom, wouldn't even call that. It's a glass cage we're in, albeit one with good food and a million streaming channels.

But it's still a cage. One we're going to die in.

The telltale burning of tears stings my eyes, but I refuse to blink and let them fall. Instead, I stare at the TV until my vision blurs, and the image of the anchor and ethicist turns into nothing but foggy colors. I wish I could tune out all her words the same and make them disappear, but no such luck. The anchor's annoying voice penetrates my weakened walls.

"*—are claiming there's no legal ground for Advangen to hand the serum for the two teenagers so desperately needing it. I must say their* *statement is quite extensive: in their eyes that serum is a trade secret and protected. They also have an NDA with Dr. Bennison, Nya's father, which means nothing else but that he legally isn't allowed to reproduce the serum outside of Advangen's walls. And, to top it off, Advangen does not have a legal obligation to share said serum. It's their intellectual property, and they can do with it as they please. Your comment on this development?"*

The ethicist clears her throat. *"Obviously, my point differs. As an ethicist, I believe that Advangen has a duty of care to the individuals whose lives have been impacted by their research and that withholding the serum is a clear violation of that duty. Adding the fact that Cris was reportedly kept in the dark about his genetic modifications and subjected to invasive procedures without his knowledge or consent is a clear violation of the Nuremberg Code, which, as you know, was developed in response to the atrocities of Nazi medical experimentation and sets out basic principles for ethical human subjects research."*

"My goodness," the news anchor says. *"Aren't you going a bit far? Nazis?"*

"I'm stretching the comparison, I know there are vast differences in scale and context between Advangen's actions and the systematic, state-sponsored atrocities of the Nazi regime, but my point is that Advangen has displayed a callous attitude toward the individuals impacted by their so-called research reminiscent of the Nazi view of certain groups as disposable and undeserving of basic human rights. I—"

"Turn that off." I make a dismissive hand motion toward the TV. "It's the same crap, just different people. I'm sick of it." Nazi-comparisons… Not that I like what's been done to us, but there are differences, people.

Gabe reaches for the remote and clicks the power button. "Better?" He takes my hand and weaves his fingers in-between mine. "I get how shitty all of this is," he says quietly, while brushing his thumb over the back of my hand. "But we're doing all we can."

But are we? I chew on my lower lip. "We have to crank it up. Advangen feels too safe, trade secret, lack of legal obligation to share, blah, blah. They need to feel so pressured to give in they want to come to us and beg us to take the serum and make them look like the good guys again, and I don't care where that pressure is coming from. Well, obviously not anytime soon from the legal system. And no, the hunger strike is out the window," I throw in when Cris pulls his eyebrows down into a V.

"Good," he mutters, throwing a somewhat sad glance into that suspiciously clean jar.

Gabe sighs. "I know what you mean, but what else can we do? We're on so many platforms, all that's missing is a Kickstarter project, and still we're at a standoff: we want the serum, and they want Cris. They don't want to give us the serum, and we don't want to give them Cris and condemn him to the same life of experimentation and benefitting Advangen he's had for the last eighteen years." He sounds frustrated. "Believe me, if I had a Nobel-prize worthy idea, I would've come clean with it. But short of going to Advangen, banging on their door and dragging out Mr. Sherman to—"

I sit up straight. "Wait. Say that again." My blood pressure spikes, making my blood pound in my ears. I think I just had an idea.

"Say what again?" Gabe wrinkles his nose. "That I want to drag out Dr. Sherman and introduce him to my—"

I swat at his fist. "So violent. Appreciate the thought, and I do feel the same way, but we have a somewhat better option." Not a perfect one, but beggars can't be choosers in our situation.

"We have a better option?" Cris repeats.

"I'm curious myself." Gabe scoots away from me to look at me, a tad too skeptical for my taste.

I punch him in the thigh, lightly and lovingly, of course, as always. "Negative Nancy. Yes, we do have one option we haven't gone for." I bring both palms out, facing up, like serving them my idea. "Open confrontation."

"Open confrontation." Gable scratches his temple. "As in…?"

"As in a showdown. I took a page from your playbook, actually, Gabe. We have a million people standing outside these walls, plus how many news vans? We leave this building, they'll follow. So, we go to Advangen. All three of us. We walk right to their main entrance and demand to speak with Mr. Sherman. What do you think will happen? All the reporters who followed us, plus the ones stationed at Advangen, will broadcast live what's happening. He isn't coming out? Nasty blow to Advangen's rep, especially when the tears come out." I pout and trace the path of a hypothetical tear down my cheek. "Or even better, when we give our passionate hero-speech, like in the movies, and again, it gets broadcasted *live*. We're hoping for him to feel pressured to the point of giving in, put on the spot. And yes, I know it's not a brilliant plan, but it's at least a plan. Our best shot for now."

For a moment, both guys are silent. Then, Cris tilts his head to the side and nods. "Huh. Not bad, actually."

"Not at all bad." Respect shines in Gabe's eyes. "Being there, in person, live TV, hero speech—"

"Which you will give. I'm just the mutant, but you were a real member of human society. That's your job." Cris nods his chin at me.

"Me?" I jab a finger at my chest. Heck no, that's not the plan! "I thought that was more of a collective thing, all of us together!" I'm not a public speaker, Gabe is much better at that!

"Cris is right, though," Gabe says. "It needs to be you. You delivering that hero speech, flanked by us..." He smacks his lips. "It could work. At the very least, it's worth trying."

I groan. Yes, it's worth trying, but man. Shot my own foot there.

"Hundred percent worth trying." Cris claps his hands. "We drive there tomorrow morning?" When Gabe and I look at each other and nod, he grins ear to ear. "Nice. Do we take Johanna—"

"No." I shake my head. No need to even think about anybody accompanying us. "Not Johanna, not Dad, nobody. We leave early, before people are up and it gets busy. If we talk to Johanna or Dad, they'll get Chelsea involved. And a lawyer by our side censoring our words would make our trip look like a calculated political move, not like the spontaneous teenage uprising we want this to come across as."

"Right. And," Cris says, pointing a finger at me, "from what I know thanks to a thorough TV-education, Chelsea might keep us from talking to Dr. Sherman all together. Because, reasons."

Exactly. "And that would negate the entire purpose of this trip."

Cris holds his hand up for a high five. "Cool. I like that we're having a plan. Much better than sitting around in this suite. Live broadcast of a passionate speech, for the win! We're *so* going to get that serum!"

I hit his palm, even though his words cause a wave of nausea to flare up. I doubt it's going to be as easy as Cris makes it seem. For one, there's the hero-speech, which isn't exactly a strength I list on my resume, and for another, there's the wild card, the man without a conscience, Dr. Sherman. I have no clue how he's going to react, he's unpredictable in a whole new way. Do I hope with all my heart my plan succeeds, and he gives in to public pressure?

Yes.

But I also wish we had something else to strengthen our position. I wish we had something more foolproof than too many variables to control.

Two hours later, I pull my blanket up to my chin, but rest my arms on top of the soft fabric. Even the sheets in this suite are high quality. If it weren't for all those other annoying circumstances, I could pretend this was the fanciest hotel I've ever been to.

I should probably enjoy it while I can.

Before that thought can get to me, Gabe exits the bathroom, dressed only in boxer briefs, tight abs on full display.

"Show off," I mutter, which makes him grin.

"You complaining?" With one elegant motion, he slides onto the bed and props himself up on his side, facing me, a mischievous look on his face.

I chuckle and turn to face him. "Not at all. I appreciate the view. Also appreciate that I can do this." I place my palm on his chest and drag my fingertips over his pecs. Gabe's body is such a contradiction. His muscles are firm, but his skin is so, so soft. It's quite the addictive sensation touching him.

He closes his eyes and makes a purring sound. "Please, don't stop on my account. All yours." He gestures down his body.

Another chuckle leaves my throat. "All mine. Do you need me to sign it? Accept delivery?" Using the tip of my index finger, I scribble a fast something onto his skin.

Suddenly, he turns serious. "Actually, do it here." He captures my hand and finger, and guides it so that my nail scratches his skin right above his heart, moving it up and down with just enough pressure to leave red, raised marks until he has spelled out the three letters of my name. "Perfect," he whispers. "That's where you are. Right here." Flattening my palm against my heart, he looks at me from under his lashes, all vulnerable and cute and—

I bite my lower lip. The surge of emotions rushing through me is beyond overwhelming, and I'm not fast enough to throw up mental walls, so sue me if my voice wavers a bit with my next words. "I like being there." In his heart. Boy, a few weeks ago I would've thought that so cheesy and made a gagging noise, but now… It's different.

"Always been there, always will be," he says so matter-of-factly, a little gasp escapes me at the certainty in his words.

Always been there, always will be.

Or at least, for as long as I'll live. Those few weeks or months. No pressure for tomorrow, no biggie if I don't convince Sherman to give us the serum.

As if he'd heard my thoughts, Gabe's expression softens as he brushes a strand of hair from my face. "Hey. What's going on in that head of yours? You seem… worried. About tomorrow, I assume? The televised hero-speech?"

Bull's eye. But while I'm nervous about speaking in public, I'm a megaton more nervous about failing. About delivering a hero-speech only worthy of a direct-to-video production instead of one featured in the biggest blockbuster of the year. The thought of failing, of letting Cris down, of wasting his only chance, gives me palpations.

"Yeah. It's… weighing on me," I say, trying to keep my voice steady.

Gabe tugs on that same strand of hair he just brushed behind my ear. "Have you thought about what you want to say?"

"You mean after you guys threw about a million buzzwords and half-sentences at me?"

"Yup. I expect you to call him a cold-blooded, calculating, blackmailing bastard, as I suggested."

I nod like a bobblehead figurine. "Of course. It'll be my opening sentence."

"Really?" A surprised look crosses his face.

"No, doofus." I roll my eyes. "I'm not going to start by insulting him." Although I'm considering ending on it. English was never my strong suit in school. Science, yes. Creative writing, no. And it's not as if they taught us to come up with a life-saving, one-chance-only hero speech anyway.

I swallow dry. No pressure.

Gabe gives that strand of hair a harder tug. "Boo for fooling me. But if I try to be serious for a second here, you got this, Nya. It doesn't have to be perfect. Maybe we shouldn't have called it hero-speech. It needs to be from the heart. What you think, what you want. Be real. Be yourself. The impact will be far greater then compared to reciting a speech that isn't yours."

That's kind of what I'm hoping for. I have a few things lined up, but nothing I could write down right now. "I've got enough ammo. I just hope I'll be able to use it right in the moment." Adrenaline, nerves, pressure…basically my regular Tuesday these days.

"You will. And even if you don't say a single word, and just stare at him—"

"Stare down, not show down?"

He grins. "Exactly. Even then, it'll send a powerful message. We can only win."

I exhale slowly. Ah, optimism. Why are you holding out on me? "Your words to Fate's ear. But what if we don't? What if our plan doesn't work?"

"If he doesn't give us the serum?"

I nod.

"Well, either way, our plan will set *something* in motion. Maybe he won't give in right away, but if more and more of his shareholders side with us, I'm sure he's going to see an upside to giving us the serum."

Eventually, maybe. Money makes the world go round, after all, but... "It could take too long," I whisper, my voice rough. "We don't know how long Cris has." And while we think I have longer, that's not what we're going by. We need that serum, ASAP.

His chest heaves up in a sigh. "It won't take too long. Your idea is good. Great even. And if it doesn't work... it's not like we'll then give Sherman what he wants and leave Cris with him, see-ya-later-buddy, have fun being Sherman's unlimited mutant stem cell supplier again. This isn't Make a Wish. Sherman's only choice is how painful his downfall will be."

Sherman's unlimited mutant stem cell supplier.

My entire body tenses. Dr. Sherman wants stem cells. *Mutant* stem cells. What if—

No.

No, no, no.

We don't negotiate with terrorists.

We won't negotiate with Sherman either.

I suck in my lower lip. But *if*... *If* push came to shove, we ran out of time, and we had no other option... I close my eyes and let fear and devastation wash over me. Then—

"Hey. Nya." Gabe brushes a finger over the puckered skin between my eyebrows. "What dark thoughts are bringing those worry wrinkles on?"

I make a non-committal grunting sound and file my idea away, under *L* as in *last-ditch-effort.*

Gabe places his hand over mine on his chest again. "You know you can talk to me. I want to know what's going on in there," he taps the blanket right above my heart, "and in here." He taps my forehead.

No, you don't. I wish I hadn't even had that idea.

Nausea rises, but I push it down and force a smile, shaking my head. "I don't want to talk about any of this anymore." It's a half-truth, a lie by omission, but really, I'm done. It's after hours. Doom and gloom need to wait until the next business day if they want an appointment with me.

"But—"

"Nope." I curl my fingers over his pec, and Gabe sucks in a sharp breath, then lets out a little desperate groan.

"Nya—"

I lean in and press my lips to his, effectively shutting him up. Gabe responds instantly, his hand sliding into my hair as he deepens the kiss and shifts my emotional overload to a whole different level, one I like much, much better.

Every touch, every caress of his lips, sends a shiver down my spine. I lose myself in the sensation of his mouth moving against mine, the warmth of his body pressed close. In this moment, nothing else matters. Not my speech, not Dr. Sherman, not that tiny sapling of an idea I would rather rip out than let it grow. None of it does. There's only Gabe and what we feel for each other, only the flame that burns between us, bright and fierce and all-consuming.

Gabe grows impatient, throwing back my covers and sneaking his hand under my shirt. His fingers skim over my stomach, leaving a trail of goosebumps in their wake. I gasp into the kiss, arching into his touch. More. I want more. I *need* more. Feeling Gabe is life-affirming, it's everything. He's better than oxygen, better than anything else people consider necessary for life. They know nothing.

We continue like this, hands roaming, mouths exploring, until my shirt is gone, leaving me in my bra. We're both breathless and flushed. Gabe pulls back slightly, resting his forehead against mine. "I wasn't lying when I said that." He taps a finger to where he scratched my name into the skin above his heart. "Always been there, always will be."

Stupid, sappy tears prick at the corners of my eyes, and I swallow hard. I want nothing more than to stay in this moment forever, to feel Gabe's skin under mine, have goosebumps pop up all over my body when he touches me, and think of nothing else but him. I want to memorize every little detail just in case I—

No. Not going there.

Instead, I take his hand and place it over my heart, repeating the same words he spoke to me. "Always been there, always will be. No matter what." And I mean it, with every fiber of my heart. The thought of losing Gabe, of hurting him, is almost too much to bear.

And yet, I know in the depth of my soul that I might not have a choice.

Gabe swallows audibly, then splays his fingers over my chest, brushing the outlines of my bra.

Both of us suck a fast breath in, a sudden charge of heady tension filling the air between us. A deep sound rumbles from his chest, reverberating through my body, and like a switch was flipped, Gabe shoots forward, bridging the few inches between us in a heartbeat.

Our bodies are flush as he slides the strap of my bra down my shoulder, lowering his mouth to mine. I tip my head back and wait for the delicious touch of his lips to add fuel to the fire raging inside me. I want to let it devour me. Let *him* devour me.

For now, nothing else counts but Gabe and me.

And tomorrow… we'll see.

CHAPTER TWENTY-NINE

The next morning, I don't feel so good.

Even though the way I fell asleep was as peaceful as can be—lying cuddled into Gabe, my head resting on his shoulder—my subconscious apparently wanted to play out some worst-case scenarios: Cris chained to the basement at Advangen, screaming as they draw marrow from him. Me, seizing, but observing myself during the seizure, like an out-of-body-experience. Gabe and me at Cris' funeral, my soul ripping apart as they lower the casket into the pitch-black hole in the ground.

Fair to say I'm still traumatized from the night.

Waking up and realizing those were nightmares was a blessing, remembering that the nightmares could be set in motion today… not so much.

"Everybody ready?" Gabe asks, one hand on the doorknob of our suite's entrance door. "Cris, stop taking the kitchen apart," he calls over to Cris, who's been opening and checking cabinet after cabinet. Gabe's brows furrow when his gaze drops to me next. "You okay? You look pale. Second thoughts?"

I shake my head. Second thoughts aren't my problem. "No. Not at all. Just want to get it over with." And make it work. Because my imagination has shown me very vividly what will happen if I fail.

Cris grunts and closes the last cabinet. "Are we out of Nutella?"

Gabe levels him with a blank stare. "I wouldn't know. Neither of us has even gotten near that stuff in the last days for fear of losing a hand if we dared to touch it."

I burst out with a small laugh and feel better instantly. "I think we're out, but I'm sure Johanna will get it restocked today. It'll be here waiting for you when we come back."

"It better," he grumbles as he walks over to us. "Guess I'm ready then."

Gabe gives us both another questioning glance before he opens the door. Nobody's in the hallway, which is great, and nobody is in the elevator down, which is also great. To be honest, it feels more like sneaking out than it actually is, really. Doesn't mean I wasn't happy not running into anybody on our way to the underground parking garage where somebody had parked our car after our somewhat unorthodox arrival.

"Poor car," Cris says and pets the scratches and dents in the car's right front. "You were very brave, breaking through those bushes."

Gabe grimaces. "I completely forgot to update Duncan about that. Whoever the person was he organized this car from, I doubt they expected *this*." He motions to all the scrapes and bent metal, witnesses to the wild ride we had coming over here.

I slide into the passenger seat. "But guess what? His car's going to be famous now."

"And probably on live TV." Gabe turns on the engine and reverses out of the parking spot while Cris still fumbles with the seat belt in the center of the back row.

Gabe drives us up the ramp, slowing down when he gets to the automatic rolling gate. It detects our arrival and slowly opens up.

"Look at that," Gabe murmurs as the parking lot comes into view. "Conveniently awake already."

Indeed.

While nobody is yelling anything yet, the parking lot is already—or still?—filled with several people. Two reporters are chatting right in front of the garage's exit, both keeping their fingers tightly wrapped around the steaming Starbucks cups in their hands. They move aside for us, their eyes widening in recognition.

Slowing down, Gabe lowers all our windows. We want them to see us. "Good morning," he says, like there was nothing extraordinary about the fact we're casually driving out of the building they've besieged for the last few days.

"Uh, good morning," one of them replies. He tilts his head to the side, as if he was trying to make sense of what he's seeing, blinking quickly as we pass him by at a walking pace. The other guy is quicker. His gaze snaps from his colleague to me in the passenger seat, then darts over to Gabe and Cris.

"Where are you going?"

Thank you, exactly the question I was waiting for. I school my expression with what I hope is steely determination. "To talk to Dr. Sherman. Our situation is life and death, and we're not going to let him play us like fiddles." First quote for the hero speech? Nailed it.

The reporter's mouth hangs open, and for a split second, he appears frozen. Then, like on command, he and his colleague both drop their paper cups and dart to their respective news vans.

Gabe chuckles. "Part one of the plan, working."

We keep the windows down as we continue down the parking lot at a leisurely pace. A good number of reporters and supporters—or haters, who knows—stay over night, and whoever wasn't awake yet, gets woken up by the noise of several news vans starting their engines. We make sure they all get a good view of us on our way off the parking lot as they crawl out of their fogged-up cars.

In fact, we're doing such a good job, we already have a following of at least six news vans once we hit the little side street, and even more once we reach the first traffic lights. I throw a glance into the rearview mirror and whistle through my teeth. "We're leading a caravan." A caravan of news vans and… yup, also some private vehicles by now. We're bringing our witnesses to where we need them. Good.

We fall into a relaxed silence while Gabe keeps us under the speed limit, making sure we don't lose our company. After about ten minutes, he sighs and wiggles to get to his back pocket. He pulls out his phone and gives it to me. "I must say, I miss the days where I didn't get a million alerts per hour."

"You could silence them," I say.

"And miss how the world is reacting to us? Not going to happen. The only thing I want to silence is that gene causing your guys' seizures."

I chuckle, then reach over and pat his shoulder. "Genetic engineering dad-joke. Nice, Gabe."

He grins as he focuses back on the road. "Thank you. Knew you'd appreciate it. Do me a favor, check those pop-ups, please."

I tap the first one, hold the phone in front of his face to unlock it, then read through the messages. "*Mutants on the Move*. That's the first one. Next one is a bit more elaborate, that's a message on X—who still uses that, by the way?—from ABC news, *Showdown at Sunrise*. Huh. Kinda stole our line there. Okay. And then here… Well, they definitely all know we're on our way. This here is a call to action, which is nice. It's from *EthicsInResearch*, and they're asking everybody who can to support us at Advangen."

"That's good, right? Lots of attention." Cris claps his hand.

"Yeah, that's good. We want word to spread that we're coming. It'll increase pressure on Sherman."

Cris responds with half a choke, half a gasp.

That weird noise—

Crap! I drop the phone into my lap and twist in my seat. "Cris, I forgot! The driving! How are you? Nauseous? Gabe, slow down!" I look back at Cris, but instead of being all white and pasty, he's actually… smiling.

"No need to slow down. I'm doing just fine. We're fast, and it doesn't seem to bother me this time."

Well. *Fast.* Not really. I look out the window into the desert landscape. We're definitely faster than Gabe drove on the way to WissenSCHAFFT, but not a tad above the speed limit, if I'd have to guess, but either way, it's progress. "Yay you then. But why that choking sound?"

He points his thumb behind us. "I saw a cool red car, a sports car, and I liked it. Thought that since I don't mind driving as much anymore, I could get myself one of those, eventually. If I don't die, that is."

Gabe chuckles and ignores the doom's day last sentence. "You, behind the wheel? I'd pay to see that."

"One, you might have to, since I don't have any money to get a license or a car and I consider you all family at this point, and family helps each other out. Two, I would be a phenomenal driver," Cris retorts, feigning offense. "I've had plenty of time to study the theory."

"Because knowing the theory has always made for phenomenal drivers. It has nothing to do with experience in traffic," Gabe replies.

"I would obviously get that experience. Learners' permit. You, me, your car—"

"My car?" Gabe yelps. "I love my Beemer!"

"Caring is sharing." Cris meets Gabe's gaze in the rear-view mirror and blinks, innocence impersonated.

"Man, you're killing me here. I—"

As they banter back and forth, I look from one to the other. From Cris, so alive, so hopeful, making plans, but also accepting what fate throws in his way, to Gabe, supporting both of us through a mess nobody could have anticipated on the day I didn't know where to go and knocked on his door for help.

A lump forms in my throat, one that's hard to breathe around. Nobody here deserves what happened to us, but least of all Cris. He can't die. I don't want to die either. No surprise there, but Cris… I've got to keep him alive.

Not sure when I started feeling so responsible for him. Maybe when I found out it was Dad who played a hand in his fate? No. Earlier: When I realized that guy in Advangen's basement was basically a kidnapping case. That's when I knew I had to take care of him. Every minute we wait, every minute *I* wait, puts Cris at risk, just to emphasize that. Backing out or failing my hero-speech is not an option.

Mr. Sherman, we've come here to—

No.

Mr. Sherman! You're an egoistic, cruel man and—

Well. It's the truth, but will probably make him angry, so not the best start.

Dr. Sherman, you—

No! I won't call him doctor, it puts him on a different plane that us, like he was better, and he's not.

Gabe reaches for my hand and squeezes. "Hey," he says softly.

"You okay? You seem like you're lost inside your head."

"Huh?" I whip my gaze over to him. "Y-yeah. Just going through my speech. Nervous. The usual, at this point." I come up with a small smile.

Bringing my hand to his lips, he presses a soft kiss to my knuckles. "We'll get through this together, I promise."

My heart nearly shatters at his words: Together. How I wish he's going to be right, but I don't dare let myself hope. If Plan A doesn't work, Plan B…

I close my eyes for one eternal moment. Plan B will hurt Gabe. Big time, and that thought, of hurting him, and worse, of first hurting him and then losing him, of not being able to be with him, is almost too much to bear.

But I can't let Cris die, not when only I have the power to save him.

Gabe adjusts his fingers to mine, squeezing the living daylight out of them, then clears his throat. "Hey, Cris?" He calls out. "I can't believe we've not talked about that yet, but: favorite TV show?"

Cris makes a huffing noise. "Easy. Anything *Star Trek*. Although *Loki* was awesome, too. *Stranger Things* made me feel too much like I was also stuck in the actual Upside Down, so that's a no."

"Okay then. Favorite *Star Trek* show. I'll go first. *Lower Decks*."

"Nice choice," Cris says, "but obviously you're wrong. *Strange New Worlds*."

"What?" Gabe taps the back of my hand with his finger and catches my eye, winking at me. *You'll be fine*, he mouths, before he squeezes my hand once more. "Nya. Be the judge. Help a guy out here."

In this very moment, my heart is full, so full, it might just burst from all these wholesome feelings. Gabe gets me like nobody else in my life. What distracts Cris also distracts me, and I'm more than thankful for it.

So, for the next forty-five minutes, we talk about everything and anything that comes to mind. I keep my fingers in-between Gabe's, the small contact grounding me in reality.

As the miles slip by, I try to memorize every detail of our ride. The way the sun streams through the windows, casting a warm glow over Gabe's face. The sound of Cris' laughter as he and Gabe move on to arguing about the best Marvel series. The feeling of Gabe's hand in mine, strong and steady and sure.

Dad calls my phone, but I let it go to voice mail.

He calls again, and I turn my phone off.

They must've found out what we're doing.

I close my eyes and breathe in over ten long seconds. Should've said goodbye, but… It would've given too much away. If Plan B comes to play, then… Then I'm sorry, Dad.

As the Los Angeles skyline appears on the horizon, the nausea churning in my gut cranks it up. After today, everything will change. I may never have moments like this again, moments of peace and love and friendship. But I will do whatever it takes to secure the serum for Cris.

No matter the cost.

⚬⚬⚬

As we hit the city limits and then the neighborhood around Advangen, the conversation becomes more strained until nerves shut us up for good. Nerves, and that churning nausea inside my stomach.

It feels weird driving the same way I took to get to my

internship, now that everything has changed. Gone is the pride, the excitement, replaced with trepidation and a generous serving of disgust. Gabe feels it, too.

"Different lifetime, eh?" he says quietly.

Definitely.

We turn the corner to the usually quiet side street Advangen sits at the very end of, and—

"Holy—! Is that—" Cris snaps his mouth shut when he sees the obvious we can't overlook: the crowd of people.

"Jesus," Gabe wheezes. "That's a lot. Way more than I expected!"

If I ever wondered how hundreds of people fit into the Advangen parking lot, now I know: They don't. People spill over onto the sidewalk, street and areas surrounding Advangen, some of them standing still, others marching with their banners and posters held high. It feels like somebody beamed over the crowd from WissenSCHAFFT with all their signs and chants and duplicated it. Or triplicated it. But hey, at least they changed it up.

"You got your wish, Cris. Fresh signs," I whisper, craning my neck to see one we just passed by.

"Lots," Gabe adds, then laughs out once. "*Pro-Life, Pro-Choice, Pro-Mutant.* Okay, I'll take it."

Cris claps his hands. "I got a better one: *Gene-ius Nya,* and they drew a beaker and Petri dish next to it as an exclamation mark, and hearts!"

I snap my head to the left. "Where?" My name and—

"Somewhere there, we just passed it. Oh, there's the old and never boring *Kill the Mutants,* now available in plural, and yikes, *Their Seizures and Death = God's Punishment.* Right. Oh, oh, there—I'm seeing some good ones! *Stop Designer Babies*—okay, agreed—then, *Your Fault, Your Responsibility, Fix Them*, ah, there's a…" He narrows his eyes then jerks back from the window. "…what's that? *Cris, marry me?* Are these people for real?"

"Welcome to the crazy world of fandom, buddy," says Gabe with a laugh, but sobers up a split-second later, when somebody throws their sign, stake and all, at our car.

"Geez!" He swerves, avoiding the car getting hit. "Okay, maybe we were a bit naive, hoping for people to come here. That's definitely gone overboard. This crowd is wild, we'll have to stick together and make sure—" He curses, barely avoiding somebody jumping into the street, fist raised, screaming at us.

Crap, crap, crap—this is way more than expected! The crowd is so thick, it's a sea of people, no, an ocean of people! No matter where I look—

I gasp. "Guys!"

"What?" Gabe's voice is pressed, clipped.

I jab a finger against my window. "They have a huge outdoor movie screen, by the back rows, and—" I squint. "There's some kind of news show projected there, from this lot, and— Oh. Right. There's our car." Holy everything, that is… I don't even know.

"Car, you're famous now. We called it," Cris whispers and pets the seat next to him.

I'm not sure getting any more famous is good right now though. Adrenaline pumps through my veins, making me jittery. The surrounding chaos makes me feel like being thrown to the wolves, only we're stupid enough to throw ourselves.

Keeping our speed low, Gabe drives us into Advangen's parking lot. The crowd parts before us, but they must've been there done that, because they're only going back just enough for the car to pass.

"Guys. I'll park by the EV charging stations in the front. I want them to see us and televise, but I don't want them to kill us while we're getting to the entrance." Tension swings in Gabe's voice. "It's a rough crowd. Once I stop and we unlock-slash-open the doors, we'll have to stick together."

I wipe my hands on my pants. "Got it. Get out, walk to the front door, make noise—if anyone can even hear us—and let Sherman come outside."

"While not getting killed by the crowd," Cris repeats. "Again, would be a bummer at this point."

"No shit, Sherlock," Gabe mutters under his breath as he stops the car nowhere near an official parking spot, but only about ten meters from the stairs to the main entrance.

The crowd pulls tighter around the car, their yells and screams morphing into one deafening blanket of noise.

"Ready?" Gabe calls out, voice raised. "And go!"

We all throw open our doors—

And we're bombarded by an even louder noise. Yells, shouts, scants, whistles, screams—

Holy Guacamoley, arriving at the Oscars can't be noisier than that! Hands reach for me, for Cris, for Gabe, as soon as we duck out of the car. I reach for Cris at the same time he fishes for my hand. We interlock our fingers so tight, my fingers hurt.

"There they are!"

"They're here!"

"No right to live! No right to—"

"Fix their genes! Fix—"

"No mutants!"

Gabe gives up to get around the car and instead slides over the hood. He lands right next to me and takes my other hand.

"Make room!" He yells at the top of his lungs. "Coming through! Coming through!" He waves his arms as if he was shooing away the masses, but there's only so much he can do. Within a few steps, the car's swallowed by the crowd, and while I catch a quick glimpse of the entrance, signs and waving arms cut off my line of sight to *any*where. There's only people and yells and whistles and—

Somebody pulls on my hair and grabs my face, fingers digging into my skin. I yelp out—

"Monster! You're an abomination! Unnatural!" A woman screams into my ear. She pulls me by my hair and I rip my hand from Gabe's, swatting at her blindly, until she lets go. What in the absolute—!

Gabe scrambles for my hand again and pulls me forward as five or six men, all dressed in Advangen security uniforms, force their way over to us. Aww, crap, more people to fight off—but no, one of the men inserts himself on my left side, separating me from the woman.

"Move, move! Don't stop," he yells, shoving the woman back and keeping himself as a barrier between her and me.

I don't think I've ever felt so much gratitude for any one person after only a few seconds. I nod at him, eyes wide, because, heck no, I'm not stopping! Adrenaline makes me jumpy, jittery, and turns my heart into an erratic bouncy ball in my chest. This is chaos, absolute pandemonium—I'm not sure how we can wait in this crowd for Dr. Sherman. There's no way we're going to stay in one piece!

The security guard who saved me from having my hair ripped out yells out commands at his colleagues until they've formed a barrier between the crowd and us, like a lipid layer in a cell membrane.

Following Gabe and pulling Cris with me, I make myself small as I push through the narrow corridor opening for us. My heart hammers like crazy, every breath is short and wheezy, but there's no time to act, no time to think or process anything, because at this point the whole crowd must've realized we're out of the car if the increase in loudness is any indication. More of the same stupid chants pop up as well, deafening and louder than the good chants:

No right to live!

Lock him up!

No wait: Lock *them* up. That's what they're saying.

I grimace as I keep my head low, forcing my way through the crowd, flanked by security. *Lock them up.* I want to say it feels great to be included, but it doesn't. Gabe jerks his head back just when something comes flying from the left, hitting another protester instead of him.

An egg.

We're being *egged.*

Somebody screams on my left side. "You have no right to take their rights! They're human—"

"And you're an idiot if you believe that," somebody else yells back, and another egg flies through the air.

Jesus!

"Cris! Faster!" I have to drag him after me, but I don't dare look back why he's so slow. Can't afford to take my eyes off what's in front of me—and to the sides—but I can wager a guess what Cris is facing: the same as me, or even worse.

I squeeze his hand so hard I might have to apologize to him later, but I can't loosen my grip. The crowd is *wild.* They're shoving and pushing, trying to get closer, either to support us or to kill us, who knows, and if it wasn't for the security guys around us, I don't think we'd have a chance to make it. As it is, I feel like in the center of a mosh pit during a death metal concert. Why is it so much worse here than at WissenSCHAFFT?

We were so, so stupid coming up with our plan. Correction: I was. It was my idea, after all.

"Almost there," the security guy next to me yells. "Keep your heads down, keep moving!" He forces some fifty-something year old man with a *"Go Gabe!"*-sign in his hand away from us. "No touchy-touchy!"

We make it to the stairs leading up to Advangen's main entrance, and relief washes over me. Almost there. This is insane, literally insa— Ugh!

Out of nowhere, I get pulled back and down before Cris' hand turns limp in mine. I grunt and stumble backwards when my foot misses the step. "What the—"

Spinning back, it takes me a second to make sense of what I'm seeing. Cris… Cris is on the ground, and—

"Shit!" I curse as realization strikes. "He's seizing! Gabe!" Horror assaults me, cold and sharp, slicing into every fiber of my being: *your next seizure might be your last.*

No idea how Gabe heard me over this cacophony and chaos, but he did. He pushes his way back to me and Cris, like a swimmer going against the stream, while the security guys build a human wall around us.

Cris twitches and stiffens, and while we've seen it before, it's a billion times scarier right now, in the middle of a crowd that wants to eat us alive and while knowing this could be the seizure to kill him. *Dizzy.* I'm struggling to pull air into the all-encompassing ball of fear where my lungs should be.

"Change in plans! We've got to get him inside," Gabe yells, his movements hectic as he scrambles for Cris' arm pits. "Nya! I need your help! I can't carry him alone!"

That snaps me out of it. Somewhat, at least. I swallow down the panic, the fear, the unbelievable anxiety, and scoot to the left so I can take his feet, while Gabe grabs Cris from behind and under his armpit. He nods at me, and together we lift him.

Oh, crap. My back protests in an enraged spasm. Cris isn't the lightest to begin with, after all, he's well built, but when he's seizing, he's close to impossible to carry. His legs jerk and stiffen at irregular intervals, and the strength he develops in his core when twitching is unbelievable. We drag him more than we carry him up the stairs while the chants never stop, the whistles, the noise—

"Faster, guys!" A news reporter aiming a camera at us uses his free hand to hold the door open, and we burst through and into the lobby, flanked and followed by the last security guys and the reporter. One of them slams the door shut behind us, bringing the noise level down to bearable. "Locked!"

Gabe and I drop to the floor, laying Cris down as gently as possible. I'm on my knees and next to him only a split-second later. "Cris…! Come on, come on, break that stupid seizure. *Please!*" I feel like I'm a foot away from a ledge and about to be pushed over into a free fall any second now. Cris is seizing, but I'm the one shaking because of it.

"We need a medic!" one of the security guys yells, but Gabe waves them off.

"No medic," he calls back, and as crude as it sounds, right he is. A medic won't help us. Either Cris makes it, or… he won't. "It's privacy we need! Take that camera down!"

The reporter flinches, and, to my utter surprise, complies. "You got it."

Gabe acknowledges it with a short, jerky nod of his head as he rips off his jacket and tries to angle it to also cut the view for the crowd behind the glass doors. Problem is, we only have one small jacket for a lot of Cris.

"Incoming!" The word is followed by fast and heavy footsteps of two of the security officers carrying over a room divider. Good.

I snap my gaze back to Cris. Even looking away for a split second makes me worried I might miss something. His last breath, his last move, his—

As they set up the divider, a shadow falls over us and the surrounding light dims. "Thank you, that's perfect," Gabe says.

The guy who saved me from the crowd nods. "No problem. Anything else you need?"

"No. We'll stay with him until he's back to normal." Gabe's voice isn't as steady as it usually is.

… until he's back to normal. Or dead.

Yeah.

"Of course. Just to let you know, it's my duty to update Mr. Sherman we let you three into the lobby."

"Got it." Gabe takes his jacket off Cris. "Do what you have to. We… we appreciate your help."

"Our pleasure. Man, they were wilder than usual today." The security guy huffs, then retreats, his steps slower and more measured this time.

And Cris is still seizing.

"Nya. Nya!" Gabe taps my arm.

"Huh?"

"Help me with his head. Come on."

I snap out of my trance and help Gabe slide the folded jacket under Cris' head. So helpless. Making a pillow for him is all we can do. That, and, well, pray.

Gabe brushes a hand over Cris' hair. "Jesus, buddy. Way to go making an entrance." Then he stares up at me with wide eyes, the shock and fear in them mirroring my own. The crowd, Cris… He doesn't say it, but I'm pretty sure we're both thinking the same: This can't be it. He can't be dying, not here, not now, of all times, not when we're not ready.

Not when I'm so close to get him what he needs, either way.

Every second, every twitch, every stiffening of Cris' body plays out in super slow motion.

He's seizing forever.

"Please wake up, please wake up, please wake up." I whisper it over and over again, like a mantra, a prayer, a deal I'm trying to strike with fate, although I have nothing to offer. He must wake up, he must, but it's taking forever, the twitching looks way more brutal than before—

But if I'm not mistaken, it's slowing down.

I suck in a sharp breath through my teeth. "It's slowing down."

"It is." Gabe blows out a puff of air, the next word filled with as much relief as I feel. "And he's breathing more regular. Halle-freakin'-lujah."

Hallelujah indeed. I let my eyes fall shut to hold back the tears of relief. Can't cry again, but knowing that Cris is fine, will be fine in a few minutes… It's more than relief I'm feeling. Like we've been granted another chance. It's not over yet, neither for him, nor for me.

I hold on to Cris' hand, not only to support him until he wakes up, but to steady myself. My hands are shaking. Actually, *I* am still shaking, head to toe.

Silence falls, only interrupted by the waves of chants from the outside. After about two more minutes, Gabe scrunches his eyebrows together and shifts so he can reach into his back pocket and pull out his phone. "This thing still won't stop buzzing," he says a half-second before his eyes pop wide when he looks at the screen.

"What is it?" I scoot a tad closer. Being at Advangen, the mob outside, and Cris' seizure have put me in a constant state of PTSD and anxiety. Not where I need to be for my impending hero-speech, so no, I don't need to add anything else, really.

Gabe huffs out. "I mean, we wanted media coverage. We got that." He turns the phone for me to see—and there we are, smack *everywhere* on his feed, from different angles: pictures and videos of us getting out of the car, ducking, hurrying through the crowd, but mostly they're of how we carry a seizing Cris inside. Some videos have a closer view, others more an overview, but all of them look as scary as it felt being in that moment.

"Oh wow," I whisper, a weird sense of apprehension tingling down my spine, "that was fast. And *not* what I was going for with media coverage." I turn my head to look down at Cris. I guess decency and privacy are out the window once the public develops an interest.

Gabe sucks in a harsh breath. "What happened to your face?" Gently he reaches up to my cheekbone. "You're bleeding."

"Oh." I touch my right cheekbone, my fingers meeting warm, sticky wetness. *Blood.* "That's why it's stinging." I hadn't really paid much attention to it.

"Did one of *them* do that to you?" Steel creeps into Gabe's voice as he jerks his chin behind us and toward the crowd.

I wipe my hand on my pants. "Yeah, somebody grabbed my face and hair." Another shudder runs down my spine thinking about it. Being grabbed out of nowhere is a violation I hadn't experienced up to now, and I hope I never will again.

"Are you fucking kidding me?" Anger hardens Gabe's voice? "Those cowardly fucking—"

"Gabe." I shake my head. "It doesn't matter."

"It doesn't matter?" Incredulity shines from his eyes. "They hurt you, Nya!"

"And that won't be the reason I'll die," I snap at him.

Gabe recoils, then closes his eyes, jaw so tight, I'm worrying he might crack a molar.

Crap. He didn't deserve that. "I'm sorry," I say. "That was uncalled for. I'm just so on edge, and…"

Gabe forces a slow inhale, followed by an equally slow exhale. When he opens his eyes again, he nods at me. "I get it. I just don't like you talking about dying. And, by the way, we don't have to take what they dish out. We fight back our way." He uses his thumb to press something on his phone. "Stay just like this, keep facing me." Raising his phone, he takes a picture, then types something and turns the screen around about twenty seconds later. "They injure you, they get to see what effect that has."

The picture pops up on top of our account, and God, it's haunting. My hair is chaotic, my eyes wide, my right cheekbone red and bloody from the scratches. I look like a panicked, wounded deer caught in headlights. The way I'm holding on to Cris, my knuckles turned white, and since Cris' eyes are closed and his head rolled to the side, it looks like…

I swallow hard.

Yeah. Not fun to think about.

My gaze drops to the very first hashtag before the dump of all the other million hashtags Gabe uses for us: *#MoreHumanThanMany*

If only they'd all understand that.

CHAPTER THIRTY

After another five minutes, Cris opens his eyes, blinking up at us with a dazed, hazy expression. The more his gaze turns sharp, the more his face drops. "Aww, man," he groans after yet another few seconds. "Another seizure?" His voice is hoarse, his words slightly slurred.

"Yup," Gabe says. "But the good thing is, you're still alive." He gives him the equivalent of a winning grin and a thumbs-up.

"And the downside is, everybody out there saw it." Cris pushes himself up to sitting and rubs a hand across his eyes, then glances around, taking in the lobby and the makeshift privacy screen surrounding us. "But I see you tried. Thank you."

"Emphasis on tried." I pat, then squeeze his shoulder. "I'm afraid people and their cell phones were faster."

He groans and rolls his eyes. "Lovely."

"Indeed." I pause. "But maybe it helps people understand what's really going on." I look from Cris to Gabe and back. "Hearing about seizures and seeing them are two different things. So maybe it actually helped us."

Cris doesn't seem convinced, but he lets the subject drop, then waves his hand at the privacy screen and the lobby. "So, what now?

This isn't exactly how we planned for things to go."

No, it isn't.

But I'm not sure where to go from here.

I exchange a glance with Gabe, who looks as uneasy as I feel. We're wobbly with our plan to begin with, and having what little strategy we had torn into shreds isn't really what I would call helpful.

I lift and drop my shoulders. "Maybe we should—"

The sound of several footsteps echoes through the lobby—and then Dr. Sherman himself rounds the corner, flanked by two security guards.

Oh, crap.

There goes making a decision. It's just been made for us.

I scramble to my feet and brush my palms off the side of my thighs. Gabe helps Cris up to standing, and within five somewhat chaotic seconds we face the man who played fate for us once before, and is doing it again.

He stops after a few steps into the lobby and crosses his arms in front of his chest, standing in a wide stance. *Tell me you're in charge without telling me you're in charge.*

We take another few seconds to realize what he wants: for us to come to him. Another show of strength. He's in control. Not us.

And, as much as I hate it, I couldn't agree more.

This is the moment Cris' life depends on as well as mine, and it's very unfortunately also the moment I realize I'm not ready for it, not yet. My hands are shaking and my thoughts are scattered, courtesy of our chaotic last minutes. Nerves bubble inside me. How am I supposed to convince Sherman to give us the serum when I can barely string a coherent sentence together? And without the pressure of an audience?

Privacy is bad.

At least in this case.

I force down a way too dry swallow.

Commence operation *fake it until you make it*, and boy, will I fake it.

As if I met cold-blooded bastards every day, I step forward, my back straight, chin held high. The boys follow me a tad slower, since Gabe is supporting Cris with an arm around his waist.

I take a deep breath, squaring my shoulders as I come to a stop about three meters in front of Dr. Sherman. That's close enough. I don't trust him to not snatch Cris and make a run for it. After all, we're in the lion's den, his building.

"Mr. Sherman," I say, mentally patting myself on the shoulder for keeping my voice steady. "Thank you for agreeing to meet with us." Dang it, that was a sentence I planned on saying *with* an audience. Without one… it changes things. Mainly, our chances.

I swallow hard as Sherman raises an eyebrow, his expression cold and calculating. "I didn't *agree* to anything. You barged into my building and caused quite the scene outside."

Opposed to the scene that was there already?

Alas, I don't take the bait, but cut right to the chase. "We didn't have much of a choice besides coming here. You refuse to give us the serum."

Sherman waves a dismissive hand. "Not open for discussion. I've made my position clear—the serum is our intellectual property."

That moment when I thought I wasn't ready? Never mind. Anger flares in my chest, hot and bright. How can he be so callous, so uncaring about two lives at stake? "If anything, it's my dad's intellectual property! He developed it specifically for us!" I gesture to Cris and myself. "And I would like you to remember that this guy here is the one *you* experimented on, the one whose DNA *you* altered without his consent! Because of what *you* did, I have the same problem, and we're the ones who will *die* without that serum!"

Dr. Sherman's expression remains impassive, even though he watches me like a hawk. "Since that seems hard to understand, the serum is Advangen's intellectual property, developed by your father, who's employed by Advangen, and as such, any discoveries he made belong to the company. We're doing nothing more than using our legal right to protect our proprietary information."

I step forward, jaw clenched tight, any thoughts making my speech or plea gone, overwritten by disgust for the man I'm facing. "Legal right? What about moral obligation? You have the power to save two lives, and you're choosing to hoard that knowledge for your own benefit? Because, who else is there who might need it besides us?" Unless— Oh God, are there others? Others like us? Horror slices through me. What if Sherman kept doing what worked so well? What if Cris is just the tip of the iceberg?

Sherman rolls his eyes. "Nobody else needs it. But that doesn't mean it doesn't have any value to me. If nothing else, it's a fantastic bargaining tool." He pointedly looks at Cris.

Without thinking, I step sideways, blocking Cris from his view. "Oh, so that's how it's going to be?" Tears of frustration burn my eyes, but I blink them back, refusing to let Dr. Sherman see. "Blackmail?"

A slow smile spreads across his face, one worthy of a horror movie. "Not at all. As I said, Advangen is well within its legal rights to maintain control over the serum. I'm only saying that maybe I could be persuaded to give you some of it, depending on the circumstances." He nods his head at Cris again. "You know what I want."

Oh, hell to the no! "First, let me make one thing perfectly clear," I growl. "I know *whom* you want. Cris is a person, *not. A. Thing*! Address him as such!"

Sherman huffs. "Sure. If it makes you happy."

"A common courtesy doesn't make me *happy*, but it makes me a tiny bit less likely to rip your head off!" I grab the air with my right hand and snatch it back to my body, imagining it's Sherman's hair and head I'm yanking. Thank you, Neanderthal-genes, for that little burst of violence.

Gabe sucks in a harsh breath, then chuckles. "You go, Tiger," he mumbles under his breath.

"Big words and attitude for somebody whose life is in my hands, don't you think?" Sherman smirks. That arrogant bastard *smirks*!

"I could say—"

He holds up a hand. "You could, but I really don't care what it is, or what either of you could say."

I narrow my eyes. "But—"

"No. I'm done with this very unfruitful conversation. You know where to find me if you want to talk business."

And with that, he turns on his heel and strides away, his security detail falling into step behind him, leaving us standing in the middle of the lobby like unwanted cargo.

I open my mouth and close it, no sound coming out.

Cris makes a weird squeaky noise, while Gabe curses under his breath.

And Sherman is still walking away.

He's walking away, and with him, our only chance. *Cris'* only chance.

I blew it. Instead of convincing him, I antagonized him, and now...

I close my eyes for one eternal second. Now I only have Plan B left.

Before I can change my mind, I call out, "Mr. Sherman."

He stops dead in his tracks and turns around, the same smirk-smile on his face as before.

I still want to punch it off his face, but beggars can't be choosers. "I have a proposition to make."

"What are you talking about, Nya?" Gabe hiss-whispers behind me.

I'm sorry, Gabe. Taking a deep breath, I step even farther away from the guys, as if the added distance would make it easier. Note to self: It doesn't. "I would like to—"

With a bang, the lobby doors burst open, and Dad stumbles through, hair disheveled, his shirt buttoned up wrong. Looks like the crowd didn't make it any easier for him than for us. He takes no more than half a second to assess the situation. "Nya! Brian! Brian, we need to talk. My serum—"

"No need to talk." Dr. Sherman holds up a hand. "I've done that enough, not interested. Security!" He waves at the guards who helped us out in the crowd, and two of the men step forward, grabbing Dad by the upper arms. Dad tries to rip himself free, but it's no use. Two trained security guards versus one untrained scientist who hates to work out—it's a no-contest.

"Thank you," Sherman says, before directing his attention back to me, a gleam in his eyes. "I believe you were going to say something before we were so rudely interrupted?"

Dad's gaze darts from Sherman to me and back, as if he was trying to figure out what he missed. A cold band of steel wraps itself around my heart, restricting every beat and squeezing it.

What I'm about to do isn't any easier with both of them here, Gabe and Dad.

But it needs to be done.

I turn back to Dr. Sherman, keeping my chin lifted in defiance. It's my decision to make, and not his blackmail forcing my hand. Okay, well, maybe both, but the point is, I'm making this decision. Not him. "I have a proposition for you."

Sherman raises an eyebrow as that glimmer in his eyes intensifies. "I'm listening."

I take a deep breath. "I'm willing to cut you a deal."

"Really?" He sounds amused and chuckles at the same time as Gabe sucks in a sharp breath.

"Nya…!"

Yup, Gabe knows.

He didn't win that summer internship for nothing.

I pay him no attention, because if I did, if I turned around and looked at him, I couldn't do what I'm about to. "You give us the serum, and in exchange, you will get your mutant stem cells." I take two long steps forward. "From me. You can take me instead of Cris—"

"Nya, no!" Gabe and Dad are in perfect sync with their outburst, the horror in their voices slicing through my heart.

"Security!" Sherman waves his hand, and Gabe grunts. I throw a quick glance over my shoulder, only to see Gabe and Cris both held down by security guards, two on Cris, and three needed to control a struggling and angry Gabe.

Sherman levels me with a cool gaze. "You're offering to take Cris' place in my company. You're offering yourself and your stem cells."

I pull my shoulders straight, so that nobody sees how wobbly I feel. "Correct."

A shocked silence descends over the lobby, broken only by the harsh sound of Gabe's breathing. "Nya, no," he whispers, his voice cracking with emotion. "You can't do this."

But I can. I have to. For Cris, for me. We're out of options, out of time. Out of leverage. "It's the only way," I whisper, my gaze never leaving Sherman's face. "So, what do you say? Do we have a deal?"

Dr. Sherman studies me for a long moment, his expression unreadable. Then, slowly, a smile spreads across his face. "You've got guts, I'll give you that." He nods once, decisively. "All right. I accept your terms."

"No!" Dad shouts and lunges forward as if to physically drag me away, but the two men securing him keep him in place. "Brian! You can't take Nya! You can't! I have custody! I'll sue—"

Sherman chuckles again, and this time the sound brings goosebumps to my spine. "No, you won't. You want your precious daughter to get the serum, don't you? I'll have a contract for you by noon. It'll specify the outlines of our agreement, and it will clearly include a clause that ties Nya getting the serum to you contractually committing yourself to *never* sue me. In short, you both sign over your rights to me. I won't be taken by surprise by an eighteenth birthday and a shift of legal responsibility."

Gabe roars. "You can't have her," he snarls. "I'll do whatever it takes—"

Sherman sighs. "Alas, I guess my lawyer will be busy today. You'll get your own contractual agreement, Mr. Hargrove. Unless you would like your girlfriend to *not* receive the serum?"

Gabe chokes on his next breath, eyes wide, face pale. He walked right into that one.

"Didn't think so." A smug look settles on Sherman's face, and it makes me sick to my stomach. "In fact, I will withhold the serum from Nya until the risk of death reaches a tipping point. Either of you do anything I don't like, I'm withholding it longer."

Dad chokes on his next breath. "You wouldn't dare—"

"Oh, yes, I would. I'm not stupid. The lawsuits will happen, but I intend to delay and drag out every single one of them. The longer they take, the longer until I'm forced to release you, and the more I can use you for the benefit of all mankind." He rubs his hands together, like an evil Rumplestiltskin.

My chained heart is twisting under its cold, metal bindings, not pumping any blood. I knew what I was getting myself into. I'm not stupid. I saw how Cris was held, what was done to him, but I expected a certain level of decency. Geneva conventions, right? Withholding the serum from me to keep Dad and Gabe under control... Nausea threatens to overwhelm me. I'll be living with constant fear of death. Every seizure could be my last.

And yet, it's the only viable option. "Okay," I whisper.

"Nya," Gabe rasps, and my soul shatters at the pain in his voice. I never wanted to hurt him, not since I got the old Gabe back. Seeing his reaction to my decision is devastating.

"Nya..." Like Gabe, Cris whispers my name, yet I hear it the loudest and over the noise of the crowd outside, because so much swings in this one word: Desperation, helplessness, fear. All of it, and more.

"Brian, please." Dad begs his boss, he literally begs him, falls to his knees and folds his hands like in prayer. "Please think about what you're doing. Give both of them the serum. They shouldn't pay for your and my mistake. Please...!"

That least *please*, it cuts deep into the bottom of my soul and releases the tears I thought I could hold back. Newsflash, I can't.

I let them stream down my cheeks as I turn one more time to Gabe, Cris, and Dad, trying to memorize every detail of their faces. "I'm sorry," I whisper. "I'm so, so sorry. Please understand."

And then, before I can lose my nerve, I step forward to Dr.

Sherman's side. He lays his hand on my shoulder, the ultimate gesture of claiming me as his property, and even though his touch makes my skin crawl, I force myself to stay still, to not flinch away. Feeling his hand on my shoulder is nothing to what my life will look like from now on.

But it's my choice.

Suddenly, a deafening angry roar goes up from the crowd outside, the sound only slightly lessened by the lobby doors. The chants, our content acoustic background, change and get louder, more aggressive, as if they got a second wind out there.

At first, I can't make out the words, but they become clearer, louder, until they're impossible to ignore:

"…*uck! … eww… uck! …eew*—"

You suck? They're yelling *you suck*? Who now? Us? Or—

A second chant becomes more and more clear: "*….eee… eee-uh! ….eeee…Nya! Free Nya!*"

Free Nya.

The surge of endorphins shooting through me from the sound of those few words, chanted in unison, is hard to describe. *You suck,* Dr. Sherman! *Free Nya!*

Dr. Sherman must've understood the crow's wild chants as well. His eyes widen, and he tightens his grip on my shoulder.

With a loud smacking sound something crashes into the lobby doors. I jerk like everybody else. No idea what it was, but where the crowd was yelling before, they're now screaming, banging against the doors' windows, rattling them.

Holy cow.

That's a mob out there!

Sherman turns to one of his security guards, his expression tight with anger and something else. "Get her out of here," he orders. "Now!"

Gabe bursts forward, trying to break free from the three guards holding him, to no avail. "No! Nya—"

Dad yells my name at the same time, full of desperation, but both of them snap their mouths shut when another voice cuts through the lobby: "I'd reconsider that decision if I were you."

We all whip our heads over to the room divider—and the reporter who'd held the doors open for us and snuck in with us. He holds his camera up and supported on his shoulder, the red recording light blinking steadily.

"Just to let you know, I got it all. Every little detail, including you admitting to blackmailing Nya and Cris with the serum." A triumphant grin spreads across his face. "And guess what? Everything you just said, everything that happened here, has all been broadcast live, and onto the big screen outside."

Live and—

He hid behind the room divider and broadcasted—

I open my mouth and close it again. My mind scrambles to adjust to the new rules of the game, but it only takes a second, exactly the second Sherman's face drains of color. His eyes dart from the reporter to the angry crowd visible through the doors, as if he couldn't believe what he just heard. But it's clear as daylight and loud as thunder: He's been outmaneuvered, outsmarted. And now the entire world knows it.

Dad, Gabe, and Cris keep yelling and cursing, but I tune them out.

We've been given a way out by the media, just as we'd hoped, albeit differently than planned

Slowly, I turn to face Sherman, my voice low and steady, my heart hammering hard, as I take the only chance I have. "I'm giving you two options. Option one, you stick to your plan, take me instead of Cris, and give us the serum only if we comply. If you choose option one, I will make a scene and you will have to drag me out of the lobby. It will be ugly, and it will be live televised. It won't make those people out there any happier. Or, oh—your shareholders. You're in deep already, Mr. Sherman, which means I would recommend option two, which I'll call redemption arc. Tell the world what they want to hear. Give them some story of how you changed your mind. How you will give the serum to Cris and me, with *no* conditions. How you won't take any legal action against us. If you choose option two, I can promise you in return, we'll leave quietly and you might stand a chance to save face, keep some shareholders, and maybe even look better at whatever trial you'll face first."

The apple in his throat moves up and down, and the muscles in his jaw tick. His gaze darts through the room, from the angry crowd outside, to my dad and the boys, fighting to get to me, to the reporter, documenting everything happening in here.

His hand cramps over my shoulder to the point of pain, but I ignore it. I look him straight in the eye. "The world is watching, Mr. Sherman. What will it be?"

For a long, tense moment, he says nothing, his jaw working as he weighs his options. But then he pulls his shoulders back, jaw set in a hard line that vanishes the moment he puts a wide, completely fake smile on his face. "I must say, I'm impressed," he calls out. "I wanted to see how the Neanderthal-genes affected a sense of family and belonging, and it turns out bonding is as strong as in humans, if not stronger." He squeezes my shoulder once, then drops his hand from it. "Of course, you both shall have the serum. No strings attached. I will have our scientists discuss with your father how to best get it to you as soon as possible."

He nods to Cris, then to me, snaps his mouth shut and pivots, striding out of the lobby and around a corner.

Relief crashes over me like a tidal wave, so strong it nearly brings me to my knees. Blood swooshes in my ears, a storming river of noise.

We did it.

We did it!

We're going to get the serum. Cris is going to live. I'm going to live, and not in Advangen's basement.

I turn to Gabe, my heart in my throat—

And get tackled full-force by him. The very moment he runs into me, he lifts me up on off the ground, pressing me so close to his body, I can barely breathe. He nuzzles his nose in the little crook under my ear, breathing hard.

"You would've given yourself up for Cris?"

I nod into his embrace and wrap my arms around his neck. "Yes. I'm sorry—"

"Shush." I hear him swallow, then grunt, as Cris tackles us as if he had spent the last years playing football on the offensive, not locked up at Advangen. He buries his head somewhere near my shoulder, gripping my side so hard it's probably going to bruise.

I'll take it any time of the day compared to the alternative I just avoided.

"You're certified mental," Cris mumbles into the embrace.

Gabe huffs out his approval. "Agreed."

I cringe. "But—"

"Shush, I said." Gabe softens his words with a kiss pressed to my temple. "That was the fucking bravest thing I've ever seen anybody do, Nya. You would've given your freedom for Cris'. Do I like it? Hell, no. Neither of you should be Sherman's guinea pig. Can I respect it? Hell, yes!"

My heart swells and bursts out of those cold steel clamps holding it hostage and takes its first real beat since we arrived here.

"You do?" He respects my decision? "You're not mad?"

He huffs out a laugh. "Mad? I was *livid*, Nya. But I understood it, of course I did. And even as you were walking away with Sherman, I knew I would've sued the living hell out of him and Advangen—"

"So would I." Dad wraps his arms around the three of us, somewhat carefully, as if he was waiting for the boys or me to call him off.

None of us do.

The crowd outside breaks out in loud cheers and *whooo*s. Guess the live stream is still on.

Despite the cheers and whistles I hear Dad swallow hard, and his voice cracks with the next words. "Screw whatever NDA Brian would've come up with. We would've gotten you out—"

"—even if we'd have to break into Advangen again," Gabe finishes Dad's sentence.

I nod like a bobble head, sniffling. "I know." A tiny part of me had hoped exactly that, only I didn't dare acknowledge it for fear it might not come true. Sherman has proven his recklessness one too many times for me to cling to hope rather than expecting the worst.

The crowd keeps up their deafening cheers, their joy and relief a palpable thing, like ours. I'm glad the reporter is capturing this moment, too. Even though it's very private, it also belongs to everyone.

We stay like that for a long, long time, wrapped in each other's arms, silent, lost in the moment, and together.

That's what counts most.

Together.

Always together.

CHAPTER THIRTY-ONE

I carefully raise my left arm, keeping the elbow at a slight bend. Don't want the IV to poke me. Yes, I know there's no actual needle in my vein, but the thought of a plastic tube resting inside my blood vessel isn't much better. Hence, I move my hand at a snail's pace to grab my little purse from the side table next to this super-comfy reclining patient chair I've been assigned to. Yay WissenSCHAFFT for yet again rising to the occasion and furnishing us a therapy room on their second floor.

Yes, a therapy room, because duh, that's where you receive therapy: gene therapy, to be precise.

Because today's the day.

I wouldn't say I'm nervous, but maybe a tad antsy. After all, Cris and I will be guinea pigs yet again, only this time with our consent and to fix what was messed up in the first place. It's still a momentous day in medical history. No pressure. Just life and death, as per the usual.

A shudder runs down my back, so I open my purse and rummage through it. Good thing I packed something to calm my—

Huh.

I pinch my eyebrows down into a V and my lips together. "Cris?"

"Ye-hes?" He stretches the word out and looks straight up to the TV hung on the wall, as if it needed his full attention and brain power.

It tells me all I need to know.

"Would you happen to have an idea where my Nutella-to-Go I had in here went?" Because it's gone. And I know I packed it to calm my nerves.

"Me?" His voice rises at the end, another clear give-away, as is the bouncing of his foot he started the moment I looked at him. Like me, he's also reclined in the medical equivalent of a La-Z-Boy chair, relaxed and stretched out, feet crossed at the ankles, an IV in one arm.

I take a deep breath in and count to three. "You know, you could've just ask—"

He waves a hand. "I have absolutely no idea what you're talking about, and shush, this interview is super interesting."

I roll my eyes. "Sure it is," I mumble. We've raised a Nutella-addicted monster.

On-screen, the CNN news anchor is talking to an ethicist. It's definitely a good conversation, Cris is right, but there's no shortage of them these days. People are seeing the light, I guess.

"*…with the Supreme Court taking up the case. They're about to set a precedent for the legal rights and protections afforded to genetically engineered humans.*"

"*You sound very excited by that prospect.*" Not sure if the news anchor meant this as a statement or a question, the way she raises her eyebrows and tilts her head.

The ethicist takes it at face value. "*You bet I'm absolutely thrilled, especially if they go ahead and require the establishment of a national registry for genetically engineered humans. That step would go a long way to ensure transparency and prevent future abuses of the likes we've seen with the current case of Advangen."*

"Are you saying we need to monitor the biotech industry?"

"I'm saying we need to make sure that every person's rights are upheld, and yes, I'm using the word person until we come up with a more precise—or more inclusive—definition of what humanity means on a genetic level. We're advancing at a neck-breaking speed, and it will only get faster. I mean, think of all that AI can and will do for us. Hence, we must ensure we don't leave ethics behind."

A brief knock comes from the door, which opens just a split-second later.

"Good morning, you two," Duncan says and waves at us. "Y'all remember Vinnie?" He points at the man following him into the room, holding a camera and grinning at us.

"Of course we do! Hi, Vinnie!" I wave with my IV-free hand, and so does Cris. "Nice to officially meet you. The man of the hour!"

Vinnie chuckles. "Well, I got lucky. And then hired by the Times, so I guess it paid for me to be in the right spot at the right time."

It paid for us for sure. Without Vinnie broadcasting what happened between Sherman and us, we'd be in a completely different situation today, especially me. So, I feel like we gave each other a hand here. Vinnie helped us get what we needed, and our story helped him go from freelancing to a salaried position with the L.A. Times.

Duncan rolls his eyes. "Well, if you want to stay hired by the Times, stop talking and get ready to make more medical history." None of his words hold any bite, though, and Vinnie knows it.

"Yessir, boss man," he says with a smile and wink at Duncan, and readies his camera.

"I have an authority problem," Duncan sighs, then claps his hands. "So anyway, you two give me a wide smile when you look over here. We want everybody to see how happy you are getting your injection. Don't we?" He claps Vinnie on the back.

"Yes, boss. Of course, boss."

I lift both palms to the ceiling. "Excuse me, I *am* happy! Six days from my idea to a working serum that will keep us from dying of seizures is *really* making me happy! I didn't think that needed extra emphasis." To say that we were lucky is an understatement: One, Sherman gave us the serum within eight hours, and we went straight to the lab. Two, my idea together with Dad's serum worked like a charm, and three, we got emergency authorization to use the serum for ourselves. With the eyes of the world on us, there was no way we could've pulled off gene therapy without going through official channels, or else Dad would've been in even more trouble. But, for once, fate was on our side: we got emergency authorization for a clinical trial, which I guess is a fancier term for us being said guinea pigs again, but then, we've basically been that our whole lives, we just didn't know it. Anyway, helps to be a high-profile case—and helps that Dad's serum was already designed after an FDA-approved method of gene editing, which made them way less nervous in granting it emergency authorization.

So yes, I'm indeed quite thrilled.

"I'm also happy. Like a clam." Cris shows his wildest, widest grin to the camera.

"No wonder, after you ate my Nutella." I'm about to cross my arms in front of my chest and barely remember the IV in time, so I don't.

He gasps in fake outrage. "Did not."

"Uh-huh." I give him a death stare, but he knows me too well.

Like Duncan, I bark, but I don't bite.

Within one second, Cris' expression turns mischievous. "Aww, Nya. You know what? You can put it in your memoir, *the case of the missing snack*, or something." Cris snickers and ducks just in time to avoid my purse I throw at him. Closed, obviously. "Hey! What was that for?"

"Annoying me," I say. He's very much aware I'm not the biggest fan of that assignment. Contract. Deal. Whatever you want to call it. Will I get a good six figures for writing my memoir about *my life, my genes, my future*? Yes. Does that make me happy? Also, yes. What doesn't make me happy is that writing isn't my thing. English is hard. Science is much, much easier. Plus, who writes a memoir at my age? It feels weird, but since I signed the contract, I guess I better come up with something.

Cris grins and makes a face at me until I can't uphold the angry facade and chuckle. He's been so giddy the last few days, but how could he not when freedom—and health—are around the corner? Especially after we both had another seizure. What a reality-check that was. Not sure what was scarier, the moment I realized I was going to seize, or when I saw Cris twitch from yet another one a few days later. Gabe says both of them got him gray hair, which is a total lie. He always will be a younger Thor. Norse gods don't get gray hair.

The door to the treatment room opens again, this time for, speaking of, Gabe and Dad. Gabe holds two large, filled syringes, one in each hand. "Are my two favorite mutants ready for their gene therapy?"

"Duh." Cris rolls his eyes, a reddish-brown lock of hair falling into his face. "Although I'd like a cookie to go with that, to sweeten it up," he adds with a dreamy smile, and I level him with a glance.

"I think you've had enough sugar for the morning." Should I

be glad he's branching out? Not sure about that. Now that Cris has discovered food delivery services, he has also discovered his sweet tooth beyond Nutella. There goes the, uh, *advantage* of being kept in a basement and having no access to junk food. Dad might've tried his best to give him healthy food down there, but since Cris has given in to the temptation called sugar, his nutrition is less exemplary. Case in point, my missing Nutella, or the Oreos Gabe couldn't find yesterday. I suspect their fate was similar.

"Cris," Dad exhales the sigh of an exasperated caregiver. "Please make smart decisions—" He frowns. "Never mind. Maybe I shouldn't be talking about smart decisions. But watch out for yourself, okay?"

Cris regards Dad from under his lashes. "I plan to."

Dad gives him a smile, one that says they're not where they were when Cris still considered Dad one of the good guys, but also not enemies. Not on opposite sides.

Placing both syringes on the tray between Cris' and my seat, Gabe clears his throat. "Okay then, attention forward, please." I hear the strain in his voice. It mirrors my own I've been trying to downplay for the last two hours. Everybody's nerves are a bit on edge, and we're *all* overplaying it. Sometimes gene therapy doesn't work. Sometimes people get reactions to the vector used. Sometimes stuff just goes plain wrong. We all hope today is a good day and fate continues to play nice with us for a change.

"Both of you feeling okay?" Dad raises an eyebrow at me, then Cris, satisfied when we nod. "Good. You'll get the injection, we'll observe you—"

"While I will take pictures and video of everything." Duncan all but shoves Vinnie forward. I honestly think he's still a bit miffed Vinnie was the only witness to our showdown with Sherman, and not Duncan himself. By hiring Vinnie, at least he got the story and a fantastic camera operator out of it. And while there are—as always—several news trucks and a bunch of people outside WissenSCHAFFT's doors, the only reporter allowed in here is Duncan. He's got the exclusive rights to our story, and the money the Times paid for that went straight into our Cris-fund, which is growing by the minute thanks to some smart strategic moves on our part.

One, Chelsea let Mr. Sherman's lawyer know that a public apology by Advangen and some financial compensation for the years spent in their basement would go a long way in front of a jury judging over Mr. Sherman. And, to all our surprise, Advangen issued that public apology to Cris and established a compensation fund, which gives the bank account Gabe opened for Cris a nice baseline cushion.

Two, the Times shelled out an even bigger chunk of money for the exclusive right to not just our story up to now, but to Cris' story as he adjusts to life after Advangen. Duncan—and Vinnie—are on contract with him and will be the brains behind the documentary series following Cris' journey *as he adapts to life outside Advangen and his life as a genetically engineered human.*

Thing is, Cris is probably going to do well financially, because three, he just signed his first contract with—yes, a talent agency. And not only that, but his agent already secured him a national TV commercial for Carver's Keto Meals, a food delivery service targeting *single, tough men.* The whole thing is supposed to be Cris digging into one of their meals while a voice-over says, *when your inner caveman craves meat, you need Carver's Keto Meals.*

The amount of money Carver will pay for Cris' participation in that spot is ridiculous, by the way, and it's the reason Cris can buy the sports car he wants with his own money once he has a license. Oh, and it's also the reason I took the stupid memoir-gig:

#FOMO, and turns out I'm not above using my genetic status to make some college money.

Gabe grabs an alcohol swab from the drawer unit next to my recliner. "For either pictures or video, make sure you get Steve when he gives Cris the serum, please. After all, we want the jury to see he's working on redeeming himself."

Good point. I mouth a *thank you* at Gabe, and he winks. He and Dad have also gotten along better since our showdown, not quite like *before*, but better. The fear of losing me united them, so yeah, you're welcome, gentlemen. We've all been talking a lot, and all three of us understand Dad more. It makes a difference hearing stories of how he and mom were longing for a healthy child. I can understand how he got sucked into the mess of secrets and unethical conduct. I do. Doesn't mean I condone it, but I understand, and I think that's making a difference. We're more civil with each other than we were in the last few years, now that we're both playing with open cards. And, all three of us working together on the serum for the last days has definitely brought us even closer again. So close, I don't mind returning home with Dad after we're done here, at least after his trial has come to a verdict, and then… we'll see. I hope it's not prison time, though, or else I'll have to join the guys in Gabe's apartment, where Cris will stay until everything is sorted out: Papers, school, money, etc, etc. It's surprising what a problem it can be if you were non-existing for close to twenty years and people have to first discuss whether you're counting as a full-fledged human or not, which is why Gabe opened the bank account for Cris.

As if he heard my thoughts, Cris makes a groaning sound as Dad readies the IV for him. "It's about time I get out of here. I've been in only three buildings my whole life. I can't wait to do whatever I want." He gives Gabe a challenging glance.

"As long as you behave, roomy." Gabe cringes. "And maybe we should limit that to a few activities first, because you know who's following."

"Right. I keep forgetting we're celebrities." Cris pouts. "We're going to have an entourage."

"We will. But I'd rather have twenty people watch me buy a Boba than be Advangen's guinea pig." I shudder. That I was so close to taking Cris' place still is scary as hell to me, even though I'd act no differently if I had to do it again.

Cris eyes light up. "Boba? I want to try that!"

"Then I guess it's a date. We might have to take this guy, though, or else he's going to be grumpy." I lightly punch Gabe in the shoulder with the hand not impaled by an IV.

He throws away the alcohol wipe he used to clean the connector for the IV. "Well, somebody has to watch you two trouble-makers. Might as well be me."

And a bodyguard. Per person, of course. While the general public has made up its mind and likes us—or at least doesn't mind us—there are still haters out there. Too many to count. We just hired people to go through the hate mail, hate comments online, etc. and follow up with what seems credible. We also have people protecting us for that very same reason, all courtesy of GoFundMe number two.

Gabe holds up the syringe and flicks it with two fingers. He looks so much like a scientist at this moment, it's almost cliché. Which means: "Stay just like that. Don't move," I say and fish my phone out of my side pocket. At least it wasn't in the purse I threw at Cris.

Gabe, the best guy in the world, doesn't question my request, but freezes, keeping exactly the concentrated look on his face that makes him so adorable. Not that I'd tell him that. His ego is inflated enough, but still.

Making sure me, the IV, and Gabe are all in the frame, I take two quick selfies, then drop the phone. "You may now move again. I'll send that to your dad later. I'm sure he can use it."

Gabe flicks the syringe one more time. "Good idea. He changed the schedule on me, so I think he now wants me to accompany him and meet with the Surgeon General tomorrow—"

My jaw drops. "He knows the Surgeon General?" Holy cow, whom does he not know?

Gabe shrugs, his cheeks taking on a slightly reddish hue. "Before she became the Surgeon General, Dad and her ran into each other at several Make A Wish occasions with sick patients who wanted to meet the famous Joshua Hargrove."

I whistle through my teeth. Both Gabe and I have about two hundred letters with job offers at home. Each, of course. To say we've got choices would be an understatement. Do we want to go into bioengineering? Research, general or specialized? Into bioethics? One offer came from a Think Tank even. Oh, advocacy groups for human rights and genetic privacy are also interested in us, and to top it off, Gabe has some additional offers from investigative journalism and public relations firms, all thanks to how he handled the media with our story.

So, yes, we have options. Gabe has options. Which is why his meeting with the Surgeon General is kind of setting a course. I peek up at him from under my lashes. "I think it's perfect you're meeting with her. Does that mean you've decided what to do? One of the advocacy groups?"

He sighs. "No firm decision yet, but since my dad is using his clout to help de-stigmatize genetic engineering, I might as well use him and his connections as well. And then, we'll see. But as I told you, I won't make any decision without you." He winks at me, sits next to me on the recliner, and takes my hand.

A little charge shoots from the contact of our hands up to my chest and explodes into bright and hot fireworks as he brushes his thumb over the back of my hand.

"Ready?" He looks from me to Cris and back.

"Ready," we both confirm.

"Then let's do it." He attached the syringe to the IV, and so does Dad with Cris.

Duncan whispers to Vinnie, who sneaks closer to us, camera directed onto our arms.

Dad attaches the syringe, like Gabe did. "You let us know if you're feeling woozy, short of breath—"

"We know, Dad." I try to catch his eye to give him a stern glance. "We've been over it a million times."

"If it takes a million and one times to keep you safe, I'm okay with that." Dad doesn't look up from the injection, as if he feared the catheter would jump out of Cris' vein if he did.

As Gabe pushes the plunger down, I feel a bit of coldness going up my arm. Amazing to think what's now racing through my blood stream: countless little viruses armed with the tools to tell my genes what to do—or rather, what not to do. Science is amazing.

"Slow and steady, Gabe," Dad says.

"On it."

And even though it looks like he's barely injecting anything, it only takes a minute and the serum is in our bodies.

I blow out a puff of air as a boulder the size of a small car drops off my shoulders. "Good-bye seizures."

"Good riddance," Cris adds, then flinches when Dad pulls out his IV and applies pressure to the area. "I don't mind taking a break from anything medical. Especially anything with needles. And you said you wanted to see me when?" He rubs his hand over the injection site and eyes the used IV Dad is discarding.

"In four weeks. The earliest. And if you change your mind, that's okay."

"I won't." Cris peeks under the Band-Aid. "I told you I won't back out."

"Then... well, thank you again for doing this. For agreeing." Dad hesitates for a moment, then lays his hand on Cris' shoulder and squeezes. "We can continue to do good with your stem cells. And yours," he adds, looking at me.

I just shrug. If Cris can donate his stem cells, so can I, especially since I'm benefitting from their use. That being said, had it been me deciding, he would never have to go back to Advangen, but Cris... Cris is more diplomatic than I am.

Cris waves a hand through the air. "I told Nya before, had I known all the marrow draws were to help me and somebody else, I would've done it. At least now they're on my terms, and they're numbing me. Us. They are numbing us, right?" His gaze flicks up to Dad's.

"Yes, they are." Dad's voice takes on a steely edge. I don't think he's gotten over the cruelty done to Cris in his name. "Advangen won't dare step a toe out of line."

Because, as I said to Dr. Sherman in the lobby of Advangen, the entire world is watching. Cris and my willingness to contribute to science and help other people despite what we've been through has brought our Kickstarter a fantastic boost. Advangen has profited from the good press as well, which is an unfortunate side effect of helping Dad: It was Dad's and my idea to look more into the epigenetic landscape of human-Neanderthal hybrids, aka, Cris and me, to potentially develop epigenetic therapies to treat metabolic disorders, or cognitive decline. Maybe even certain types of cancers. After all, our immune system and genome work differently.

But to do all of that, we need a controlled environment in a specialized lab, and that's where Advangen unfortunately is still the best, not that I'm happy about that.

What I *am* happy about is that Chelsea gave us a good legal cushion to rest on. Like Dad said, Advangen won't dare to step one itty-bitty pinky toe out of line, but since Dr. Sherman resigned as CEO, the company tries to make amends, and I'm okay with Dad, Cris, and me going there. It's for science, after all.

Gabe holds out his hand and helps me off the chair. "Ready to face the music?"

I hold on to his hand, because, duh, why would I ever let go of him when it took us years to get to this point? Gabe is like a newly found addiction, a good, healthy one. "If you tell me what you mean by that, because, as always, we have options."

Grinning, he circles his thumb over the back of my hand. "For now, I mean the reporters waiting outside."

"Not the court date for Dad?"

"Nope."

"Or the court date about more restrictive genetic engineering laws where we are called as expert witnesses?"

"Nope."

I pretend to think hard. "Maybe the trial against Advangen?" Although I heard rumors their willingness to give us the serum and to work with us reflected positively on their future charges and sentencing. Bet Mr. Sherman was happy to hear that, although if I'm to believe Chelsea, Sherman and the men doing the tasering and marrow draws from Cris won't get away unscathed. At all.

I'm just relieved they're judging Dad on a different trial, as it should be. His tally has more positive points than any of Advangen's and Sherman's combined.

Gabe shakes his head. "Not talking about the Advangen trial, either."

"Okay." I look up at him. "You also don't mean the interview with Jimmy Fallon, or with the Society for Humane Genome Editing? Because that's also on the list."

Gabe sighs. "I know. We're going to be busy. So much for choosing a job. *This* is like a whole new career already."

I snort. "Oh gee, totally. Can you believe that if all had gone to plan, you and I would still be at Advangen?" Going through our internship day by day, probably still ignoring each other or making life difficult for one another. Ah, what a ginormous difference a few short weeks can make.

Cris huffs. "Excuse me, so would I. I'd also be at Advangen, so I don't mind having to give interviews and talk about being a mutant. And I'm looking forward to doing something with my life. It's not like I ever expected to have an option, so now…" He shrugs, then stuffs his hands in his pockets. "Maybe I'll work on a cruise ship. I get to be out on the sea—"

"Maybe you learn to swim first?" Gabe cocks an eyebrow at him.

"Yes, that, but then I'll be working on a cruise ship. Two benefits: I get to see the world, and hopefully people won't recognize me all the time."

I cringe. "Yeah, that has definitely put a dent in my excitement at going back home." After we returned from Advangen, we tried going home instead of to WissenSCHAFFT for like a hot minute.

Literally a minute.

We didn't even get through to Gabe's driveway. That's how overcrowded the sidewalk was. So, we made an executive decision and moved back in with WissenSCHAFFT for the time being. We're lucky Johanna is stepping up as the godmother she never officially became, housing us and spoiling us with food and attention.

"Security should have taken care of the situation," Dad says, disinfecting his hands after throwing the used IVs and syringes out. "That's what you pay them for. There won't be reporters peeking through every window. Am I correct, Duncan?"

"From what my colleagues are complaining about, yes. You have a safe perimeter. And believe me, right now you're hot news, but that's going to change. Give it some time, and somebody else more interesting will come along." He fastens the Velcro on his camera bag, then swings it over his shoulder. "Some new story line, some new drama. But my bet will be that whenever a new step in anything genetic is being taken, they'll ask the three of you for your opinion. Prep for that and you'll be able to use the attention instead of it crashing over you, as it was at the beginning of all this... fun adventure."

"Wise words," Dad says with a sigh, probably thinking about the official trial coming his way. Compared to how the prospect of a trial unnerved me, he's quite calm about it. Resigned. As he's said, he knew he would one day have to pay for what he did, and in the end, he got a healthy daughter out of his action *and* finally cured Cris—and me. *I sleep much better now*, he told me when the letter from the DA arrived.

And I guess... I guess that's one way of accepting your guilt and potential punishment.

"Not wisdom, experience." Duncan opens the door to the hallway for us, and we all file out. "And I appreciate you guys keeping me in the loop."

"Not as much as we appreciate your help," Gabe replies, wrapping an arm around my shoulders as we walk toward the elevators.

Silence falls as we wait for the elevator, but it's neither heavy nor loaded, rather more at ease. I let my gaze drift over the people who enter the cabin with me. Kind of amazing how the last weeks have changed all our lives. How they've changed science. How they will change the law.

A chuckle breaks from my throat, and I shake my head.

"What?" Gabe asks.

"Just thinking about how it's going to be tough for anything in my life to measure up to what happened over the last few weeks." I've had enough excitement for two lifetimes. We all have.

Gabe slides his arm from my shoulder down to my hand and weaves his fingers in-between mine. "Regarding action, point taken. I'm putting a checkmark behind that bucket list item. But that being said, I'm sure there are some other areas in life we can make memorable." He gives me a heated glance as Dad opens his mouth and snaps it right back shut.

Warmth swamps my cheeks. "Also point taken," I echo him.

The elevator doors open toward the lobby and the huge glass entrance doors.

I hold my free hand out for Cris. "Ready?"

He takes it, and, just like Gabe, interlaces his fingers with mine. "Never been more ready."

"Then let's do this." I take the first step forward out of the elevator, flanked by Gabe and Cris, and followed by Dad, Duncan, and his photographer.

The moment we're visible from the entrance doors, a jolt of energy shoots through the media gathered outside. Finally, they get to see and document what they waited for.

"And here we go," Dad murmurs.

Here we go.

I lift my chin high and nod to Keith to open the doors for us.

We're going to be healthy, and we're going to live a free life.

Keith opens the doors, and the noise level jumps from serene and quiet to overwhelming and chaotic within a second.

"Nya! Nya! How are you feeling after—"

"Cris! You'll be free for the first time—"

"Mr. Hargrove! Gabriel! What are your plans—"

"—if you end up in prison, Mr. Bennison?"

I squeeze the hands of both the guys, and together we step out into the chaos, not running from it, but embracing it.

It's our story, and we're going to tell it.

Together.

* * *

ABOUT THE AUTHOR

Micky O'Brady is a pediatrician-turned-writer living in beautiful, dry Southern California with her husband and two critters (one son, one dog). Micky loves to write YA thrillers and sci-fi with a romantic twist, mainly because she wishes her life had been such an awesome mix of action and cute guys when she was a teen.

When she isn't up at around 3 a.m. (with a cup of tea, Earl Grey, hot) drafting stories she can't get out of her head, she can be found at a martial arts dojo, though maybe not at 3 a.m. She holds a first degree black belt in Krav Maga and a second degree black belt in Judo, and is convinced every girl should know how to kick some butt.

Micky also is a firm believer in the healing powers of Nutella eaten straight from the glass and in the magic that can happen on a rainy day, as long as there are fuzzy socks and a cup of hot tea involved.

Her previous publications include a doctoral thesis and several medical articles as well as a medical book about emergency communication. None of them are as fun to read as her YA novels though. Her first YA-novel, THE PRESIDENT'S DAUGHTER, and its sequel TRIAL BY ICE, are published by Curiosity Quills and available through all major retailers, such as Amazon, B&N, Kobo, and Smashwords.

Through Snowy Wings Publishing Micky is the author of the YA-sci-fi romance BETWEEN WORLDS, a super-cool contemporary romance-slash-pro-wrestling-story PLAYING WITH #FIRE, as well as another sci-fi romance, TIME WARPED, and its sequels TIME BOUND and TIMED OUT.